MW01064135

UNDER WATCHFUL EYES

By

CARLTON LOFTIN

Hope you like my book.

Carlton Loftin

This book is a work of fiction. Names, characters, places and incidents are either the product of the author's imagination, or are used fictionally. Any resemblance to actual persons, living or dead, or to actual events, or locales, is entirely coincidental.

This book is licensed for your personal enjoyment only. This book may not be re-sold or given away to other people. If you'd like to share this book with another person, please purchase an additional copy for each person you share it with.

Copyright © 2018-Carlton Loftin

All rights reserved; including the right to reproduce this book, or portions thereof, in any form. No part of this text may be reproduced in any form without the express written permission of the author.

Version 2018 (03-29-18)

Under Watchful Eyes

Mark Wakefield was taken at age six from rural Wichita, Kansas. He escaped from an underground facility, where aliens were raising young people, and experimenting with their minds and bodies. He walked into a police station in Pahrump, Nevada, and began telling the officer at the desk, how he wanted to find his biological mother and get help to rescue the others.

Trying not to snicker in front of a female officer standing near, the officer said with a comical, raised voice, "So, let me get this straight. You were taken at age six by aliens, and now you are how old?"

"Thirty," Mark answered, a little aggravated. "Look, I know this all sounds weird to you, but I am telling you the truth. I was finally able to escape. If my biological mother is alive, I want to find her. The others being held by the aliens need to be freed."

Looking in the other officer's direction, he said, "Susan, can you help this gentleman? I have to go to the men's room" smirking, with his back to Mark.

The brunette (with her hair in a ponytail) stepped forward, and the officer handed her the form he'd been filling out.

"Make sure you get all his information down correct," he added, "Oh yeah! Make sure to fill out a fingerprint card." Smirking he continued, "You know, to help him find his mother." While he walked away, he whispered to himself, "Yeah, in case we have to arrest this nut case for something we don't know about yet."

"I can give you our address at the time I was taken, and the phone number,'' Mark interjected, "Mother's name is Carolyn Wakefield. I'm pretty sure she was born there in Wichita. I don't know anything about my father. I remember asking her about him one day on a swing in the park near our house. She just said he was out of the picture and it was just her and me. Mother promised she would explain it all to me when I got older."

The male officer walked away holding his mouth, so he wouldn't burst out laughing.

Susan asked, "Why didn't you just borrow someone's cell phone and call the number?

Mark asked, "Would you have loaned me your phone, if you heard my story?"

"You've got a good point there," she nodded and continued, "There are still a few pay phones here and there. There is one on the back wall for people to call a bail bondsman, or someone to pick them up, if they don't have a cell phone."

"Lady, I don't have a dime to my name," I told the other officer that I just escaped last night, and here I am."

Susan, wanting to get the form filled out to pacify this nut and get him out of the building, continued, "Ok! Let me get a little more information from you and we will be finished with this form. Where were you being held?" She tried not to grin.

"At an underground facility in a hilly area between Las Vegas and here," answered Mark as a matter of fact.

Not so much of a smile now, she asked, "Could you lead us back to the area where you were being held?" She thought, "Just in case there was anything to his story."

"Ma'am, I crawled out of a vent pipe on the side of a hill right at dark. For what seemed like hours, I stumbled, fell down hills, stepped in holes I couldn't see in the dark, crawled under fences, and eventually made it to a main road."

She leaned forward peering at his ragged dirty jeans, and then took better notice of his shirt that hugged his chest, and the short sleeves that exposed his biceps. His dark brown hair was cut short. She saw his face had dirt on one side, like he'd been sleeping in the park.

Glancing at his body and wondering what she was looking at, he continued, "A truck driver picked me up, and dropped me off here in town. He drove a Mayflower truck and his first name is Kent. He never said his last name. He's the one that told me where we were, when he stopped to pick me up. He let me out, and continued down the road."

"Did you tell him your story?" she inquired.

"No! I was afraid he'd make me get out. I just told him I was trying to get to a police station to find a certain address. At least that way I wouldn't be lying. I told him I was exhausted and extremely thirsty. He gave me a can of soda. As I gulped down the drink, he said, "Guess you've got good reason for wanting to keep all your information to yourself. Maybe it is better that I don't know, anyway. You get some rest and I'll wake you in Pahrump. Just dropped a load in Vegas, and when I drop this one, I'm off for a whole week. Family and I are going to Disney World. We've been saving for this trip for a good while."

She interrupted, "You remembered every word he said?"

Mark nodded and continued, "He turned the music down a little. I couldn't keep my eyes open and must have drifted to sleep. Next thing I knew, he stopped to let me out, and wished me luck, as he pulled away. I didn't try to get another ride. I just kept walking until I saw this station."

"Did you get the number of the truck?" she asked, feigning interest.

"No! I was barely awake when I climbed out of the vehicle, and said thanks."

She continued, "You said there were others being held by these aliens; how many?"

"There were 38 where I was being held. Twenty were female and the rest of us male. There were other females who were removed for one reason or another. Usually, the ones who were pregnant were returned after delivering the baby, but without their new-born. Sometimes they didn't return. We guessed those died during childbirth. A few were taken away because they seemed to go crazy when the aliens wouldn't return their babies."

"This guy has a hell of a story," she thought, as she jotted down his information. "They didn't return any of the babies to their mothers?"

"No! They said the babies were the answer to the continuation of their race, as a mixture with humans."

By now her female brain had to know, "Were any of the babies yours?"

"Probably," he answered with a frown. "We were encouraged to have sex with all the females, from the time we turned eighteen. It is almost certain that one or more had to be part mine."

Frowning, she asked, "It didn't bother you that some of these babies might have been yours and they were taken away?"

"As I got older, of course, it began to play on my mind. Knowing there was nothing I could do about it, left me totally frustrated. Even though males and females were given medicine to make you want to have sex, I got to where I would finish the act but not deliver the semen. I'm sure the females were feeling the frustration; too, because they never let the aliens know what I was doing. If they had, I would have been put in the chamber, where they hooked up leads to your brain to make you conform. Even they didn't like having to put you in a chamber, because those who came out never seemed to be quite all there."

Finding herself a little intrigued by his information, she asked in a lower, softer voice, "Did you ever fall in love with any of these women?"

"Not sure exactly what love is," came his solemn honest answer. "I do know the definition of the word, but it was not dwelled upon in our teaching. The females were taken at an early age, too, and we grew together under the control of the aliens. We were given regular injections, fed and trained together. However, we were kept separated during sleep time until the age of eighteen. At that time, we were encouraged to sleep together and have sex. We were shown males and females in the act of having sex to keep us aroused. Some females seemed to enjoy having sex with certain males, and it was similar for us, too."

A male officer who'd come from the back to hand her a paper, said, "Don't know where you were, but I'd sure like to have been there."

Knowing he hadn't heard much of Mark's story, for he just came on duty, Susan ordered, "Go find something to do, if you want me to file this report for you." The officer grinned, nodded and proceeded out the back door to his cruiser.

In a crowded big city station, there would have been a line of people with some kind of problems waiting behind Mark. However, this was a new small, satellite station. No one was in line behind him. A few officers were at desks answering phones and doing paperwork.

The only other interruptions were a few officers bringing in a man and woman, who had too much to drink, and doing drugs. Those two had been hurried off to booking.

Finding she wasn't in such a big hurry to get him out of the building anymore, she questioned, "You mentioned injections. What kind of medicine were they giving you?"

"They would never tell us what medicines they were giving us. They would only say it would make our bodies stronger and our brains more functional."

"Did this medicine do as they indicated?" she found herself wanting to know, as she looked over his physique again.

"Yes!" came his answer somewhat blunt, but not bragging. "Our strength was constantly put to the test, and we could see we were getting much stronger at everything they had us do. Our minds were often flooded with information, to see how much we could remember, or understand. Most of us realized our brains were improving. Some were much slower at retaining, but even they slowly improved. We were taught to use our minds to do specific things, which were much harder to learn."

"Explain that last part more fully," she asked, with pen in hand.

"From the time we were taken, we were trained to concentrate on objects like an empty matchbook on a table, and think about it moving. Over a short period, as we all stared and thought, it would eventually move slowly to the edge and fall off. As children, thinking that was neat, we'd think together to move larger objects and make them fall off the table. Under instructions, we learned to make them levitate. As we aged, we were taught to use our own singular thoughts to do these things. Some of us were better than others and eventually could make the items fly through the air in the direction we wanted them to go. As we got older, we were taught to use our thoughts to heat objects and bend them."

Susan hesitated, and then began searching the desk for her pen.

"It's in your hair above your right ear."

"Do you read minds, too?" she asked, as she removed the pen from her hair."

"Not really" he answered, "But by a process of deduction and observation of a person's words and actions, you can often know what they must be thinking, and sometimes even what they are going to say next."

With pen in hand now, she began again, "The aliens," as she was cut short.

"They have gray colored skin and their bodies are similar in some ways to drawings of aliens that humans claim to have seen. They only have three long fingers, and one that must be the thumb, for it is a little shorter. Their heads are more like a cross between those alien drawings and a human. They have eyes, ears, nose and mouth."

At that point she interrupted him, "You said they told you things. Do they speak English?"

"Sometimes, they speak their own language, but not often enough for us to learn what they are saying to each other. They get their point across to us telepathically, using what English words they have learned. However, most of the times, they use some type of language translator, when they want to say something or teach us. We suspect by their physical body actions that they communicate with each other telepathically, also."

The pages were beginning to mount up, as she grabbed another and began writing. Looking up she asked, "What kind of teaching did these aliens give you other than what you have mentioned, and why?" For a second she thought to herself, "I can't believe I am asking these stupid questions."

"Daily, we spent time in front of information screens concerning everything you could possibly imagine. Physically, we were trained in all sorts of exercise, and the use of many weapons."

"What type of weapons?" as she thought of some possible weapons stashed away the police might need to find.

"Bows, knives, spears, swords, rifles, shotguns, a variety of pistols, and we were taught to dismantle them and put them back together."

"Weren't these aliens afraid you might use the weapons on them?"

"They had no fear of what we might do with the weapons. They could make you do whatever they wanted, with their minds. They could cause severe pain to any part of your body, just by looking at you. They demonstrated some of what they could do when we were very young. They could look at things and cause their destruction in one way or another. They could make extremely large objects, such as a boulder; fly through the air in the direction they wanted."

"Why would they even want to teach you about weapons?" was her next question.

"They said it was part of us having a more rounded knowledge of as many things as possible."

"You described the aliens, but you didn't say if there were male and females?" she inquired for her own information. She wasn't prepared to write down his answer.

"Yes! There were male and female," he informed.

Her feminine mind made her ask the next question, "How could you tell the females from the males?"

He continued, "They all wore black shiny uniforms over their bodies, but you could tell the females had breasts. Their voices were different from the males; still stern sounding, but somewhat softer."

She couldn't stop herself from asking the next question, even though she wasn't going to write it down either, "Did they make you have sex with the alien females?"

She was surprised at his answer, "No! I'd come to know one of the female alien teachers pretty well, so I asked her that question one day. She informed me, they'd found in past experiments that sex with human females and males by them, produced deformed or dying babies. After many experiments and trying, they finally gave up hope of having offspring in that manner. She related, the injections they gave us, would cause the new babies to be part human and part of their species. As I grew older and absorbed information from the screens, I realized they must be injecting us with some of their DNA."

Susan had become so interested in the information he provided, she hadn't noticed her fellow officer had returned from the men's room and break. The officer chuckled and Susan frowned toward him.

Mark and Susan were interrupted by a commotion on the other side of the room. Two brothers, who had been brought in for booking, escaped from their restraints. One of them had a handcuff key on a string around his neck and managed to use it to remove both of their shackles. They seized officer's weapons, took hostages, and threatened to kill them, if they couldn't get out of there alive.

Mark walked toward one of the men, who held a gun to a female officer's head. As the guy threatened to shoot her if he came closer, one of the other officers grabbed Mark. Mark kept his eyes on the man's weapon. The weapon got extremely hot. The guy dropped the confiscated officer's weapon, and held his burnt hand.

The brother had been watching Mark closely. Knowing he'd done something, he turned the weapon he'd been holding at a male officer's head, and fired at Mark. The officer he'd been holding around the neck, back head butted him and dropped to the floor, knowing his buddies with drawn weapons would take him out. They did just that and emptied their weapons into his body, causing his weapon to discharge wildly several times.

The one, who'd dropped his hot confiscated weapon, learned what it's like, to go up against a trained female officer hand to hand. She put some moves on him he surely had never seen. Chop to the throat, kick to one leg causing bone to protrude out of the back of his leg, and a stiff-arm under his chin. A kick to the chest sent him flying back against a wall, which he bounced off of and onto the floor. When he landed, his hand was near the weapon he'd dropped. He grabbed for the weapon, which no longer felt hot. Before he could fire, officers now trained their weapons on him. Bullets entered his body in many locations. He soon lay dying on the floor. Officers rushed to the two bodies making sure the threat was over. No one noticed Mark leaving the building, and slowly walking away holding his side. Blood soaked his shirt and upper part of his pants leg.

Marked and unmarked cars came to a screeching halt, as officers entered the building with drawn weapons.

Ambulances could be heard in the distance, as a female detective's car came to a halt. Mark was beginning to stagger, as she came to a stop beside him.

She rushed to the other side of her car, as he dropped to one knee, and said, "Two men with guns inside." She opened her passenger door, and grabbed a towel from the front seat. She helped him sit down on the seat with his feet out of the car. She raised his shirt and saw the entrance and exit wounds. She wrapped the towel around his side trying to cover both wounds. She told him to try to keep pressure on the wounds, and that ambulances were on the way.

Her partner, Jack Caruso, was inside on desk duty, as the result of a shooting he was involved in a few nights prior. She needed to get in that building. She drew her weapon and headed for the door. She was oblivious to the news truck that arrived, with news reporter and camera crew approaching the building.

The news lady pointed to Mark at the car, saying, "Get a quick shot of that man in the unmarked car, and then focus on that female officer hurrying into the building. She is Detective Sarah Sidwell. I did a piece on her a few months back."

As the well-trained camera crew obeyed, the cameraman said, "You are live in 3, 2, 1," and nodded.

"This is Danah Polero, PVT News (short for Pahrump Valley Times) covering a shooting inside the police station. I see Detective Sarah Sidwell rushing inside with her weapon drawn, with fellow officers still arriving. By the empty vehicles and doors open on site, there has to be a multitude of officers in there. We are working our way into the danger zone." She and her camera crew entered the front glass doors. Inside they saw Sidwell had holstered her weapon and was talking to her partner. The cameras shifted to the backs of officers surrounding two bloody bodies on the floor. They, too, had holstered their Glocks and Sigs.

Danah spoke into her mic, "It is obvious the danger is over, but there appears to be some wounded officers." A female and a male officer sat in chairs, as fellow officers applied pressure with handkerchiefs, to a shoulder and arm wound, while comforting them.

Officers cleared a path, as EMS rushed through the doors. They proceeded to the wounded and treated their wounds.

The watch commander finally came to his senses enough to call out, "Get these people out of here. This is a crime scene." Officers hurriedly escorted the reluctant Danah and her crew from the building. One officer found a roll of crime scene tape and stretched it across the front doors. Other officers took up vigil at the doors to make sure no one else entered.

Out of the building, Danah looked toward where the guy had been sitting in Sidwell's car, but the car was gone. She began to interview people in the area, as to what they may have observed.

Once Sidwell made sure her partner was ok, she came out of the building to make sure the wounded guy wasn't bleeding all over her car. She saw him trying to walk away holding his side. She rushed to him, saying, "Another ambulance is arriving, and they will take you to the hospital."

"No hospital," he muttered weakly, "Can't, they may find me."

"Who will find you? Who are you running from? The law or someone else?" asked Sidwell, quickly, and somewhat annoyed.

"Never done anything wrong," he answered softly, as he grimaced.

"I know I'm going to regret this" she thought as she said, "Let me get you back to my car." She helped him in that direction and eased him into the passenger seat. She fully intended to rush him to the hospital and let them deal with it. His wound was severe, and he'd lost a lot of blood. In her mind she rationalized, "Surely she wouldn't get in trouble for taking the man to the emergency room."

As she sped in that direction, she asked again, "Whom are you running from?"

It was somewhat of a shock when he answered, "The aliens. I escaped to find my biological mother and get help for the others. None of my internal organs feel damaged. If I stop the bleeding, I will heal."

Agitated, she answered, "Aliens, are you some kind of a nut case? What do you mean you escaped?" Before he could answer she added, "Unless you are a damn doctor, you don't know what damage that bullet did."

He didn't answer her.

When she glanced his way, she saw he'd passed out. She knew she should rush him on to the hospital, but what he said was intriguing. What her partner had told her inside the building, about this man walking toward one of the shooters who dropped his gun like it was hot, also added to her inquisitive nature. Also, her partner would be on desk duty or off without pay, because he'd used an ankle holster to fire at the two shooters in the building. He wasn't supposed to have a weapon on him while under investigation from the first shooting. Of course, she was thinking she would have done the same thing as her partner. It may be policy, but it would be stupid not to have a weapon of some kind on you. You can't be a police officer and not make some enemies. All this ran through her mind, as she glanced at her passenger again.

She trained as a nurse before she decided to become a cop. She still had plenty of bandages, antibiotics and pain pills, from when she was recovering from a bullet wound in her leg, shortly after she made detective. She got a leg wound, but the two shooters were killed. She was a much better shot.

She could tell this guy probably just had a flesh wound; but how much blood had he lost. If he died in her car or her house; if she took him home to treat him, she'd be in a hell of a lot of trouble. If anyone even found out she didn't take him to the hospital, it could damage her career on the force. All kinds of negative thoughts rushed through her head. She came to a stop at a red light that was just about to change. She didn't want to use flashing lights to draw attention to her vehicle.

She looked upward and saw the sunlight reflecting off a figure of the Virgin Mary on a church window above the doors. Turning right would lead her to the hospital. Turning left was toward her house.

The light changed and there was no one behind her, as she glanced into her rear view mirror. In this city, with no cars behind her on a busy street, these had to be omens. She immediately turned her car into the left turning lane and sped down the street, whispering out loud, "Sarah, what in the hell are you doing?"

As she arrived at her home, she pushed the garage door opener and brought her car to a stop inside. She opened her door and rushed to the passenger side. As she opened the door, he opened his eyes.

"Don't you die on me, after all this," she ordered, half smiling.

She helped him into the house and into one of the bathrooms. On the way, she'd glanced back on the kitchen floor, expecting to see a trail of blood. She didn't know whether to feel good about only seeing a few drops along the way, or to worry whether he'd lost too much blood, and was going to die in her bathroom. What would she do if he did? Why did she do this? Why did she take this chance for a stranger?" These were just a few of the questions running through her mind, as she sat him on the toilet and began taking medicines and bandages from the cabinet under the sink.

She removed his bloody pullover shirt, and tossed it into the shower stall, as he leaned back against the toilet bowl. She grabbed a clean washrag, wet it, and wiped the wound area. As she cleared the blood, she saw the wound was only oozing. When she turned him where she could wipe the blood away from the exit wound, it took her by surprise. The fresh blood was also only oozing and she could swear that exit hole was much larger, when she first saw it.

He was looking at her, but wasn't making a sound, as he let her treat him.

"Damn" she thought. "This guy has to be in a lot of pain, but he's not showing it. He's probably on cocaine, or something else. Here I am treating a bloody addict in my home. I must have lost my mind."

Her thoughts were interrupted, as he weakly said, "No, I am not on any kind of drugs."

She wondered how he guessed what she was thinking, as she applied antibiotics and bandages. She reached into the cabinet, retrieved a bottle and ran some water in one of the throwaway mouth wash cups.

"The pain medicine will not be necessary, but I do need to rest, and then I will be on my way. I have to find my mother." Weakly he added, "I thank you for your help, but I don't want to be the cause of any trouble for you. I can't let them find me here. You would be in great danger. We will be safe for some hours yet, but not for long. "

She set the pain medicine down and helped him to his feet saying, "I'll let you lie down in the spare bedroom. We'll talk more about it when you wake. For now, I just have bandages on the wounds, but tomorrow when you are stronger, I'll have to find a suture kit. I've got an EMS friend who will help me. I don't need you in my clean bed with bloody pants and shoes on. Lean back and I'll remove them."

He unbuckled his pants, unbuttoned them, and attempted to do it himself.

He was either too weak or didn't want to object, she thought, as he fell back on the bed. She removed his shoes and socks. Then she pulled the pants off, exposing his underwear. She couldn't help but see the bulge and pictured him being well endowed. She half folded the pants, as she laid them on the floor. There was some blood around the top of one side of the pants, so she folded them with that side up, thinking, she'd deal with them later.

She pulled the covers back, helped him ease more comfortably into the bed, and returned the covers over his body. She saw he was already beginning to fall asleep. She left the door open, as she left the room saying to herself again, "Sarah, what in the hell are you doing? Have you lost your mind completely? A stranger is in your spare bed with a bullet wound. You are breaking all the rules, girl. You may have just shot your career to hell and you may end up in jail."

She went back to the bathroom, cleaned the sink and floor. She disposed of the bloody towel, his shirt, and the washrag in the garbage bag, like a criminal getting rid of the evidence. She wiped up the blood off the tile floor in the kitchen with a wet towel, and threw it into the garbage can. She did the same for a few drops on the garage floor, and began to clean the blood from the car seat and edge of the floorboard. The wadded towel she'd given him to put pressure on the wound had soaked up most of the blood. A friend had shown her how to clean the blood from her driver's side, when she'd been wounded. She still had some of those chemicals. She retrieved them from a cabinet and began the cleaning process. Soon she could see no evidence of his sitting in her car, as she stood there inspecting it.

She went back inside and peered out the window. Most everyone in houses around her was hard working families. Mom and dads were both at work this time of day, and it wasn't time for school kids to be at home. Still, she didn't know everyone's work schedule. She wondered if anyone was home and saw her enter her garage with a passenger.

She heard him groan and went to the door to look in. He was still asleep. He was a good-looking guy with muscular arms and chest. As he moved the arm that was out from under the cover, his bicep flexed. She imagined him being very strong.

Since her divorce from a defense lawyer, only one man had been in her house. She and her partner occasionally spent some time together in her other bed. She forced herself to not let him make a habit of it because of police rules about partners' cohabitating. It irritated her, because he was good in bed, and she wasn't happy about living in the house without a man around. The divorce had been a messy one, but she came out ahead on the deal, with the house, car, money in the bank, and a monthly income unless she remarried. She definitely didn't need her ex husband finding out she was sleeping with her partner. He might use that information against her in some way to hurt her career. Maybe she was being too cautious, for he had remarried, moved on with his life, and they were expecting their second child.

Sarah was glad there were no children involved when they divorced. She remembered sitting around crying her eyes out, after finding out he was sleeping with this woman that he married after their divorce. He told Sarah she was always working crazy hours, stakeouts with other men, having to leave at odd times when the phone rang because of a case, and they didn't have much of a life together. He told her it got to him and he lost his love for her. He met Connie, they fell in love, and then he told her the truth, and asked for a divorce.

Sarah got over the hurt much faster than she'd expected and put it all behind her. However, she felt sure that marriage to someone else would be a long time coming.

He moaned some words in his sleep. She neared the bed, felt his forehead for a fever, but found his forehead relatively cool. She pulled the covers back far enough to see the bandages, to make sure they weren't blood soaked. Finding all looked as well as could be expected; she placed the cover back over him.

She'd been off duty when she heard the voice on her police radio about the shooting. She was on her way down town to do a little shopping. That would definitely have to wait for awhile. Since her partner was going to be on desk duty a lot longer now, she considered calling in, and taking some much needed vacation time. Her captain was always telling her she needed to take some time off.

She made herself a sandwich and a bowl of soup, glancing over her shoulder now and then. She placed them on the bar, and retrieved a glass of ice water from the fridge door. She made one more trip to the spare bedroom door, and then came back to sit and eat.

After finishing her meal and washing a few dishes, she checked again at the bedroom door. She took a bottle of wine from her wine rack, opened it, and poured herself a glass, sitting both on a table by the recliner. She picked up her kindle, turned it on and tried to read, as she sipped on her wine; but found it hard to concentrate. She thought about the few words the stranger said, and worried about the choices she'd made this morning. That first glass was soon empty, and another poured. Her Glock .357 caliber service weapon made her uncomfortable in her chair, so it was removed, and placed on the side table. Her eyes glanced toward the bedroom door, and then to her kindle, to resume reading.

The next thing she knew, she woke up to the sound of the shower in the spare bathroom. Sarah palmed her service weapon and checked to make sure it was still loaded. She rose from her chair and approached the open door to the bathroom, with her gun in a raised position.

Inspecting the area with her trained eyes, she saw the bloody bandages in the trash basket. His pants were lying on the closed toilet seat. She saw him soaping his body in the shower through the curtain. She wanted to check his pockets for identification. Before she could move, the shower water stopped, and he threw the curtain back to retrieve a towel.

It caught both of them by surprise. He was standing naked, and she stood just inside the door with her weapon in her hand. Her eyes took in his masculine figure, and his eyes looked at her weapon.

He said, "I've already been shot once, today. Are you going to make it twice?"

Finally able to remove her eyes from below his waist, she sheepishly said, "No! Of course not, I just," as she hesitated trying to think of something to say.

"Good. You had me worried there for a minute." He reached for the towel. "Hope you didn't mind me using the shower. I felt a little grungy."

Still not able to take her eyes off him completely, she noticed the area of the wound was not bleeding, and the skin appeared to be healing over the area. She still found herself unable to move, as she watched him drying his body, seemingly without any inhibitions about being naked in front of her. When he turned where she could see the exit wound, she almost dropped her weapon. Where there should have been a gaping hole, the skin was red, but the wound was closed, as if healing. As the towel slid over the exit wound, he flinched a little, saying, "It is still pretty sore in that area."

Pulling her detective self together, she stated, "I would ask who are you, but after seeing your wounds better and you in the shower, I should be asking what you are? No one can heal that quickly." She brought her weapon to the front of her own body.

Noticing her tenser movements, as he donned his pants, he assured, "I promise you that I am human, and if you don't shoot me, I will be glad to explain or answer anything you want to know."

When he approached, she somewhat nervously backed out of the bathroom and let him pass.

He walked past her recliner. "You seemed to be getting some much needed sleep, so I didn't wake you. Yes, I saw your weapon." as he stopped and looked back at her.

"How'd he know what I was thinking?" she asked herself.

Her thoughts were interrupted by his words, "I apologize for any mess I may have made. I'm sorry for the blood on my pants and the fact that I don't have a shirt to put on. Mine wasn't in the bedroom or bathroom. I am extremely grateful for everything you have done for me."

Still holding her weapon, but much lower, she stated, "With a bullet hole and blood soaked, I threw it in the trash."

Not wanting to say ex, she continued, "I'm sure one of my husband's old shirts will fit you. You appear to be about the same size. However, before I go digging through the closet to find you clothes to wear, you have a lot of explaining to do."

"I will answer any questions you may have, and again, I appreciate your doctoring me, instead of taking me to the hospital. I hope you don't get in any kind of trouble because of me. Before I begin answering your questions, could I ask if you have anything for me to eat? It would help the healing process."

Not feeling that she was in any kind of danger, she holstered her weapon, and followed him to the kitchen. She told him to have a seat on one of the stools at the bar. That way she could keep an eye on him, and she'd have the bar between them, while she was in the kitchen. She watched him flinch, a tidbit, when he climbed shirtless onto the stool.

"All I have are frozen dinners and beer in the fridge. I haven't had a chance to go grocery shopping." She was still trying to keep up the pretense that she had a husband. "My husband," she started but he interrupted.

"You do not have a husband. You don't wear a wedding ring. There are no wedding pictures, or any pictures with you and a man, except for the pictures of you and your fellow officers. You only have one bowl, one plate, and one glass in your dish drainer. You do not have to pretend. You are in no danger from me. I will bother you for some food, drink, and that shirt you mentioned, and then I will be out of your hair. I must keep on the move."

Before she could say anything, he glanced past her, seeing an over the counter microwave, and a smaller one sitting on the counter.

She saw his eyes going from one to the other and she explained, "The big one broke. Cheapest one I could find was about $800.00, and I didn't need to spend that for only me," as she looked at him and smiled.

"What time is it?" he asked anxiously.

Glancing at the clock, which he couldn't see from the other side of the bar, she related the time.

He startled her for a few seconds, as he rose, coming into the kitchen. He didn't see her hand going to the butt of her weapon, for he was looking toward the small microwave, as he approached it.

"I need to borrow that for a few minutes." He moved back to the other side of the bar, retrieved the barstool, and placed it in front of the microwave. He tried to brace himself on the counter and raise his right leg onto the stool.

Seeing he was unsteady, she rushed to his side and helped support his body, until he got the leg situated on the stool.

"What are you doing?" she inquired.

"Got that frozen dinner? No need to waste electricity," he answered.

She cautiously moved to the freezer, prepared the frozen dinner for the microwave, and handed it to him.

He placed it inside and asked, "How many minutes?"

"Ten," she answered without thinking, "Then, I'll have to peel back the top and let it go for another five."

She watched, as he tensed himself and pushed the button to start cooking. She watched him grit his teeth, and noticed a spot under the skin on the back of his leg beginning to turn red.

"The back of your leg is getting bright red. You need to stop whatever you are trying to do."

"Not yet, he said through gritted teeth, as he watched the clock on the kitchen wall. Then, as if he couldn't stand any more pain, he removed his leg from the stool. Sweat beaded on his brow, as he leaned against the counter to compose himself.

"Just what was that all about?" she asked nervously, handing him a few paper towels off the roll.

"They planted a tracking device in my leg when I was a child. I discovered when I grew older, that waves such as the ones produced by your appliance, would disrupt the signal from the tracking device. It will scramble the signal for approximately thirty-six hours, and the aliens can't track it precisely. However, they can locate the vicinity of the scrambled signal within a few miles, I would suspect. "

"Why don't you just remove it?" she wanted to know.

"I'd still have to destroy it somehow, and I am not quite sure how to accomplish that task. They evidently are very durable and waterproof.

Secondly, I'm not exactly sure what it would do to me. They always told us we would die if we ever removed the device."

"Did you believe them?" she added, "Most likely they wanted to scare you to make sure you didn't try to remove it." She suddenly realized she was talking as if she really believed this stuff he was telling her.

"Of course, I considered that might be the case, but I was never in a position to try to remove it, anyway."

Her ringing phone interrupted their conversation. She removed it from her pocket, putting it to her ear. "Captain, I was just about to call you, and request a couple of week's vacation. Caruso is under scrutiny for awhile, and I have no desire to work with anyone else at this time."

On the other end she heard his reply, "No vacation right now. The news video showed you entering the building with the other officers with your weapon drawn. Now, you and the others have to answer IAD, about the shooting."

Trying to get out of her situation she stated, "Captain, by the time I got in there, the shooting was all over. All I did was say a few words to Caruso and leave."

"I know, but you still have to come in here today, and give your statement to IAD, just like everyone else. Then we'll discuss your vacation. By the way, the news showed some guy sitting in your car. You got a new boyfriend? I couldn't see him clearly through your windshield."

"Yeah," She answered, "We were going shopping."

Laughing a little, he stated, "Get you ass in here later, talk to IAD, and then come see me."

"Ok, but be thinking about my vacation request. It's short notice, but you've been telling me to take some time off."

"I'll keep it under consideration," he muttered, as she heard him end the call.

She turned to Mark, "I've got to go in today, and talk to the Internal Affairs Division about what I know of the shooting you were involved in."

"As soon as I eat, I will leave your home. What are you going to tell them about me?"

"I'm not going to tell them anything about you. The captain thinks you are my boyfriend, who was sitting in my car waiting for me."

Suddenly, she found herself making excuses to keep him from leaving. "Listen, while I'm at the office, I'll look up the information report my partner said they were taking before the shooting. I'll get the address and phone number for your previous home and see what I can find out."

Not seeing an agreeable look on his face, she continued, "Also, a guy I know is one of those scientific nerds. Well not really a nerd. He is much more book smart than the rest of us, but he's a real nice guy. He continued his study in radio waves and that kind of stuff, after he graduated. He works for the government in some top secret building near here. He lives in a cabin about ten miles outside of town. We get together once every couple of weeks for pizza and beer. Maybe he can tell us something about that device in your leg."

She saw his face light up, as he heard her words.

"Anyway," she cautioned, "You are healing fast, but you don't want to disrupt that process. A day of rest around here can do nothing but help."

His face turned serious, "I can't scramble the signal from the tracking device from this same location a second time. It would be a dead giveaway to my position."

"I'll do what I have to do at the office as quickly as possible," she said, "Then we'll go to another location. There are no shortages of microwaves. They are everywhere, but putting your leg up next to one in a store might draw some attention."

He agreed, and they talked more about his confinement by the aliens, as he waited for his meal from the microwave.

While he ate, she went to change blouses. She didn't feel safe enough to jump in the shower with this strange man in her house. She sure didn't get dirty yesterday, anyway. However, she thought it would probably be an exciting time in the shower with him, as she pictured his naked body pressed against hers. When she returned wearing a tight fitting black pullover blouse, she noticed his eyes fixed on the way it hugged her breasts. She raised the blue pullover shirt she held in her hand, and disrupted whatever he was thinking, "See if this will fit."

He grinned, as his eyes moved to her face. He slipped the shirt over his head and adjusted it. He muttered a slight groan, as he raised his hands in the air to check out the snugness of the shirt. "Like a glove," he assured.

In her other hand on a hanger was a pair of pants. "I think these should fit you, also." The clothes were actually some old clothes her partner had left there, when she bought him new clothes for his birthday a few years ago."

As he started to unbuckle his belt, she stopped him by saying, "I laid some clean underwear and socks on your bed. I need to throw your old clothes away in case there is any trace of blood on them."

Seeing her face was a little blushed, he agreed, "Oh, Ok! I'll change in the bedroom," and headed in that direction.

She smiled, as she watched his butt all the way to his room. She liked the thought of it being his room. At least the thought comforted her for now. Soon he returned fully dressed, with his old clothes in his hand.

She liked the way the clothes looked on him, for they fit much better than when Caruso wore them. She took the soiled clothes from him and threw them into the garbage bag. As she removed the bag from the can, she thought, "Last bit of evidence."

Before she left for the office, she made him promise to stay inside and not answer the house phone. She didn't want him walking around in the yard and maybe talking to someone. She pulled on the jacket she wore to cover her weapon and badge. She saw him watching her movements. She knew she had a nice body. Hell, she worked hard enough to keep it in shape, and was pleased to see the admiration on his face. She told him to make himself at home, and that she'd be back as soon as she could. She reaffirmed she'd get in touch with her friend to see if he could help.

Not being able to think of any more excuses to keep him from leaving, she placed the garbage bag with all his clothes, rag and bandages in the trunk of her car. There was a dumpster on the way to work, where she could dispose of everything.

When she backed out, she looked up to see his figure at the door watching her. Like a wife waving at her husband, she threw her hand up and waved.

When the garage door closed, and she backed into the street, she began talking to herself again, "Sarah, you idiot. You may come home and everything you own will be gone. You don't know anything about this stranger, except that he sounds like a nut case. There could be some gangsters looking for him." She remembered what he looked like, as he threw back the shower curtain, and whispered out loud, "Damn, he looked good naked."

A few blocks away, she found the secluded dumpster and disposed of her garbage bag. There was no one in the vicinity, and she knew there were no street cameras in this area to capture her actions.

As she sped away, her cell rang. She retrieved it from her jacket. It was her best friend, Kate Brewster. Kate was a patrol officer. They met at one of Sarah's crime scenes, and became best friends in no time.

Sarah answered, "Aren't you at work, girl?"

"Yeah, but I'm in the ladies room. What's this about you have a new boyfriend you haven't told me about? I thought we told each other everything."

"We do," confirmed Sarah, "I was just about to call you. I've got a lot I need to tell someone, and I want it to be you."

Kate replied, "You've got to talk to IAD this morning. Get your ass in here. By the time you give them your statement, my shift will be over. We can go somewhere for lunch, since you are still off, and you can tell me about this new guy. I'm dying to hear all about him."

Sarah heard the door open, as Kate said, "Gotta go," and hung up.

When she put her phone down, she wondered how she was going to explain this guy at her house. She could already picture Kate telling her, "Are you nuts?" She made up her mind right then and there. She was taking Kate back to her house to see the guy in person, if he was is still there when she got back home.

Chapter Two

When she arrived at the station, Kate met her and whispered, "Caruso doesn't seem too happy that you have a new boyfriend." Kate knew all about her relationship with her partner.

Sarah saw Jack look up from his paperwork, then nonchalantly back down to his desk. "Yep, he's a little teed off, I can tell," whispered Sarah. "Let me get this IAD thing over and we'll get out of here. You're going to wait for me if this takes longer than expected aren't you?"

"You know I will," as she walked back to her desk. The patrol officers had to rotate now and then to a desk inside. They had to learn the usual mundane job of taking down complaints, or helping booking and fingerprinting. It was Kate's turn today. Sarah was glad it wasn't Kate's turn yesterday during the shooting.

As Sarah walked toward IAD's office, she glanced again at Caruso. His phone rang and he looked up for a second or two, but not in her direction. Talking, his head went back down to the papers he'd been reviewing. She always liked looking at him. His physique and short military style hair cut was always impressive. He had a reputation for not being someone to make angry. She'd seen firsthand, how criminals, who got unruly, were thrown around like dishrags. She hoped he wasn't, too, mad. She was sure she could convince him that this guy wasn't her new boyfriend. After all, he wasn't anything to her, yet. He was a weird, wounded stranger that she took home. Now she found herself whispering, "Oh! Yeah! Sarah! You just might be nuttier than the guy you waved goodbye to, who was standing at your kitchen door."

Giving IAD just the facts without elaborating, she was soon out of there, and made a stop at the desk, where they kept the reports from the previous night. She found the report about Mark, and quickly checked the computer, to see how it was put into the system. It wasn't in the system with the other reports. She surmised; because it was Susan who was the female wounded officer. With the commotion and crime scene thing, no one had gotten to it. She found a large brown envelope and slipped the report inside. Her eyes went toward the ceiling, as she told herself again, "Sarah, you just broke another rule."

From there, she went to the captain's office, to inquire about her vacation. He already had the vacation request on his desk ready for her to sign. "I put you down for two weeks, paid vacation, but if you need to come back sooner, just call in. I'll make up some excuse for needing you."

"Thanks, Captain, I'm going to take the whole two weeks, whether I need it or not," she nodded, and hurriedly signed the forms.

"It's about time," he agreed, "Now get your ass out of here before something happens and I change my mind."

She grinned back over her shoulder and closed the door, just as Kate met her saying, "Are we through here now?"

"We are so out of here, girl," was Sarah's answer, "You are not going to believe what I have to tell you, and hopefully show you. First, I've got to call Charley."

She saw Kate's eyes light up at the mention of Charley. Sarah had introduced them some time back, while they were sharing beer and Pizza. He and Kate hit it off, and dated off and on. Sarah had trouble believing these two liked each other. Kate was a wild child, and Charley was a bookworm. Still, the two were seeing each other, and Kate told her that he was a good lover in bed. They'd made no commitments to each other, and Kate had been seeing other guys. Neither she nor Sarah knew if Charley was seeing anyone else. He kept to himself. He wasn't a party-going type of fellow.

"Remember to watch what you are saying to Charley on the phone. Remember where he works," cautioned Kate, "And put your phone on speaker so I can hear his voice."

"Yeah!" she answered, and then, "Charley, good to hear your voice. Are you working hard?"

"Nah! It's been kind of a slow week. What's up, girl?"

"Kate and I want to know if you can come over to my house for pizza and beer tonight." She glanced at Kate's wide smile.

"Sure, you know if Kate is going to be there, my ass will be there."

"It may be a very late party," she continued, "Bring extra clothes and a shaving kit. You can spend the dark."

At that statement, Sarah saw the inquiring look on Kate's brow.

"What time do you want me there?"

"Soon as you can get off from work, grab some things from your place and make it to mine."

"Do you need me to bring anything, beer, ice, chips and dip?"

"Nope, got most of what we need. Kate and I are going to the store for the rest. Then we're going to her place to pick up a few things so she can spend the night, too. "

"I get off at 3:30. I should be at your place by quarter till five. Is Kate with you right now?"

"Yeah, I'm here," Kate said loudly, "I'm looking forward to seeing your handsome face again. It's been a few weeks, and you haven't even called."

Defensively, he said, "Not because I didn't want to. Had some important things around here I had to get done. It was crazy for awhile. Getting some breathing room now; looking forward to the beer and pizza, and being near you again."

"I promise I'll make it worth your while, dear boy," Kate smiled.

"You're making me want to leave right now, but I can't, so I'll look forward to seeing you guys before five."

"It's a date!" Kate finished, and said goodbye, as she saw Sarah put her phone down.

"You, your new boyfriend, Charley and me on an all-nighter; what's your new man going to think about this?"

"Guess we'll find out later today, huh?" She didn't want to tell Kate anything about the stranger yet. She'd have way too many questions. "And don't start asking me a bunch of questions about him. After you meet, you can ask me then. I'm not answering shit right now."

"Ok! Keep it a secret, but he must be something special," Kate grinned.

"He's special alright!" was all Sarah was going to divulge.

Kate changed the subject. "Are we going to get something to eat? Right now I'm starving. I wasn't hungry last night at work. Well, maybe a little, but I'm still trying to keep my weight down. Got to keep the boys watching me walk."

Sarah laughed, "You're so full of it. You could eat all day and never gain an ounce. I'm the one who has to watch what I eat, and work out at the gym all the time. We'll get a sandwich at the deli."

"Sounds like a plan." Kate agreed.

Soon they'd made their stop for food, and proceeded to Kate's to pick up her overnight things, and then Sarah hurried back toward her place. It was then that realization began to sink in. What if he wasn't there? What was she going to do? She resigned herself to thinking she'd have to go looking for him. She'd picked up the report they'd been filling out before the shooting, but she hadn't made the call, or tried to find out about his mother. There was just too much going on. She'd tell him she wanted to make the call in his presence, just in case his mother answered. Yeah! That's how she'd explain things. She neared her house and saw a vehicle parked in front of her house. She slowed her car, and came to a stop a few driveways away.

"What's wrong?" inquired Kate, looking a little worried at Sarah's actions.

"I just don't recognize that car." She eased her vehicle forward, pushed the garage door opener button, and entered. Shutting the engine off, she looked toward the door, but no one came to open it.

The two girls exited the vehicle and went into the hallway to the kitchen, as the garage door closed behind them.

Danah Polero sat on a sofa talking to Sarah's guest. Sarah, a little nervously, "I didn't recognize your car, Danah." Sarah wondered what in the world she was doing here, and what this man may have told her? She hadn't talked to Danah since the live interview the paper had done on Sarah. The article was about women on the force and Sarah recovering from her wounds.

"You wouldn't," she smiled, "Just got it a few days ago."

Introducing Kate, Sarah said, "This is my best friend, Kate Brewster ," and turning toward the reporter, "This is, Danah Polero, from PVT News."

Danah and the man stood, and Danah shook Kate's hand.

Kate remarked, "Oh! Yeah! I recognize you now. You are prettier than you are on TV." Kate was being honest. Polero's svelte shape, dark sultry eyes, and shiny black hair could have tempted any man to go wrong.

"You are being kind, dear girl, but thank you."

Realizing she hadn't even looked at the report and didn't even know the strangers name, Sarah faked it, "I see you've already met this handsome gentleman," as she nodded toward him.

Danah turned to him and remarked, "Yes, Mark and I were getting acquainted. You are correct, he is handsome."

Before Sarah could say anything, Danah turned to her saying, "I have to apologize for being here today. We had a news shot of your boyfriend in the car through the window. When we came out of the building you car was gone. When we interviewed passersby, one said a wounded man was sitting in your car. He was holding a towel to his left side.

We went to the hospital thinking you hurried a wounded man to the emergency room, but found you had never been there."

Looking toward the silent Sarah, she continued, "Obviously, the person gave us erroneous information. Mark said it was him in your car waiting. He kindly raised his shirt to show me both his sides. He has no wounds. He does have some red skin areas, but he explained it was a rash."

Now, Sarah could breathe enough to speak, "Yeah! Mark woke up with a rash he must have gotten when we were walking in the park yesterday. I gave him a towel and told him to keep it dry while I was in the office." Evidently no one had told Danah about her having to coax the bleeding Mark back into her car before she sped off. As she thought back, she remembered people looking at the front of the building, as if they expected shooters to come running out. They weren't paying much attention to her or Mark.

Wanting to change the subject, Sarah said, "I've wanted to thank you about the flattering article you wrote about me, after the live interview. I'm sure there are a lot more deserving females on the force."

"I don't know about that," defended Danah, "You made detective faster than anyone ever, and the way you handled yourself when you were shot was totally remarkable. Your male counterparts did a lot of bragging on you. Anyway, I've got to get going. There's news out there waiting." Looking toward Mark, "It's been very nice meeting you.

Looking toward Kate, "And thank you, young lady, for your kind remarks," as she shook her hand again.

Turning to Sarah, "I'm going to have to keep a closer eye on you, girl. You seem to be where the action is a lot."

"No more than I have to, I assure you," as she stuck out her hand to Danah.

In a minute or so, Sarah escorted Danah to the door, and said goodbye. She breathed a sigh of relief, and waved, as Danah pulled away.

When she returned to Mark and Kate, she heard them introducing themselves.

"Mark, I see you are already getting to know my best friend. I'll warn you ahead of time. We tell each other everything."

"I don't have any problem with that, but I'll let you stop me, if you think something I have to say should stay private between us," as he grinned.

"No, really, we don't keep any secrets from each other." Suddenly she remembered the report in the car. "Oops, I forgot the things we bought at the store and the report. I'll get them from the car, while you two get more acquainted."

Kate grinned, "Oh! Yeah! I want to know all about this man you've been keeping to yourself."

Sarah just rolled her eyes, as she headed for her car in the garage. When she opened the back door to get the articles, her cell rang. Seeing it was Caruso, she answered, "Jack, I wasn't sure you were speaking to me."

"What? Oh, you mean because of your new boyfriend."

"We're just friends, Jack. There is nothing going on."

"That's not what the captain said," he replied.

Sarah, defensively, "You know how rumors get started around there. I was going to talk to you when I came out of IAD, but you disappeared."

"I was in the bathroom. Had the shits from something I ate the night before. When I came out you had already left. Then I had to go talk to IAD. Guess I'll be on desk duty, or off with pay, since the shooting at the precinct. They haven't made up their minds yet." Continuing, "I didn't think much about the rumor. I figured if I was out of the picture, you would let me know. We've been through a lot together."

Feeling somewhat guilty, she assured him, "You know if I found a new boyfriend, I'd have the decency to let you know. I'd tell you in person."

"Yeah, I Know. What I called for was to tell you that IAD might call you in again. There was some kind of information that you may have been seen outside the station with a guy that was wounded. Also, before Susan was wounded, she was taking information from the guy that Jeff had to hold back before the shooting started. That guy disappeared in the commotion. Now they know when one of the shooters fired at the ghost guy, the bullet hit Susan. This guy has become a person of interest, and IAD wants to find him. To make things even worse, the report Susan was handwriting never got placed into the system, and it has disappeared. There was speculation our magician may have grabbed the report during the shooting, and took it with him."

Glad they thought Mark had taken it made her sigh as she said, "Possibly."

Caruso added, "No one said anything to IAD about this, but Nick said you were looking over last night's reports. He saw you leave with a brown envelope."

"He saw correctly," she admitted calmly. "Everyone looks at those reports when they come on duty, if they give a shit about what is going on. Since I had to be there, of course, I went through them out of habit. I didn't see that report (Well almost true she thought, for she didn't read it.) What the hell would I need with one of last night's reports?"

Before he could continue, she said, "As for the envelope, did the captain also tell you that I am taking two weeks off? I had some information on where I might go in that envelope (Not totally a lie, for what ever is in that report may lead her anywhere, and she would be on vacation.)

"Hopefully, not with a new boyfriend," he interrupted.

"Cute, Jack." She didn't want to tell him anymore about that situation. "Kate and Charley are going to be at the house tonight for pizza and beer. I wanted to get these two back together. I think their relationship was failing. They are perfect for each other."

"Want to make it a foursome?" he asked hopefully.

"Don't know how this is going to turn out. If I think they want to be alone, I'll give you a call."

"I'll be at home. I'm not planning on going anywhere tonight. If you want to sneak off somewhere, you know we can," he said a little softer.

"Are you still at work?" she asked, after hearing his voice drop almost to a whisper.

"Yeah, but I came out to the car to get something so I could place this call. If yours rings and you see it is from the precinct, I wouldn't answer if I were you. Might be a good idea for you not to stay home tonight either."

"Thanks, Jack, I'll keep you posted. Gotta go for now."

"Later," was all he answered before ending his call.

She realized there were no comments like "Love ya," "See you later sweetie," or any other words that would indicate a commitment. Their relationship wasn't that kind. It was more of an attachment to each other as partners, and an occasional night of hot sex. However, they both knew if they needed each other for anything, the other would come running. They knew they made a good team.

Maybe she was fooling herself. He'd told her many times she was very special to him. There was several times when she was almost sure he was going to tell her he loved her. When she was wounded during the shootout, he was at the hospital every minute he could. When she went home to recover, he was there almost every day, doting on her, doing the grocery shopping, and even cooking. He didn't catch much flack from the department. After all, she was his partner, and a wounded fellow officer. Several of the male and female officers came to visit, brought food, and offered to help in anyway they could.

She knew she had very strong feelings for him. There were times when they sneaked out on a date, or a night of hot sex, that she felt herself wanting to say those three special words. Something always held her back. There was probably no doubt if it wasn't for the force they'd be living together somewhere. Of course, if they ever made that commitment, one or both, would have to quit the police force. Neither was ready to take that step. She wondered if she was going to need him before her present situation was over.

She took the report and bags of pizza, beer, chips and dip from the back seat. Once inside, she sat some of the items on the bar and put the beer and in the fridge. The carried the report into the room where Kate and Mark were talking.

She knew by the bewildered look Kate gave her that Mark already told her some things she was having trouble believing.

"Kate, before you get too wrapped up into what Mark is telling you, we need to read this report together," as she sat down between them.

The doorbell rang. "Shit," she uttered, as she rose, stuffed the report under a cushion, and headed toward the door, thinking, "Damn, IAD already here?"

She peered out the window, and opened the door. "Charley, thought you wouldn't be here till around five." She gave him a big hug and a kiss on the cheek.

Coming in, he answered, "Boss heard our conversation this morning. He's been real pleased with what we got done the last three weeks. He insisted I take the rest of the day off, and be with friends. He also handed me a paper informing I've been given a big raise. I'm ready to celebrate." He raised a box of hot wings, and held an eighteen case of beer in his other hand.

"Congratulations! Kate is keeping my new friend occupied. We were just about to read a report. I'm glad you got off early. Now, we can read it together."

Kate came running, wrapped her arms around his neck, and gave him a big kiss, "I've missed you, Teddy Bear."

"I'll put your beer with mine in the fridge, let Kate take you in and introduce you. I'll get the pizza and hot wings warming."

As they walked toward Mark, she headed for the kitchen.

By the time she rejoined them; Kate had retrieved the report and handed it to her. She pulled the report out of the envelope and began to read. She only got started, as she read Mark's words about being abducted by aliens, when Charley held up a hand and stopped her.

"Is this some kind of joke you are pulling on me?" he questioned barely smiling.

"No! It is a real report they took at the station last night."

Charley quickly stood, saying, "Don't read anymore until I get something from my car."

"Ok!" she said with a confused look toward the others.

In a few minutes, Charley returned with what appeared to be a radio with headsets. He didn't speak. He just held his fingers to his lips in the hush sign, and began walking around the room. He pulled his cell phone out of his back pocket, and motioned for them to do the same.

Not having the faintest idea what he was doing, but trusting him completely, they obeyed. He passed the radio by each of their phones and looked toward Mark, who just shook his head.

Charley walked toward him anyway, holding the small radio in front of him. Suddenly he stopped.

He moved the machine upward toward Mark's head, then down his body, and stopped when he got to his lower leg.

By now, Mark surmised this wasn't a radio. He raised his pants leg so Charley could see the red area on the back of his leg.

Charley removed the headsets saying, "It's not short-wave radio frequency, or high tech listening device, but there is some kind of signal similar to a tracker."

Kate was bewildered at Charley's actions and now she looked even more so.

"Scrambled tracking device," answered Mark matter of fact.

"Better sit down, Charley. I'll read this report out loud," Sarah interrupted.

Mark asked, "What made you go get this machine when you heard the word aliens? Something tells me you know a lot about them."

Charley sat saying, "Let's just listen to the report."

He and Kate sat speechless as Sarah read. Occasionally, they glanced toward Mark, who would nod in agreement to what she was reading out loud.

When she finished, Kate spoke immediately, "Mark, I don't want to be unkind, and I'm sure you are a nice guy, but this is all a little farfetched."

They were all surprised when Charley spoke softly, "Not necessarily. Before I say anymore, I want to know what you meant by scrambled tracking device. I've never encountered the type of signal, that I picked up on my machine. I've never seen a pitch that high from evidently a small device in your leg. That kind of signal is usually produced by large pieces of equipment, and heard by satellite in space."

The women remained quiet, as Mark repeated what he'd told Sarah, and how he'd used the microwave to disable the tracker for thirty-six hours.

"Now that's one for the books," Charley said smiling. His smile went to a frown just as quickly, "How much time do we have left?"

Looking at her watch, Sarah answered for him, "Twenty-five hours."

As if he was not the least bit worried, he continued, "Sounds like we've got plenty of time for food and drink. Didn't take time to eat today, and I am starving. Right now, I could definitely use one of those beers."

"Me, too," agreed Kate, as she wrapped her arms around Charley's waist.

"I'll bring the beer, and the wings should be ready. It will probably be a little longer for the pizza. Want to help me, Kate?"

"Sure," Kate kissed Charley on the cheek, and rose to accompany Sarah.

Charley turned seriously toward Mark, "That thing has got to come out of your leg, or they will find you, sooner or later."

"They always said it would kill us to remove it, but I'm not sure that is fact."

"I doubt it," replied Charley, "It's just a device they implanted in your body. However, if it is alien technology, I can't be positive."

The girls returned and Kate spoke excitedly, "You've been held captive all these years and you escaped to find your mother. Let's call the number."

Sarah interrupted, "What about your father. Was he alive when you were taken?"

"Not sure," he answered, "I was only six. I remember asking Mother about him. She said he was out of the picture, and she would tell me all about him when I got older. That was enough to appease me at the time."

Kate and Charley already started on a wing and beer while they were listening. Mark and Sarah did the same.

Kate wiped her mouth and handed Mark her phone, "Call the number. If she's still alive and answers, what a moment this will be for you, and her. For us, too, for that matter, so make sure you put it on speaker."

Somewhat nervously he accepted the phone, looked at it and began dialing. They were all disappointed to hear the recorded voice, "This is not a working number. Please check your number and dial again."

As he ended the call, Sarah comforted, "Didn't really expect her to have the same number after all these years. She probably moved, maybe remarried, or maybe just went to a cell phone, and no home phone like a lot of us now days. I hear the beeper on the stove. Pizza is ready. I'll bring it."

Everyone nodded, as Sarah walked toward the kitchen.

Kate helped herself to another wing.

Mark turned to Charley, saying, "Nothing I've said about the aliens has surprised you. Why is that?"

It kind of floored both of them, when he grinned, saying, "Because I believe you."

Now Kate looked intently at Charley, as Sarah returned with the hot pizza. Charley continued, "I'll put it this way. The CIA and NASA are friends where I work. What I am going to say from this point on would put all of us in great danger, if any of it were ever repeated. Do all of you fully understand what I am saying?"

As the girls nodded, he began again, "This is no joke, and I'm not kidding in any way. If you leak any of this, you could be in deeper shit than you could ever imagine. You could be here one day, and gone the next. Never to be heard from again."

"We understand," Sarah agreed, biting into a slice of pizza.

He took a bite of his, swallowed some beer, and then started, "I must be out of my mind for what I am about to tell you, but here goes. For years there's been sightings of UFOs, in the area Mark talks about. My company has monitored signals coming from that area for our friends in higher places. They've been trying to pinpoint the location. However, aerial observance day and night, satellite and ground search have proved fruitless.

Two years ago, a woman was found on the side of a road near that area. She was picked up by military on a search mission that night. The friends in high places I mentioned have held her. Just as Mark, she'd escaped and could not lead them to the location. Ground search from the point she was picked up has been extensive, but to no avail. I've been busy the last three weeks installing sophisticated listening devices in that area for our military. Some of which I personally designed."

They were silent, and munching on their food, as he finished off a wing, took another bite of pizza, and chased it down with beer.

Seeing his bottle was empty, Sarah jumped up, saying, "I'll get us all another one. Don't start again until I return."

He was glad to oblige, as he continued eating.

As she passed around the beers, he took a swallow of his, and continued, "This woman, whose name I can't mention, related that there were humans helping aliens at this underground facility. She said they must have been high ranking, because the aliens seemed to be bidding their commands. Also, the underground secret place was definitely built by humans."

Mark jumped in wide-eyed, "How did she escape? I know what I went through to get out of there. It took planning for several years."

Charley began his answer; "According to her, there was a box truck that arrived at night, once every three weeks. It was always the same two men, and they delivered all kinds of food and cooking supplies. She related how, another of her duties along with other women, was to prepare food for the young people in another part of the facility."

Mark again, "We were always taken to a lunchroom per se for each meal. The food was always hot and ready in buffet style, but there were no servers anywhere. We'd been taught to eat healthy foods and small portions, so we helped ourselves to the food. There was never a shortage, and the food was always good. Many of us wondered who prepared the food, and we doubted if it was the aliens. We figured the aliens added some ingredients of their own to the food, to make us become what they wanted us to be."

Charley nodded, "Probably. That sounds logical. Let's get back to her escape. She was around twenty-eight, and the men supposedly were two brothers, approximately her age. She made sure she was on the night shift each time they arrived. She said the aliens had grown used to these same two men arriving, and they knew they already had to come past a checkpoint that the men had said were human.

The aliens would check to make sure everything looked normal, and then disappear. The woman also knew there were cameras watching the huge storage room where these men unloaded the supplies. The aliens also grew used to her entering the truck to help the men unload, and tell them where to put things in the room.

She made herself attractive, and started coming on to one of the brothers. She told of how she wore a loose blouse, a skirt, and no underwear. She mentioned to the brothers how her tubes were tied, and she needed a man. It didn't take long, of course, before the one who was a target of her affection, got a quickie, while his brother kept unloading.

After a few more trips, the brother wanted some of the action. Since she was more than agreeable, this other brother was soon having sex with her in the truck. Every third week this scenario repeated itself. I'm sure the brothers looked forward to this delivery.

This went on for several months. On one of their deliveries in the back of the truck, she showed them her baby bump and told them she was pregnant. She made them aware that the aliens would know the baby had to be from one of them, and they weren't going to be happy about it. As the months went by and her pregnancy continued, she wouldn't be able to perform the work she was supposed to do.

This had been her plan from the beginning. Her tubes really had never been tied. She convinced them to sneak her out of there in the back of the truck. She told them they could drop her off on the road. If the aliens caught her, she'd tell them she hid in the back of the truck to escape. She related how the men went into a panic, fearing she would tell someone who may pick her up on the road, about them, the facility, and the aliens.

She sweet talked them into believing that all she wanted to do was get away, hide from the aliens, and get back to a normal life. She also convinced the brothers she liked making love to them, but it would be better if they never saw each other again after her escape. That way the aliens couldn't blame them. The brothers came to the conclusion her plan was the only way out of the mess they'd gotten themselves into.

The men were extremely nervous, but sneaked her out in the back of the truck. The human guards at the checkpoint didn't even look in the back of the truck where she was hiding. They, too, were accustomed to seeing these same two men coming and going. This was also verification that these guards were human, as she heard one of them talking to the brothers.

She told of how she was in the back of the truck going down some type of bumpy road, a seemingly endless time. She feared the men might kill her, out of desperation, and leave her body in the desolate area along the road. She admitted she was terrified when the truck finally came to a stop and the door was lifted on the back of the truck. The men helped her out of the truck, and she saw town in the distance, from the hill they stopped on. The brother she'd had sex with the most pointed down the road on the other side of the hill, and she saw lights from a row of vehicles. They were far enough away she could not hear their engines.

He told her it was a military convoy and she could flag them down. The man laughed, saying, "We always know where the convoys are, and when the military will be in this area." According to her, they both kissed her, and got one last feel of her breasts. Then they jumped in the truck and sped away toward town.

She stood patiently, hoping the aliens didn't find her before the convoy got to her.

When the military found her, she told them about the brothers, the facility and the aliens. They took her into custody, and she remains today in a government facility supposedly run by NSA."

"Poor woman," Kate sighed, "She went from one captive situation to another."

Charley nodded, "I think she is much happier where she is. According to rumored information, she is basically treated like a queen. First of all, they don't need her talking to anyone else, but they would need her to identify the two brothers when they found them. There have been many trucks stopped since her escape. Anyone remotely resembling the descriptions of the two young men is put in a room for her to possibly identify. These two would be a direct link to finding the location of the facility."

Mark asked, "What happens to her, when and if they find these guys, and discover how to get to the facility?"

"That, my friend, is the million dollar question." Charley frowned, "It's for sure they won't need her much longer. However, now there is a child in the picture. The baby was a boy. If they find the brothers, they will also have DNA from the baby to match to one of the brothers."

Sarah had been silent up to this point, "What will our people do, when and if they find the location?"

Charley gave an answer that neither was ready for, "For years, it is believed that there have been men, who are descendents of a group called, The Majestic Twelve. This group was developed in the 50's, and worked outside of, and above any other government agencies. They have apparently unlimited untraceable funds, and such a secret society that apparently no one has ever broken their silence. Probably for fear of death, or just to have the knowledge that they have so much power. Anyway, this group was originally organized to work with aliens to obtain their craft propulsion, and other types of technology."

Charley continued, more sternly defensive, "You need to understand this will be a matter of national security. For years, our government has tried to find this group, and destroy them. Of course, we want to abstract any alien knowledge that is possible for our own military purposes. Our people know this group has developed, and are flying, craft with alien technology. Hell, a lot of UFO reported sightings are probably their experimental crafts. You can imagine how much this is pissing off our military."

Mark mentioned seriously, "I have doubts that our normal military could win, if it came down to a battle with the aliens."

"That's always in the back of their minds, of course," Charley agreed, "That's why there is a lot of brainstorming, as to how to convince the aliens to work with our military, if they get the opportunity."

With a worried look Kate asked, "What about the humans being held? They will be in great danger, if our military has to pull a full out attack on the place."

Charley placed an arm around her, comforting, "That's why I love you. You're always thinking of the other person. I imagine our government would like to get all of these people out alive. They'll want to know everything about each one."

Kate said, "All this is hard for my pea-brain to believe. You are telling us that all this is true, and there really are aliens here on earth?"

He laughed, "Kate, have you been living under a rock? Aliens have visited earth since as far back as any type of recording took place. Egyptian scrolls and cave drawings for instance. Our friends in high places know that aliens from different planets have been here from time to time; for what reasons they are not sure. Some seemed to have been friendly, some not, and some didn't seem to give a shit, one-way or the other. Those appeared to be just passer-bys."

They were interrupted by Sarah's cell, "It's Jack, I've got to take this," as she rose, and headed toward the kitchen.

"Yeah, Jack," she answered.

"Just wanted to let you know you may be off the hook with IAD for a little, anyway. After all the interviews, they seem satisfied that our ghost guy was a nut case and just tried to help, before the shooting started. They think he took the file and left because he didn't want to be involved with the shooting. CSI team found traces of blood where Jeff was holding him. He must have been wounded, and they are checking hospitals, etc. for anyone with a gunshot wound. How is the cupid thing going with Kate and Charley?"

"Okay so far," she said, stepping on out into the garage and closing the door behind her, "Are you still going to be available if I need you later tonight?"

"Honey, I'm available anytime you need me and anywhere."

"Jack, I," she caught herself. She almost said I love you. "I'm just glad you are there when I need you."

He could tell there was something different in her voice, "Are you sure you are alright? I'll come over right now, if you want."

She tried to laugh a little, saying, "Let's just see if Cupid works his magic for Kate and Charley. I'll probably call you later."

As she hesitated, he told her, "I'll go right home and be waiting when I leave here."

In a serious tone Sarah mentioned, "You know that cousin of yours who works for the FBI in Kansas?"

"Kenny, he's my favorite cousin. Why?"

"Do you think he would do something for you off the record?

"I imagine he would, Sarah, where is this leading?

"I need you to have him find out everything he can on a woman named Carolyn Wakefield. She'd probably be in her late or early fifties, and may live in Wichita, Kansas."

"What's so important about this woman?"

"I'll explain everything later. Call me as soon as you hear from your cousin."

"Ok, but this is going to cost you," he answered laughing.

"You know I always pay my debts. Later," and she ended her call.

When she walked back into the living room, Charley began, "We need to get that thing out of his leg. I want to get a look at it. I have the equipment at my place to find out more about it, but we can't take my car. The company installs special GPS systems in all employee vehicles, and they are equipped with listening devices. I don't need any of what we are doing brought to their attention."

"No wonder you always wanted to use my car when we went on a date," Kate quipped.

"Where is your car anyway?" asked Sarah, "I didn't see it at the station."

"At my apartment," I've been carpooling with, Tilly, the redhead in booking. Why?"

"I didn't see it at your apartment complex when we went by there today."

"My Dad took it to have the brakes repaired for me this morning. It was an early appointment and it will be there now. He has a key and I have my keys."

Sarah explained, "Don't want to take my car to Charley's place. It has a GPS in it they can activate. We don't need IAD showing up at his place tonight."

Kate said, "My car it is, then. It doesn't have one of them ON STAR, or fancy GPS systems. Hell, I'm lucky if the air condition works when I get in it. Every couple of months I have to put another can of Freon in the thing."

"Ok, we'll drop you off at your apartment. You follow us, and we'll stash my car in an all night parking lot somewhere."

Mark interrupted, "Mind if we finish this good food first?"

They all had to laugh a little, as they saw him cramming the butt end of a slice of pizza in his mouth.

Charley rose from the couch, "I'll get my bag with a change of clothes, razor and stuff. I was under the belief we would be staying here tonight."

Sarah asked Kate, "Want to help me gather some things to take with us?"

"Sure," she answered, standing.

"Grab chips, dip, bread, beer and sandwich meats, and wieners out of the fridge. There is a small cooler with wheels in the garage, and a big bag of ice in the freezer out there. I'll pack some change of clothes, shoes, and women things."

Mark had also stood, and added, "I'm afraid I don't have anything to gather. I don't even have a tooth brush."

Sarah smiled, "Don't worry, Handsome. We'll stop at a drugstore and pick you up some toiletries. However, I don't have another change of clothes for you, so try not to get those dirty."

Noticing he and Mark were similar in height, Charley said, "I've still got some clothes that are too large for me now, since I went on that weight loss program two years ago. Some may fit you, if you need them."

Kate turned on the TV handing Mark the remote, "We'll get everything collected and be ready to leave shortly. See if there is anything on the news we need to know about. It should be on in about five minutes."

Taking the remote, he looked at it strangely. Realizing his situation, Kate pointed to the channel and volume buttons and grinned. He nodded as she walked away, and began searching channels.

A news anchor said something that made him stop on that channel, "It isn't unusual to hear reports of UFO sightings between here and Las Vegas. However, UFO sightings in the sky here above Pahrump are very unusual. Our own field investigator, Danah Polero, caught the following on film just as daylight began to fade."

The scene went to Danah reporting, and beginning to show her video, of a red light in the sky moving slowly in circles over the town. Excitedly, she described how they first thought it was a satellite, but soon realized it was something else. The light was too high in the sky to make out a shape. The video kept showing the light moving around, and then in the moonlight, two smaller objects approached the red light, which almost immediately shot off in the distance, and out of sight. As the camera went back to Danah, she said, "We'll contact the Air Force Base, and see how they explain what we've just witnessed. One thing for sure," she added, "It wasn't a weather balloon." She turned things back to the news anchor.

Sarah had been listening from her bedroom while gathering clothes. When she came out, Mark affirmed, "They know I'm here somewhere."

Nervously she added, "We need to get to Charley's and get that tracker out of you. That is, if you are ready to take the chance and remove it."

"I'm not going through the rest of my life with that thing in my leg. Yeah! I'm ready."

Charley came in the front door with his bag.

Kate came in from the garage, "I've got the food and beer in the trunk. There is still plenty of room for other things. Of course, you'll have to move the shotgun, boxes of ammunition, flack vest, and numerous other things around," as she grinned. "Hell, girl, you've got an arsenal in that trunk.

"Never know what we will run into. I don't have a personal car, remember? Besides, you guys keep a bunch of shit in your patrol cars, too."

Soon they were loaded into her car and headed down the road.

A short stop at a pharmacy for Mark's things, and they headed to Kate's apartment.

There they switched everything to Kate's car. She and Charley followed Sarah to a parking lot. She and Mark climbed in Kate's back seat and they cruised down the road out of town toward Charley's cabin. As they traveled, they made light of their situation, by making joking comments, until they saw a red light high in the sky. It wasn't blinking, so they knew it wasn't a plane. They knew a satellite looked like a star going across the sky, so they eliminated that possibility.

Things were quiet and tense, as they continued to observe out the windows.

Charley wisely kept the vehicle at the same rate of speed to avoid suspicion, just in case they could see the roads from that high up. The object moved in the opposite direction. They were relieved when it could no longer be seen.

Finally, they turned off the main road and proceeded down a winding dirt road. Eventually, they began climbing a small hill. When they leveled off, the cabin could be seen in the distance. Headlights reflecting off the area behind the house indicated there was a body of water.

Having never been to his house, Sarah excitedly announced, "Charley, you never told me you had a lake behind your house."

"Oh! Yeah," Kate confirmed, "He and I have caught some nice fish and had them for supper a couple of times. Wait till you see the deck on the back of the house."

Charley said apologetically "Didn't know you were into that kind of thing. I've never known you liked anything but work. Well, except for beer and pizza."

As the car came to a halt, they began finding their bags of things.

Charley announced, "I've got to check the house before we go in and shut off the alarm."

That was nothing unusual, so they nodded in agreement. When they saw him drop his bag at the door, and take out his little gadget before turning the key, they looked toward Kate.

"He shuts off the alarm and checks the house for listening devices every time I've come home with him. He says he's never found one, but he doesn't take any chances."

Charley came back to the door and waved for them to come in.

Once inside, he gave Sarah and Mark the short tour of inside. His home was country looking but clean as a pin. The bed and bathrooms were immaculate, and looked as if an interior decorator had set them up. Then he opened the back door and they stepped out onto a covered deck. They saw the moonlight reflecting off the calm lake water. They could see a short dock and a boat with a motor, secured to the dock edge.

"Charley, this place is beautiful. I never pictured you living in a place like this."

Charley laughed a little, asking, "Just how did you picture me living, Sarah?"

A little embarrassed, but answering honestly, "I pictured you living in a very small cabin, with books and computers stacked in every corner."

Turning toward Kate, she said, "It's obvious that we don't tell each other everything. You've never said anything about this place and how beautiful it is. All I ever hear is how good the sex was," as she grinned toward Charley.

You could almost see the blush on his face in the moonlight as he invited them back into the house.

"Kate and I will be in my bedroom. You two can share the spare bedroom, or one of you can have the couch, whichever way you want to work things out. I'm kind of in the dark about what's going on between you two."

Mark said he would take the couch, and sat the bag from the pharmacy down beside one arm on the floor.

Charley nodded, "I'll get blankets and a pillow for you. Sarah, you've got the spare room." He and Kate carried their bags into his room.

Sarah looked toward Mark, with a small smile, as she headed to the other bedroom with her belongings.

Mark went back to the car to bring in the cooler and the bags of food.

In Charley's room, Kate placed her clothing in an empty drawer, and her toiletries on a dresser. She pulled out a sexy nightgown, placing it on the bed.

Charley grinned, took stuff out of his duffle bag, put them back into the drawer, and his shaving kit on the dresser.

When she saw him remove a Glock 9mil, and bullet pouch with two clips, she said, "Charley, I didn't even know you owned a gun."

Easing her mind, he explained, "It is company policy to carry a weapon, and know how to use it. Each year, we have to re-qualify, just like you officers. You didn't expect me to work at a top secret facility, and not own one, did you?"

She walked toward him explaining; "I've never seen you with one."

"Kate, I'm never far away from my weapon." He reached into the large bag, pulled out a small satchel that he knew she was used to seeing, and held it in front of him.

"I always thought the bag just contained your gadgets." I never knew I was in love with a super spy," as she placed her arms around his neck and kissed him.

"I wouldn't call it anything that exciting," as he wrapped his arms around her. They kissed more deeply and lovingly.

When she released his neck, she said, "Even with all the possible danger lurking out there for us, there is something very special about tonight."

With his arms still around her waist, "And just what would that be?"

She gazed warmly into his eyes, "Tonight, is the first time we both told each other I love you."

"I should have said it a long time ago, but I was never sure of your feelings."

"Charley, I didn't tell you for that same reason."

Soon their lips met again, as their hands roamed over each other.

Charley separated them from their hot embrace, "We better get back to the others. We'll replay this later tonight."

She grinned wider, as she took his hand and they started out of the room.

Chapter Three

Sarah found empty drawers, chose one to place her changes of clothes, and sat her bag of makeup and toiletries on the dresser. Her eyes took in all the pictures here and there. She noticed pictures of Charley and his parents at different stages of his life. She'd never met the couple, but he mentioned they'd come to visit him over the years, from their home in Ohio. Charley's schooling led him to this job far from his home. He'd told her many times how he missed his parents and back home, but he had a good paying job doing the kind of work he loved.

When she picked up a small picture of his parents holding him in the hospital at birth, she sat down on the edge of the bed, and a tear formed in her eye. Her mind unlocked memories that had been blocked away for years. She pictured when she was pregnant, and the night her husband had to rush her to the hospital. It was early in her pregnancy and she was in severe pain. At the hospital they discovered the baby was dying inside her. The doctors operated immediately, but couldn't save the child. It was devastating to both her and her husband.

Things got even worse, when her doctor told her it was best that she never try to have children. Because of some of her female internal organs, she, the baby, or both, would most certainly perish, if she tried to have another child. As she looked back, she could see this probably put the first wedge in her relationship with her ex. After getting several second opinions, she'd decided to have her tubes tied, so she could never get pregnant. He understood, but things just didn't seem to be like they were between them. Though sex was regular, she felt there was always something missing.

Kate called her from the living room, "Sarah, Charley got his equipment ready to deal with the tracking device. Bring the medical kit and bandages out of the bottom drawer of the nightstand."

She wiped the tears from her eyes, "I'm coming."

Mark was lying on his stomach on the couch, with a plastic tablecloth under him.

Charley sat in a kitchen chair beside him, with a machine on the floor and headset on his ears.

She kneeled on the floor beside his legs, and removed articles from the kit.

Mark looked at her face, and asked, "Are you alright?"

"Damn his observance," she thought, "Yeah! I'm ok, but this is going to hurt some," as she held the surgical knife where he could see it. "Are you sure you want me to do this?"

"Yes!" was all he answered, as he looked forward toward the wall.

Kate stood nervously behind her, gritting her teeth as she watched.

Sarah made the incision and blood ran down his leg. She quickly glanced toward Mark's face, but could not see him showing in any kind of pain.

Charley scared her, when he yelled, "STOP!" She picked up a towel, as Charley ran his equipment over the area of the device in Marks leg. She waited for a second or two, then she saw the red blood beginning to flow more out of the wound. She covered it with the towel, putting pressure on the area. "What, Charley? You scared hell out of me. It's a wonder I didn't put a big slice in his leg."

Not apologizing, but explaining, "When oxygen reached the tracker, its radio waves went off the charts."

For the first time, Mark's face showed he was dealing with extreme pain. He strained to say, "That definitely is not good. I can just imagine an alien looking at a screen right now, and saying, "Ah! There he is. Sarah, get that thing out of my leg; and hurry."

Charley stopped her for a second, "Mark, I can't tell for sure by my equipment what it will do to you when she removes it. I've never seen oxygen affect a radio wave."

Mark gritted his teeth once more, "I appreciate everything you are doing, but I am not going back under their control. If I die here, dispose of my body, try to destroy that thing, and get the hell out of here."

Kate questioned, "What if it is attached to an artery?"

Mark didn't answer her. He saw Sarah's eyes beginning to water, and said, "Whatever happens, do it."

She looked into his eyes once more, as if trying to search his soul and feel his pain. She looked back toward his leg, and removed the towel. Through the blood running out of the hole, she made the slice deeper and wider.

Kate tore open the sterilized extractors, handing them to her. They looked like the ones you see on TV, when bullets are being extracted, but these were shorter. Sarah laid down the knife, and slid her fingers into the scissor like loops. She inserted the forks into the hole. She saw the device, and it was beginning to glow redder. She was past the point of no return, and she pushed the extractor forks deeper to encompass each side of the tracker.

At this point, Mark grabbed a thin book off the nightstand at the end of the couch, and placed the edge of it between his teeth. He was no longer looking their way. His head was forward, his eyes were closed, and he groaned. His body became rigid, as Sarah dug deeper.

Years of tissue had grown around the device. Sarah glanced toward his head for a second, but couldn't see his eyes. Maybe that gave her the strength to continue. She began to slowly pull, and saw it glowing more. As she struggled, in a raised voice, "Charley, what's this thing doing? It's getting redder and I can feel it getting hotter."

In a half-panicked voice, he checked his machine, and answered, "The signals coming from this thing seem to be rerouting inward instead of outward. They are constantly changing. It's almost as if it is trying to repair itself, so it can send a clear signal again."

His answer made her pull harder at the object with the forks. As she did so, Mark let out a much louder, longer groan.

The machine flew out of Charley's lap pulling the headsets off his ears. It went flying across the room and slammed against the wall. The bloody knife Sarah had laid aside flew into the air, and stuck in the edge of the wooden door. The bulb in a lamp on the nightstand in front of Mark's head exploded.

Kate went to her knees, ducked her head, and covered it with her arms.

Charley couldn't move. He was in a semi state of shock, as he saw different objects in the room beginning to move around.

The forks in Sarah's hand were getting almost too hot to hold. She strained hard and pulled one more time. The device came out still in the prongs.

Not able to withstand the heated instrument, she threw the extractors and the tracking device on the floor away from them.

Red blood ran more freely from Mark's wound. She placed a bandage pad that Kate had prepared for her over the wound. She put both hands over it, and applied pressure.

Suddenly, everything that had been moving stopped.

She looked toward Charley, whose eyes were still wide as saucers, "Charley, what now? What do we do with that thing?"

Sitting there dumbfounded, he collected his senses, "Kate, get me the tinfoil out of the kitchen cabinet."

Danger or not, she jumped up to do as he bid.

Charley rose, approached the tracker, and kneeled beside it. He saw the glow becoming weaker.

Kate returned, and he rolled out a long piece of tinfoil. He picked up the extractors, encased the prongs around the tracker, and placed it on the edge of the tinfoil. Then he rolled the tinfoil around the device in the shape of softball.

Sarah glanced toward Mark's head. Seeing he wasn't moving, she turned toward Kate, "I need some help here."

Kate rushed to her side as Sarah ordered, "Get some more pads and a big patch bandage ready. As Kate began to fulfill the order, Sarah looked toward

Mark's head. He was completely motionless with his eyes still closed. She couldn't see him breathing. Was he dead from the ordeal? She felt a whirlpool of sadness trying to overtake her thoughts. She had to stop the bleeding. There was no time to check anything else on him. She removed the blood soaked pads and replaced them with fresh ones. In doing so, she noticed there was less blood trying to flow out of the wound. She quickly placed the large bandage over the pads.

Kate handed her a clean wet rag. Sarah softly wiped the blood that had run down the side of his leg onto the shower curtain under him. She refolded the towel she'd held on his wound, so the blood was within. She lifted his leg, placed the towel over the blood on the curtain, and gently lowered his leg onto the towel. Mark's head moved a little, and she felt the smile forming on her cheeks.

He raised himself onto his elbows. With a sweat beaded brow, he slowly looked her way, "Is it out of me?"

Both Kate and Sarah grinned from ear to ear, as Charley held up the ball of tinfoil, "I don't think it's sending a signal anywhere right now except back to itself. However, it is alien, and I can't be sure."

Kate and Sarah helped, as Mark struggled to his feet. When he was able to stand, Kate folded the bloody towel and patches into the shower curtain, and took it to the trashcan in the kitchen.

Sarah was partially supporting him, as he said, "Thanks, I owe you."

"Oh! Hell yes you do, and one of these days I will collect," she agreed.

He began to support himself more, as he looked toward Charley, "How do we destroy it?"

"I've been thinking about that. Since we don't know what would happen if we tried, I think I've decided on another fate for this little booger. You and I need to take a little ride. Do you think you are up to it?"

He removed his arm from around Sarah's shoulder, "Give me a few minutes. I'll be alright."

"Where are you taking, Mark?" Sarah inquired.

"It might be best if you don't know that answer. I'll have him back in an hour."

Her cell phone ringing interrupted them. "Damn, my battery is almost dead," as she answered, "Jack, my battery is almost dead. I may lose you, and I've got you on speaker."

"I'll talk fast. My cousin checked out that woman for you. There was a woman by that name, who lived there about twenty-four years ago. At least she used that name when she lived there. Turns out she'd been married to a man in another state. He'd been abusive to her, and they were in and out of court, while the child was young. Seems the husband found out the child wasn't his. He put her in the hospital, beat to a pulp, and they put him in prison. She took the baby, named Mark, moved to Wichita to live with her grandmother, and began using her grandmother's last name. Grandfather was already deceased. The grandmother died of a stroke, when the boy was about three. Now comes the real strange part. When the boy was six, she went to the police, and claimed aliens had abducted him. The police arrested her, suspecting she was the cause of the child's disappearance. They could never find any evidence to convict her, and eventually had to set her free. Though she was basically a laughing stock, she went to the papers and told her story. She placed ads with his picture, and the paper put her picture on the front page. You know, woman claims son was abducted by aliens. Most everyone that knew her figured her to be a nutcase, and no trace of the boy was ever found. She's deceased. Kenny forwarded a picture of the woman to my phone, and I'll send it to you now. "

"Hurry and send it. Thanks, Jack, I'll explain all this soon. I'll put my phone on charge after the pic comes through, and I'll call you later."

He said ok and ended his call.

While she was waiting the minute or two for the picture to come through, she and the others were looking at Mark. He'd sat down on the couch, and his head was buried in his hands. He looked up; when the sound of the phone let Sarah know the picture had arrived. They saw the tears swelled in his eyes. She opened the phone, looked at the picture, handed it to him, and softly said, "She was a beautiful woman."

He stared at the picture, and ran his fingers across the face, as tears rolled down his cheeks.

Kate said sadly, "Mark, we are so sorry."

When he looked up, they could see he was heartbroken. Charley softly spoke, "Kate and I are going to step out on the deck, and leave you two alone for a bit." He took Kate by the hand and led her out the door.

Trying to hold back the tears, he finally spoke, "All this for nothing."

Sarah dropped to her knees with tears in her eyes, as she placed her hands on the outside of each of his arms, "Mark, your Mom would have been so proud to know that you went through all this to escape, and try to find her. She'd be ecstatic to see the man you have grown to be. All this doesn't have to be for nothing. We need to find someway to help our government find that facility, and free those other men and women."

She saw the tears drying and a sense of purpose filling them, as he agreed, "I don't know how, but I know you are right. Somehow I have to do something to free those people. They are the only friends I had for all those years."

Charley and Kate came rushing in, "I know this isn't the proper time, Mark, but Kate and I just witnessed that red light easing across the sky. You and I need to take that little ride."

Mark stood lifting Sarah off her knees. As he did so, "I'm ready."

Charley said, "Got to get something out of my room first. Hold this, Sarah," as Charley handed her the ball of tinfoil. Within two minutes, he came out of the room with his weapon and the clip holder on his belt. The gun was in a holster above his hip. He gently removed the tinfoil wad from Sarah's hand. Kate wrapped her arm around his waist as they headed to Kate's car. She gave him a long tender kiss at the driver side, but Sarah interrupted them, "Pop the trunk." He reached in and did so.

She retrieved a black leather case. She unzipped it and removed a Glock .357 caliber pistol. She handed it and two clips to, Mark, saying, "You said you were weapon trained."

He took the weapon, and shoved one clip into his front pocket. The other clip he slapped into the butt of the weapon, and jacked a shell into the chamber. He moved the slide backward enough to make sure the bullet was in the chamber, and placed the weapon in the small of his back.

As she watched, he suddenly pulled her to him, and kissed her tenderly. "That's for luck."

She put her arms around his neck, and just before kissing him again, said, "You may need a lot of luck."

This was like a cue for Kate and Charley as they tenderly embraced again.

When they stopped kissing, he and Mark entered the car, and as the car pulled away, the women waved.

The women watched until they were out of sight, until Sarah said, "I've got to take a shower. I didn't take one last night."

Kate agreed, "I'll take mine after you. I'm so ready to get out of this uniform into something more comfortable." When she and Sarah picked up some things at her place, she didn't take time to change out of her uniform. She'd planned to do it later. Her blonde hair in a ponytail and her sparkling blue eyes complimented her figure. She followed Sarah inside.

Sarah soaped her body under the hot water from the shower. Her mind raced over all that happened to her the last couple of days. She pondered her deep feelings for, Jack, and now these new feelings for, Mark. She could almost feel his lips on hers again. Soon she dried her body, and blow-dried her hair. When she came out with a towel wrapped above her breasts, she saw Kate wearing a towel the same way, as she proceeded to the other shower in Charley's room. Sarah began laying clothes to sleep in on the bed, but put on a pair of pajamas, and came out into the living room. She got out the chips and dip, and opened a beer. There was no TV in the cabin. She saw a radio, stereo, and other music equipment; but she didn't need that noise right now. She wished Charley had told her where they were going. After consuming a few chips and a swallow or two from her beer, she took the bottle and went out onto the deck. Clouds had obscured the moonlight. Not being able to see much, she began to get that unsafe feeling. She went back inside and locked the door behind her. She went to the front door and dead-bolted it, also. She walked into her room, removed her weapon from its holster, and carried it back to the couch, laying it beside her.

Kate finished her shower and came out of Charley's room, also wearing PJs.

Seeing Kate also had her service revolver in her hand, Sarah laughed, "Great minds run together," as she looked down at her Glock. "Grab a beer and come have some chips and dip."

Kate obliged. As she sat down, "Sarah, looks like you and Mark have a thing going."

"Honestly, I don't know what Mark and I have going. I've only known him for two days, I know very little about him and he's already got me breaking every police rule in the book. I'll be lucky if I can salvage any of my career before this is over. Then there's, Jack. I've never told him, but I think I've loved him for a long time. Now, I have these new strong feelings for Mark. He's so strange but exiting. You know what I mean?"

"Mark seems to be a real nice guy, and yes he's a hunk. Jack's good looking, too, and I think he really loves you. It's the force that keeps your love from growing, or showing itself. I can't be of much help with your situation. I am your best friend though, so I've got to say what I'm thinking. You've got to consider what you might be throwing away, whichever one you chose to be your mainstay."

"I know! All this is running through my brain like water falling over Niagara Falls. I'm not sure of what I'm feeling."

"Take it slow, Sarah. You're not even sure what Mark's feelings are, or Jack's either for that matter.

Just roll with the flow for a little while, and see what pans out."

"I know you are right. Maybe I'll figure all this out soon. Where do you think Charley was taking, Mark?"

"Who knows? I just hope they return soon. I don't feel warm and fuzzy way out here in this cabin without them around."

"Me neither," Sarah agreed, nodding at her weapon.

To lighten things, Kate said, "Right now it's chips and beer," holding hers toward Sarah.

She tapped her bottle to Kate's and they drank their beer toast.

They continued catching up on what had been taking place in their lives.

Occasionally, one would go to the window to look out. Clouds would pass sometimes obscuring the moon. At other times the light from the moon seemed exceptionally bright, and they could view the area surrounding the cabin.

At one point, they were both at the window at the back of the cabin. They were excitedly observing a doe and two fawns walking to the lake to drink water. The girls were at the window for a long time, as they watched the animals slowly feed their way back past the cabin. They were irritated, when another large cloud passed overhead, and they could no longer make out any images. So, they returned to the couch to talk and snack some more.

Chapter Four

Miles away, in a Kansas FBI Office, Kenny Sanchez was finishing some paperwork just before leaving for the day. His secretary's voice sounded from the intercom on his desk, "Ken, there are two men here with NSA credentials to see you."

A little confused, he answered, "Send them in."

Shortly, she opened the door to let the two men into his office. He immediately knew it was unusual for Diane to precede a visitor. Dianne had been a field investigator, and wounded twice, before she decided an office job was much safer. He knew by the look on her face, she was trying to let him know she didn't trust these two men.

He nodded, so she'd know he got the message. As the men entered, he stood saying, "Come on in, gentlemen. What can I do for you?"

The first one in came toward him, shook his hand, and introduced himself and his partner." He began, "You've been inquiring about a woman named Carolyn Wakefield."

"Yes, I have. What's so important about that? Before the man could answer, Kenny spoke defensively, "I investigate people all the time. How did you know I was investigating her, and exactly what are two NSA agents doing in my office?"

Not happy about Kenny's statements, the man informed, "Information on this woman is a matter of national security. It's imperative that you cease any further investigation on her, and explain exactly why she was chosen to be investigated."

Kenny was high ranking in the FBI and one of the most respected in the total FBI system. He'd earned his office and reputation along the way. "I'm not used to having to explain anything I do."

"It would be in your best interest to answer our questions, and truthfully. I will answer one of your questions, as to how we knew. In your computer searches, you triggered a red flag in our field office. We were sent to find out why you were searching, and to terminate your searches."

Kenny's gut feeling told him these were not normal NSA agents, if they were real agents at all, but they sure knew a lot about what he'd been doing. "You gentlemen don't mind showing me your identification, do you?"

The second man in his office spoke sternly, "Your secretary already checked our identifications."

"I didn't," Kenny answered a little sternly.

The first one nodded toward the second one, and said, "No problem. I would probably do the same thing." He handed his credentials to Kenny, as did the other man.

Kenny could spot fake ID's in a heartbeat. These appeared to be authentic. He scrutinized the information, looked back at the men, and then returned their badges. NSA took precedence over FBI and CIA. He knew he had to answer the questions truthfully, but he'd do it as sketchy as possible. "A detective friend of mine in Pahrump, Nevada asked me to find out about her. He's a good friend, and I didn't care why he needed the information."

Taking a notepad from his jacket pocket the first man inquired, "What's your friend's name?"

Ken hesitated, but knew he had no choice. He had to divulge his friend's identity. His name is, Jack Caruso. He's a detective in a new satellite police station on the edge of Pahrump."

The man closed his notepad, placed his pen back in his jacket, smiled a little, and acknowledged, "We'll take it from here. We appreciate your cooperation." The two men turned and were soon out the door.

Diane stepped back in, "Those two gave me the creeps."

Diane was a sharp looking woman with a shapely body. She and Kenny knew each other very well. They shared a nice home in the suburbs outside of town. FBI rules about agents living together were much more relaxed than other agencies. Diane had been out of the field for a good while now, anyway. She also knew Caruso. She was with Kenny, when he and Caruso visited each other.

He answered, with a concerned look on his face, "Yeah! They weren't your normal NSA. Too bad I can't investigate them, I'd sure love to. Those credentials were top of the line, maybe too perfect. Get Jack Caruso on the phone for me. I'm not very good at taking orders. I need you to use the back door to find out more about this Carolyn Wakefield. You know, yearly census, births and deaths; things that won't draw attention."

She nodded, closed the door, and soon Kenny was on speaker saying, "Jack, two NSA agents were just in my office wanting to know why I was searching information about the Wakefield woman. I didn't ask before, but now I need to know why you needed the info?"

"Damn! NSA! Sorry I brought that upon you. However, I can't clarify everything for you. Sarah wanted me to find out the information for some reason. She hasn't explained why to me, yet. I've been involved in two shootings in less than a week. Today they put me on administrative leave with pay. Sarah started vacation yesterday. Her phone was dying when I gave her your information. She said she would charge it, and call me when it was charged."

Kenny had heard Jack speak of Sarah many times, he knew Jack cared a lot about her, but Kenny had never met her. "I know she's probably a good agent. I also can tell by the way you talk about her that your feelings are more than just respect for her. However, she has apparently opened up a can of worms. I had to give the NSA agents your name. They'll be knocking on your door soon, so you need to have your answers down pat. I'm sorry, Jack."

"Not your fault. You did what you had to do. I'll deal with them when they show up. I just hope I didn't get you in any kind of trouble."

"Jack, don't worry about me. I can handle any flack I catch. You just be careful. These guys look like they could be nasty business."

"I can handle myself. I've got broad shoulders. I'll try to find out more information from Sarah, so I will be more prepared when the men in black show up. I'm on admin leave, and I'm walking out of the office right now. I'll try to make myself unreachable, until I can get back in touch with Sarah."

"Good idea, Jack. Also, it's best we don't contact each other on this matter after today. I'm sure it won't take long for them to start monitoring my phone, if they don't find out what they want to know soon."

"Take care, Kenny. Thanks, and I hope the next time we see each other, it's fishing on Lake Mead."

"Looking forward to it; see ya, Jack."

As the phone line went dead, Jack hung up his desk phone. He grabbed the few pieces of paper off his desk, where he'd written the notes about Carolyn Wakefield. He shoved them into a briefcase, and headed for his vehicle. He drove the speed limit, but hurried to his place. Once there, he found a suitcase and threw things into it. He walked to his gun safe and spun the combination dial. When it opened, he removed a spare Glock and two more clips. Suddenly he hesitated. He caught himself feeling like a criminal on the run. He knew that wasn't the case, but he also knew that dealing with NSA you could disappear never to be seen again. He hadn't gone on a long vacation in years, and he'd put money away, for when that occasion arose. He'd wanted to have plenty of cash to spend, and no credit card bill to pay when the vacation was over. He grabbed a stack of $100 dollar bills, stuffed them in an envelope, and threw it into the open briefcase on the bed. It wouldn't be as easy for NSA to find him, if he used cash wherever he was going. "Where was he going?" he suddenly thought to himself. He'd run by Sarah's. Sarah mentioned that Charley and Kate were coming for beer and pizza. That way he could warn her.

In short time, he drove to her house. When he arrived, Charley's car was still out front. Jack recognized his car, and hoped they were all still inside. He rang the doorbell and knocked, but there was no answer. He walked around the side of the house and looked into the window of the garage. Sarah's car wasn't in it. He pulled out his phone and tried Sarah's number, but it went to voice mail. He put the phone back into his jacket pocket, saying out loud, "Now what? Where are you, Sarah?"

He got in his car and drove aimlessly. Wherever he was going, he couldn't make it look like he was hiding from something. He decided to go to Vegas. He had a friend that worked in one of the casinos. At least this way, he'd appear to be just going somewhere to have fun, and do a little gambling, if NSA found him.

It wasn't an exceptionally long drive, but it sure seemed longer tonight. Alone in the car, he had plenty of time to think about everything. His mind went over the day of the shooting, and everything that took place. He remembered the information that IAD had gathered. The confusion about Sarah confronting a wounded man outside the station became fresh again in his mind. The man, whom the news people took a quick shot of through her car window, was also bugging him. She'd said he was a friend. Where'd she meet this friend? How long had she known him? Was he only a friend? The captain had mentioned the guy was her new boyfriend. He probably would have kept that to himself, if he'd known Sarah and Caruso were occasional bed partners.

That was another thing that was eating at him on this long drive. Had he waited too long to tell her he loved her? He was pretty sure that he did. If she loved him too, one of them would have to quit the force. This was all he'd ever wanted to do, since he graduated with an AS degree in Police Science and Administration. He knew he could have moved up the ladder many times, but he liked doing what he was doing. He liked being with Sarah everyday on the job. If he couldn't be with her every night, he could at least have her at his side every day of work. Had he lost her by not making a commitment? Had he drove her into another man's arms? He was aggravated at his thoughts, and slapped the steering wheel hard.

Rationalization took over. It was her that limited their times in the sack. He felt they could sleep together much more than she let him, and still not have gotten caught by someone. He thought she loved him, but she never said it, even when the sex was hot, and great. Maybe he was wrong. Maybe she just cared a lot about him, and settled for sex now and then, until someone special came along. Still, she was one hell of a partner on the job. He knew he didn't want to lose that.

He looked out the front windshield, and was glad to see the lights of Vegas coming into view. He calmed down, as he considered his options. He'd check into the hotel casino, get a room, get settled in, and then try to get in touch with his friend Tony. If he was working, they'd hook up for some drinks after his friend's shift, unless he already had other plans.

Soon he valet parked at the Mirage, checked in at the desk, paid cash for three nights, and opened the door to the room. Tossing the briefcase on the bed, he went to the window to check out the view. He could have probably gotten comped a room from Tony, if he'd checked with him in advance.

Vegas always amazed him. It was the city of lights that never slept. Most people who came to the town for vacation got little sleep. If they weren't gambling, they were checking out the themes of the casinos. They were all different. You could spend hours touring the outside and inside of each casino, and never spend a dime, if you so chose. However, he and the casinos knew that was unlikely.

Here at the Mirage, a man-made volcano would erupt several times nightly, amongst an array of breathtaking lights. Anyone visiting the casino, or walking by, could watch the event for free.

At Treasure Island you could see two ships battle it out in the moat on one side of the casino.

At the Luxor, which was shaped like a pyramid, you could witness the light show at night from the sphinx eyes.

Circus, Circus always had free circus acts going on upstairs.

In most, if not all casinos, there was something free to see. In recent years, the casinos had catered to families, instead of just gamblers. Many of the casinos now had rides, water slides, arcades, and many other attractions for families to enjoy.

After all, if they could get you inside, it was almost certain many would want to dig in the old wallet or purse, to participate in the paying attractions. Of course, they also knew, at least two thirds of the patrons who were old enough, would gamble on the slots or tables.

However, the food was good and plentiful most everywhere, and finding cheap drinks was extremely easy. In most casinos, drinks were free if you were gambling. If you tipped the waitress, you were sure to have her stop by you many times with a tray of drinks, and your choice would definitely be on it.

"Lights, lights, lights, everywhere," he thought to himself, as he gazed out his window.

He whipped out his phone and tried Sarah's phone again, but only got the voice mail, so he tossed it on the king bed.

Nothing to do now but take a shower, put on casual clothes, go get some food, and see what he could get into.

His room had a safe, so he opened it, and placed both of his weapons and clips inside. He removed some $100 bills out of the envelope, and placed the envelope alongside the weapons. Securing the safe, he put the room key in his pocket. There was no number of the room on the key card, so he wasn't worried too much in case he lost it. The hotel might charge him, but they'd supply him with a replacement.

He tried to forget everything, as the hot shower cascaded over his head and down his body. He stood under it for awhile just letting it run. It was as if the water kept him from thinking. Eventually, he put soap on a rag, and before long, he'd rinsed and shut off the shower.

He reached for a towel and dried. Here came the thoughts again, as he found himself asking aloud, "Sarah, what in the world have you gotten yourself into?"

When he looked at his phone again, "low battery" was flashing. He pulled his charger cord out of the suitcase, and found a wall socket next to the dresser. He turned the phone off and plugged in the charger cord.

Soon he was dressed, in the elevator, and making his way into the casino.

He was hungry; and tried to decide on what kind of food he wanted to eat, as he walked passed slot machines. Bells and whistles going off near and far drew his attention. "What the hell he thought," and sat down on a stool in front of a machine, with red, white, and blue sevens. Maybe it was the pretty brunette with the outstanding figure on the machine next to him that made him take this seat. He inserted a hundred into the slot, and the machine acknowledged his credits.

The light on top of her machine started blinking, and the buzzer in the machine sounded loudly. She excitedly jumped up and down.

He looked over at her machine, saying, "$500 dollar winner. Hey! You did alright there." He noticed she still had $200 worth of credits left, along with the $500.

She sat back down, still a little breathless. "I'm here visiting from Jacksonville, Florida for a teacher convention. It was over late last night, but I allotted myself one more day to take in the free sights around Vegas. I'm leaving in the morning, and I saved $100 for gambling tonight; $50 for a nice evening meal, and breakfast in the morning before my flight."

Glancing toward her machine again he laughed, "Don't think you have to worry about what you can afford tonight. That is, if you don't put it all back in."

"Oh! No! Not me. I work too hard for my money. If I get down even close to $500, I'm cashing out."

"Wise woman," he smiled to her, "If you don't mind me saying so, I sure wish I had teachers that looked like you in my classes at school."

She laughed at his comment, but asked, "Are you here on vacation?"

"Sort of," he said with somewhat of a frown. "I'm a police detective in Pahrump. I was involved in a shooting, and it is standard procedure to put officers involved on administrative leave with pay. By the way, I'm Jack." He reached a hand out to her.

As she gently shook his outstretched palm, "Lillian," she answered smiling.

He couldn't believe he was telling this stranger all this crap. He never had a habit of disclosing information about himself, or his job.

As their hands separated, "Where is Pahrump?" she asked, "If I pronounced that correct."

"You did a fine job. It isn't very far away. I decided to come to Vegas to get away from it all. (He was being honest there, he thought to himself.) I checked in and was going to get something to eat, but like most people, I was lured to the machines first."

"That's understandable," she admitted. "Kind of wish you hadn't mentioned food, though. I haven't eaten since breakfast. I started playing this machine, hours ago. My credits went up and down. Each time I thought my money was almost gone, the bells would ring again, and I'd win some amount."

He noticed her eyes seemed to be glued toward his, as she pushed her machine button without looking. He also noticed there was no wedding ring on the left hand lying on her leg.

"I'm not going to stay at this machine long," he laughed, "I'm starving. I haven't eaten since early this morning, either. I rarely come to the casinos, and I really hate eating alone. Would you like to cash out now and join me? There's a real nice restaurant here, and I've been meaning to try out the food." Once again he was being honest, though he spent many meals alone, he thoroughly hated it.

She was still looking into his eyes, as if she was trying to decide if that would be a good idea or not. He could almost tell she was wondering if she'd fallen prey, to a pickup artist.

"The drinks and meal are on me, of course," he added, solidifying his request for her to join him.

Her face broke into a smile, as she said, "You're buying supper. I get to keep all this money I won. Sounds like a plan to me."

Jack had also been pushing the button on his machine without looking. Suddenly the light and buzzer on his machine went crazy, as three sevens lined up for a $1,000 dollar winner.

"Well, I'll be damned," he uttered aloud. "I never win much on these machines, just a little here and there. You must have brought me luck." It wasn't a come on, he was just being politely honest.

"I don't know about all that, but at least I won't feel bad about you paying for the meal," as she giggled.

Seeing him push his cash out button, she did like wise. She followed him to the nearest money-changer window. Cashing in the little paper from the machine, they each stowed their winnings away.

They found the restaurant and ordered. The food was exquisite, as they sipped on drinks, and talked for several hours.

He was amazed that it seemed they'd known each other for years, as their conversation had drawn on. There didn't seem to be any inhibitions, about what they discussed. One subject just led to another.

During their talk, he even learned that when she was fourteen; her mother and father came home early one evening from a party, because her dad got ill. They found her naked on the couch with her boyfriend. She'd made him use a condom, and it wasn't her first time. From that day forward, her mother made sure she was on the pill.

At fifteen, she thanked her mom, because two of her best friends got pregnant, had to leave school, and were discarded by their lovers.

At seventeen, her best friend got pregnant, and she was on the pill. That scared Lillian. She began making any boy she had sex with; use a condom for her double protection. She found that turned many boys off, but she was determined not to end up like the other girl. So her dates got a lot less.

When she graduated, she attended a tech school, to continue her education, and become a teacher. She had love affairs there that didn't materialize either, and some of them were for the same reasons as in school.

When she was twenty-one she gave herself a birthday present. She had the reversible tubal ligation.

Two years later, she married an insurance salesman. He traveled a lot and didn't want children. She was devastated, a year later, when she discovered he was living a double life. He had another woman, and fathered two children in another town. She divorced him shortly after.

Jack realized during her conversation that he'd never wanted children either. Even before he finished school, he was working, trying to establish a career. He made sure he didn't get some girl pregnant, and interfere with his plans. He'd achieved an AS degree in a community college, before going into law enforcement.

He began to realize how appealing Lillian was to him. It had been several weeks, since he'd been able to climb in Sarah's bed and wrap around her. He didn't have time for other women, though he'd turned down some invitations from a few lovely creatures. Her low-cut top exposed the top of firm breasts. The slit in her dress on the stool at the machine had exposed tan taut legs and calves. Her sparkling green eyes complimented her wavy brunette locks.

Her voice brought him back to reality, as she smiled, "Looks like you're paying more attention to my breasts than just to me."

Being embarrassed was new to him, as he confessed, "I apologize. You are a very pretty woman, and easy to like. I don't think I've enjoyed being with someone like you for a long time now."

She detected the honesty in his voice, and laughed, "Boy, you got yourself out of that one, didn't you?"

"I hope so," he said, in somewhat of a giggle.

A young couple next to them hurriedly got up to leave. They heard the young woman say, "Come on, slow poke. We don't want to miss the last volcano eruption."

As he and Lillian turned back to each other, she said, "I've never seen it erupt. I thought earlier about watching it tonight."

He'd already paid the bill and left the tip. He stood and held out his open hand. She stood grinning, and clasped hers into his. Hand in hand they headed for the door with others who rushed out to see the action. They just made it; as the volcano began to rumble, lights flickered, and smoke eased out the top. His arm went around her shoulder. As she glanced up at his face, her arm went around his waist. They turned back toward the volcano, as the rumbles got louder. More smoke and fire came out of the top. The special effects made it seem like lava flowing from the top into the lights below.

Excitedly, she looked back at him with a wide grin, and then back at the show.

He'd seen it many times, but he enjoyed seeing the excitement on her face. His eyes drifted down to those partly exposed firm looking breasts, and he wished his hands were wrapped around them.

"Busted," he thought, as her words made him look up, "There you go again staring at my breasts."

This time he was ready with a comeback, "Couldn't help myself," he answered with a big grin. "I've seen the volcano before, but not those pretty breasts."

Her next words kind of took him by surprise, "If you are going to take me to bed tonight, now would be a good time, while I'm feeling warm, fuzzy, and happy."

Now he had a grin so wide he looked like a child who'd been offered a big bowl of ice cream. "I can't think of anything I'd like better."

Still looking into his eyes, she placed her hand in his. He began leading them back into the casino. They made short talk as they walked to the elevator. Alone in the elevator, she looked him in the eyes, and admitted, "I haven't been with a man since my divorce, so you'll have to excuse me, if I seem a little nervous about this."

"I'm feeling like a very lucky guy tonight," as he pulled her close, and slowly but tenderly let their lips meet. Her lips were warm, soft, and inviting, as her return kiss wanted more.

They separated and laughed, as the elevator stopped. A young couple was waiting to come in, as they exited.

There were no evident inhibitions now, as they walked toward his room with arms around each other's waist.

He wanted to remove her clothes and see the rest of that lovely body, as soon as they were inside. Instead, he led her to the window with their arms still around each other, so they could look at the view.

Then he turned her to look directly into her eyes, "When I checked into this room, I came over here and looked at the view outside. I thought what a great view. Believe me; it is pale in comparison to looking at you."

She beamed with pride, as she wrapped her arms around his neck. They passionately kissed, and his hands found and cupped those warm breasts.

He slowly removed her top, and she his pullover shirt. He unbuckled his pants, as she removed her bra, and dropped her skirt.

Each smiled, as they saw he had no underwear and she no panties.

Their naked bodies seemed to mesh together, as they ravished each other's lips, and hands roamed. He wrapped his strong hands around each of her cheeks, and lifted, as her legs went around him, and he carried her to the bed.

No time to pull back covers; adjust pillows, or any of that. It was time for action. Neither wanted to wait any longer; lips and hands searched body parts.

He felt her warm moistness, as his member entered. She gasped for a second, and then held him tighter, as they began moving together, slowly bringing each other to that magic height of pleasure. As she collapsed lying back on the bed, he struggled to remain in the standing position. She looked into his eyes, and sweetly asked, "Could we take a shower, and then try this slower? Don't get me wrong. It was wonderful, but I want to enjoy more of it."

"Those were my thoughts exactly," taking her hands and pulling her to her feet, as he backed away.

In the shower, they soaped each other's parts, holding each other in different positions, and kissing. His hands cupped her breasts, and her hands finding his manhood standing tall, led them to drying off, and climbing into his bed. This time things went much slower, as they slowly ran their hands over each other's body, and lips met special places. When the moment of complete ecstasy engulfed their bodies, they collapsed in each other's arms.

What seemed another hour, they lay talking, laughing, and enjoying being next to each other, with nothing but air between them. Fingers and hands were still occasionally touching here and there.

She brought it all to an end, when she softly admitted, "Jack, part of me wants this night to never end. It's been wonderful, but I've got a 5:00 a.m. flight to catch, and it is way after midnight. I've got to get a little sleep, so I can function tomorrow. I'm not used to these late nights. As it is, I'll have to request a wakeup call, and set my alarm, to make sure I wake up."

Her words made him realize he wished they'd make love one more time, fall asleep together, and wake up holding each other.

"Lillian, our time together will be something I will never forget. There will be a big piece of happiness in my life leave on that plane with you."

"You couldn't have said that any sweeter," as her finger touched his lips. "Will you walk me to my room?"

"I wouldn't let you go alone," he assured, and they both eased out of different sides of the bed. They were looking at each other, but not talking.

They watched each other dress, as if they wanted to see each other's naked body as long as possible.

When they eased out of his room, arms were wrapped around each other, but it was if they'd said it all back at the room. They just seemed to look at each other tenderly. Inside the elevator to her room, she wrapped her arms around his neck. They tenderly kissed until the door opened, and they stepped out. They were mostly oblivious to the couple headed down to gamble, and a man pulling a small suitcase and talking on his phone.

It wasn't until they reached her room, she swiped the key and pushed the door open, that the silence was broken.

"Jack, you've made this trip so very special for me," I truly hate for this to end."

"It doesn't have to end at this door. I could come inside and be with you till that alarm goes off."

"Believe me. I'd love that, but I know if you stayed with me, I wouldn't get any sleep. I'd want to hold and touch you. I've got a long hard day ahead of me tomorrow. I've got to sleep."

Maybe it was the policeman in him, or maybe he was just trying to get his foot in the door, "I'm not letting you walk in that room, until I know it is safe and no one else is in there. Remember, I'm a detective. There might be someone lurking in there."

"I appreciate you worrying about me, Mr. Policeman. You can check out my room, but I mean it, you can't stay; promise?"

"It'll be a hard promise to keep, but I promise."

She moved aside grinning, and let him enter first. She stood holding the door open as he checked the bathroom, the closet, under the beds, and made sure the window was secure.

"Seems like all is safe and secure, Ma'am!" as he walked back toward her.

She waved her free hand toward the door opening, letting him know she was sticking to her guns.

As he passed, he bent down and kissed her one more time. When he stepped out and looked back, he watched her ever so slowly close the door, until they couldn't see each other any more.

When he heard the deadbolt inside, he felt like it was a gunshot sending a bullet to his heart. He actually felt a pain in his chest. His legs wouldn't move. He wanted to beat on the door until she opened it, and make love to her again. He wanted to tell her he didn't want her to ever leave. Tonight was like the first time he and Sarah made love, and she had to leave, and go back to her own house, for fear someone would find out. That first time with Sarah had been wonderful, too, and he'd wished that night would never end.

Now, as he slowly moved away from her door, he began to wonder if his destiny was to lose special women in his life. As he walked down the hall toward the elevator, he turned looking back at her door. If she'd opened it, and looked down the hall, he'd run back to her arms. Sadness engulfed him, as he stepped into the elevator with his back against the wall, and watched the doors close. Those doors seemed to be closing a chapter in his life, one he wasn't prepared to be over.

When he entered his room and threw his key on the dresser, he noticed his phone. When he picked it up, he unplugged the charger cord. He turned it on and saw there were no messages. Damn the late hour. He dialed Sarah's number. If she was with the other guy tonight that just didn't matter, as long as he knew she was safe. She was his partner. He needed to know, for she'd been acting strange for several days now. Again his call went to voice mail, and he had to end his unanswered call. He shut it off, put it back on charge and laid it on the dresser. He undressed, brushed his teeth, rinsed off in the shower, dried himself, and climbed into bed.

Tonight's scenario played again in his mind. He'd had the best night in his life, for a very long time. Tonight was so much more than just the hot sex with Sarah. He wished he and Sarah had spent hours talking, seeing things, going places, and having fun together. He felt it could have been that way, if it wasn't for those stupid damn rules. It wasn't long before his eyes began to get heavy. The long day had taken its toll on his body and mind. Soon, he rolled onto his side, as sleep overtook him.

Chapter Five

Charley wasn't saying much at first, as he drove with Mark as passenger. Mark sat silently, also. He watched out the side window, and through the front windshield. Both wouldn't have been surprised, if an alien ship came down from the sky in front of them.

Charley had turned onto the main road, drove for a good while, and turned onto a side dirt road. As his car proceeded down the spooky-looking winding road, Mark finally broke the silence, "We don't have much more time before that tracker reactivates. My thirty-six hour window is just a good calculated guess. I doubt we are going to find a microwave out here anywhere."

"Not much further to our destination," Charley glanced at him. He had things he'd been thinking. Mark breaking the silence made him get them off his chest. "Mark, what are your feelings for Sarah? She seems to care a lot about you, to do some of the things she's done. She's one of my best friends. I care a lot about her."

He looked toward Charley with apparent honesty across his face, "I'm not sure exactly what I feel. I like being around her, I like the way I feel when she's near, and I think she's a special person. I know it's hard for you to understand, but I spent all these years with women who were more like friends. I truly am not sure what love is, or what those feelings would be like."

He hesitated for a few seconds, and then continued, "Even if I wanted Sarah to always be near me. What kind of life could I give her? I don't have a home, car, job, or any kind of life any woman would want to be part of. There is not even a record anywhere about me since I was six years old. I'm not even sure I'm all human anymore, after all the alien injections over the years."

"Mark, Kate and Sarah think I'm just a smart guy who gets to play with his toys. I've been with the CIA since graduating. I've climbed the echelon chain to as far as I want. Along the way, I've made a lot of friends. I guess you could say that I have long arms, and can reach way up for help, if I needed it. What I'm trying to say is, when this is all over, I can probably get you a job and a place to live, if you want my help. I can almost assure you the pay would be substantial. You seem like an honest, trustworthy person. You've been through a lot and deserve to have a real life. I'd be glad to help if I possibly can."

"Even though it is happening, it's hard for me to comprehend you three placing your lives and careers in jeopardy, for me, a total stranger. Especially, since I sound like an idiot to others, with my alien stories. I can't find the words to thank you enough, or even begin to think of how I could repay any of you."

"I'm sure the other two feel as I. We only want to help. However, there is one thing I personally need to make clear for you to understand. If you make Sarah fall in love with you, and you break her heart, I'll spend the rest of my life making yours miserable."

"I would never hurt her on purpose. I'm not that kind of person. There again, it's strange for me to see someone care that much about another human being. I've never had those kinds of feelings."

The car lights reflected off an overpass ahead, as Charley brought the vehicle to a halt. He shut off the engine and they opened doors. They walked upon the overpass, with Charley carrying the ball of tinfoil.

Marked asked, "Where does the road lead to? Why did we stop here?"

"It's actually a road to nowhere now. Back in the western days, there was a small settlement at the end of this road. It eventually became a ghost town that no one remembered. Some investors found out about it, and had big plans for building some kind of attraction on the property. They talked the state into building this nice overpass on this dirt road. The agreement with the investors was when they began some type of construction on the property, the state would put in entrances and exits to the main highway below. When the investors started having perks done, and water from wells tested, so they could begin building, it was discovered the water and land were laden with radioactivity. Unscrupulous companies in the past had used the area for radioactive waste dumping, without having to pay for dumping through proper channels. So, the construction never began, and the road is blocked with warning signs, just before you get to the old settlement."

"Why did we stop here with this tracker?"

Charley explained, "When I first bought my property, and was having the cabin built on the lake, I would sometimes ride around in the day or nighttime, just to see what I could see. Being a long way from anything at my cabin, I wanted to make sure there was nothing weird going on that I needed to know about. I found out about the old settlement and this overpass. While standing here one night, I noticed dump trucks going and coming. I watched them several nights, and discovered the trucks were using the main road from dark till early morning. At first, I was suspicious as to what they were doing, for they weren't traveling on the road after 5:00 a.m. However, I checked it out thoroughly. I found there is a huge rock quarry where the state gets gravel for the roads being built. Right now there is a big road project on the other side of Pahrump. The trucks operate at night, for the road construction crews only work at night in the area the new road is being built. Every 45 minutes or so, one of those trucks will pass under this overpass, going one way or the other. You can see one coming now in the distance. It will be fully loaded. "

Marked looked in the direction he nodded toward, and saw the truck lights approaching.

Charley started unfolding the tinfoil under the moonlit sky. The tracker began to slowly glow. Charley grinned, and continued, "This little fellow is going to take an unscheduled ride in the back of that truck."

The truck would be under the overpass soon. It was evident the driver was trying to make as many runs during the night as possible.

"Mark, it's only fitting that you be the one to toss it in that truck, and send it on its journey."

Mark grinned, as he saw the truck almost under the overpass, and his hand reached for the tracker. Suddenly his hand stopped. His eyes seemed to glow in the moonlight. Charley was a little unnerved, when the tracker began to rise off the tinfoil a few feet above them. When the truck passed under them, and came out the other side, the tracker flew through the air like a bullet, and embedded in the gravel in the bed of the truck. They saw the object getting brighter and brighter, as the truck continued down the dark highway, until it was no longer in view. They both were silent that whole time, until Mark explained, "It was only fitting that I used what they taught me, to put it in the truck."

"Shocked hell out of me," Charley laughed, as he hit him on the back of the shoulder, saying, "Let's get back to the girls."

Soon they laughed and talked, as they headed back to the cabin.

The girls saw the lights from the vehicle coming down the road. They stood by the windows with weapons in hand, until they were sure it was the two men in Kate's car. They laid the weapons aside and met them at the door.

As the men came in, Kate was the first to speak, "What did you guys do with that thing, Charley?"

He laughed, answering, "It took a ride to Pahrump."

"What?" asked Sarah, "You didn't destroy it?"

Charley took the time to explain the whole scenario, as they sat drinking beer and eating snacks. He excitedly told how he witnessed Mark using his mind to lift the tracker, and send it flying into the gravel in the back of the truck."

Kate questioned, "What if someone finds that device?"

Charley defended his and Mark's actions, "Hopefully, by now it is buried under tons of rock at a road construction site."

Everyone voiced his or her hopes that he was correct.

Kate grinned, and said, "Charley and I are going to call it a night. We'll see you two in the morning," as she stood, and took Charley by the hand. He said goodnight, they disappeared into his room, and shut the door.

Sarah finished her beer and rose from the couch, "I don't need to tell you I haven't had much sleep, so I'm going to pack it in, also."

He jumped to his feet, reaching behind him, and retrieved the weapon she'd loaned him, "Forgot to return this."

"Keep it for now. You still may need it," as she said goodnight, and entered her room.

He placed the sheets and quilts on the couch making a bed. He put the pillow at one end, with the weapon underneath, and lay down on his back, with his hands behind his head. His eyes were wide, as he thought of all that had taken place. He thought about Sarah and what his feelings were. He found himself wondering if she was going to sleep in those pajamas or if she slept naked, as he usually did. He realized he needed to be more comfortable, so he stood, removed everything but his underwear, and covered up with the sheet and blankets. Still, he was wide-eyed, thinking.

In her room, Sarah hadn't laid down. She sat on the edge of the bed considering her feelings for, Jack, and her new feelings for this strange man. There was only a nitelite glow from where it was plugged into a socket low on the wall. Though they were trying to be quiet, she heard the noises that let her know Kate and Charley were having sex.

Jack would never make any kind of commitment because of the job. He'd even seemed kind of distant, since she wouldn't agree to let him climb in bed with her the last three or four weeks. Sure, she loved their time in bed, but there was too much at stake to get caught at it. She had to make herself say no. It made her a little upset that he just didn't seem to understand her feelings. Maybe she'd been distant to him, also, because of how she felt.

Mark on the other hand was attracted to her, she could tell. He was strange, but somewhat exciting. When she heard about him being encouraged to make love often to the other women, she felt herself being aroused. Now, he was lying in the other room, thinking what, she didn't know. Maybe he was thinking he'd like to jump in the bed with her and make love.

She stood, opened the door slowly, and walked to the couch. She saw his upper torso and strong arms above the covers. When she stopped and looked down at him, he rose to a sitting position, with a questioning look on his face.

She stuck out her hand for him to take, and he stood letting the covers fall to the floor. She could see his muscular legs, chest, and the bulge in his underwear. She knew exactly what he looked like without underwear. She couldn't take her eyes off of it, when he'd thrown back the curtain at her house. She quietly led him to her room, and closed the door. As they stood by her bed, she wrapped her arms around his neck, and they tenderly kissed.

He pulled away, whispering, "I don't have any protection."

Knowing he meant condom, she whispered, "It's ok. I can't get pregnant."

As they locked in embrace, his hands touched breasts through the cloth. She gently pushed him back and removed her clothes, letting them fall to the floor. She watched, as he dropped the underwear, and then they were entwined once more. He laid her back on the bed, and began using all the information he'd learned on those sex videos. He found he was more aroused than he could ever remember, as he performed, and could tell she liked everything he was doing.

To her, liking wouldn't have come close to describing what she was feeling. He knew all the right places to touch and caress. His strength and stamina were amazing, as they moved back and forth. She found herself having trouble holding back the flow of juices that wanted to erupt, and her body began moving faster meeting his.

He began thrusting harder and faster, as his hands and mouth found other parts to play with.

As her climax reached its peak, her body shook with pleasure and arched upward. She felt him turn rigid, as he let go of the essence he was keeping from her.

They collapsed on the bed and wrapped around each other. They didn't talk. They just lay there together, as if one didn't want to let go of the other. Their eyes met. She knew he wanted to say something, but she put her hand behind his head, and pulled his head to her breasts.

His mouth and hands enjoyed her breasts and nipples, as he gently toyed with them. She felt her womanhood reawakening. She pushed him to his back and climbed on top.

At first, it was slow and easy, as she looked down at him, and held her hands on top of his, at her breasts and nipples. Then her speed began to increase, and her eyes closed. He found he needed to hold onto her hips, if he was going to stay with her. One last arch of her body and they both let go of their juices.

As their tensed bodies relaxed, she lay down on the bed beside him looking into his face. Shouldn't they be saying something to each other? She couldn't find any words she thought fitting to say. Her mind raced with emotion, or lack of it, she couldn't make up her mind. The sex was way above describing. However, there was something missing. Something she always felt, when she and Jack made love. Maybe that was the answer. Maybe this was just sex to her, for that same feeling just wasn't there. Still, she didn't want to let go of him right now. She wanted to feel those strong arms around her, and his body pressed to hers. She turned on her side and put her backside against him, as she pulled his arm around her, and placed his hand on her breast.

She was extremely tired from hardly any sleep the day before, everything that transpired today and evening, and now this wonderful round of sex. Maybe that was her problem. Maybe she was just too tired to think straight, or know exactly what she was feeling. Before she knew what was happening, she'd pulled the covers over them and fallen to sleep.

A hand was shaking her arm, and a soft voice whispering, "Sarah, wake up. Wake up." It startled her, and she rose to a sitting position. She saw it was a fully dressed Kate, with her weapon on her side. When she jumped up, she felt Mark's hand slide off her side and onto the bed. She quickly glanced at his still sleeping face. Before Kate could whisper another word, Sarah was already thinking Jack would have been on his feet with a gun in his hand, if he'd been the one beside her. He was a very light sleeper.

Seeing Sarah was awake enough to comprehend, Kate continued, "Get dressed. Charley has equipment in his bedroom that he turns on at night. Sensors pick up signals on the road to the cabin and send signals to that equipment. A vehicle is easing down the road. It may be someone lost, or young people looking for a place for sex. Charley isn't taking any chances. He's already dressed and armed. He's in the living room watching a piece of his equipment now."

"Yeah, ok!" She started shaking Mark, "Mark, wake up. We may have unwanted company approaching." She hurried out of bed, threw on pants and a blouse, and secured her weapon to her side.

Mark was wakening, "What's happening?" She didn't bother to tell him what she'd said, she just told him, "Get up and meet us in the living room."

As she started for the door, she glanced at the clock, seeing she'd been asleep only three hours.

In the living room, only light from the screen lit the room.

Charley pointed to the screen, explaining, "The large signal on the screen is from a vehicle that has now stopped down the road. I could see the lights out the window for a little while till they were apparently extinguished. You see these four signals appearing on the screen and moving?" as he saw her and Kate nod. "Those are four people spread out, and easing through the woods in this direction, two on each side of the road."

Mark ran into the room in just his underwear. Kate smiled at Sarah, and watched him put on his pants and shirt. He pulled the pistol from under the pillow on the couch.

He approached, and listened as Charley continued, "These signals indicate planned movements. They are getting closer and I feel trouble brewing. Anyone moving through the woods like that at night will have to be using flashlights, or night vision goggles. He rose from the chair in front of the screen as he turned it off, and quickly went to the front window peering out. They could only see parts of each other, by the moonlight coming through the open blinds. "There are no lights shining, and that means night-vision equipment. That also indicates they mean business, and are most likely professionals."

He looked at the three huddled next to him, so they could see and hear him, and whispered orders. "Sarah, take up a position between the fridge and the bar counter, you'll have a clear shot at anything coming through the back door. Stay low."

Mark, get behind a chair or couch where it will be harder to be seen. Try to place yourself where you can get a shot at anyone coming out of either of the bedrooms. If they have heat sensor equipment it won't do any of us any good to hide. Also, since they are using night vision equipment, it will almost be certain they are wearing bulletproof vests. So, aim for the head and legs as much as possible. Head first, of course."

Turning to Kate, he softly said, "Angel, I love you. Put your back against the front wall between the window and the side wall, and don't move. You'll have a clear shot at anything coming through the front windows or front door."

Charley took up a position near the other front window, and they waited. Time seemed to stop, as they listened, but could only hear their own heartbeat.

Suddenly they could make out muffled footsteps on the front porch and the back deck. Kate and Sarah were seasoned police officers. They'd both been in shootings, and knew they'd do what they had to do, as both glanced toward Mark behind a recliner in the corner. He looked prepared with his weapon ready, but they wondered if he really was.

Charley was also seasoned in shootouts that were far more dangerous than either of the women could have imagined, yet neither of them knew anything about it. He wondered what they were thinking about him right now.

As he heard the faint sound of lock picks at the front door, he pointed.

Sarah also pointed to the back door, indicating she'd heard the same barely audible sounds.

Charley had purposely chosen his spot. Above him was the switch to the battery operated emergency lights he had installed throughout the house. He was almost certain by now they'd cut the electric wires.

The front and back doors swung open, and two armed men came charging through the front, and two through the back.

Charley immediately threw the switch and the lights all came on. The intruders weren't expecting this, and were temporarily blinded by their own equipment.

Charley and his companions opened fire on the enemy. Bullets poured into the attacker's night vision goggles and face. Automatic weapons fired wildly from enemy weapons, as Sarah and the others delivered well-placed death delivering bullets.

As the shooting stopped, the attackers fell lifelessly bleeding to the floor. Charley and Sarah checked each body to make sure they were dead. Kate picked up their automatic weapons and removed side arms from their holsters. Mark helped her with that chore.

"Is everyone alright?" Charley inquired, as he scanned each of them.

They all responded with positive answers. So, he began again, "It's highly unlikely they left the vehicle unattended. More than likely, the driver is waiting and heard all this shooting. He or she will know it wasn't just their buddies' weapons. The driver is probably also professional. They will do either of two things, when the companions do not return to the vehicle. One, they'll start the vehicle, get the hell out of here, and bring back reinforcements. Two, they'll be one of those cocky son of a bitches, and come to finish the job."

"How do you know all this stuff, baby?" Kate asked somewhat bewildered.

"There is a lot about me that you don't know, and I can never tell you." It was a weird time to ask, but he did anyway, "Is that going to stop you from loving me?"

"Of course not," she answered, "As long as you love me, I'll always love you."

"Ok. Let's take up our positions and wait for this next round, or listen for the engine to start and roar away."

"Not this time," Mark announced, "I have more rods and cones in my eyes than the rest of you. In case you don't know what I'm speaking of; I can see at night like a deer or an owl. I'm not going to let you people be in more danger tonight because of me."

As he rose, ejected a spent clip, replaced it with a full one, and jacked a shell into the chamber.

Before he headed for the door, Sarah put a hand on his arm, "You don't even know it is because of you."

"It doesn't matter, Sarah. I'm the most logical one to end this confrontation. If I fail, then you guys will have to handle it." He removed her hand from his arm gently, and disappeared out the door.

"Make your rounds count if he fails," Charley ordered, to bring them back into focus, "And check the rounds in your weapons."

Sarah and Kate did so, and took up positions.

It seemed like an eternity with nothing happening, until they heard two shots from a pistol. In a few minutes, they heard a vehicle start and saw lights coming their way.

"Stay ready," Charley ordered.

When the vehicle came to a halt and the lights went out, they heard Mark's voice, "The threat is ended," and they saw him get out of the driver side and walk toward them. All three went out to meet him.

The two women went to his side to make sure he was ok, as Charley shined his light into the vehicle. He saw the man dead, against the passenger door. Mark had pushed him over there after putting two bullets in the side of his head.

Charley came back to talk to them, stating, "That's a government type SUV. With all this sophisticated equipment, I'm beginning to wonder if they were after me. It may sound ridiculous, but it isn't impossible. I didn't get where I am, without making enemies along the way. Whichever the case, we need to gather our things, and get the hell out of here. Problem is; I haven't the faintest idea where we can hide, until I can find out more about what is happening."

Kate interrupted, "I think I know where we can hold up, but we need to get to Vegas. I've got a favorite uncle who is high up in one of the casinos. He has a huge boat on Lake Mead. I'm sure he'd let us stay there, no questions asked. It's a beautiful party boat to say the least, and easily sleeps eight people. He used to spend a lot of time on the lake, but he doesn't go there much anymore. His daughter and I were like twins, and inseparable, until she was raped and murdered. My aunt lost her mind after that, hit the drugs hard, and eventually killed herself. Occasionally, he'll take some girls and gambling whales (big spenders) out there to make sure they stay happy, and keep coming back to gamble. Otherwise, he just has cleaning ladies go out there once every three weeks, to make sure the boat is in tip top shape, and stays clean. He pays one of the guys at the marina to make sure the boat stays fueled, and run the engine often. I'll have to see my uncle and get the key from him. I don't think anyone would find us out on the lake."

Sarah worriedly stated, "If they are looking for me, and by now I can imagine they are, they will most assuredly know that at least Charley and I are together. If I leave the scene of all this, I can almost surely kiss my career goodbye. If you leave here, Charley, you may be in big trouble, too. It might be best for you to stay here, call the law, and wait. So far, you've done nothing illegal. You were just defending your home by attackers. Kate, the same goes for you. You haven't done anything wrong, either. You just helped Charley defend his home. You should both just stay here, and wait for the cavalry. On the other hand, I've broken too many rules already, and probably already in deep shit. I'm not ready to see the other side of those bars yet. If these guys were sent by this Majestic Twelve group to retrieve Mark, I'm not ready to let that happen, either. I've got to get him somewhere safe, until I can figure out how to help him find those people he left behind. I've got money saved. Just give us a head start in Kate's car, and I'll find somewhere for us to hold up."

Charley finally interrupted her, "I can't stay here in case they were after me, and I can't be hauled in for questioning, until I know from higher up, just how I'm going to answer those questions. I do have to make a call right now," as he took out his phone and walked out the door.

Kate added, "If Charley leaves, you know I'm not staying. I'm going wherever he goes, no matter how this ends. I know a place for us to go, and I doubt if you do, Sarah."

Mark spoke, "I'm saddened that I have caused so much trouble for all of you. Until I came into the picture, Charley didn't have any problems, so it is almost certain these men came to extract me, and probably kill anyone else that was here. It's best for all three of you to stay here and wait for the authorities, and for me to leave. Without that tracker in my leg, maybe I can become invisible for awhile."

At those words Sarah broke into the conversation, "How did they find us so quick anyway?" Mark, are you sure there are no more devices in you somewhere?"

"Probably not," Charley said, as he returned. "My boss says we are picking up information here and there, that men with NSA credentials have been asking questions, and researching computer files on Jack, Sarah and me. That caused my people to get in the picture, and start absorbing any information on the three of us they could find. My people don't like the NSA getting the upper hand. Anyway, my boss says they've seen news videos where Sarah is helping a wounded guy. The news station also reported that before the shooting, a man fitting the wounded guy's description came into the station claiming to have escaped from aliens."

He nodded toward Mark asking, "Are you wounded?"

"Not anymore," Mark answered.

Charley continued, "The news also mentioned that the stranger somehow caused a shooter's weapon to get hot enough for him to drop it. Those reports alone would draw the attention of the Majestic group helping the aliens. It's plausible they'd send these men to get Mark, instead of letting an alien space ship be seen more than they have to. Also, there was a rumor spreading that Sarah and I may have been kidnapped, when they found my car at her house, and hers broken into at a parking lot. With their connections, they probably satellite tracked mine, or Sarah's phone, or both. Give me your phones. I'll put them in my safe. The satellite can't pick up any signal from them through that metal. Luckily they can't trace or track the call I made to my boss. Awhile back, I invented a tracing blocker for specific phones. They can't trace his incoming or outgoing calls. I didn't think I'd ever need one for my phone, too."

As he removed his phone from his pocket, Sarah handed him hers.

Kate asked, "Mine too? They may not know about me yet, and we may need a phone."

Sarah confirmed, "If they're tracking our phones, and all of a sudden they can't get the signal, they'll start tracing all calls from our phones, especially mine. They are sure to see you and I have talked to each other, and they will start tracking yours."

Realizing she was correct, Kate handed over her phone.

Charley moved a nightstand and rug exposing a floor safe. He entered the combination, opened the lid, tossed in the phones, and secured the lid. Soon, he placed the rug and nightstand back in place.

Then he continued, "I've been ordered to get you three out of here. My people want to talk to Mark, and I've been ordered to keep him away from these supposedly NSA people at all costs." He walked over to one of the battery operated emergency lights on the wall. He moved a lever on the left side, and the light swung away from the wall exposing a very small safe. He spun the dial and opened it. He retrieved a stack of $100's and $50's, some ID's, and credit cards. As he turned back to them, he saw them all staring in disbelief at what they were seeing. Holding the items up in front of him he said, "None of this is traceable. I'll pick up a burn phone and check in with my people from wherever we go."

Looking toward Sarah, he seriously said, "You need to get a burn phone and call your partner. Jack needs to know you are safe. I'll use one, to place an anonymous phone tip that there was a shooting at this address. When they find this mess, all hell is going to break lose. Your people, my people, and no telling who else are going to be involved."

"Then let's get out of here," Kate said quickly. They all nodded and began packing belongings and weapons.

Charley came out of his room with a small duffle bag, and handed it to Mark, "I threw in some of those clothes I mentioned earlier at Sarah's, and an empty travel case for your little stuff."

Mark thanked him, and put the things Sarah bought for him at the pharmacy into the kit.

Before long, they were in Kate's vehicle headed toward Vegas.

Chapter Six

Jack awoke in his hotel room with a dire need to relieve himself. At first he was disoriented, but soon remembered where he was. He glanced at the clock. The red numbers illuminated 3:30 a.m.

The memories of his night with Lillian came rushing back, as he quickly headed for the bathroom. He wondered if he was ever going to stop urinating, as he remembered her flight time.

He hurriedly brushed his teeth, splashed on some cologne, applied underarm deodorant, and donned some clean clothes. His thoughts seemed to be rampant. "Her flight is at five, and she'll probably leave her room by at least four, and get a cab to the airport." He glanced at the time on his watch, as he slipped it on, thinking, "3:52 a.m. If she's not in her room, I'll try to catch her downstairs. If I don't see her, I'll take a cab to the airport. There can't be that many flights at 5:00 a.m. headed to Jacksonville Florida, or connecting flights to get there." His room key was in his wallet in his pants, so he shut the door making sure it was secure, and headed to the elevator. It seemed like it was creeping, but finally the door opened, and he rushed to her door. He felt a big smile stretch across his face, when he saw her coming out of her room, pulling her suitcase in one hand, and holding a piece of paper in the other.

She heard him approaching and looked his way. Her face beamed with joy, as she admitted, "I never dreamed I'd see you again this morning before my flight. You've just got to know that I'm pleased beyond words that you are here."

Making light of the situation, he laughed, "Hey! As a police officer, I wouldn't feel like I'd done my job, if I didn't make sure you made it on that plane safely."

"You're going with me to the airport?"

"All the way, Beautiful; I'd be a very sad man if I couldn't at least see you every minute we have left, before that plane leaves the ground."

Her eyes began to water, as he took the handle of her luggage. She placed her arm around his waist, "It's still hard for me to believe I met someone so special. You are something else."

They laughed and talked in the cab to the airport. He paid the cab driver, and helped make sure her luggage was checked in properly at curbside. They went as far as they could go, before reaching the security station where only passengers could proceed. There was a coffee shop near, with coffee, Danish, sandwiches, and other foods. She only wanted coffee, so he paid for two. They sat in the flight waiting area enjoying each other's company, for what seemed way too short, for now it was time to board her plane. They rose from their seats and discarded the empty coffee cups.

One last time she placed her arms around his neck. There were other teachers from her school in the waiting area she knew, but they were politely leaving her alone with Jack. She didn't care who was looking, or what they thought, as their lips met tenderly and longingly.

When she eased away from him, she handed him the folded paper. "I was going to slip this note under your door before leaving the hotel. Please, don't read it, until I am on that plane and in the air. Jack, thanks again for being so special."

He noticed her eyes beginning to water again. He was speechless. Was this a note telling him she was really married and this was a fling? What was he expecting? She just met him last night. Did he expect her to just fall in love with him, and forget about going back to her life in Florida? He found himself walking hand in hand with her, as far as he was allowed, as he told himself, "Jack, are you some kind of idiot? Say something."

Before she could pass the security person, he spun her around slowly, "Lillian, you are an amazing woman." He pulled her to him, and they kissed wantonly.

Her face got a little red, as she heard one of her teacher friend's giggle, and other people grinning as they passed. He and Lillian waved until he could no longer see her. He walked away clutching the folded paper, with a sick feeling in his stomach. He wouldn't be able to see the plane leave from this waiting area, and rushed to the flight observation deck elevator. Even with all the airport lights, he could still see the star lit sky with clouds in the distance, and planes arriving and departing. He went over the layout of the airport in his mind, and pinpointed where her plane would be backing away from the loading ramps. Soon, he saw he'd been correct, as her plane headed to the runway. He stood thoughtless; as he watched it sitting on the runway awaiting take off. His eyes stayed glued to the plane, as it taxied and rose into the sky. He watched until it slowly banked, and the rest of the airport blocked his view.

He looked down at the paper clutched in his hand, and said aloud, softly, "Ok, Lillian! I kept my promise," as he began to slowly unfold the paper. He eased under an overhead light, so he could read the note.

Her words began, "I've never met a man that I've known for so short a time, yet enjoyed being with so much. Not even my ex husband. You turned a humdrum trip into a wonderful occasion. Leaving your room last night was one of the hardest things I've ever had to do. By the time we got to my room, I was kicking myself in the butt for not letting you stay, even though I thought it had to be that way. It's hard for me to believe some special woman hasn't won your heart. Though your face and words showed nothing but honesty, I couldn't fathom you not having that one person to bestow all your love upon. Tonight, in my heart, I found myself happily pretending I was that woman."

As his eyes read her signature, tears filled his eyes. He was glad no one could see him wiping the teardrops with his handkerchief. He'd never been married, but he'd had lots of girlfriends in the past. No woman had ever made him cry with her words. Emptiness was probably the best way to describe how he felt inside. He placed the note in his front pocket and took the elevator back down. Soon he was in a cab and headed back to his hotel.

He opened the door to his room, and laid the key on the dresser. Noticing his phone, he removed the charge cord, turned it on, sat down on the bed, and waited for it to boot up.

There were eight messages in voice mail. The first was the lead IAD investigator, "Caruso, Nelson here. There's been new evidence in this investigation. I need you to return this call as soon as possible."

"Maybe!" he uttered out loud, but hit save so he'd have the number.

The next call was the captain, "Jack, IAD is bugging me about you and Sarah not answering your phones. Between you and me, I know there is more to your relationship with each other than just partners. If you two are shacked up together somewhere, you need to get separated fast, before IAD finds out about it. When you get this message give me a call, and I'll bring you up to date on new evidence.

I'm afraid that Sarah is going to have a lot of explaining to do."

As Jack deleted the call, he began talking to himself, "Shit, Sarah, now what have you done?"

The third call was from his friend Barry Anderson, a patrol officer, and a good friend. "Jack, this is Barry. Keep this under your hat, and you didn't hear it from me. A woman, who read about the shooting at the station, sent a phone video to the news people. If you haven't watched any news you sure need to. The video clearly shows Sarah helping a wounded guy on the street, with blood all over the side of his shirt, and putting him in the passenger side of her car, before she ran inside with her weapon drawn. Now IAD is hot about her not divulging this information, and why she didn't file a report about a man with a gunshot wound. You are her partner, and I knew you'd want to know. Don't take this wrong. I know she's a good officer, and she must have good reason for her actions. Later, buddy."

As he deleted that call, Jack shook his head, saying, "I don't know what she's doing either, old friend."

Fourth call was from several hours later, and it was from the captain again, "Jack, something strange going on. Sarah's car was found in a Wal-Mart Supercenter parking lot. Driver's window was smashed, and the car was apparently ransacked. All her duty equipment was missing from the trunk; weapons, ammo and everything. Officers sent to her home could not bring anyone to the door. A vehicle parked out front was registered to a Charles Decker, no wants and warrants. There is speculation Sarah may have been kidnapped. Call me as soon as you get this message."

Fifth, sixth and seventh calls were IAD requesting him to call in immediately, and if he was in touch with Sarah, to tell her to do the same.

The eighth call was from Barry's personal phone, "Jack, I and other officers have been dispatched to the address of one Charles Decker. He lives out of town and we are on the way. His car was parked in front of Sarah's house. IAD is beginning to suspect this guy might have abducted her, or maybe the wounded guy abducted both of them. If they are not found at Decker's address, the captain is going to call in the FBI. I'm taking a big chance here, buddy, giving you this info. Make sure you keep it to yourself."

"Damn," he moaned out loud, "I should have called Charley when I saw his car at her house." At the time, he'd supposed they didn't go to Charley's house, since his car was still there. Maybe somehow they did," as he quickly dialed Charley's phone. Hearing it go to voice mail didn't surprise Jack. Charley hated phones. He very seldom had his on if he was at home.

A knock at his door got his attention. "Surely IAD didn't find him this quick. May as well face whatever music," he thought, as he opened the door. "Delgado, how the hell are you?" He was glad to see it was Tony, and not someone he didn't want to see. Before he could answer, Jack continued, "How'd you know I was here?"

As he stepped in, "I'm fine, and you must be, too. Where's the brunette you were with last night in the casino?" look.

"Early flight; how'd you know I was with someone in the casino last night?"

Tony cocked his head with a questioning "Are you stupid, look?"

"Oh, yeah, those little bubbles on the ceiling," as he shook hands, and they gave each other a friendly hug.

"I was doing my weekly check of all the screens, and I recognized your ugly mug. Of course, I was trying to get a better look at the fox you were with, as he shook his fingers together with "HOT" sign.

"Didn't see you after that; I had to go to a special room upstairs, as security for a few tables with high dollar whales gambling. That lasted all through the night. As head of security, I had to oversee the security detail. You would not believe how much money is won or lost at those games. When I came in this morning, I checked the front desk, to find if you got a room for the night. So, how long are you here for? You should have called me. The room would have been on the house. Scratch the "would have been," I already took care of that. You didn't check in last night. As of yesterday, this room is listed as a comp room for a male high roller." He handed Jack an envelope. "Here is the cash you paid for the room."

"Thanks, you know I appreciate you doing that. To tell you the truth, I really had no plans when I checked in. I'm on admin leave, with pay for two weeks or so, because of two shootings I was involved in. I just wanted to get away from everything."

"No bullet holes, I hope? The room is yours, unless you'd like an upgrade. I could handle that quickly."

"Shit no. This room is fine and a great view. Don't know what I'll be doing today, but if I'm still here, we could have a few drinks when you get off."

"Sure, we can tie one on if you want, but I don't get off till nine tonight. You know my personal cell, which you should have used before checking in. Here is one of my new cards with my casino phone number. If you need anything, and I do mean anything, call me. I'll see if I can make it happen. Right now, I've got to get back to work." He stuck out his hand to Jack, and added, "If something happens and you check out without seeing me, just leave your key at the desk and tell them your room number. They'll see it's all taken care off."

As Jack thanked him again and closed the door, he felt proud to have friends like Tony. "Wow, now that I'm not registered here, IAD will have a little harder time finding me." He shook the envelope, saying aloud, "And now I have more gambling money."

His phone rang. It was Barry again, so he answered, "Yeah, Barry."

"Jack, glad I got you this time. I'm sure you got my other messages by now. We are at the Decker resident, and it looks like a war zone inside. There's bullet holes and blood everywhere. Four guys dressed to the hilt in tactical attire, night vision equipment, and automatic weapons, are dead on the floor. A fifth one is dead in the passenger side of a black SUV out front. Two bullets to the left side of his head ended whatever career he had. CSI has already been called. Their ETA is probably ten minutes. Jack, I found three of Sarah's cards you detectives hand out, lying on a dresser in one of the rooms next to a set of earrings. I shoved them in my pocket. What do you want me to do with them?"

"Put them back where they were before CSI arrives. You've done enough for me keeping me posted. I appreciate what you've done and being a good friend. I owe you, man."

"You don't owe me shit, Jack. I owe you my life. I can never repay you for that. Shit is starting to get deep for Sarah."

"You don't owe me, you know that. As for Sarah's mess, there's nothing we can do right now. I still haven't been able to contact her, so I'm still in the dark, too." Jack's memory shot back to the day Barry was referring to. He had just made detective. Jack heard the radio crack about a robbery going down at a convenience store and heard the address. Knowing he was close by, he spun his vehicle around and headed in that direction. Before he could even get there, he heard the chilling "officer down" in the dispatcher's voice. As he arrived, he saw one bloody patrol officer face down. One of the robbers was lying against the store outside wall with gunshot wounds to his chest and stomach. Barry was on his back with a bullet wound to his shooting shoulder, and trying to get his weapon to his other hand. One of the robbers walked toward Barry to put another bullet in him. Jack hadn't used his siren, so the robber was startled, as he heard Jack's vehicle screeching to a halt. He turned quickly to see Jack jump out of his car with weapon drawn. The two exchanged fire. Jack was hit in his shoulder; but the robber took two shots to the chest and one in the head.

Both Jack and Barry spent several days in the hospital together, before being released to recuperate at home.

"Ok. I'll put the stuff back on the dresser. Now that CSI is involved, I'll have to cool it on these phone calls."

"You've gone overboard already. Thanks again, Barry."

"Anytime, Jack, anytime," and he ended the call.

Jack was still shaking his head and wondering what the hell was going on, when his phone rang again. It was the captain. Jack had a lot of respect for the man. He was a black man in his middle 50's. He'd earned his stripes as he moved up the ladder. He was one of the most respected men on the force. Jack keyed his phone.

"Captain, are you looking for me?"

"Don't be cute, Caruso. Why haven't you returned my calls and where the hell are you?"

"Since I'm on admin leave, I came to Vegas for fun, drinking and relaxation. Haven't had time to mess with this phone, I've been too busy. You know, the "What happens in Vegas stays in Vegas kind of thing." He was being partially honest, he thought.

"Sarah there with you?"

"Nope, I've been with a woman, but not her." He was being honest once again.

"Jack, you better not be lying to me. Your job may be in jeopardy."

"Captain, I promise you that I have not seen nor heard from her, since I left the office." He didn't want to mention that he'd tried many times to reach Sarah, but to no avail, since he'd just told the captain he hadn't messed with his phone.

"You got a pen?"

Jack pushed down on the top of his pen and reached for the little notepad the hotel rooms always have, "Yeah, I'm ready."

"Charles Decker," and he rattled off his address. "Uniforms are on site, and you need to get your ass out there right now. Nasty crime scene. CSI on the way."

"Captain, I'm on admin leave, remember? If it's a crime scene, I can't be on site."

"Not any more. IAD has cleared you. You've been reinstated. Now, quit wasting my time and get your ass in gear. Other dicks will be there, but you are in charge. Don't screw things up."

"Ok! I'm on my way. Thanks, Captain." He knew the captain didn't have to call him back in. He could have let other detectives handle things.

"Yeah, Yeah, Yeah," Just get it done. If you really are in Vegas, it will take you long enough to get there, as it is." and he hung up.

Well, at least he still had a job so far. He wondered how Sarah was going to be able to hold onto hers.

He threw his stuff in the suitcase, unlocked the safe, removed his money, weapons, ammo, and threw the extras in his suitcase.

Like a young boy rushing to a first date, he hurried downstairs to the desk, turned in his keys, and gave them his room number.

As the desk girl checked the room info, she asked politely, "Was everything suitable for you?"

"Everything was great," he smiled back.

"We hope you stay with us again soon. Have a nice day."

He nodded and headed for the valet to hand them his ticket.

Soon, he'd paid and tipped the valet, and was en route to Charley's place. He'd never been there, so he entered the address into his GPS system, and the directions appeared. Now that he was back on duty and en route to a crime scene, he pushed the pedal down a little farther watching his speed increase. He didn't want to over do it, but he did want to get there soon as possible.

Still, it would be a long ride, so he thought about Sarah again, and tried to put some of the pieces of the puzzle together. "Ok, Sarah! You come say a few words to me at the shooting and disappear. Though you didn't admit it, you probably did take that report. Why would you do something that stupid? You neglect to tell anyone that you helped a wounded man outside the station, who was probably the same guy who bled in the station. You didn't take him to the hospital, so you must have taken him home. If you did, that was real stupid. Did you know this guy or what? Anyway, since Charley's car was at your house, you must have called him to help you with this wounded guy. Then you all left in your car, left it in a parking lot, and made it look like a break in."

He was a good detective, and now he was proving it with a clear mind. He continued talking to himself, "How did you leave the parking lot? You wouldn't call a cab. Neither you, nor Charley have a second vehicle. Ah, Ha! There's only one person I can think of that would help you at a time like this. Kate. It had to be Kate Brewster, your best friend." She was supposed to be with Charley at

Sarah's. He didn't have Kate's number, but he'd get it. He did know her address. He'd been there with Sarah, to pick her up sometimes for a night out together. That would be his next stop. Right now, he had to get to that crime scene.

He continued to think, and time passed quickly. Finally, he arrived at Charley's cabin. He had to park a bit away, though. There were two uniform patrol cars, a detective car, two CSI investigator vehicles, and one CSI meat wagon.

As he entered the front door, he saw Barry and nodded.

Another detective team from his office approached.

He acknowledged them with, "Jim, Terry, fill me in." He knew these two burly guys well, and they were good detectives.

Terry said, "Heard you were back on duty, and on the way. I'll try to walk you through what we think happened. By the way the bodies are lying, and the path of bullets, it appears two came in from the back and two from the front. There was no forced entry, but we found lock picks on one body from each entrance. As you can see, they were wearing tactical attack attire and armed to the hilt. At least they were; their handguns are missing."

Barry grinned, as he pretended to be doing something else, for he knew Jack already knew the information.

"Electricity was cut outside. Looks like they came in thinking they had the upper hand, but were surprised. Bullets to the head probably took them out, causing their weapon fire to spray wildly. From four places in the room, there are 40 calibers, 9 mil. and .357 casings scattered on the floor. I'd venture to say, those four were lying in ambush when the intruders came through the doors. It looks like they were lucky, also. No blood at any of the four positions. I know you probably saw the other guy in the SUV out front," as he saw Jack nod.

Jim interrupted concerned, "Jack, there is a picture on the wall of you and Sarah with this Decker guy and another female. These guys are pros. Do you have any idea about what happened here?"

Knowing Jim was fishing for information, Jack answered, "No! I have no clue what happened, and yes, Charley is a friend of Sarah and me." He figured he better divulge what would become obvious, "The other woman is Kate Brewster, Sarah's best friend. She's a patrol officer."

Jim answered, "Yeah! I recognize her now. The short hair and sunglasses threw me off. That explains why Sarah's cards and earrings were found on the dresser in one of the bedrooms." Jim continued, "They're taking finger prints everywhere. Have you ever set foot in this place, Jack?"

He knew his associates were worried that Jack might be implicated in what took place at this scene. Thank goodness, he could honestly state, "Nope!

I've never been here and didn't know Sarah had either."

A CSI investigator, whom Jack didn't recognize, said, "Looks like she's done more than just be here. We already collected semen samples from that bedroom."

Terry and Jim saw Jack's face turning red with anger, so Terry turned, saying, "Cards and a set of earrings don't mean your samples came from Sarah Sidwell. She's a good detective, so watch your mouth."

The guy didn't have a come back. Realizing he might have stepped on somebody's toes, he went back to collecting evidence.

Jack let it go, as his face slowly returned to normal color. He began walking delicately around looking at the evidence. When he got to the bedroom, he pictured Sarah and some guy in the bed having sex. He felt his face getting hot again, so he went back into the main room.

Jim placed a hand on his shoulder, "Jack, we've got this, unless you just want to be here."

"No need for me to be here. I just wanted to get a look. You two are top notch investigators."

Terry added, knowing the captain put Jack in charge, "We'll have a full report on your desk as soon as possible."

Jack nodded and proceeded out the door to his vehicle.

As he started his engine, he hesitated, and whispered out loud, "Sarah, you are getting deeper and deeper into a hole you may not be able to climb back out of."

When he pulled away, he headed for Kate's, before Jim and Terry headed to her address themselves, as soon as they finished their investigation at the cabin. He hoped that was where he'd find Sarah, Kate, and Charley, and find out what the hell was going on.

He was on Hwy 160 and just entering the busy streets on the outskirts of Pahrump, when he realized he was being followed by a black SUV, similar to the one at the cabin. He placed a quick call to the station, leaving it on speaker, "This is Jack Caruso. I'm on Hwy 160 headed toward the station and just passing Wal-mart. I have a suspicious black SUV on my tail. Tinted windows are too dark to see occupants. Occupants are suspected to be armed and dangerous. Request immediate backup, to help intercept," as he gave the cross streets to achieve the ambush.

He heard, "Officers on the way," in the dispatcher's concerned voice, "ETA three minutes."

Soon he approached the intersection and saw patrol cars approaching from streets to the left and right.

The SUV was still staying almost a block behind him.

Two more SUV's intercepted the one that had been following him. Armed men in suits and ties quickly surrounded the other SUV and extracted four men from inside.

Jack and the patrol cars stopped, and exited their vehicles with weapons drawn, as they watched what was taking place.

They saw the four men being handcuffed and placed into the other two SUVs, while one from the intercepting SUV's quickly climbed into the driver's seat of the one that had been following him.

All three SUV's sat still, as one suited man walked a little toward Jack, and stood in the middle of the street facing toward him. Traffic in the area had come to a standstill, observing what had taken place.

Jack, with weapon still drawn, walked toward the man standing.

Before Jack could reach him, the man ordered, "That's far enough, Jack,"

"The hell it is," he thought, as he continued his approach, but saw two more suited men join the first one with hands on their weapons but not drawn. He stopped his approach.

However, the officers in the two intercepting patrol cars didn't like what they were witnessing. They came closer to him, with their weapons ready. Jack held up a clinched fist, which meant for them to hold their position.

The man, who'd been standing alone, continued, "We'll handle these four men."

"Just who the hell are we?" Jack asked loudly, with his weapon still trained on the man.

"Far above your pay grade, Jack. Tell your officers to stand down, before all of you get in a world of shit. These four are our jurisdiction now."

"Haven't seen any ID's yet," Jack said sternly.

The man continued, "And you won't. I stayed long enough as a courtesy to give you this information. You need to find your partner, and her friends Kate and Charley. They are in grave danger. We will help when we can, but I can't get it done standing here talking to you. Now, tell your men to stand down, while we disappear."

Jack knew these guys had to be above FBI, or they would have been flashing badges. They weren't afraid of anything, and it was obvious they weren't going to answer to Jack and his fellow officers, even if it meant a shoot out.

"Stand down," Jack ordered, as he holstered his own weapon, but started approaching the one talking, and ordering, "You, me, closer."

They met in the middle of the street, as Jack questioned, "What the hell is going down? Men in tactical attacking my friends, some guy talking about escaping from aliens, what's this all about?"

"We aren't positive about exactly what is happening, but we know it is a matter of national security. These four may be a key to finding out. We will use means to abstract information from them, which you cannot lawfully use. I promise that I will relay any information they divulge on why they attacked your friends. Just as we, you need to devote your resources to finding your partner, before whoever sent these four finds her." As he turned to walk away, he said over his shoulder with a grin, "Nice meeting you in person, Jack."

Jack and his men let the suited guys mount up and leave the area.

As he walked toward his car and the patrol officers, one officer asked, "What was that all about, Jack?"

"It has to do with Sarah and the shooting at the station. These guys are untouchable, and you know what I mean. We'd be wasting our time trying to haul them in."

"What about the four following you that they took into custody?" another officer asked.

"Obviously, they are the bad guys, and I wouldn't want to be in their shoes," Jack answered, "And they saved us a lot of trouble and paperwork. I'll make a report on this call. I sure appreciate you guys getting here fast."

"No problem, Jack," one answered. They nodded and headed for their patrol cars. Soon they and Jack headed in opposite directions.

Jack finally made it to Kate's apartment complex. He didn't see her car, but went to her apartment and knocked on the door. There was no answer, and he figured he didn't have probable cause to kick in her door.

Returning to his vehicle, he sat there feeling helpless, wondering what he was going to do next. He keyed his radio saying, "Requesting APB on Officer Kate Brewster. Vehicle is a dark blue

Dodge Charger. Tag on file at the station; forward Officer Brewster's photo to sheriff and state. Officer may be in the company of Detective Sarah Sidwell and one Charles Decker. All three subjects may be in grave danger from unknown suspects. Follow protocol."

He felt like he was somehow ratting on friends, but since they were keeping him in the dark, he knew he'd better take the appropriate steps to keep himself out of trouble, and maybe keep them from getting shot by police. Also, the more agencies he got involved, the more likelihood of finding his friends.

He asked himself out loud, "Now what, Mr. Detective?" His thoughts rushed back to the bedroom at the cabin, and pictured Sarah and that guy having hot sex in the bed. Maybe it wouldn't have bothered him so much, if she'd told him she had a new boyfriend. He realized that was bullshit, as he felt anger creep up once again.

He started his car and pulled away. He'd done all he could do on the road. The best thing now would be to get back to his desk at the station, and get on his computer. He knew he'd better get a report on the captain's desk soon, about this latest encounter with the suited guys. He wasn't quite sure how he would explain his actions, but it had to be done.

As he drove, his eyes scrutinized every dark blue car in sight, hoping he'd be the one to locate Kate's vehicle. However, he reached the station without having any luck.

When he came in, the captain saw him and motioned for him to come to his office. Jack closed the door behind him. Knowing the boss had probably heard some things, Jack quickly said, "I'll have a report on that back up call on your desk shortly, Captain."

"Already heard about it. Who do you think they were, Jack? FBI, CIA, or NSA?"

"At least CIA; but probably higher. It was evident they meant to keep the four that had been on my tail, even if it meant a gunfight. I wasn't prepared to put the patrol officers in danger over four assholes that really hadn't broken any laws. I'd sure like to have gotten my hands on them, though."

"You made the right call, Jack. All this involvement from higher agencies is becoming a pain in my ass. I'm more worried about Sarah and Officer Brewster. Get in there to your desk, and do what you do best. You're the best detective I've got. If anyone can find them, you can."

Jack nodded and closed the door behind him. He went to his desk and started searching information on Charley and Kate. His main concern was to find any known associates, in hopes that someone who knew either of the two could point him in the direction of their whereabouts. He knew they and Sarah were in a lot of danger from someone, and he needed to find them. He realized he didn't give a damn about the stranger being in danger, but believed that somehow, this guy had to be the key to everything.

He'd started with Charley's info. They'd been friends for a long time, but he realized little was known about him. As he researched the information, he found that after college, information about Charley ground to a halt. It didn't take Jack long to figure that Charley was CIA. All this time, they'd thought of Charley as a guy with a plush government job working with wave signal equipment. Although Jack thought of Charley as being tough if he needed to be, he didn't picture him as working for a government spy agency. Now other thoughts entered his mind. Maybe Charley was dirty and selling government information. Maybe he was the one that caused all this trouble. Still, where did this weird stranger fit into the picture?

He got as far as he could with Charley's information and started with Kate's. Everything he found seemed normal. High school, two years of college, and odd jobs here and there before joining the force. One of those odd jobs caught his eye. She'd had a part time job parking cars at the Mirage in Vegas. He thought of Tony. He'd be working right now and wouldn't answer his personal cell. Jack took out the card with Tony's work phone and dialed.

When Tony answered, he began, "Tony, it's Jack."

"Saw where you checked out without even saying goodbye," Tony laughed.

"Got called back to work. Back on duty now. This is really a business call, sort of. There was a young woman named Kate Brewster, who had a job at the casino parking cars. Do you happen to know anything about her?"

"Yeah, I know her well. She's my boss's niece. I remember her and his daughter ran around together, until his daughter was raped and murdered. Kate's still family, and comes around to visit the boss now and then. She's a pretty girl, but I had to stay away from that, if you know what I mean. You should know her; she's a patrol officer in Pahrump."

"Yeah, I know her. She and Sarah are best friends. They have dropped off the map and I'm trying to locate them."

"They didn't drop too far. At least Kate didn't," Tony informed, "I saw Kate on the screens visiting the boss less than an hour ago. She wasn't with him long, and I saw her leave. If I'd known you were looking for her, I would have flagged her down, or at least have let you known. I didn't observe anyone else with her."

"Damn," he thought to himself, "Tony, I need a big favor. I need you to find out from your boss what she wanted to see him about, and if he knows where she's going."

"Sure, Jack. I'll do what I can. Just a minute, Jack," and he heard Tony ordering someone, "Get security down there now."

"Jack, sorry about the interruption. Look, I've got to go. There's trouble on the floor near some tables. I'll get back to you as soon as I can."

"Thanks," Jack said, "Go take care of business."

As he ended his call, he contemplated everything he knew about this situation. He wondered why Sarah hadn't called back to explain why she wanted the information on the Wakefield woman. He guessed things got too hot for her on the run, and she was afraid to call him.

When Susan was able to talk to IAD at the hospital, she told of how she took over the report from the other officer, after the ghost guy had given his name. She remembered glancing at it, and was fairly sure it was Mack or Mark, but couldn't remember his last name. The first officer who started the report couldn't remember. He was too busy laughing to himself, and wanting to pass off the report to Susan. She felt sure the guy had said his mother's name was Carolyn, but couldn't remember where he said she lived. Without the handwritten copy of the report, there was no way to prove her memory was correct.

Now, Jack had the information from Kenny about Carolyn Wakefield in Wichita, Kansas; the information that Sarah had wanted so badly, but didn't call him back to say why. He could no longer withhold the information, so he knocked on his captain's door.

"Come on in, Jack, did you locate, Sidwell?"

"Not yet, Captain, but I do have a few leads. I need to relay some information to your ears only. It's up to you how you handle it." Jack sat in a chair in front of the captain's desk. He began, "Before Sarah was in any kind of trouble; she called me, and asked to have my FBI agent cousin, Kenny, in Kansas, find out about a woman named, Carolyn Wakefield, who lived in Wichita, Kansas. Sarah didn't tell me why?" He continued with the whole story, including everything he knew. He divulged how it seemed the ghost guy the day of the shooting was the son of Carolyn, Wakefield. Carolyn had died, still claiming that aliens abducted her son, whose name was Mark. Now, this guy had walked into the station claiming to have been abducted by aliens, and looking for his biological mother, Carolyn. Jack explained how he thought this was the same guy who Sarah had been seen helping, and the same one probably still with her. Jack went on to explain how Kenny called him back to let him know about two NSA agents coming to his office about his inquiries of this Carolyn, and he had to give them Jack's name.

Jack's boss had been silently listening to everything, but suddenly asked, "Do you think this guy really was abducted by aliens? When the men in black come into the picture, it makes me wonder if there might be some truth in all this."

"Captain, I'm not sure what to believe. Sarah's doing all this strange stuff, and hasn't contacted me. I can't find her yet, to figure out exactly what is going on. I'm as frustrated as everybody else, maybe even more so."

They were interrupted by a knock on the door. A female officer manning the front desk said, "Jack, two men with NSA credentials need to speak with you."

As Jack nodded, he glanced toward the captain, who suddenly said, "Send them in here."

"Yes, Sir" was her answer, and soon the two men in suits and ties stepped through the door.

"Gentlemen, what can we do for you?" The captain asked.

Looking toward Jack, one announced, "We'd like to talk to Detective Caruso in private about his partner, among other things."

Jack and the two men were a little shocked, as the captain, who had stood, said, "Afraid that isn't going to happen. Whatever you have to ask my officer, you can ask in front of me. That way there won't be any misunderstood information when you leave."

Before they could get over their shock, he continued, "Before you ask any questions from, or about, two of my detectives, I need to see your identification."

"What are you trying to pull here?" one of them asked, but flashed his badge.

"Afraid that won't do, just flashing a badge that you can get out of a magazine. I need to see your ID's up close, take down your names, check with your supervisor, and confirm where his office is, before we give you any police information."

"You are stepping over the line, Captain. I suggest you start backing down."

Jack remained quiet. He could hardly believe his captain was talking to NSA agents in this fashion.

"I didn't get where I am from backing down from anything." The captain answered, somewhat angrily.

"You are putting your career and that pension you've got coming in jeopardy, by your actions."

Now, the captain was closer to the guy, and stated firmly, "If something happens to cause me to lose the career and pension that I have earned, and worked so hard for, then I would have nothing to lose. I'd spend the rest of my life trying to find the person who caused me to lose it."

"Shit," Jack thought, "Now I know why this guy is the boss."

His captain continued, "Cough up those credentials, I'll contact your supervisor, and then we'll answer any questions that you might have."

"You are going to be very sorry you did not cooperate with us, Captain."

The captain pushed his intercom button, "Send some officers in here immediately."

Never having heard the captain call out over the intercom, detectives and patrol officers came barging into the room. The first one through the door with a hand on his weapon asked, "Everything alright, Captain?"

He answered with, "See these two gentlemen to the door. It's time for them to leave."

As they turned to leave, the NSA agent said softly, "Some other day, Captain, some other day."

His men made sure they were clear of the building.

When they left the captain's office, Jack said, "I'm sorry I brought all this on you, Captain."

"You didn't bring shit on me, Jack. In the first place, I'm not even sure they were real NSA agents. Even if they were, I don't believe for a minute that they were operating under orders or permission from a NSA office. I believe these are rogue agents, or fake agents working for someone else. Don't worry about those two. Get back out there and follow those leads you said you had. It's even more evident now, that we need to find Sarah, for her sake."

Jack nodded and hurried back to his desk. He continued gathering information on Sarah and Kate, and hoped his friend Tony would call back soon.

Chapter Seven

In a small conference room at a secluded location outside of Las Vegas, General Arthor H. Gilliam was just walking in with two military advisers. Through his years in the military, when someone asked what the H in his name stood for, he told them, "Hardass." They placed their hats on the table and sat down. There were two military guards at the door.

Across from Gilliam and his men sat three men in suits and ties.

One gentleman in a suit, but no tie, patiently stood at the head of the table. As the others sat, so did he, as he began, "You were all called to this meeting in light of new evidence concerning Area 69. As you know we've had nothing but frustration concerning that area. We've come to the conclusion that all our operations in that area, including use of satellite visual, was somehow disclosed to concealed occupants in that hilly area. That makes it almost impossible to locate our targets."

Everyone glanced at each other, and then back at the speaker. He continued, "Our CIA office has performed a slow and meticulous surveillance video and audio of each of you six at this table. We purposely excluded a joint effort with NSA."

General Gilliam spoke angrily, "Why in hell would you have an investigation on any of us? We all worked together on many projects with no problems."

The speaker calmly answered, "For the enemy to know exactly what we were doing at all times, we determined it had to be done by someone who sat in on these meetings."

"That's ridiculous," one man added, "All of us have proved our dedication to all our projects, past and present."

The speaker again, "It was troublesome to us all, to believe there could be a traitor among us, but I hate to inform you; that is exactly the case. Also, our investigation showed there was more than one individual passing on secret information."

With those words the door opened, as two more armed military came to the table on one side, and two armed secret service agents approached the other side of the table, with stern looks across their faces.

The speaker pointed to a screen that dropped down from the ceiling behind him. Upon the screen were lists of bank accounts for one of the army advisers, and one of the NSA men.

"As you can see, the deposits to these accounts far surpass the normal payroll deposits, and clarified income. You will also note large money transfers to selected offshore accounts in these two individuals' names."

As he hesitated, the General and one advisor quickly looked at the guilty ones. Gilliam surprisingly said, "Harry, tell me this is a bunch of shit, and they've got their wires crossed. You've been like family to me all these years. I would have trusted you with my life."

Knowing he was busted, the guilty man just stood, as the two military police placed handcuffs around his wrists.

The guilty man across the table was already standing, so the NSA agents could place handcuffs on him. He gave no excuses for what he did.

As the two men were led away and the door closed, the speaker waited for the murmur among those still seated to die down. Then he spoke again, to solidify the guilt of the two who were just arrested. "Using new sophisticated listening devices developed by one of our agents, we've been monitoring voice and text messages from all of you. I'm proud to say the rest of you are squeaky clean, and maybe we can make some headway in our endeavors. By using this new equipment, we tracked texts and calls from our two traitors to a string of phones, with one passing the info to another. As our investigation continued, it led us to the two mystery brothers, who'd reportedly delivered food supplies to the target area. Our female guest has positively identified the two. DNA samples from the two have proved the boy child is one of the brothers'."

"Now we're getting somewhere," Gilliam stated. The others around the table nodded.

The speaker continued, "The brothers have not divulged the location for their deliveries, but it is only a matter of time before they do. We will use every means at our disposal to obtain that information."

"Also," he added, "There has been a new twist in this situation, which also may be in our favor. One of our trusted agents has another escapee from our target area. He is a male, and is showing alien tampering with his maturing from childhood. He is friendly, and cooperating with our agent. Unfortunately, our agent had to temporarily drop off the grid. Their lives became endangered. Apparently, rogue NSA agents working for Majestic Twelve, ordered a mercenary military-type attack on our agent's home. The attackers were killed. Not knowing where the next attack might come from, our agent had to dispose of known phones, and go into hiding. We are awaiting contact via burn phones in the near future. Once this escapee is safely in our custody, we should be able to find out much more about our adversaries, and what they've been doing to the humans they've abducted. We've also managed to take into custody four rogue NSA agents. I don't need to explain the extent of questioning these men will endure, before we obtain the answers we are looking for. We are hoping they will lead us back to the head of these operations."

As the ones at the table grinned and murmuring resumed, the speaker concluded, "I want to thank you men for your dedication to the service of our military and country. Without men as yourselves, this country would fall to our enemies, be they human or otherwise. Because of men and women like you, we will never let that happen. Thank you for your continued efforts."

There were no goodbyes or any normal parting. He just gathered his info and prepared to leave.

The other men rose to depart, as they shook hands and rekindled friendships. Each expressed their sad feelings for losing their arrested associates.

Just before they exited, the speaker said, "General, a word with you."

The others knew well enough to keep walking. If the speaker wanted them there, he would have said so.

When the door closed, the speaker confided, "I appreciate all the hard work you and your troops have put into this Area 69 thing."

The general was wise enough to add, "I'm sure you didn't detain me just to tell me what a good job we've been doing."

"Of course, you are correct. General, I need to ask a favor."

"If I can do it, you can be assured that I will," he answered militarily.

The speaker explained, "We have no idea how far-reaching, or how many out there, are on the Majestic's payroll. That's why all our correspondence is face to face, or in sealed government envelopes, and delivered by tried-and-true. However, as we saw today, money talks and bullshit walks. I'm worried about my agents in the field. Sure, they can handle themselves under normal conditions. Now they are dealing with heavily-armed rogue mercenary. I'd like to know I can count on you, in case things get too hot for my people to handle."

"You've known me a long time. In any situation when you need me or my soldiers, all you need do is ask. We'll take care of it."

"I appreciate that very much, General. I'd like you to have small groups readily available in Pahrump, Las Vegas, and the roads in between. I'd rather it not look like planned exercises, but more like just giving your people something to do. However, any soldiers you send to these destinations need to be apprised of the dangers involved."

"My people can handle most anything, but I personally will express the need to be extra attentive. Anything else we can do for you?"

"Can't think of anything right now, General, but you never know when I might come knocking."

The general shook his hand, adding, "You know how to get in touch."

Soon the general and he proceeded out the door.

Chapter Eight

When Kate visited her uncle and asked to use the boat, she also mentioned she needed the use of a vehicle. She explained she might be in a little bit of trouble, and didn't want to be found until she cleared things up. Her uncle had several cars at his disposal and gave her keys to a new Cadillac SUV. Kate left her car in the parking area.

With the key to the party boat, the four headed to the marina. They stopped long enough to pick up some extra supplies and groceries, while Charley and Sarah obtained several burn phones. When the trip continued, Kate let Charley drive. They headed southeast out of Las Vegas toward Boulder City. Then they took hwy 93 out of Boulder City toward the Colorado River, and Lake Mead. Except for a few tense moments, when sheriff or state troopers passed, the ride was uneventful. They spent the trip pointing out beautiful scenery and making small talk.

Always being the inquisitive one, Sarah said, Mark, "You have a nice tan and you don't have a tan line," as she noticed Kate smiling at her. "Your skin tone doesn't look as if you got your tan from a tanning booth. You can almost tell by looking at someone if that was the case. If you have been held underground all this time, how did you get the tan?"

"I can see where that would be a question in your mind, and one very easy to explain. The aliens knew the human body couldn't live without a certain amount of natural sunlight. We were often escorted out of the hillside to a flat area, basically with beach attire and lotions, until we reached the age of eighteen. At that point, those eighteen and above were encouraged to sunbathe in the nude. Remember, it was during this time they were trying to encourage sexual behavior between us. This just added to their plan."

Now Kate had to jump in, "And did their plan work?"

"Of course, it did at first," he grinned, "Rubbing suntan lotion on a naked woman, arouses a young man very quickly. There were no rules about not having sex right there under the sun, and more often than not, it did happen. However, as we grew in age, sex in front of others got less and less. Mostly, sex occurred while sleeping together away from the others."

Sarah looked irritated, as she continued questioning, "Weren't the aliens afraid you sun bathers banging each other would be seen by airplanes, or even satellite, since they had to know the government was trying to find their location?"

"No, they somehow knew when it was completely safe for us to be out there without being seen. If what Charley told us is correct, and they are being helped by these high-ranking Majestic group, it's logical to assume they were feeding the information to the aliens on when to, and not to, let us in the sun."

Charley grinned into the rear view mirror saying, "Sounds like it wasn't a bad place to be." Of course, Kate who was up front with him frowned and punched him on the shoulder, causing Charley to laugh.

Before they knew it, they saw the great Hoover Dam nestled between the mountains. The dam held back the teal blue water, forming one of the largest man-made lakes in the Western Hemisphere. To their left they saw water of the lake extending up into the hillsides of red sandstone and black lava, some of which was over six million years old. On the lake they saw all kinds of boats, jet skis, and other craft enjoying water sports. Soon they turned down the road that led to the marina. Everything from small fishing boats to huge party boats, were either out on the water, or secured at the dock.

Charley had an urgent need to take a leak, so after parking; they headed for the bait shack. Mark pulled the cooler on wheels. Walking out on the dock, they saw literally thousands of carp with their mouths out of the water. People were feeding them popcorn. A few brave souls were on their knees, placing the popcorn into the fish's mouth. Others

Inserted a thumb in the mouth of the fish, and tried to lift it out of the water. The slippery carp were impossible to hold. Below the carp, large bass, bream, and other species of fish, swam un-bothered by the commotion above.

While Charley and Mark took care of business, Sarah and Kate slipped into the women's restroom.

Charley purchased two bags of ice. He dumped one in the cooler, but left the other intact lying on top of the things in the cooler. The lid wouldn't close fully.

Before long, they rejoined the women, and headed for Kate's uncle's boat. Kate explained on the ride from Vegas, that the boat had a gas stove and gas refrigerator. She had only to throw a switch and push a button, and the refrigerator would start cooling. The gas stove could then be used at their discretion.

As they walked along the berths, Charley stated, "Man, there are some expensive craft docked here, and on the water. You can tell there are some rich people around."

Kate walked a little to the front, and finally stopped, saying, "This is it."

The other three stood there in amazement, until Sarah said, "Kate, when you mentioned big party boat, I pictured a huge pontoon boat of some kind with sleeping quarters. This isn't a boat, it is a frigging yacht."

"And a very costly one at that," Charley added.

As they climbed aboard, Mark passed the cooler up to Charley. Kate began to tell about the boat and give them the tour. She'd been on it many times with her uncle and his family, but she hadn't been on it in quite some time. She related the story of how he came to own it. An Arab oil sheik had the company who built it deliver it to Lake Mead, when he purchased the craft. He was going to be in Las Vegas for a few weeks of gambling. He wanted the privacy of his own boat for his harem and bodyguards. He'd won and lost millions; on earlier gambling sprees. On one of his trips, he was down a little over a million in a private game against one of the big wheels at the Mirage, who was Kate's uncle. The sheik had been given special privileges and exquisite sleeping quarters, with plenty of beautiful women coming and going, so he had spent little time on the yacht. He offered the yacht against his losses. A one-card draw from the deck, with high card takes all. Kate's uncle agreed. He let the sheik draw both cards from the deck face down. When he turned his card, the sheik happily showed a king card. Kate's uncle nodded toward his card, which was still face down, and asked the sheik to do him the honor of turning the card. When he did, the card was the ace of spades. Supposedly, the sheik only laughed at his own bad luck, and Kate's uncle now owned the yacht. The next year, when the sheik returned to gamble, he took Kate's uncle to see his new yacht. It was larger, plusher, with all the bells and whistles.

As they saw the large dining table on the fly bridge, fully stocked bar, and spa bath that easily held six, there were a lot of oohs and aahs.

Kate proudly explained the yacht was fast, and designed to run in open water. It would probably never reach its maximum speed on this lake. However, it was possible, of course, with the lake's 1.5 million acres and 820 miles of shoreline.

As the tour continued to the aft section, they were shown the crew quarters and dining area. Her uncle didn't have a ship crew, but the sheik did.

The guests' sleeping quarters were elegant, to say the least. The four guest rooms easily let four couples sleep comfortably on queen-size beds.

An oversized shower and bathroom pleased the ladies. Hot water came from solar recovery cells strategically placed along the top and sides of the yacht. Quick showers would allow the four to bathe without running out of hot water. Kate explained there were huge holding tanks for gray water and from the toilet. Non-dumping rules on the lake required her uncle to pay a company to come pump out the tanks from time to time.

Charley finally interrupted, "If you've got to be on the lam, then this is the place to get it done. Only one question, how do we get this thing out of the marina?

"Baby, I've guided it out myself, with my uncle standing near me. I've heard you talk about driving boats before. I'm sure you can handle it," as she wrapped her arm around his waist.

"We'll see," he smiled, "But if I crash this damn thing, you're going to take the blame."

"No problem, we'll tell my uncle that I was the pilot."

Mark may have known about weapons, but he didn't know anything about boats. However, Kate and Charley had their sea legs, so to speak. They were up front, piloting the boat toward open water.

Sarah and Mark sat in the back of the boat talking.

He broke the silence. "I noticed you seemed upset when I spoke of having sex in the sun, why is that?"

Sarah answered with shortness in her voice, "Most women who just had sex with a man, doesn't particularly want to hear about his sexual activities with other women."

"I apologize if I caused you any hard feelings, Sarah. You've got to remember, this is the way we were taught, with no inhibitions when, where, or how we had sex."

"That brings something else to mind. Last night, when I led you to my room and we had sex, what exactly did you feel?" The cause of her question was the feeling she'd had when it was over, that there was something missing. He'd pleased her at the time beyond words, but something didn't feel just right inside her.

"I'm not sure exactly what you are asking. I'm sure you could tell that I was pleasantly aroused, and pleased with the way our bodies worked together. It was a very enjoyable experience."

His answer didn't come close to what she'd hope for. His reply more readily described the mechanical act. "That's it," she suddenly realized, the whole sweaty body grinding act seemed mechanical. There was no feelings deep inside her, that she was making love to someone she loved, or even liked a lot. She realized she'd brought it on herself. He was new, strange, exciting and physically attractive. She wanted to feel him next to her and experience what he had to offer. Her mind raced back to the times in bed with Jack. He made her feel special, and filled the moment and after hours with ecstasy, when they made love. She wished he were here right now, making love to her on the back of this boat. She wouldn't care who was looking.

Their conversation was interrupted, as Kate came down from the bridge, "Mark, Charley wants to show you how to operate the boat just in case."

Mark looked toward Sarah with a questioning look on his face, but only said, "Sure," as he stood and went toward Charley.

Kate sat down by Sarah. As soon as Mark was out of hearing, she asked, "How was he in bed? I know you two were reeling and rocking last night."

"He knew all the right buttons to push, and was totally amazing in the sack," Sarah answered forcing a smile. She'd rather Kate not know what was going through her mind right now.

"Uh, Oh," Kate said, as she read through Sarah's guise, "I get the feeling there is something amiss."

"Sometimes you are too smart for your own britches," Sarah commented, as her eyes began to water.

"Just not the same as with, Jack, huh? I've had those same feelings when having sex with other men. Yeah, some of them drove me wild during the act, but it just wasn't the same as when Charley and I make love."

"Kate, I suddenly feel that I've burned a bridge, and can't get back across to Jack."

Kate tried to comfort her; "I think Jack has been somewhat in love with you for years. I've told you that before. I wouldn't throw in the towel just yet, Sarah."

Kate wrapped her arm around the shoulder of her best friend. She needed to get Sarah's mind off things. "Before they stop this boat somewhere, let's go fix some sandwiches and beer for everyone."

Sarah agreed and followed her.

With Charley's instructions, Mark guided the boat to one of the many secluded coves along the hillsides. They'd observed a lot of coves being used by other boats along the way. People were swimming in shallow areas of almost crystal clear water, from melted snow mixing with lake water. Others tried their hand with rod and reel. Some were doing "whatever" inside their boat.

Mark slowed the craft in shallow water, and Charley lowered an anchor. They were unreachable from the barren hillsides. Not even a mountain goat survived in that area. Anyone approaching would have to accomplish that by boat or air. Under either of those conditions, Charley and the others would know immediately.

They were well-armed by this time. Before they left Charley's place, he'd opened another secret panel and removed two AR-15s, clips and ammo. They also had the attackers' side-arms. Their assault weapons were left, so authorities could see they had attacked Charley's home.

With Sarah's weapons from her trunk and extra Glocks, they could put up a decent fight, if it came down to that. However, they felt they were safe where they were for now. It would take some time for anyone to find them.

With two anchors out to hold the boat parallel with the hillside, Mark and Charley joined the women for food and drinks. They laughed and made light of their current situation, as they snacked on sandwiches and cold slices of leftover pizza. It was a Nevada hot day. Temperatures broke the triple digit mark. There was no shade anywhere, and even inside the boat, they began to sweat profusely. They could have started the generator and ran the air conditioners inside, but decided they'd better save that option, just in case. The twelve-volt lights would run off the boat extra batteries, but if they went dead, the generator would be needed to recharge the batteries. Tonight, it would be just the opposite. It would get extremely cold on the water in the desert air. Right now, the heat was very uncomfortable.

Mark rose, went to the edge of the boat, shed his clothes, and dove into the water.

Sarah saw Kate's eyes light up, as she watched Mark undress.

Charley had seen Kate watching Mark. Knowing he was fairly well endowed, and in good shape, he shed his clothes and joined Mark in the water.

It was the first time Sarah had seen Charley nude. It was obvious that Charley should have no trouble pleasing Kate in bed.

As the two women nodded to each other, they also shed their garments and entered into the water. The water was cold enough to make their nipples rigid, when they came up and stood in the shallows. They swam and enjoyed the water like a bunch of school kids out for the summer. You'd never guess they'd just managed to not get killed the night before at Charley's cabin.

Charley and Kate began getting amorous under the water. Sarah just wasn't ready for that kind of thing with Mark again. She swam to the boat and climbed the ladder at the back. By the time Mark decided to come aboard, she'd dried, donned her clothes, and was drinking another beer.

After Kate and Charley's quickie, they soon joined the other two.

Mark was dressed, so he and Sarah got to watch Charley and Kate dress.

Then they began choosing sleeping quarters and placing their belongings inside. Charley and Kate, of course, chose one together. Sarah chose one of her own, and pointed at another for Mark. He shook his head and obliged. The extra large, exquisitely decorated, old sheik room was left empty. It was as if no one wanted to be any better off than the other. Then it was more beer and food, as they began to try to figure out exactly what they were going to do from this point forward.

With half the country probably looking for them, how were they going to do anything to help Mark find where he'd escaped from, and free the others? It would be a monumental task. Even if they weren't apprehended, they didn't have the resources to find the facility. So far, they'd only managed to stay one foot in front of their adversaries and the law.

Tonight, they felt relatively safe. They'd come in a vehicle not registered to either of them, and were on a yacht. Surely no one they knew would expect that.

Charley asked Kate, "Do you think your uncle would care if we had a few drinks from the bar? I'm about to get burned out on beer."

"He wouldn't care at all. I'm sure we won't make a dent in his bar supplies."

"Whoa," Charley said, "I know that's right. There is every kind of liquor and mix you could think of behind these cabinet doors, besides everything that is visible."

The others joined him to place their preferences. All except Mark, that is. He'd never tasted any kind of alcohol, so he had no preference.

The sun began to set and they already felt the welcome change in temperature. They sat around drinking and talking like four friends on a normal boat excursion.

As the sky around them began to darken, Kate switched on the twelve-volt system. Lights came on around and throughout the yacht.

They shared their drinks on the open deck under the moonlit sky.

Mark enjoyed the taste of the mixed drinks and was having more refills than the others. They warned him he'd better take it slow, since he wasn't accustomed to drinking. They'd mentioned how his alcohol tolerance was probably very low. However, he didn't heed the warnings. Before long, he was slurring words and staggering. Soon they helped him to his room and piled him onto his bed.

Not too long after that, Kate went to take her shower and put on some nightclothes.

As soon as she was out of sight, Charley looked toward Sarah, "I'm going to make a call to the boss. Now is a good chance for you to place a call to Jack. I know you've been putting it off, but he's got to be worried sick about his partner, if for no other reason. He's a good man, Sarah. No matter what your feelings are for Mark, he doesn't deserve to be kept in the dark about whether you are ok or not."

"I know. I've wanted to call him, but I just don't know what I'm going to say."

"You can tell him what you want to about everything that has happened up to now. However, don't tell him anything about Kate's uncle or this boat. His phone will probably be monitored, and the less we involve him in our situation, the safer he will be. Knowing Jack, he'd come charging out here to try to help us. We don't need to put him in danger, too."

As Charley stood, she nodded and watched him go to the top and front of the yacht, until he was out of sight.

She sat there, dumbfounded, for a few minutes. What was she going to say to him? Most assuredly by now, he knew she'd lied to him about the report, holding back the information about Mark being wounded, and not taking him to the hospital. What excuse could she give for her actions? Hell, she wasn't even sure why she did what she'd done. She tried to find some words of rationalization to give him, but nothing made any sense. She knew Charley was right. She definitely needed to tell him she was alive and ok.

She stood and went to her room to get the burn phone. She heard Mark snoring from his quarters. She walked to the back of the deck and looked up at the moonlit sky. She found herself wishing this was a romantic occasion for her and Jack; and they were sitting under this bright moon. She wished he was holding her and watching the moon reflect off the lake water. She felt her eyes starting to water, as she wiped a tear and dialed his cell. Part of her hoped her call would go to his voice mail. A deeper part needed to hear his voice again. She could tell the inquisitiveness in his voice, not recognizing the number, as he answered, "This is, Jack."

She still found it hard to find any words and was silent, as she heard him again, "Hello! This is, Jack. Who is this?"

Finally she spoke weakly trying to hold back the tears, "Jack, it's me, Sarah." She didn't need to add her name. He'd recognize her voice anywhere, anytime.

"Sarah, didn't recognize the number. Are you alright?" Jack wanted to say a lot more, but refrained for the moment.

"It's a burn phone. We discarded our other cells. Yeah, I'm ok." She wanted to blurt out how good it was to hear his voice and how warm it made her feel inside.

"By we, I'm sure you mean you, Charley, Kate and your new boyfriend. Don't try to feed me that shit about he's just a friend. CSI found the semen in both beds at the cabin."

She could tell the anger and hurt in his voice, and she felt sick inside.

"Jack, I promise you. He isn't a new boyfriend."

"Oh! Just someone you may have thrown away your whole career for, and someone you enjoy screwing? Sarah, you've gone to hell in a hand basket. You were lucky to get out of Charley's alive. Those guys were professionals. What in the hell brought that down on you?"

There was no use arguing with him about Mark, she'd already screwed that up. Now, it was time to give Jack the whole story. She needed to get it all off her chest. He deserved to know everything.

"Jack, when I pulled up at the station the day of the shooting, there was a man wounded outside. I put him in the passenger seat of my vehicle and rushed in to make sure you were ok. I didn't want the wounded guy bleeding all over my car, so I rushed back out. He was trying to walk away, so I got him back into the car, and was headed to the emergency room."

"Well you never made it there and no record of any gunshot wounded checked in."

"I know," she admitted, "It was stupid, but because of things he'd said about someone looking for him, I took him to my place instead. I don't know what made me do it. Something inside just made me head to my house."

"So you take a wounded nut case, who by your words was on the lam from something, to your home and doctor him. Sarah, you have definitely lost your marbles."

She could tell he was angrier, but she'd started confessing, and she needed to get it all out.

"Yes. I treated his wound and put him in a spare bed. I knew I'd already broken the rules, but now I had to see it through."

She'd leave out the part of seeing him in the shower, as she continued, "When I woke up later, he no longer had the bandages on, and his wounds were already healing over."

"Sarah, the guy was hit with a bullet from a Glock .357 mag. You don't just heal over night. It had to leave a gaping exit hole wherever he was wounded."

She interrupted, "Jack, I'm serious, he was already healing. He told me he'd been held for years by aliens and he had a tracker device in his leg."

"Sarah, you need mental help if you believed all that shit."

"Jack, it's true and I'll get to that, but back to when I returned to the station and saw you and IAD. When I looked at the previous night's reports, and saw Susan's report hadn't been entered in the system, something made me take the report. When Kate and I left, I called Charley to meet us at my place. Charley checked Mark's leg, and sure enough, there was a tracker signal coming from his leg. Charley assured it was high tech. Charley told us more than he should about aliens. I knew I couldn't let them find me, until I knew more about what was going on with this stranger."

Referring to the statement he'd made earlier about the semen, he said, "It's obvious he isn't a stranger anymore. Really, Sarah, a tracker put in his leg by aliens?"

She was past making excuses, "We got rid of my car in a parking lot. We took Kate's, and went to

Charley's cabin, to lie low, until I we could figure things out. Later that night we were attacked, as you know, and none of us know exactly why. I could tell you what Charley thought, but not over this phone. Now, Charley was sure we needed to get somewhere off the grid."

It was evident he wasn't ready to let it go as he said, "So, after you got through banging your new friend, and these guys came in and shot up the place, all of you left and went into hiding some place.

What could she say? All of it was true. As far as Mark, she'd done all the damage with Jack she could do, so she simply answered, "Yes."

Her reluctance to give any excuses kind of caught him off guard. For a second or two he was silent. He suddenly realized she was his partner. No matter what, he needed to get to her and make sure nothing happened to her. "Sarah, where are you? I'll come to you. I'll bring you in, and we'll let the captain straighten everything out."

"Jack, I can't. There is more to Charley than you, Kate or I ever knew. Mark's story is for real. There are others being held where he's been all these years. Aliens have experimented on their bodies. That's how Mark was able to make the weapon hot at the station, causing the shooter to drop it. I can't let you know where we are right now. We've got to figure out how we are going to find the location where Mark was held, and somehow free the other people."

His voice was a little calmer, as he remembered his friend Kenny, and his visit from the men in black. "Let's assume that some, if any, of what you are telling me is true. You've definitely stepped on somebody's toes, and they sent troops to take care of you. You do not have the resources to fend off future attacks. Since this one failed, they will be more prepared on the next try. With the remote chance that any of what Mr. Wonderful has told you is true, how in the hell do you think the four of you can find that place, since evidently, he doesn't know how to lead you to it."

She'd leave the Mr. Wonderful comment alone. No need to get into that and aggravate Jack any more than he already was. Besides, his voice was becoming less aggressive.

"Jack, we aren't sure what we'll do, or how we'll accomplish it. Charley has a lot of connections, and we'll work out something."

"Sarah, you'll be lucky if you can take a leak without someone finding you. A sketch of your friend was put together from his picture through your car, and descriptions from Susan and others at the station. An APB has been put out everywhere with all of your faces, and description of Kate's vehicle. Also, the FBI is now involved, for we had no way of knowing if some type of abduction had taken place. The FBI showed up at the crime scene at Charley's and so did two men from CIA. However, the CIA just seemed to want to observe, they didn't take over jurisdiction from the FBI."

Now she knew Jack had to know there was something weird going on, for all these agencies to be in the picture.

"Jack, I've got to keep where we are a secret for now. I just needed to let you know I was alive and safe for the moment. Trust me, I'd feel safer if you were here." She knew her last statement was so true, but she didn't say all she was thinking. She wished he were here to take her into his arms and hold her. It was sickening to think that may never happen again.

"I don't think I'd want to be there to watch you screw this Mark Wakefield. However, you are still my partner, and everything inside of me wants to make sure you are safe. Tell me where you are. I won't tell anyone else. I'll come join you and we'll work on your situation together. The captain is on our side. He's already run off two NSA agents. I'm sure he'd help us if he could."

"Jack, I'm not ready to put you in danger and put your career at risk. I promise I'll try to keep in touch to let you know I'm ok. Whether you believe it or not, I still care for you very much." She didn't give him a chance to say anything else, as she ended the call.

Charley heard her last statement, as he returned. "Time to toss these," and he threw his over board. It was like casting away a link between her and Jack. However, as hers went over the side and she watched it sink, she consoled herself with the thought she had more burn phones.

Kate returned, and after a few more drinks and small talk, she and Charley retired for the evening.

Sarah remained in her perch under the stars and continued to think and drink, as she searched her memories and feelings for her partner. There were several trips to the bar, and each time the drink was a little stronger. She felt herself wanting to wash away all the pain and thoughts, and managed to do a fairly good job of it. Eventually, an empty Solo cup fell from her hand, and she passed out on the long deck seat.

Chapter Nine

When Sarah hung up on him, Jack was frustrated and threw his phone angrily upon his desk. He looked up and saw his boss locking the door to his office. He knew he'd better not keep this information from him.

As he approached, Jack began, "Just got a call from Sarah on a burn phone. The four of them are safe, somewhere. I couldn't get her to tell me the location. They've ditched their cells so they wouldn't be traced. She says there was no abduction and that she and the others are trying to help this Mark Wakefield guy. She swears he was held by aliens in an underground facility, and others are being held there, also."

"What do you believe, Jack?"

"I'm not sure what to believe. I've never seen Sarah do anything this far-fetched. Apparently, our friends Kate and Charley believe her enough to try to help her."

"Jack, I've been running all this through my mind. NSA agents showing up in my office, rogue military attacking this Decker's place, guys following you get intercepted and whisked away by some unknown agency, which seems to know what all of us are doing. Looks like the water is getting deep around us, and we don't even have a canoe yet."

"Captain, all the eggs in my basket aren't broken, I still have some leads to follow up."

"I'd tell you to get to it, but you look like you are running on fumes and need some rest. Maybe you need to go home, get a few hours sleep, and come back in refreshed. That's what I'm fixing to do right now, before something else happens."

"Maybe, Captain, but I've got to at least check on one hot lead, before I call it a day."

"You mean call it a night. Have you even looked at the time?"

Jack just glanced at his watch and shook his head.

"Do what you've got to do, Jack, just watch your back. Call my cell if you need me. If no call, I'll see you here in the morning."

Jack held his cell into the air and smiled.

"Make sure the damn thing is charged."

Facetiously, Jack grabbed the end of the charger cord he kept plugged into the wall by his desk. He held the phone up again so the captain could see him putting the phone on charge.

"Smart ass. Go get some coffee. Looks like you need some bad." He didn't wait for Jack to comment. He just turned and threw a hand up in the air.

When his boss left, Jack's eyes scanned the area within the station. Officers were answering phones, desk duty, and other mundane tasks, to get their shift over with. No one had even been brought in for booking, at least not any he'd noticed. He realized the other officers were purposely leaving him alone, as he saw them glance his way now and then. They were all good officers, and knew what he was going through, with his partner missing.

He was tired, real tired. It had been a late night with, Lillian, and up early to see her off at the airport. He realized food had not been one of his priorities all day.

Tony hadn't returned his call and that was bugging him. He decided to get coffee and something from the snack machine, before he returned to his desk. Then he'd give Tony a call, to see if he found out where Kate had gone. He had purposely not mentioned Tony to Sarah.

He bought a turkey sandwich and tossed it on one of the small round tables in the break room. Coffee was free, and someone had made a fresh pot. As he poured a cup and sipped on the way back to his table, he made a mental note to ask who made this pot. It tasted pretty good.

After his first bite of the sandwich and slowly washing it down with the hot coffee, he tried to rationalize things in his mind. Sarah, Kate and Charley were in great danger from something, but didn't want to put him or his career in jeopardy. So far, he was helpless. He'd involved his friend Kenny, and hoped he hadn't gotten him in trouble. The captain threw the two NSA agents out of his office, if they really were agents. He was followed, until a mystery agent from some unknown agency intercepted them. "What the hell is going on?" ran rampant through his mind.

After another long sip of coffee, he wondered why he was so angry with Sarah for banging the stranger. Just last night he'd done the same with Lillian. Sex with Sarah was no less than amazing. She made him feel like she loved him at those times, even if she never said it. Down inside, he'd fallen in love with her, but never told her. Maybe if he had, things might have been different between them.

His thoughts went to his hotel room at the Mirage and making love to Lillian. She made him feel special, and he couldn't even find the words to express how good the sex had been. Maybe she'd been telling the truth about not having sex since her divorce, because she sure put it on him last night. The note she left was the clincher. Now he wasn't sure about his feelings for Sarah or Lillian. They both had become very important to him.

The turkey wasn't great, but it took the edge off his hunger. He refilled his coffee cup and headed back to his desk.

He left his cell on charge and picked up the desk phone. He dialed Tony's work number, but heard it go to voice mail. After the beep, he said, "Tony, it's Jack. I'll try your cell number, old buddy."

He dialed that number. Just before it went to voice mail, he heard a woman's voice answer softly, "Hello." He thought it sounded like his wife Nancy, but he wasn't sure, so he just said, "This is Jack Caruso. I was trying to get in touch with, Tony."

"Jack, this is Nancy," as he heard her voice breaking up.

"Nancy, I didn't recognize your voice. Is something wrong?"

"I'm at the hospital. Tony just got out of surgery and he's in ICU."

More softly now, he asked, "What happened?"

"Apparently, some members of different motorcycle gangs got into a fight in the casino. Tony joined his security people on the floor to try to calm the situation. One of the gang members pulled a gun and shot him in the stomach. Tony's security people killed that guy, but a woman on vacation was also wounded. She's up here in the hospital, with a shoulder wound."

"Nancy, you don't have to say any more. I'm out of here right now. I'll be there as fast as I can. I'm at my office in Pahrump. Do you need anything?"Jack grabbed his phone off the charger cord, putting it into his pocket.

"No! I'm just like a zombie, sitting here wondering why this happened. I called my sister in Phoenix. She's headed to the airport right now. She'll arrive later tonight. Jack, they say Tony made it through the surgery ok, but the road to recovery will be a rough one."

"Nancy, Let me call you right back. I'm on the desk phone. I'll dial you on my cell."

"Ok, Jack."

Jack was already headed to his car with his keys in hand, as he dialed, "I'm getting in my car right now, Nancy. I'll be there as soon as I can."

He heard her answer tearfully, "Ok, Jack!" Then the call ended.

Jack plugged his cell into the car charger and fired up his engine. He didn't have the authority to use his flashing lights for personal use, but his foot could sure push that pedal down. On the open road he kept glancing in his rear-view mirror for any suspicious black SUV's. He didn't need any of that right now.

Things were mounting up, with everything else that had occurred, and now Tony. What next? He really wanted to be there for Nancy, and now he doubted if Tony had the chance to ask his boss anything about Kate. Frustrated, he decided to talk to Tony's boss himself. How he was going to accomplish that, he didn't know. You don't just walk up to the desk and say, "I'm a detective from another town and I want to talk to the big wig here."

A dark colored SUV in his side mirror approaching fast distracted him from the thoughts. "I don't need this shit right now," he said out loud." As the SUV came along side, Jack's hand went to his weapon. He relaxed, as he made out the female figure in the passenger side on her smart phone. The SUV passed and pulled ahead.

"Damn," he thought, "I'm doing close to eighty and that vehicle is pulling ahead of me." He wasn't pushing his pedal any farther down, though. He didn't need to be pulled over. Sure, the officer would let him go, especially after explaining about Tony, but that would take time. Time he didn't have to spare.

At least the tense moment with the SUV had made him more awake. For a second or two, he didn't feel as tired. However, he knew that would wear off as the night went on.

At the hospital, he checked the information desk for the location of the ICU waiting room, and headed in the direction. Walking in, his eyes picked out Nancy. She was a pretty, petite, dark-haired woman of partly Hispanic descent. He always thought she could have been a model, if she had wanted.

"Jack," she called out, as she stood and they hugged.

"Any more news on Tony's condition since we talked?"

"They are watching him closely. He's sedated to restrict his movements. The bullet missed vital organs by centimeters, and came out his back, above his hip, close to his spine. They are not sure if he will be able to walk again. Right now they are just trying to keep him alive." Her tears started flowing.

"Tony is a strong man and a fighter. He'll get through this, Nancy."

"I've been to his bed, held his hand and talked to him," she said through her sobs, "Do you think he knew I was there?"

Trying to comfort her, but knowing he didn't have a clue, he answered, "I'm sure he did. I've always heard your subconscious knows what's happening around you at times like these. You just keep holding his hand and talking to him now and then. You're going to need a lot of patience. It may take some time. Am I allowed to go in and see him?"

Standing, she answered, "I'll take you in with me."

Tony looked like a cyborg in one of those space movies, with tubes sticking in him everywhere. To solidify what he'd just told Nancy, he put his hand on Tony's arm, and said, "Tony, this is Jack. Just wanted you to know Nancy and I are here with you. The doc said you came through the operation with flying colors. You'll be out of here in no time. Nancy will take good care of you."

Of course, there was no response of any kind from, Tony, as they stood around speaking to him now and then. Eventually, they headed back to the waiting area.

"Jack, I sure appreciate you being here. I know he would, too, especially with whatever is going on with Sarah. I saw the pictures of her and three other people on the news. The reporter said the FBI was now involved in the search for her and the others. They mentioned they might have been abducted. The news said four armed men were found dead in a house that held evidence she'd been there recently."

"Keep this under your hat, Nancy. We don't know exactly what is going on with Sarah or her present location. She called me just before I came here. She says she's ok. She was in the house that was attacked. She and her friends managed to get the upper hand on the intruders. Sarah and the three managed to come out of that without a scrape. Now, she's afraid to come in out of the cold, so to speak. None of us know why they were attacked. We are still gathering evidence. Let me worry about Sarah. You've got enough worries here. Are you sure there is nothing I can do for you, like go get you some food, or anything from the house? Do you need money or anything?"

"Jack, there's nothing I need, except for Tony to get well. As I said before, my sister will arrive later tonight. She's reserved a rental car, and she'll stay with me until Tony is out of danger. Her husband is fortunate enough to make the kind of money that allows my sister to stay at home. I'm so glad she'll be here. Sarah is apparently in big trouble and needs your help. Tony is in good hands and I'll be ok."

"Ok! I'll keep my phone on. You call me if you need me for anything." They both stood and hugged. He waved from the door, and then was out of sight.

He valet parked at the Mirage and went to hotel check-in. He noticed the clerk with her head down writing something, was the same girl who'd been on duty when he checked out. He searched his brain trying to remember her name, "Alexi, isn't it?" he said, as she looked up.

"It is," she answered sweetly, "And you are, Mr. Caruso, if my memory serves me correctly." Knowing she was correct, she continued, "How can I help you today? Are you checking back in with us? Your room is still available and has been cleaned. I'm sure Tony would still want you to have the room under comp. Have you heard what happened?"

"Yes! I just came from seeing him at the hospital. His wife and I were at his side for awhile. He made it through the operation. He's sedated and resting in ICU."

"I'll let the others know the good news. We've all been worried sick about him. He's a real good man and everyone loves him. If you are not checking in, how can I help you?"

"Here goes nothing," he thought, "Before Tony was shot; I asked a favor of him. He was going to ask his boss something for me, but of course, he never got to ask him. I'm a detective with the Pahrump Police Dept.," as he showed his credentials. "Do you think there is anyway I could talk to Tony's boss for a few minutes?"

"Being Tony's friend, I'll be honest with you. I doubt very seriously if that will happen. However, let me call the fill-in security manager. You just never know." She punched some buttons and spoke into her mouthpiece, then looked at him, and nodded, "He's coming down."

"Thanks, Alexi, you've done all you can do," as he stepped to the side and waited.

Within minutes, a sharp dressed gentleman in dress suit with no tie introduced himself, "I hear you are a friend of Tony. What can I do for you?"

"I'm working on a case concerning the whereabouts of your boss's niece, Kate. She's possibly in great danger and I need to find her."

"I'm sure he will appreciate your concern. If you leave me your card, I'll see he gets your information."

Seeing he wasn't going to get anywhere, Jack threw in a little more information, "It's possible she was in a cabin with my partner, Sarah Sidwell, when the cabin was attacked by four armed men. Those four men are dead. I'm sure you can see why I need to find them both."

"I can understand your deep concern and I will deliver your message and card. I'm afraid that is the best I can do for you at the moment, Mr. Caruso," and he stuck out his hand.

"At least I tried," he thought, and there sure wasn't any need to make this guy angry. He shook his hand saying, "I'd appreciate it very much."

They parted. Jack nodded toward Alexi, who shrugged her shoulders, and he headed for the valet door.

Soon he was back on the road toward Pahrump.

His thoughts were like a whirlwind spinning around in his head. A good friend in the hospital, his wife hoping he makes it, Sarah and other friends in a world of shit, his own love life a total mess; and he had one hell of a headache. He was pretty sure the headache was from lack of sleep, for he was getting more tired with each passing minute. He was too wrapped up in himself to notice a black SUV coming up on his rear. As it came along side, it forced him off the road, with both vehicles sliding to a halt. Four men in suits rushed his way.

"Oh, hell no!" he said to himself, as he swung his door open, stood behind it, and drew his weapon. As he aimed, they stopped approaching, and put their hands on their weapons. He said out loud, "I don't know what you had in mind, fellows, but it ain't happening tonight."

One spoke where he could hear, "You are coming with us."

"Don't think so. I've got other fish to fry."

The one to the left drew his gun and Jack's bullet smashed into his shoulder, causing his weapon to fall.

The other three drew theirs, as Jack's next bullet tore into a second one, in the opposite shoulder. Jack was aiming at the shooting shoulders. He ducked behind the open door.

Before the other two could fire, a red Cadillac came off the road, sliding to a halt, on the right side of Jack's vehicle. Two men in casual suits exited with weapons trained on the two still standing with hand weapons. The guy who'd been driving the Cadillac hollered, "How's this going to end? It's your choice," as two from the back seat also exited with weapons.

The two looked toward the Cadillac, Jack and their wounded partners. Still holding weapons, they gathered the two wounded, their weapons, and jumped back into the SUV.

As they sped away, Jack stood confused. The Cadillac driver stated, "It's a good thing Tony is your friend, because it looks like you have enough enemies."

"Who are you?" Jack asked in a confused state, "Where did you come from?"

"Been following you since the casino," the one on the passenger side spoke, "Boss said to make sure you didn't bother his niece. He also said not to hurt you, too bad. So we figured we'd better not let you get hurt while we were watching you. Otherwise, you are in no danger from us." They both placed their weapons back into the vehicle. The two from the back seat followed suit.

Jack holstered his weapon, but said, "I owe you, but don't get in my way, or try to stop me from doing my job." He got in his vehicle and pulled back onto the road. So did his tail. However, as they neared Pahrump city limits, the Cadillac shot around him. He watched them disappearing up the road.

"Where's a cop when you need one?" he said facetiously. They'd probably just saved him from being taken by whoever those guys were. So, he just let them go, while he stayed at his present speed. There was no need to hurry, because he didn't know where the hell he was going. He began to feel he'd run out of leads and options. He also realized he'd better not go to his house. Whoever was trying to capture him now, would most likely be watching his home. He realized they had to be tracking the GPS system in his vehicle or his phone. When he got to the station, he parked the vehicle and opened the trunk. His suitcase, extra money and second weapon were nestled among his duty equipment and weapons. He removed the suitcase and his extras. He shut off his phone, tossed it in the trunk, and closed it.

When he walked out of the parking garage, a patrol car was coming in. Barry stopped, "You going on a trip, Jack?"

"No, old buddy! I just had a run in with another black SUV. I feel sure they are tracking my phone, vehicle, and probably watching my house. They are still trying to abduct me for some reason. They probably think I know where Sarah is, but I don't."

"Hop in, Jack, I may be able to help. Throw your stuff in the back seat." Barry turned around in the garage and they headed out to the street. "Wife flew out of town to visit her mother for two weeks. Her car is just sitting in the driveway. You can use it, but I'll need it back at least the day before she gets home. You can stay at the house if you want."

"I can't promise I'll keep your car in one piece, the way things are going for me."

"It's insured," Barry laughed.

"Ok, I'll use her car and return it full of gas. I sure appreciate what you are doing. These guys in SUV's are getting to be a pain in my ass."

"Want to crash at the house?"

"I don't think that would be a good idea." He frowned, "You might come home to find the place blown to bits. I've got an idea of where I'm going to stay. I do need you to tell the captain what I said happened. Black SUV ran me off the road and four men tried to abduct me. I put a bullet in one guy's left shoulder and one in the right shoulder of a second abductor." He purposely left out the bit about the guys in the red Cadillac, "They gathered their wounded and hauled ass."

"Yeah, it might be a good idea that you don't stay at the house, we've only got a few more payments to make on it," as he grinned.

They were still laughing when they pulled up to Barry's place. He got his wife's keys from inside, and helped Jack load all his stuff into her car.

Jack thanked Barry again, and they drove away in different directions.

He figured it wouldn't be wise for him to try to go to the station again, so he decided to head for Boulder City and get a room.

Tomorrow, he'd purchase a couple of burn phones, and use one to call the captain. He was a little pissed, because now Sarah wouldn't know how to contact him, but he felt he used the smartest route. Barry wouldn't say anything about what he was doing for Jack. No one would expect him to be in this vehicle. He'd pay cash for the room wherever he stopped for the night. So, he thought he'd be able to get a good night's sleep, seeing as how he was tired as hell. Just to make sure, he'd stop at the nearest liquor store for a half-pint of something strong.

When he reached Boulder City and checked in at a hotel, he took everything to his room. He took a big swig out of the whiskey bottle, and then entered the hot shower. He could definitely feel the tiredness in his back and other muscles, as he let the hot water cascade over his head and body. He didn't bother to turn on the TV after he dried and came out of the bathroom. He just took another big swig of whiskey, and climbed under the sheets and blankets. He didn't feel he'd be any good to anyone tonight, so nothing kept him awake, and sleep overtook him.

Chapter Ten

In an exclusive hotel in Las Vegas, a meeting was about to take place in one of the smaller rooms dedicated to that purpose. In the hallway was one suited serious looking man on each side of the double doors to the meeting room. A few steps in either direction stood two men in the same attire blocking the hallway to the room. The looks on the faces of these six let you know right away that you were not about to come past them. Though you couldn't see the weapons, it didn't take a brain surgeon to know they were heavily armed.

At the end of the hall, the elevator was locked in the open position, with a sign saying, "Out of order." There was a similar sign on the closed door of this elevator, in the lobby.

Inside the room, six men in suits, but no ties, sat quietly at a table, three on each side. The room was specifically designed to be virtually sound proof.

Two men walked around in the room with bug detectors looking for listening devices. When the search was completed, they nodded toward the six and left the room, closing the door behind them.

One of the men at the table broke the silence, as if giving a report, "So far we have not been able to locate our male escapee. We continue to be one step behind him. Since his mother was dead, and we knew he now had that information, we ruled out the search in Kansas. Thanks to the news reports, we know he was in a Pahrump police station, and was wounded. We know he has somehow enlisted the help of two women and one man."

One from the other side of the table spoke, as the first speaker hesitated and looked in his direction. "Efforts to extract our subject from a cabin in the woods outside of Pahrump were unsuccessful. The five mercenaries sent in were all terminated. There is no possible way to track them back to any of us in this room."

He looked toward another man, and that person began, "One of the individuals that our subject has befriended is a female Pahrump detective. We have attempted twice to take her partner into custody on the open roads, in the event she has disclosed her location to him. The first time, NSA personnel intercepted and took four of our men into their custody. There is very little information they can disclose, other than the location they were supposed to take her partner. That location, of course, was only a drop off, so more of our people could take him somewhere else. Unknown occupants in a red Cadillac foiled the second attempt with weapons. The detective wounded two of our men. The rest withdrew carrying the wounded with them to avoid capture.

He hesitated, and then continued, "We know her partner has been in touch with the security manager at the Las Vegas Mirage Casino. For what reason, we have not been able to ascertain. There was an incident at the establishment, and that person is sedated in ICU at a hospital. We will follow up on that situation when he is able to talk. We also know the detective visited him and his wife at the hospital, but could not have learned anything. We've monitored the cell and home phones of the casino security manager since the detective's first contact with him. The casino man's wife knows nothing."

A fourth man then spoke, "All GPS and cell devices we were observing have been terminated, or are of no use to our cause; such as the detective's vehicle and his cell. They are both in the parking garage at his police station. We do not know the detective's location, or his present mode of transportation."

A fifth man continued the reports, "No checks, debit, credit cards, or any type of bank transactions have been used by either of the individuals of concern. Wherever they are, or whatever they are doing, they are obviously using cash. Since none of these individuals are of impressive means, it seems obvious one will attempt using plastic before too long. When that happens, a flag will be triggered and we will immediately know the location it was used."

Now all five looked toward the last man, who seemed to have more authority, as he spoke in a gruff voice, "We are the descendents of the twelve, who were the most powerful men of their time. Now there are only six of us to carry on the cause. We have billions at our disposal, and countless personnel, who are either sympathetic to what we believe, or are happy with the fat paychecks they receive each month. You five are telling me we can't get our hands on our subject and four pathetic normal individuals. We need that male escapee. Our gray colored ugly friends at the facility are not happy that we have not been able to locate him. However, neither have they. He managed to remove his tracking device. It was located miles from the cabin in the woods, at a construction site. Our cohorts have been in the sky searching, much more than they should have been.

Since the military recovered the female escapee, they have increased operations in the vicinity. We've recently learned through channels that the two brothers, who delivered food supplies, have been captured. They have the ability to lead the military to the facility. They'll try to keep silent as long as possible. They know if they talk, their lives won't be worth a plug nickel. However, the military, under the rules of National Security, can use any means they see fit to abstract information. Therefore, these two will eventually spill the beans.

We have set an operation into effect, for NSA agents sympathetic to our cause, to try to get to these two men and terminate their existence.

If it becomes evident that extraction of our male escapee is impossible, before the wrong people have him in their hands, orders have been issued to also terminate him, and whoever is with him. Anyone who might even remotely come into information that might lead back to our alien cohorts, and us, must be terminated.

We have amassed tons of information and knowledge from our space visitors, thanks to our forefathers who made contact with them in the 50's. We've managed to build and operate superior crafts, right under the noses of the army and air force. Our small secret production plant has not had one single iota of information leak, thanks to the amount of money each individual working there receives. Scientists and engineers have diligently added to the success of our productions. Those who came before us have always hoped for a mass production of these superior crafts: in the hopes that in the event the total United States was ever attacked, we'd be able to strike out at our enemies, and save our great country. Our nation's military might is spread way too thin over the world. The way our military can handle situations has been crucially limited, because of all the bleeding hearts and goodie-two-shoes in government positions, and the news media scrutinizing everything they do. The government and the people are blinded to the fact that outside forces are dedicated to destroying the United States from within. They are weakening the military, lessening the worth of the American dollar, countless money distributed to illegal aliens and foreign immigrants. The powers that be continue to let the U.S. borrow money from foreign countries, so they can turn around and give it away to other countries in foreign aid, or to the non-workers in our country, who have never paid a dime into social security. The U.S. probably owes China more money than we can ever repay, yet we continue to borrow.

Our government, in an effort over the years to encourage foreign trade and imported goods, has destroyed the American people's ability to produce quality products and earn a decent living.

Taxes on everything keep climbing. The cost of homeowners' health and life insurance has skyrocketed. Many have to go without insurance, so they can buy gas and food. Greedy oil and gas companies keep gouging the population, as they raise prices, drop them a small amount, and then raise them again.

Two thirds of the people in the U.S. are on welfare or social security for a means of surviving. The news is constantly reporting that may not be available to them, if our government keeps going broke. How much more the normal American people can withstand is unknown. Anybody with any common sense knows what will eventually have to happen, if things keep going in its present direction.

When millions can no longer pay their bills, buy food and gas, to survive and work, there will be a mass revolt. There are no people in any other country, who have the power to revolt against their government, or match the strength of the American people. Nine of every ten homes own guns, and those who do own weapons are continually amassing more. They live in fear that what I have predicted will eventually happen. Do they want it to happen? No. Will they fight to survive? Absolutely! When this happens, probably a small group at first, such as a town or city, there will be a domino effect that will spread all over the U.S.

Military intervention will meet far more resistance than if they were fighting in another country. It's almost certain many will desert the military to join friends and family to help them fight against authority.

I could go on and on about the terrible mess this country is going to be in and already in. I've said all that to say this. No matter what shape the U.S. gets itself into, this group must survive. We must be ready and able to take over; and with the help of all those loyal to our beliefs, take our country back from the idiots who are letting it be destroyed. If it comes down to keeping these secret operations, or letting them lead back to any of us, they must be destroyed. Of course, we will try not to let that happen. We'll always have the money, gold, silver and information to start all over again. We've got the weapons at our disposal to keep it.

Our underground facility with our sky neighbors is becoming a liability. They've been collecting the new baby specimens for years. They may have to be happy with what they've been able to achieve, and depart, if it comes down to it. We have our ways of regaining contact in the future. They, of course, may not see it that way. If they are attacked by the military, they may use their ship, which is hidden underground, to defend the facility. They've never wanted to show proof of their existence, but they may contact their planet for backup. Who knows what they might do? Their craft here is small but powerful. If more come from their planet, none of us may survive.

Because of the concentrated military efforts in the vicinity of the facility, supplies have not been able to reach the location. That means the humans, who are detained, will soon run low on rations. It is extremely important to the grays, for the humans to be well nourished, and along with the injections, produce superior offspring. There is no telling what these alien idiots might do, to obtain food and supplies for their subjects. Hell, they might take their ship, land at a Wal-mart, go in, and take what they need. That of course, would cause all hell to break loose across the world. There would be no more wondering if aliens existed. Panic would most assuredly spread like wildfire. Stocks and banking institutions across the world would go bananas. The largest stock market crash of all times would occur. We do have one lonely ace card to play."

As he hesitated, the other five looked curiously at him, and then he continued, "As you know, we keep a few of our people at the facility at all times. Before the grays arrived; and while we were building the facility, a nuclear device was installed at a secret location and secured from their detection. One of our people has the keys to detonate the bomb, if he receives our instructions. He has always been faithful to our cause, and we believe he will detonate, if he feels the facility is about to be overrun. That, of course, would solve all our problems at that location. However, we cannot be positive he will push the button.

When we walk out those doors today, it is up to each and every one of us to try to make sure our projects stay as they are. If that cannot be accomplished, then all individuals and information that could lead back to us must be destroyed."

As he stood, the other five did likewise. Each of them placed an open palm over their heart. They turned, facing a large American flag on a pole at one end of the table. They held their position, as if they were silently repeating an oath. Removing the hand from the heart, they each shook hands but said nothing more to each other. When they entered the hallway, the armed men outside placed themselves three to each side, and escorted them to the elevator. The meeting group went to the rear. While one armed man removed the out of order sign, the six stood to the front, and watched the elevator close and begin its descent. As the door opened in the lobby, that sign was removed by one of the men. Each member from the meeting left the elevator in different directions, with an armed escort at his side. Within moments there remained no evidence that this meeting had ever taken place.

Chapter Eleven

When Sarah came to, she felt a cool breeze. She realized she was covered with a blanket, and had a bed pillow under her head. She had a hell of a headache. There was an aroma of coffee brewing and bacon frying in a pan. The last thing she remembered, was having a drink out of a red Solo cup, and thinking about Jack. The cup was nowhere in sight. Inside the open cabin doors, she saw Kate and Charley at the gas stove. She stood slowly, with the palm of one hand on her splitting head.

Kate noticed her, and came out, saying, "Bet you don't feel too chipper this morning."

"Feel like shit," as she looked down at the blanket still in her hand.

Kate said, "Mark snored all night. I never heard you come to bed, so I came out to check on you. You were passed out on the bench seat. I put your feet up on the seat. Then I got a pillow and blanket to cover you. It wasn't real cold, so I didn't bother hauling your ass to your bed. Your Solo cup was empty, so I didn't have a mess to clean up."

"Thanks for taking care of me. Right now I need two BC powders and a Coke to wash them down. I'll get the powders out of my purse," as she headed toward the cabin.

"I'll pour some Coke over ice for you." Kate said, as she followed her.

Sarah stepped into the cabin, and said, "Morning, Charley."

"Ah! The queen has risen. Coffee is ready if you are?"

"Not just yet; got to get headache powders out of my purse."

When she passed on by him to the sleeping quarters, she heard Mark's soft snore, and shook her head, which caused it to hurt worse. When she returned, Kate handed her the Solo cup, and watched Sarah chase down two powders she'd dumped in her mouth. Kate said, "I don't see how you can take those things like that. I have to mix mine in a soda and drink it."

Sarah couldn't answer at first. The powders seemed to stick in her throat, as she continued trying to wash them down. Luckily, Kate still had the rest of the can in her other hand. Sarah held out her cup, and Kate emptied what was left into it.

"That did it," she thought as the powders finally went down her throat. To make sure, she kept sipping on the Coke and said, "That's cause you aren't as tough as I am," and smiled.

"You weren't so tough last night, angel."

"Touché," Sarah smiled a little, putting her other hand to her head.

Charley interrupted, "We don't have a lot of supplies. We should be able to stretch what we have today and tomorrow. After that, we'll have to make a quick trip to Boulder City."

Kate was facing the hallway between the sleeping quarters. She saw Mark come out of his room naked and head for the john. She got a good look at the normal morning male rising. She grinned, "Mark is up; and I do mean up."

Sarah, looked in his direction, but only got a view of his naked butt.

Charley was busy with the bacon, and ignored what they were saying.

Mark was in the head a good while. Charley finished cooking the bacon, and said, "Since Mark is awake, I'll wait to cook the eggs when he joins us." He took his coffee and went to the back of the boat. Both of the women drank their coffee black, so Kate handed Sarah a cup of coffee, and they followed Charley.

The three were still making small talk, when Mark came out the door with a cup of coffee in his hand, "That whiskey tasted good last night, but I think it will be a long time before I drink anymore of it. I've never had a headache, but now I know what one feels like."

"I've got powders for that in my purse, if you want some."

"It's going away," he answered, "But it is nice to know you have a remedy if I do need it."

Charley smiled, "The bacon is done. Kate has the bread buttered on one side, and ready to throw in the oven. A few more sips of this brew, and I'll start frying the eggs, unless one of you want yours scrambled." They all agreed that fried would be fine. When Charley headed for the stove, Kate followed him to put the bread in the oven.

"I've never been drunk before. I hope I didn't make a fool of myself." Mark said apologetically.

"No more than the normal sot," Sarah answered, adding, "I had one too many myself last night."

He had a serious look, as he softly said, "Sarah, I thought our sex together at the cabin was special. Yet afterward, you made yourself distant from me. What did I do wrong?"

Now it was time to be honest, but how was she going to put it? The old saying, "The truth will set you free," came to mind. "Mark, you performed like a champion race horse. Any woman would have been pleased. However, I felt like there was something missing. I realized it wasn't you, it was me. I care deeply for someone else. When we make love, the feelings inside me are much different, and I miss that feeling. I'm sorry, Mark, but I need to be honest."

A sad look came across his face, as he commented, "I wish I knew those feelings. I had preferences of the females that I enjoyed sex with, but I've never had real strong feelings for any of them."

"And with me, either," Sarah confirmed.

"Not because I didn't want to. I like you a lot. I just don't know how."

Kate saying, "It's on the table," interrupted them. "Bring your cups for a refill."

As they enjoyed breakfast, Sarah stated, "It's going to be hard sitting on this boat with nothing to do. I'm used to being busy all day every day."

Charley comforted, "You need a break now and then. I'll make a few phone contacts to find someone to help us. Staying here out of sight for a couple of days is the best thing we can do. Sarah, you know as well as I, that the first few days APB's are initiated, are the days they are looked at the most. After a few days, more have popped up on your screens, and more attention is paid to those, instead of the previous ones."

"Yeah, I know you are right. I'm guilty of that, also. There will be less eyes looking for us after awhile."

"We'll just lay low the next few days," Kate agreed, "Then we'll be forced to go to Boulder City for supplies. Maybe by then, Charley will have formulated a plan."

When they finished with the meal, the men took inventory of the cabinets in the crew quarters. That part of the boat was at water level. Kate had said her uncle kept canned goods in those cabinets, because in was cooler down there.

Kate and Sarah were washing dishes, and heard the motor of a boat coming into the long cove. They ran to their quarters, retrieved their weapons and alerted the men, as they hurried back to the rear of the boat.

Stepping into view, they held their weapons behind in one hand. Seeing it was game wardens, they both waved with their free hands. They knew the wardens could board, check licenses, check for drugs, check safety equipment, or any number of things. If they continued to approach, the women would have to return the weapons to the bedrooms. If these wardens weren't already looking for them, they'd sure know who they were after checking their licenses.

The wardens seemed to be scrutinizing the yacht. The women saw the driver of the boat hold up a two-way radio. The game officer on the outside edge of the craft turned and went toward him. They both raised a hand and waved to the girls. They turned the boat around and motored out of the cove. Once out of the cove, the women heard the officer's boat rev to maximum speed. It was evident they were needed somewhere else, and in a hurry.

The men had made it back to the deck with weapons of choice.

It was a huge relief for all to hear the warden's boat fading in the distance.

With the danger ended, Charley broke the silence, "There are some large cans of beans, carrots, corn and that sort of thing in the crew cabinets. We'll do all right for a few days. Hopefully, we won't have any more visitors."

Mark had a hat on his head, and added, "There are hats, sunglasses, and some clean clothes in the other cabinets, for both male and female. Maybe we can use them as disguises when we leave the boat."

They all nodded in agreement, and went to see what was available.

Kate remembered her uncle kept attire for gambling whales, and the women he arranged to accompany them.

The men found beach shirts, swim trunks, towels and shorts. The women also found clothing items that would fit. Maybe not perfect, but they would do. An assortment of different bikini sizes let the two women pick out the ones that would complement their figures. There was plenty of suntan lotion. The swimsuits would make it more comfortable for everyone, when it was time to dive into the water again. Or, would it make the time in and out of the water, less enjoyable. They couldn't help but wonder. They donned the new outfits, and were soon lounging on the open decks of the yacht.

Large fish swimming by caused the men to go to the front of the boat following the school of fish.

Kate took the occasion to ask Sarah, "Charley said you talked to Jack. What did you tell him?"

With a serious look she answered, "The truth."

"All of it?" Kate questioned.

"Yes," Sarah answered, "He already knew Mark and I had sex. CSI had discovered that much at Charley's cabin."

"What did he have to say?"

"He was pissed, of course, or maybe he was hurt, or both. Anyway, it didn't go over well. He wanted to come to us, but I refused. I didn't want to involve him in any of this, or put him in danger. He doesn't deserve that. I made this bed, and now I have to lie in it. I'm just sorry I pulled you and Charley into this. I wouldn't have, if I'd only known how this would go down."

"It was our choice, Sarah. That's what friends are for. There are some nasty people out there, trying to get at us. Do you think we would have wanted you to deal with that alone?"

Sarah felt a tear forming and gave Kate a big hug, saying, "I'm so lucky to have friends like you and Charley. I just hope I haven't lost Jack's friendship."

"I doubt it, Sarah. He may be angry, but I doubt he could ever not be your friend. I imagine if you get the chance to put some good loving on him, it will make all that's happened become a thing of the past."

Feeling there was little chance of that taking place, Sarah sighed, "I can only hope so."

"Hope what?" They heard Charley say, as he appeared from the side of the yacht.

"None of your concern," answered Kate.

He let it go, and said, "All these damn fish and no fishing equipment. Now that's a pisser."

The others just laughed, but Kate added, "There's probably a safety pin somewhere on this boat, and there may be some fishing line in a drawer somewhere."

"Now that's an idea, come on Mark let's start investigating." And the two men disappeared into the cabin.

Sarah looked toward Kate, "You know men can't find diddlysquat. We may as well go look. It could be right in front of them, and they'd never see it."

Kate laughed as they stood to go join the search.

Chapter Twelve

General Gilliam called a briefing with his top aides. The eight men were seated at a table when he came through the door. All eight immediately stood and saluted. He acknowledged with a return salute. "At ease, gentlemen. What I have to say is not for non-military ears outside this room. Each of you, are well aware of all the man hours and hard work we have put into our objective in this area. Yet, we have failed to locate our target. However, there has been a milestone overturned in our favor."

As he hesitated to collect his thoughts on how he was going to deliver this new information, the eight looked at each other with surprise and bewilderment.

"Many of you, who have been here for some time, should remember the female escapee that we picked up on the side of the road, a few years ago. Of course, NSA took her away, to abstract information. She has been in their possession since that first day. During her stay with NSA, she had a baby boy."

The ones who knew about it nodded in agreement.

He continued, "The woman described two brothers, who reportedly delivered supplies to the secret location. I am happy to announce those two men have been located, and are in custody. They have been positively identified. DNA samples proved one of the brothers was the father of the woman's child."

With this news, the eight smiled, commented to each other, and held the thumbs up signal to their cohorts.

The general continued, "It's only a matter of time, before our spy boys extract the information we need from these two men. No method will be spared until we get the information we need. I'd venture to say that after a few rounds of intense interrogation, one, or both of these individuals would tell, and probably show us how to get into that underground facility.

From this moment forward, you will step up all operations under your command and guidance. I want the area saturated with troops, tanks, and every kind of ground attack equipment at our disposal. I want Special Forces sitting ready and waiting at all times."

All the men took notes and nodded to each other. A few whispered comments to a fellow officer.

"I want twenty-four hour drone coverage. So, make sure the flight patterns do not let one single minute go by without eyes on the target area.

Contact with our flyboys have assured, there will be two stealth bombers, along with all types of fighter planes, sitting ready at NAS Fallon, Creech and Nellis air bases. There will be scheduled and unscheduled flights with different types of aircraft over the area. Higher-ups with the authority are using satellite visual at every opportunity. Air Force, Navy, Army, Marines and National Guard are primed to aid in our endeavor."

He added with a more serious look, "Gentlemen, if our information is correct, some of the newer soldiers will have their first battle with aliens. In the past, our seasoned flyers and troops have been able to damage some of their ships, and even shoot some of them down. However, we've also taken great losses in those skirmishes. Why they haven't returned to attack with more ships, we have no frigging idea.

When we attack, we expect heavy resistance. According to information received, this facility is of monumental importance to these aliens' survival, or continuance. They will not give up easily. We've also been informed they will be aided by a rogue group of humans with updated and possibly superior weaponry. However, make no mistake in your thinking. We will win one way or another. I'm depending on each of you, and your people, to make sure that I did not just tell a lie. That will be all, gentlemen, and God be with us."

The eight immediately rose to attention, as he saluted. They returned his salute. The general left the room and the others departed.

Chapter Thirteen

The officer on desk duty at the Pahrump police station called out to a female officer walking by, "Escort, Miss Polero to Captain Chandler's office. He knows she's here."

As the officer complied, Polero nodded toward the desk officer.

"Captain, Miss Polero here to see you."

He nodded at the officer, and then, "Danah, come on in. What did you want to see me about?"

As she shook his hand, "Henry, I feel honored. You don't usually let people off the street come to your office, especially news people."

"You know I don't mind talking to you one on one, when you don't have a camera man with you."

She laughed, and then her face turned serious, "Sorry if the news reports have been giving you a headache lately. I tried to keep the ones about Officer Sidwell off the tube, but the boss went over my head. She's a good officer, and I can't see her getting mixed up in anything illegal."

"Neither can we," he agreed.

"Can you give me any information? I like her as a friend, and as you know, I had a great cover story about her on the force. I hope that isn't going to blow up in my face."

"I doubt if that will happen," he answered, "Is this off the record, no recordings or any of that crap?"

"I promise. It's just for my information. All these conflicting stories and video have been confusing, to say the least. What in the hell is going on with her?"

"Danah, I wish I knew. I'm sure you know by now she is in the company of a stranger, and two of her friends. One is Officer Brewster, her best friend. Officer Brewster did not show for work today, nor did she call in sick."

She interrupted, "I was at Sarah's house just before all of this got blown out of proportion. Yes, she was there with Kate, and Sarah's boyfriend Mark. Everything seemed normal. Now everything seems weird as hell. I've received information that a man claiming to have been held by aliens was wounded in the station during the shootout. The passerby video clearly shows Sarah helping a wounded man with a bloody shirt. In the video, I could easily identify him as the one sitting in Sarah's car, and he is the Mark at her house. Yet, he showed me his upper body, both sides. Henry, there were no gunshot wounds. No wounds of any kind. He had a red skin mark on his side front and back. Sarah said it was a rash. I had to believe her.

I covered enough stories of people who have been shot. I know what an entrance and exit bullet hole looks like. Is this guy human or what? She hesitated to catch her breath.

She continued, "Then there was the gun battle with trained assassins at Kate's friend Charley's cabin. What the hell was that all about and was Sarah or her friends wounded?"

Henry glanced down at a folder on the desk for a second. It was the DNA report on the stranger's blood from the shooting. A note on the report stated, "If the sample was not contaminated by some chemical, this DNA sample can't be compared to any known type of DNA analysis. It has the appearance of being from a male subject, but that can't be confirmed. It can't be confirmed as to whether the sample is from a human or animal. Another sample from this subject is needed for comparison and further tests."

He looked back at Danah, "We've known each other for a long time. All the way back to when I walked a beat and you became a reporter. So, I'm going to tell you what I know. I swear, if you leak any of this information, you will never get any kind of information from this office. Also, anything you might repeat could put one of my detectives in more danger than they already are."

"On my mother's grave, I swear I will not divulge anything you tell me. I'm here, for my own satisfaction. All this is driving me nuts."

"Join the crowd," he said in agreement. "Yes. This guy Mark Wakefield was the nut at the station claiming to have been held by aliens. Yes, it was his blood they found at the station."

She interrupted, "Henry, I saw his body up close. There was no wound."

"I can't explain what you saw. I'm giving you the facts. Somehow this stranger hypnotized, or convinced Sarah and her friends, to help him find his biological mother. Sarah asked Jack Caruso to make some calls for her about his mother. That caused trouble for Jack."

"I heard he was in an incident with NSA or CIA men," she butted in.

"You've got way too many connections," he grinned. "Anyway, Sarah, the stranger, Officer Brewster, and her friend Charley have dropped off the grid. Jack has been pulling all the strings he could to find them. We don't know who they are in danger from, but we know they have deep pockets and mean business. Now, there is a new twist to all this. NSA agents looking for Jack found his car still here at the station and his phone in the trunk. He has not been home. Now I can't get in touch with him, and have no damned idea where he is. He should be scared for his life, but Jack doesn't scare too easy, and he still wants to find Sarah and her friends. That's it, Danah. You've got the whole scoop."

"Henry, this is deep shit. Your people are in a mess of trouble, when NSA starts digging around."

"That's why I'm going to ask you a favor. You know a lot of people. I'd appreciate you contacting anyone you can, who might know the whereabouts of any of my people. I need to find them before anyone else does."

"I'll do what I can, Henry. I'll shake the sheets and see what falls out. But I have to admit, if NSA agents come knocking at my door, I'll be stopping any of my investigating. I don't need that kind of worry."

"I've always known you were a wise woman, Danah," as he smiled, and led her to the door.

"You're going to owe me, if I find them first," she grinned.

"Yeah, I know. Give me a call if you turn up anything."

She nodded and left his office.

He sat down and reread the DNA report. He was beginning to ask himself the same question Danah had put to him, "Is this guy human or what?" He shook his head. He was frustrated at the fact that two of his best detectives were unreachable. A good patrol officer was now also breaking the rules. He was receiving calls from the Governor, telling him too many people wanted an explanation of what was going on in Pahrump. Many of his detectives and officers wanted to know what was going on. Here he was the captain, and he didn't know shit. He tossed the report onto his desk, and got up to get a cup of coffee in the break room.

He assessed his feelings. Sure, the things he'd been thinking about were aggravating, but so was most of the rest of his job. He realized what was bothering him the most was the helpless feelings. Those feelings he'd never experienced before. His people were out there, needing help, but he had no way to help them. He realized his patrol officers and other detectives would be looking at the APB photos, but most wouldn't know the scope of the situation.

He threw the cup in the trash and took a walk to the dispatcher office. Those officers were surprised when he walked into the room. He approached one saying, "Open communication to all patrol and detective vehicles." He knew that non-police personnel would be monitoring the communication, but right now he didn't give a damn.

As the female dispatcher handed him the mic, he began, "This is Captain Chandler. All of you know we have two of our detectives and one patrol officer unaccounted for. What some of you may not know is they are in extreme danger. From whom we have not discerned, but they are powerful with deep pockets. Some of the perpetrators may be posing as high-ranking officers of the law. Their credentials may seem legit. Trust no one but your known associates. If you are approached by anyone else, send him or her to me. Do not divulge any information as to what you know, see, hear or learn. That information is for our ears only. Choose your words wisely during radio communication. We need to find our people before they do. Our friends need help. Do what you do best." As he returned the mic, nodded, turned, and walked away.

Chapter Fourteen

The shower and whiskey did wonders. Jack was in a deep sleep, reliving meeting Lillian, the warm happy feelings, and the amazing sex they had shared. He was still hugging his pillow when he awoke. Realizing his surroundings, he headed for the bathroom. On the way, he turned on the coffee maker.

After the normal morning ritual, he came out with a towel wrapped around his waist and brushed his teeth. When he looked into the mirror, he realized he had no clue as to what he was going to do next. He had no idea where Sarah and the others were, or how he was going to find them.

The casino goons in the red Cadillac had sped away, out of sight. They'd said they were supposed to make sure he didn't bother the boss's niece, yet they pulled away from Jack, and went on their merry way. He never caught a glimpse of their car after that. They weren't following him when he got his new ride from Barry, so he didn't have to worry about them.

He realized they left him behind, because they knew where Kate was and headed in her direction. They'd probably set up some type of perimeter around Kate and the others, to keep Jack from reaching them, if he ever managed to locate their position.

He couldn't get anything done in this hotel, and he was getting hungry. He dressed, skipped the continental breakfast, and headed to a nearby restaurant. He looked at his watch. It was 9:00 a.m. He observed the businesses on each side of the street. He located the store where he could buy the disposable phones, stopped and entered. He paid cash for several. It was unusual for someone to purchase several phones of that type, so the clerk looked at him kind of strange. However, he was making a good early sale, so he didn't ask any questions.

Jack opened the package of one of the phones, before entering the restaurant. After placing his order, he dialed the captain's private cell. When he heard his voice saying "Hello," Jack began, "Captain, it's Jack."

"Jack, NSA found your car and phone here at the precinct. They weren't too happy about that. Glad you were smart enough to call in. I was wondering how in the hell I was going to reach you."

"I'm afraid it will just be me reaching you for awhile. This phone will go in the trash when we are done talking."

"Where are you, Jack? Do you need some help?"

"Can't disclose my location, just yet. Besides, if you don't know, you don't have to lie. I'm a big enough headache for you already."

"Yeah, no shit, but that ain't nothing new. I'm here to help if you need me. Have you located Sarah and Kate?"

"No! I was hoping you might know something by now."

"Don't know squat yet. They are still managing to stay off the grid. The station has been flooded with calls, reporting UFO sightings again. Ever since this stranger appeared, these sightings have become more frequent. Also, the DNA report on his blood sample couldn't make out if he was human or animal. Do you think this freak could be an alien? I never believed they were real until all this started happening."

Thoughts of a possible alien having sex with Sarah wasn't making him feel warm and fuzzy. "I don't think he is all alien, but it may be true they experimented on him. If that is true, he may have more alien blood in him than human."

"Weird shit, Jack. Anyway, now there is an APB out for you, and NSA requested an APB on a red Cadillac with four occupants armed and dangerous."

"Tell our people to go light on the red Cadillac. They are friendly. They saved my ass last night. Four guys in suits in a black SUV ran me off the road and tried to abduct me again. I wounded two just as the Cadillac showed up to my rescue. They are casino goons. Their boss is Kate's uncle, and they were sent to keep anyone away from Kate, wherever she is. That may work out in our favor with four more people to protect Kate and the others."

"It may work against us, Jack. With the APB, it may lead the bad guys to them, if the Cadillac is found in the vicinity of wherever Kate and Sarah are."

"You may be correct; Captain, but we can't do anything about that right now. We can only hope for the best. There is a lot of crap going down. Are you and I still tight, Captain, or am I, Rogue?"

"You are still my detective doing what you are supposed to be doing. I'll let everyone know you checked in, and are continuing your investigation. You keep in touch, Jack, and I mean it. That is the only way I can help you."

"I promise, Captain. I've got several of these throwaways and I'll get more if I need them. I'll keep in contact."

When he ended the call his food was ready. He took his time thinking and eating. He had no idea in what direction he should turn. He began thinking his only hope was to go back to Vegas, and try bugging Kate's uncle again. He doubted he'd have any better luck.

He finished his meal, paid the bill, and slowly walked out of the restaurant toward his vehicle. He'd just reached his car when he saw a red Cadillac approaching. As they passed, he saw it was the same four guys who'd helped him. The two on this side of the car had toothpicks in their mouth. He guessed they'd also just finished eating, somewhere. They didn't see him.

He discarded the phone in a trash can, jumped in his car, and followed. First he considered following them to where Kate was located, but seeing a state trooper car at a café, he realized that was a bad idea, with the APB on the Cadillac. Shoving his foot down on the gas, he caught and passed the Cadillac, putting a little distance between the vehicles. Then he slammed on breaks, and came to a screeching halt. The vehicle behind him nose-dived as it came to a stop.

Jack quickly exited and walked back toward the four men. Two of the men got out with hand weapons drawn.

Jack held his hands high and open-palmed away from his body, as he approached.

"What the hell do you think you are doing," the driver asked loudly.

"Returning the favor," Jack answered, "NSA put out an APB on your vehicle."

"What would NSA want with us? Even if those were NSA boys we foiled. I doubt if they'd bother trying to put out an APB on our vehicle. Once they left, it was all over."

"By now they probably know that Kate is with my partner, Sarah Sidwell, another friend, and some other weirdo. They probably already traced your car back to her uncle. Now, they probably figure you will lead them to Kate."

The four looked at each other, as the two with weapons holstered their hardware. It was obvious they were wondering what they should do in this situation.

Jack took the chance to say, "They've already tried to kill Kate, Sidwell, and another friend, Charley; just so they could get at the stranger. He is high priority to them and no one else matters. Furthermore, these guys are rogue NSA agents and will stop at nothing. I know you know where Kate is. She and the others are good friends of mine, except for the nut with them. The best we can do is work together on this, find and protect them."

"What if we just ditch this car, and you, and take your vehicle? It definitely isn't a police vehicle, so I'm assuming no one knows you are driving it."

"Your assumption is correct. However, you aren't taking the vehicle. He slid his hand around to the butt of his weapon. You've already seen me shoot. I'll drop two, maybe three of you, before I go down. All that is going to do is lessen the protection for your boss's niece."

Looking at each other again, the one in charge agreed, "Where do we ditch this vehicle?"

"There is a parking garage just down the street. I'll follow you, and then you can pile in my car. It will be a little tight with all four of you and weapons, but we'll make do."

They agreed, soon ditched the Cadillac, and were jammed into Jack's car. Jack was elated at his good fortune. These guys could lead him to Sarah and the others. With their weapons, that made it an even better situation. Plus, now he would be the one in charge giving the orders and directing these guys on what and what not to do.

They led him toward Lake Mead and Hoover Damn. They wouldn't tell him exactly where they were going, for they figured he'd dump them and go there on his own. They worried for nothing. Jack was happy to have them along. He figured he would need all the help he could get, since he couldn't depend on the police. These extra weapons might come in mighty handy.

When they arrived at the marina, the casino boys explained they needed to rent a boat, and look for a yacht, where Kate and the others were hiding. Since the men had no clue where the yacht was located, it would be search and find.

Soon a fast boat was rented and the five cruised on the water. With many miles of shoreline, they knew it might take a lot of searching. There were literally hundreds of coves where the yacht could be. They spent several hours in and out of inlets. They even pulled along several large and small boats, to ask if they'd seen a yacht that fit the description. The answers were never favorable.

As dark began to fall, they made a beeline for the marina and turned in the rental, but paid for the same boat when they returned the next morning.

It was extremely frustrating to Jack they hadn't found Sarah and the others, but these guys were his only lead. Five sets of eyes were better than one, and they knew what they were looking for. They were elusive with their description of the yacht. He was sure they were afraid he'd strike out on his own to try and find it. For tonight, they'd have to find rooms and get an early start in the morning.

The casino guys liked some of the restaurants in Henderson, Nevada. Since it was only ten miles from Lake Mead National Recreation Area, Jack agreed.

Upon arriving they secured three rooms, and then headed out to get something to eat. They settled on the Claim Jumper restaurant. They all agreed you couldn't go wrong at getting good food, and a couple of stiff drinks, there.

As they sat around drinking like a group of old chums, Jack couldn't help but think they looked like mafia members. Hell, some of these chubby guys were having trouble keeping their weapons hid from view.

Still, the small talk was interesting enough, and they really didn't seem to be bad guys. However, he was certain if their boss told them to get rid of Jack, they'd have no second thoughts about following orders. He discerned from the conversation that all four of these guys had been working for their boss for many years, and he treated them real well.

After the meal, they made a stop at Lee's Discount Liquor, and each paid for a bottle of their own. Back at the motel, they asked if Jack wanted to join them to continue socializing, but he declined. The one in charge let Jack know if he ran off without them, they'd hunt him down and cut off his testicles. Jack assured him that he believed his warning and was too fond of his manhood, to take the chance.

Before long, he'd taken a shower, watched TV in his underwear, and drank most of the liquor from the pint he'd purchased. When the show he watched was over, he channel surfed.

Next-door, one of the casino guys was standing outside having a smoke. He observed two black SUVs pull up at the office with four suited men in each vehicle. As one man went into the office, the casino guy beat on Jack's door and the door to the other side. When Jack and the others appeared, he said pointing toward the office, "Trouble has arrived." They darted back into the rooms, and were just as quickly back outside with weapons locked and loaded.

Jack was at a dilemma now. These could be the good guys or the bad guys. If he let these goons start firing, they could be killing friendly, or get killed by friendly. They strung out behind parked vehicles, and Jack stated, "Let's see what they want before we start slinging bullets."

They saw the one come out of the office and both vehicles came to a screeching halt facing their rooms. Men piled out with weapons drawn.

Jack hollered, "What do you want?"

One shouted back, "Throw down your weapons we are National Security Agents," as he flashed his credentials.

Jack continued loudly, "You didn't answer my question."

The man commented, "I'm not sure exactly who you are, but the other four are a matter of National Security."

One of the casino guys hollered out, "How'd you know where to find us?"

A second NSA man said, "You used your credit card, asshole. Now drop your weapons before this turns into a blood bath. You are out numbered."

The leader of the casino guys looked at Jack saying, "The boss gave us an order. These guys are not going to stop us from doing what we were told to do. Sounds like you may have an out, if you just walk away."

Jack stood up from behind the vehicle and showed his badge, "I'm a Pahrump Detective on a case. These men are with me. Let me call Captain Chandler, and he will verify my credentials."

He saw the NSA guys look at each other for a few instances, and then shake their heads. He could barely hear one say, "We need at least one of them alive."

The casino leader next to Jack heard it, too. He swung his weapon over the hood and began firing, "Take this alive, you son of a bitch." His bullets wounded two, but they and the others returned fire from behind their vehicles. The other casino men did likewise.

Jack had no choice now. He was in too deep, and he also picked targets. He saw one of the casino guys shot in the head and fall backwards. Another was wounded in the shoulder, but he continued firing.

They may have been outnumbered, but they had better firepower. Their weapons put bullet holes everywhere in the black SUVs, and the NSA guys dropped like flies.

It seemed like an eternity, as bullets hit all around him. Jack ejected an empty clip and inserted a fresh load. He jacked a shell into the chamber, and saw the last NSA guy get hit in the head and chest.

The casino men moved toward the wounded and put a few more bullets in the bodies.

Jack holstered his weapon and approached the bodies, also. He hoped these weren't the good guys. He went through one of their pockets and retrieved a cell phone. He was dialing his captain's personal cell, when another black SUV came hurriedly into view, and headed their way.

Before the goons could start firing again, Jack had a gut feeling and yelled, "Hold your fire!"

They obeyed, but held weapons at ready.

The doors opened on the SUV and the four exited, but didn't draw weapons.

One approached with his hands in the air. Jack immediately recognized the NSA or CIA agent he'd talked to during his first abduction attempt.

Jack approached him, saying, "If you are here to save my ass again, you are a little late."

The agent looked around and slowly lowered his arms. "Looks like you did fine without my help this time. Any of your people hurt?"

"One dead, and one wounded. What are you doing here?"

"Following their trail; I do wish you had left one or two alive. They might have had some useful information."

"If you expect us to lead you somewhere, it isn't going to happen."

The agent came closer speaking softer, "We paid a visit to the casino boss, but unfortunately they'd already been there. He told us the same thing he told them, so we tried to intercept. We got a tip one of the casino men used his credit card at a liquor store, and to secure a room at this hotel. We hoped to beat them here. For your information, we don't need you to lead us anywhere. Decker called in with extraction co-ordinates and time schedule."

"Where are they?" Jack enquired.

"Sorry, Jack, I can't divulge that information. I'll do you a favor, though. I'll take care of your dead, and get your wounded friend to a hospital."

"What's going to happen to the wounded one?"

"He and the dead man will be innocent bystanders during a shootout with NSA agents, and a group of terrorist. You and the other two take your belongings and get the hell out of here. You can hear the sirens coming now. I suggest you get rooms somewhere else and use cash this time."

Jack couldn't help himself, and had to ask, "Why are you hell bent on keeping me out of trouble? Do I know you from somewhere?"

"Jack, let's just say you remind me of someone I used to know. Now stop wasting time."

The two casino guys heard the conversation and helped their wounded friend, as they looked sadly at the one on the ground.

The NSA agent motioned for his men to help take the wounded man. The goons were reluctant at first, but Jack convinced them it was the only way for all of them to stay out of trouble.

Jack and the two hurriedly gathered their things and jumped into his car, weapons and all. Jack peeled out of the parking lot, as patrol cars from each direction pulled into the parking lot.

They headed for Boulder City. It was fairly quiet in the back seat. The two talked about their friends, and how the boss wasn't going to be too happy with what went down.

Jack consoled them, by letting them know if the NSA agent kept his word; it would keep their boss out of the lime light.

Before long, they paid for two rooms, and this time everyone used cash.

Jack removed his weapon and slid it under a pillow. He sat down and considered the current situation. The real NSA agents had the co-ordinates and extraction time to pick up Mark; and probably

Charley, since he evidently was one of them. What would they do with Sarah and Kate? What if more of these rogue assholes got to Sarah first? Damn, he hated being in the dark. He stood and set the alarm by his bed. He and the other two would get an early start, but they'd still be searching for the yacht.

He concluded he was very lucky with the way things turned out earlier tonight, and should be thankful he wasn't in leg irons right now. He didn't ask the NSA agent for his name. He figured it wouldn't be revealed. However, it was puzzling how this guy kept coming to his aid.

He took a big swig from his pint, and decided he needed to get some sleep. No telling what tomorrow might bring. He'd use a burn phone in the morning, and call the captain to fill him in on what went down, and what he was doing.

Chapter Fifteen

While searching through the yacht cabin drawers, they did indeed find a roll of line with a hook. It was in the crew quarters, so it was obvious it had been used to try to catch fish to fry.

Sarah cut up one of the wieners they'd bought into little pieces. There was a broom on board with a hard plastic handle. Kate removed the bristle part and tied the line to the end where it had been screwed on. She started fishing, and soon had everyone laughing at the small bream she caught and released.

Mark watched intently, since he'd never been fishing. Kate handed him the rod and line. He caught a few and missed a lot. Soon Sarah cut up another hot dog. As she brought the pieces back to them, she said, "The object of this game is to catch something big enough to eat."

Kate just giggled, but asked, "Do you want to see if you can do better?"

"Nope, don't want any fish smell on my hands. You catch it, you clean it. I'll fry it, though," she answered.

Charley had been at the front of the yacht, out of hearing and on a burn phone. He appeared, and motioned with the phone for Sarah to join him. She followed him back to the front of the craft. He looked back to make sure the others hadn't followed. "Rogue NSA agents have been spotted everywhere it seems. Jack's vehicle was found at the station with his phone in the trunk. No one knows where he is, not even my people. NSA intercepted four trying to abduct him earlier. The rogue agents probably want him to get to you and Mark. My people want to get their hands on Mark before the bad guys do. I'm running out of options here, Sarah."

Sarah felt a sick feeling in the pit of her stomach. "Damn, now I can't reach, Jack. What are you going to do, Charley?"

"The big wheels think it's not a good idea to do anything today. There are too much rogue NSA movements in the area. Not only the ones that are looking for us, but others, have tried to get to the two truck delivery brothers. They weren't successful, but we lost three good agents. The brothers have been moved to a military facility for more protection. I've set up an extraction time just before dark tomorrow night. Choppers will land on the shoreline, "as he pointed to the spot." I've given them our co-ordinates. I'm sorry, Sarah I don't have a choice."

She looked irritated. "You said choppers. It only takes one if they are retrieving Mark."

He answered, "There will be three helicopters. One for the three of us, one for Mark and his escorts, and one gun ship in case there is trouble. I've convinced the higher-ups that you and Kate were operating under my orders to keep Mark from the bad guys. You and Kate will be taken into protective custody, until the CIA can square things with your boss."

"What about the other people being held at that facility?"

"According to my superiors, the military is gearing up to attack the facility. The brothers have agreed to lead them to the entrance in exchange for immunity and induction into the witness protection program."

"A full scale attack could get those people killed, Charley."

"There is always that chance, but the big guys want all those subjects as bad as they do Mark. They'll do everything in their power to not bring them harm. If aliens are in that compound, the military will want to collect all the technology they can, and at any price. If any aliens put up a fight, then it will get real messy."

"I feel like we are betraying a friend."

"Friend, or lover, Sarah?"

Aggravated at his choice of words, she spat out, "What difference does it make? We are still throwing him to the wolves."

"Sarah, since the beginning of all this, and you found out about him; how did you think it was going to end? Did you think you'd just ride off into the sunset and have a happy life together? All he has done is put you in a precarious position with your boss, the law, CIA, the bad guys, the real NSA, and Jack. You'll be lucky if I can get you out of this mess, and you still have a job."

"No! I don't expect Mark and me to have a life together. I realized it was just a fling, and I hate that I lost Jack in the process. My intentions were to help Mark, and I made a lot of mistakes trying to. Are you going to tell him what your plans are?

"Yes, he deserves to know. I'll tell him later this evening. For today, we'll just enjoy being on the water in a yacht and having fun."

Kate screaming interrupted them. They rushed toward their friends with weapons drawn. However, they put the weapons away, when they saw what all the noise was about. Kate and Mark were both on their knees trying to pounce on a large bass. They looked up to see Sarah and Charley burst out laughing.

They finally subdued the flopping fish, and Mark and Kate headed to the kitchen area to filet the catch. There would be plenty of fish for the four later tonight.

With the filleted fish in the cooler, everyone decided it was swim time. It was hot and not a cloud in the sky. Soon Kate, Sarah and Mark were in suits and in the water. Charley decided one of them needed to stay on board with the weapons. His eyes suspiciously scanned the sandstone shoreline, and the inlet leading to their cove. He'd done what he was supposed to do and informed his superior. However, he'd learned over the years that money turns the heads of even the most honest and dedicated. He'd always trusted his boss, and he hoped he could depend on him now to keep his word on everything.

Every now and then, he glanced down at the three in the water having a good time. They had purposely anchored the yacht in the shallowest area the boat could be in, and still be afloat. Kate swam over to the shore and climbed up on the barren rock. She laid on her back to let the sun warm her body. This mountain lake was a might chilly. Sarah soon joined her and did the same. Mark swam to the back of the yacht to the ladder.

Charley threw him a towel, "Were you about to freeze?"

"It was getting pretty chilly, I'll have to admit."

"Why didn't you just use those super eyes and heat up the water?" Charley asked grinning.

"Afraid I don't have that ability. I can only do it to small objects. Mind if I ask you a personal question?"

"According to what it is, Mark?"

"You've known Sarah a long time. I don't understand her. We had great sex and then she almost ignores me. What's with her?"

"Mark, you were someone new and different. You had bullet holes that healed themselves. You have the ability to heat a weapon and make a criminal drop it. You've already mentioned other things you can do with your mind. Like most women, she was intrigued, and possibly excited by all that. However, my personal opinion, for what it is worth, is that she still loves her partner. They never committed to each other, possibly because neither wanted to admit the love they felt. Everyone that knew them well could see it. Maybe they both were just too devoted to their job."

He hesitated and took a swig from his cup. "Now he knows she's had sex with you, and a man sometimes has trouble getting over that. Some men can let that kind of thing roll off their back, and some are even turned on by it. However, I don't think Jack is either one of those." He didn't want to be cruel to Mark with his honesty; he just wanted to set the record straight. "So, you've had time to think since our talk on the overpass. What are your feelings for Sarah?"

"I've given it a lot of thought. I've realized that I don't know how to love someone. I like her a lot, and, of course, I'd love to have sex with her again. I've thought about the women I had sex with over the years at the facility. There were a few that I really enjoyed being with, not only for the sex, but just being around and having fun with. What I was feeling inside for any of the females, I'm not sure."

"Mark, it sounds to me that the few women you enjoyed being with the most was as close to love as you've ever been; especially if one of those few got pregnant by you."

His eyes turned sad, as he admitted, "One I'm almost sure was pregnant with my baby. She was a very pretty woman named Kathy, and it was always fun being around her, even when we were young. We'd been sleeping together for months, and neither of us had sex with anyone else at that time. Even late in her pregnancy, when we couldn't have sex, I enjoyed just holding her while we slept. When they came to take her away, I tried to stop them. One of the aliens used his mind to throw me through the air and onto the floor. When I was able to pick myself up they had taken her out of sight."

"How did you feel about her, when she returned after having the baby?"

"They took her way before the baby was due, and she never returned. It's possible they felt we'd become too close and would interfere with their experiments. Maybe they were punishing me, by not letting her return. It was after her, that I began faking orgasms while having sex with other women. I never slept with just one woman after that. I made sure it was a different woman all the time, sort of a rotation thing I guess. That was short lived, because I soon escaped."

"Mark, it is sad what you went through; never getting a chance to be a father to any of the children that were born. I've never been married, but if Kate and I tie the knot, I hope I'll get a chance to be a good father to our child, if we are lucky enough to have one."

Off in the distance they heard a boat motor slowly sounding more prominent. Charley yelled to the women, "Boat coming! Get Aboard!"

They watched, as the women entered the water and swam to the back of the yacht. They helped the women on board. Each of them drew weapons and held them out of sight.

As the approaching boat got nearer, tensions grew, until they saw it make a quick turnabout. Two couples waved, as their craft sped away. As they watched it going around the bend at the mouth of cove, they laid the weapons aside. Kate spoke, "I'm getting hungry. Sarah, you want to help me get something prepared to go with that fish?"

"No problem. I'm about half starved, too. I'm definitely ready for a strong drink, also."

It wasn't long before bass was frying in a skillet, and beans simmering in a pot. The aroma filled the air around the yacht. Bread was in the oven, and everyone enjoyed their drinks.

They ate on the back of the boat where they could view the surroundings. No one felt safe at this point. There was still daylight left. They discussed the oncoming night, and agreed it would be best if someone stayed awake on guard.

Sarah volunteered to be the first watch, and promised she wouldn't get soused this time. Kate would be second, Mark third and Charley would follow. The shifts were evenly divided.

While the women washed dishes, Charley took Mark to the front of the boat, and explained how the choppers would pick them up the next day. He apologized for what he had to do, but Mark seemed to understand, and agreed he could probably never have a normal life in society.

Later, the others prepared for a night's sleep, leaving Sarah to watch after them. She took it serious and sat scanning the shore, water and sky. Her Glock lay beside her and one of Charley's AR-15s was propped near. Her thoughts went to Jack. Now she couldn't reach him or hear his voice. She had no way of knowing if he was alive or dead. She was angry with herself for dragging him into all this mess. If she ever saw him again, how would she get him to forgive what she'd done? How would she convince him she still loved him? She hoped Kate had been right about putting some good loving on him, if she got the chance. She'd definitely try to screw his brains out, and make him forget about her little escapade with Mark.

With every good thought that entered her mind, an opposite one seemed to take its place. She wondered if Jack would hate her. She whispered, "Sarah, you are one mixed up woman."

The sky began to darken and she could no longer see the shoreline, or very far down the cove. She'd have to depend on the sound of a motor. Looking up to the sky, she saw billions of stars. She began picking out the Big Dipper, Little Dipper, Orion and other star constellations, like she did when she was young. She realized she hadn't even looked up at the sky at night in years. Her whole life was consumed with her job. She liked what she did every day, and it came natural to her. She'd climbed in rank quickly, and was proud of it. However, it had become her only life. Other than occasional loving sizzling sex with Jack, she had no other life. Kate and Charley were her only two good friends. She didn't pal around with anyone else at the station. If she went out for a drink with the group, she always left alone. She had no hobbies, and seldom even had her hair and nails done. She learned very young how to make herself look good, with her own makeup and nail polish.

She thought about the captain and how he was a fair man, but she had screwed up royally. She hoped Charley's boss could smooth things over with Chandler. Even if that happened, she doubted if the captain could ever trust her completely again.

With all these thoughts, she made a mixed drink, and returned to her guard post.

The sound of a small plane and the sight of its blinking light caused her to grab the AR. Her eyes were glued to the plane, until it was far past, and the engine barely discernable, before she put the rifle aside.

She heard a small sound in the water beside the boat. She rose with her Glock and looked over the side. In the boat lights reflecting upon the water, she saw small fish gathering. A much larger fish swam through the group causing some of the smaller fish to fan out. It was just nature's fight for survival. She returned to her post to continue vigil and sipped her drink.

The night air got cooler, so she found a blanket to wrap around her. She made a fresh drink to sip on. She continued thinking about everything that had taken place, and what kind of future she might have after all her mistakes. The night was uneventful, and it really didn't seem like such a long time, before Kate approached, and asked, "You still thinking about Jack?"

"Among a lot of other things," she answered. "I was wondering what kind of a future I might have, if I have any at all, except being behind bars. I know I can do other things. I've had some secretarial experience, and I can type fast, but law enforcement has always been what I wanted to do."

"Sarah, now that I know a lot more about, Charley, I think he'll be able to keep us from going to jail. Hopefully, he has enough pull and connections to get our old jobs back. If not, we'll just have to do whatever we have to do. It isn't like we are old people. We are both fairly nice looking with a head on our shoulders. My only concern is staying out of prison. As long as we don't get a criminal record, we shouldn't have any trouble making it in life."

"That's what I've always liked about you, Kate. You're always so optimistic."

Kate just laughed, "Time for you to get some sleep, girl. I'm relatively sure tomorrow is going to be a full day for all of us."

"Guess you are right," she handed Kate the AR, but stuck her Glock in the small of her back. Kate didn't need it. She had her own pistol with her.

Kate wore a coat when she came out. She made herself a drink, and settled in for a shift of watching and waiting for any kind of surprise. Noise around the boat made her check over the sides, to make sure divers weren't trying to climb aboard. She also saw a few small planes fly by. One helicopter made her a little nervous for a few minutes. By and by, though, her shift finally came to an end. She was glad to see Mark approach, with the weapon Sarah had given him. She handed him the AR and a few extra clips, and asked, "Did you have training on this type of weapon?"

"Yes and many others of this kind."

"I thought I'd have to knock on your door. How did you know it was getting close to time for your shift? You don't wear a watch."

"Your body internal clock knows what time it is, even when you are asleep. While going to sleep, I repeated over and over to myself that I needed to get up at the appointed time to dress and relieve you. It works well."

"Don't think I would depend on that type of alarm, if I had to get up and go to work," she said. "It's been fairly quiet. Staying awake has been the only problem; that and staying out of the booze."

"Leaving the liquor alone won't be a problem for me. I don't think I ever want to feel that bad again."

She laughed, and added, "Oh! I've made that statement many times before. Anyway, I hope you have a peaceful night, until Charley relieves you."

"Before you go, Kate, I wanted to thank you again. You, Charley and Sarah went way out on a limb to help me. I can only hope things work out well for you in the end. Whatever happens to me, I will remember the three of you, always."

Kate walked toward him a few steps saying earnestly, "Hopefully, everything will work out for the best for all of us." She gave him a hug, kissed his cheek, and then headed for her room.

Mark sat down by the AR and laid his hand weapon beside him. He looked up to the stars, and contemplated his situation. He thought of tomorrow evening and getting to the shoreline to be picked up. He'd noticed the two inflated life rafts on the side of the yacht, so he got up to take a better look. Beside each raft were oars on racks held in place with clamps. There was a glass case beside the oars with a trolling motor. It wasn't locked, just a lever to move to the side to open the glass door. Below the glass case on the deck was a plastic boat battery box. He undid the snaps on each side and observed the new-looking marine battery inside. "They thought of everything on this yacht," he whispered to himself. Now he knew how they could get to the shoreline without swimming. He went back to his post and pondered his plight.

Charley came on deck to relieve Mark, but didn't see him. The AR was propped against a seat. He thought Mark had to go take a leak, but picked up the AR just in case, and began a search of the outside of the boat. After a thorough search and knowing Mark had time to finish relieving himself, he went to check the toilet but found the door open. "Surely he didn't go back to sleep in his room," crossed his mind as he went to his quarters to check, but found the room empty. "Was it possible he was banging Sarah?" he wondered, but doubted after what he'd seen and heard so far. However, he stood beside her door and heard her softly snoring.

He walked to the back of the boat to make another search, only observing everything closer. He soon realized one of the life rafts was missing, its oars, trolling motor, and battery by the open battery box.

There was a hand held spotlight under a cabinet inside. He got it and shined it down the cove. There was no sign of the raft, as he scanned the shoreline and surrounding water.

This new development put a damper on the plans. He'd thought Mark had been ok with the way things were supposed to happen. Charley was upset with himself that he had no clue Mark might try to take off, especially at night in a raft.

There was no sense in waking the women to go look for him in the darkness. The yacht had a huge spotlight, but it would draw too much attention for them to be cruising around at night searching with the big light. Game wardens would surely come to check out what they were doing. This time they might be recognized and taken into custody, or have to fight their way out of it.

They had come a long way on the water to get to this isolated spot. At daybreak, he'd have to wake the women so they could go look for him. Charley hoped the trolling motor battery was not at full charge and Mark wouldn't get too far.

The thoughts of this new twist of their situation made him fix a good strong drink. At the first sign of daylight, he'd get the coffee started. For now, he found a few snacks, while he thought and observed the water and surroundings. His shift seemed long and aggravating. His bosses were counting on him to have Mark ready for the pick up. Now, he didn't even know where Mark was. They'd have to spend the day looking for him until they found him. It was also possible the law or the bad guys might find him first.

Making the search, instead of staying where they were, also increased the chances of him and the girls being recognized and hauled off to jail. It could also put them into a gun battle with the bad guys, who were definitely looking hard for the four.

Shaking his head, he went to make himself a drink. Next to the whiskey bottle he found a handwritten note from Mark and a small flashlight. As he shined the light on the note, he read, "I found this pen and paper so I can leave this note. As I told Kate earlier tonight, I really appreciate everything you three have done for me. However, I have decided that since there is no way I can help the others at the facility, I do not want to become a prisoner of CIA or NSA. I will try to disappear on my own and find somewhere I can fit in. If I am captured while trying, then so be it. I have taken one of the rafts and equipment. By the time you come on duty, I hope to be well on my way to somewhere on the main shore. Please tell Sarah and Kate goodbye for me, and I hope they don't hate me for what I am doing.

We all know that as long as I am with you, there will be great danger for the three of you. I've been the cause of enough trouble. I'm sorry I left you unguarded tonight, but I truly believe if someone found you, and I wasn't with you, there would be very little need for him or her to cause you harm. Please do not try to find me. I will not let you take me into custody. If the military, CIA, NSA, or the bad guys get to me first; at least they will leave you guys alone, and you can get back to your normal lives. I do hope you can straighten things out with Kate and Sarah's boss. You are good people and I won't forget you.

Mark"

Charley laid the paper down and felt sadness inside for the man. He made his drink, drank about half of it, and refilled it to the top, before moving back to his post. Once again he thought about waking the women and going to search for him.

Maybe they could find him before he reached the main shore. This was a fast yacht and they had the spotlight.

Just as quickly as those thoughts resurfaced, he remembered Mark's words, saying he would not let them take him. He knew Mark could be a formidable foe if he really wanted to be. Mark kept the hand weapon and knew how to use it. He was also able to use his mind to do certain things and who knows what else. Would he really cause harm to any of them? That was a million dollar question. If he became that desperate, it was entirely possible.

He decided his original plan of trying to find him after daylight was the best thing to do. Even if Mark made it to the main shoreline, the raft would be tied up. At least they'd know where to fan out and start looking for him. The only reason Charley wanted to stay hidden was for the girls' safety. He wouldn't mind a chance to throw some bullets at the bad guys. It had been a long time since he'd seen some heavy action. Once you've been there, you kind of miss it. The little skirmish at his cabin was far from what he'd experienced in the past. Now he had no choice, looking for Mark would put them in an area that would be much easier for anyone to find them.

Mark was an ace in the hole for him. By turning him over to his CIA boss, he was assured of obtaining his help to keep him and the girls out of trouble and getting their jobs back. Now that he'd let Mark escape, he wasn't quite sure how the cards would fall. He'd just have to roll with the flow and play out the hand. He killed that drink and made another. He returned to sit, watch and wait while sipping on the booze.

At the first sign of day, he got the coffee perking and turned on the overhead light. He was taking his first sip from the cup, when Sarah appeared from her room in the doorway. He saw she was dressed for business. She was wearing her pants, blouse and jacket. The jacket was open and he saw her weapon in its holster. He knew how she liked her coffee, so he poured her a cup and handed it to her.

"Good morning, Charley. Did you have a peaceful night?" as she accepted the warm brew.

"Too peaceful, Mark is gone,"

"What do you mean he's gone?"

He handed her the note. He stood silently drinking his coffee, as he watched her face when she read his note. He was inquisitive as to what her reaction would be. She was much calmer than expected.

"He probably left at the first of his shift. He's had several hours toward the main shore. I assume you want to wake up Kate and go search for him. We know everybody and his brother are searching for any clue as to where he is, and now he's walking right into their hands. What's the plan now, Charley?"

"Yeah, you basically guessed it. We've got to go find him. He'd be better off in the hands of my people, but I want you to understand something. He is desperate and armed. He stated he would not let us take him into custody. I will not hesitate to put a bullet in him, if he tries to harm either you or Kate. I want to make that perfectly clear."

"I've learned a lot about you lately, Charley. I know you mean business. It would be hard for me to believe that he would do anything to harm us, after we've done all this for him. Just for the record so you know where I stand. I would not hesitate to stop him if he tried to harm you or Kate, no matter what it took."

Charley nodded over his coffee cup, but wisely refrained from adding any more to the subject. "I'll wake up Kate, and we'll get this show on the road."

He poured an extra cup of brew and headed toward their cabin.

It was light enough to see a good way down the cove and the surrounding barren rock shoreline. There was no sign of Mark. She managed to finish that cup and top it off before Charley and Kate resurfaced.

Sarah asked, "Need me to make another pot before we get going,"

"No! He's got a good head start. He's also put us all in a lot more danger, whether he thought his leaving would, or wouldn't. Now we'll be close to the main shore looking for him. We may even have to dock and search for him. That means not only looking, but also asking questions of people to find out if they have seen him. Maybe we'll get real lucky and the trolling motor battery died. If he had to row the raft, we might still catch him. I'll bring in the anchors. Kate, you start the motors. I may need you to back up or pull forward to dislodge an anchor."

Kate finished the last bit of coffee in her cup, and replied, "Eye, eye, my handsome, Captain!"

Sarah grinned and secured the AR and the cups.

They'd keep the jackets on for a little while this morning while the boat was moving, but it wouldn't be long before they discarded them, as it heated up outside. They soon had the yacht headed down the cove. They motored slowly until they cleared the mouth and entered the open water. Charley increased speed, as they scanned the boats and other craft coming into view. It was still early, so it was easy to check out the few in the vicinity. They were a long way from the marina, and there would be many to check out along the way. Charley assumed he'd try to make a beeline for the dock at the marina, or at least somewhere close in that area. He hoped to overtake him, somehow get him back on board, and back to the pickup spot from where they'd just come.

Chapter Sixteen

Mark left the yacht as soon as he could leave the note, lower the raft into the water, place the oars inside the raft, and hook up the trolling motor to the battery. He ran the motor on low until he was a good distance down the cove and then kicked it up into high gear. The trolling motor was made for getting the raft to a short distance, or helping keep it straight while someone was rowing. It was not made for pushing the raft for long distances. Mark kept the motor on high until it ran out of juice. Then he put the oars in place and rowed. He was a strong man and kept rowing without resting. Occasionally, he slowed down enough to catch his breath, and then begin another round of steady rowing.

By the time daylight filled the sky, he had the marina in sight. A few boats with fishermen had passed him, and looked his way. Since he didn't wave for help, they continued to their destination.

He was getting tired, but, the sight of the dock coming closer fueled his determination to keep rowing. Finally, he pulled up to one of the ladders on the edge of the dock, and tied off the raft. He sat there panting, as he rested. He opened the bottle of water he'd saved and sipped. He was wise enough to not gulp it down, even though he felt dehydrated. He was way too tired to just jump up out of the boat and take off on foot. Rest and sips of water were the order of business. He managed to look in each direction and scrutinize anyone looking his way. No one seemed to be paying much attention to him. They were busy getting their own gear loaded for an outing.

Someone not far from Mark was loading blanket-covered weapons, a cooler with water, drinks, and sandwiches into a rental boat. Jack and the two goons were preparing to start the search for the yacht. It didn't take them long to start coming off the shoreline. As they cruised along the boats tied to the dock, they weren't looking for a raft. They were looking for a big yacht. They almost passed Mark completely until the main casino guy recognized the name of the yacht on the raft.

Jack was piloting the boat. The guy jumped up and tapped him on the shoulder, pointing toward the raft. Jack slowed the boat and turned it around. They observed Mark weakly climbing onto the dock, and oblivious to Jack and the other two.

"I'm relatively certain that's the guy who has been with Sarah," Jack said softly to the two men, as he began nearing the dock and raft.

"If he did anything to the boss's niece he's going to be dead meat, and I wouldn't advise you to try to interfere."

Jack only commented, "Right now, we just need to get him and make him lead us to Kate and the others. Believe me, if he as done anything to hurt either of them, I could give a shit less what you do to him."

That seemed to appease their concerns, as they soon tied off and climbed onto the dock. They saw him way ahead of them and headed his way. They left the weapons covered in the boat and only carried their concealed hand weapons. They walked so as not to draw attention from Mark, or anyone else watching.

Jack knew from the scene at Charley's cabin that this guy was more than likely armed, and he relayed that information to his two cohorts. What Jack didn't want was a shootout, with a bunch of people around, who could get hurt or killed in the crossfire. In a whispered voice, he told the two they needed to take Mark discretely. They nodded in agreement.

By the time they reached the end of the main dock, they saw him a good distance heading for a building. They continued in his direction.

When two police officers approached, they turned toward each other and pretended to be talking about fish they'd caught. Jack was describing a rather large bass that had broken his line and got away. As the officers passed, they made sure their faces were not discernable.

With them out of the way, they continued, and saw Mark enter some new bathrooms. Shortly he was out of sight inside, so they picked up speed, but didn't run.

Mark was just coming out as they reached the entrance. The three blocked his path with hands on their weapons.

Jack spoke seriously, "I know you are Mark. I know you have been with Sarah, Charley and Kate. I also know you are going to lead us back to them, and for your sake, they better be in good shape."

"Kate damn sure better not be harmed in anyway," the casino leader blurted out.

Jack continued, "Before you even think of using those eyes of yours to heat one of our weapons like you did at the station, one of us will put a few bullets in you."

Mark looked concerned, but answered, "You have got to be Jack. The one Sarah cares so much for. You are a very lucky man."

"That's none of your business right now. You need to just go with us to our rental boat and lead us to the others."

"And if I refuse?" Mark answered.

"Oh! You're going, alright," the second casino man stepped forward.

"Mark glared toward him. The guy flew backward and onto the ground.

Before Mark could even look toward Jack and the other guy, their weapons were drawn and aimed in his direction.

As Mark hesitated, the man on the ground drew his weapon without even getting up, and trained it on Mark.

Jack quickly pointed out, "You may heat one weapon, but the others will put holes in your arms and legs."

Mark raised his hands part-way saying, "If I lead you to the others and confirm they have not come to any harm, what happens to me?"

"We could care less what you do after that," the main casino guy snapped, "You can take your happy ass and get lost as far as we're concerned."

Luckily there was no one else around, or they would have initiated quite a stir with weapons drawn.

"I'm asking Jack," answered Mark as he looked toward him.

"If Sarah and the others are ok, you can do whatever the hell you want to. However, if they are harmed in anyway I can assure you will never have to worry about anything again."

As the one on the ground got up, he noticed four men in suits headed in their direction. "I think someone better make some kind of management decision quick, because I don't think the four approaching are friendly."

Mark lowered his hands, as they placed him between them, and headed for the rental.

Unfortunately, it drew the attention of the suited guys, and they were running, drawing weapons.

Good guys or bad guys, they weren't going to stop Jack from finding Sarah, since he was this close. He drew his weapon, as did the others including Mark.

Bullets flew. One slammed into Jack's left shoulder, and a casino guy caught a bullet in his right upper leg. The suited men would have probably been better shots if they weren't running. Jack and his associates were definitely placing bullets in kill zones. The casino main guy was shot in his lower shooting arm, causing him to drop his weapon. Mark was a good shot, and his bullets hit his targets.

As the last suited guy fell to the ground, Jack quickly spun, placing his weapon to the side of Mark's head, and placed his bloody hand over Mark's weapon. Mark slowly released his grip and let Jack take the pistol. The other two held their wounds. They went to the guys on the ground making sure they were dead.

"Those two police officers had to have heard the shots and will be headed this way. There are already people from the dock and other areas coming to see what all the noise was about. Put your weapons away. We've got to make it to the rental and draw the least attention we can along the way. "

They complied, headed toward the craft, holding their wounds. As people came running from the dock, they pretended to be doing something to another boat. When the people passed, they put pressure on their wounded areas and continued.

The casino guy with the arm wound saw some towels in a boat and retrieved them.

Jack placed his handkerchief under his jacket on his shoulder wound, and they hurried to the waiting craft.

As the four climbed aboard, Jack instructed Mark to start the boat and drive. Mark obeyed. Soon the boat cleared the dock area, and plowed through open water.

The main casino guy wrapped a towel around his friend's leg, and another around his own arm.

Jack looked at Mark and explained, "You need to lead us to them quick. Sarah saw something in you, so I'll give you the benefit of the doubt." He held up the weapon he removed from Mark in his bloody left hand. He placed his other hand on his weapon in the back of his pants, saying, "But if you cross me, and don't lead us to them, I will kill you."

He sat down on the seat behind Mark. The casino leader handed him a hand towel. Jack crammed it under his jacket and over the wound. He looked at the wounded two, and inquired, "How bad are you hit?"

The leader answered, "Looks like you took the brunt of it. Harry over there had a bullet pass through his upper thigh. No bones were hit; he should be ok for awhile." Holding up his arm with a towel around it," a bullet grazed my arm, but no arteries hit. I'll heal. How about your shoulder?"

"Hard to move my arm up and down, but can't tell if it hit any bone or not. Pain is at a ten plus since I used it to take this guy's weapon," as he looked toward Mark. Jack handed the weapon to the casino leader saying, "If I lose consciousness; and this guy isn't on the up and up with what he says about our people, then shoot the son-of-a-bitch."

The casino man grinned, "It'll be my pleasure."

Mark heard what they said and glanced toward them, but said nothing, as he piloted the craft onward.

Chapter Seventeen

In a black SUV, on the road approaching Lake Mead, an agent touched the earphone on the side of his head, saying, "Conners."

In his ear he heard his boss's voice, "There has been an incident at the marina at Lake Mead. Police are reporting four men dead with NSA identification. We know they are not ours and their ID's are bogus. Not quite sure who they are working with, but they are not legit."

"Probably more of the Majestic group."

"Evidently someone took care of them for us," was his boss's reply.

"I'd put money on it being Caruso and two men traveling with him," added the agent.

"If that guy is still alive when this is all over, you just might want to see about recruiting him. He's either the luckiest son of a gun, or he's damn good."

"He'd make a good agent," Conners replied.

His boss cut the short talk, saying, "Get over to the marina and take charge. Don't let any local law give you any flack. Get that mess cleaned up and out of sight. Any news people show, get rid of them."

"No problem, Sir! We are pulling into the marina as I speak. We'll take care of it from here."

"I'll notify you if there are any changes in our plans. Locate Caruso and those other two. We don't need them throwing any more wrenches into our well oiled machinery."

"Understood, Sir."

The agent's phone went dead as he stepped out of the vehicle. The four approached the yellow taped off area surrounded by a slew of police and detective cruisers. Sirens in the distance were becoming louder, and they were probably the meat wagons.

Conners flashed his identification as he approached the nearest officer at the tape, and inquired, "Who is in charge?"

The officer pointed toward a male detective with a phone stuck to his ear, and said, "That would be, Detective Jenkins, the one making the call."

Conners and the others climbed under the tape and headed toward the man. As they reached him, he hung up on his caller.

Showing his ID, Conners stated, "Detective Jenkins, we are here to take over, but before we do, can you fill me in as to what you have learned so far?" He'd discovered long ago it was better to be cordial to other agencies than to just push his authority around.

" Figured more of you guys would show up soon. Looks like these four ran into a heap of trouble. They did some damage, though. There are three areas near the bathroom entrance with blood spatters. Don't mind you guys taking precedence, either. It saves me from having to do all the paper work," as they shook hands.

Jenkins pointed to a young boy between his mother and father, being calmed and questioned by a female officer. "The kid was on the toilet when the shooting started. He said it sounded like someone was trying to take someone named Mark into custody. He also heard a few more names, but being scared, he could only remember one more name, Kate. Apparently he peeked out the door when the shooting ended. He saw your four men on the ground and four men in civilian clothes with weapons. One looked to him like a detective with coat and all. The kid was pretty sure he saw a badge on his belt. After that, the kid ran back inside and hid, until his dad found him."

He hesitated and took a sip from a store bought coffee cup, "Hell. I haven't even had time to finish a cup of coffee this morning and shit has already started happening."

Conners didn't bother to explain the four on the ground were not his men. He asked, "Anything else that could be of importance?"

"Nothing for certain. A fifteen year old with his dad and uncle were on the dock when the shooting started. As they ran this way to find out what the noise was all about, the boy said he saw four men at a boat acting like they weren't concerned, and that seemed strange to him. Can't verify any of that, but we did find what appears to be small drops of blood where the boy said he saw them. Won't be sure till CSI can investigate. However, I guess you guys will have your own CSI check things out."

"Not really," Conners informed, "We'll rely on the cooperation of your CSI people. After all, we are all on the same side. Thanks for your help, Jenkins," and they shook hands once more.

Jenkins ordered his detectives away from the scene and instructed the local police to keep the onlookers away from the taped off area.

Conners motioned for his three other men to join him away from the others. Out of hearing he began, "Both boys mentioned four men. One heard the names Mark and Kate. We know our subject escapee is named Mark, and we know he was supposed to be in the company of CIA Decker and two females Kate and Sarah. However, this sounds more like it was Caruso and the casino boss's men. If it was Caruso that means our subject is now in his custody. That could mean CIA's whole extraction deal could be jeopardized."

Pointing to two of his men, he ordered, "You two stay here and take charge. Mack and I will check at the boat rental. Caruso has probably rented a boat. Where he's taking our subject is a zillion dollar question. However, we know he is desperate to find his partner, and we now know she is on a yacht somewhere out there on the water. I'd venture to say that Caruso either knows where the yacht is, or he is making our subject take him to it. Either way we need to find him. I'd rather not call in the cavalry if we can locate them ourselves. However, if we don't find them soon, I'll consider the extraction null and void and order in search choppers."

As the other two nodded, he and Mack headed toward the boat rental shack. It didn't take Conners long to ascertain it was Caruso who had rented the boat. He took down the numbers that would be on the side of the rental. He also asked the guy about the yacht, but the only information he could be given was where the yacht was usually moored. Conners wanted to rent the fastest boat available. The man told him to just sign for it and return it, and there would be no charge. Conners thanked him and took the keys to a pleasure craft. He and Mack headed for where it was tied at the dock. Soon they cruised past the dock into open water. Conners had been informed as to the coordinates for the scheduled extraction, so he figured the yacht would be somewhere in that area. Soon he had the craft at full throttle.

(Far ahead another meeting was taking place)

Mark saw a familiar sight coming into view. The yacht was coming toward them. He turned toward Jack, sitting and holding the coat tight against the towel over his wound, and his weapon still in his hand. "The yacht is up ahead."

Jack struggled to his feet.

On the yacht, Charley and the two women were on the bridge. Kate had a pair of binoculars she'd found in a cabinet. She announced loudly, "Mark is driving that boat coming this way, and if I'm not mistaken, Jack is standing behind him."

Sarah snatched the binoculars from her hand and focused.

Kate saw the smile on her face, when she knew Sarah had him in her lens.

Sarah grinned at Kate and Charley, but didn't comment.

Charley slowed the boat, saying, "Go to the rear and help them tie off the boat. I'll idle the engines and join you in a few minutes."

The women gladly rushed to follow his orders.

By the time the smaller boat came around to the back of the yacht, Charley appeared with his gun in his hand.

The girls didn't pay any attention to him, as they secured the landlines.

Mark was the first to come aboard. Charley got the women's attention, as he asked, "Where is your weapon, Mark?"

The casino leader held it up by the barrel so it could be seen.

Jack was in much pain as he tried to climb aboard. Sarah rushed to help him. She looked into his eyes but couldn't find the words to say anything. She helped him to a seat, removed his jacket, and inspected the wound entrance and exit. She finally spoke, as she placed the bloody towel back over the entrance wound, "The fact you can move your arm at all tells me the bullet didn't hit bone, but you need a doctor, Jack."

He didn't answer her, he just mentioned to Kate, "Weapons under the blankets in the boat."

She nodded in compliance.

The casino leader was helping his friend onto the yacht. Kate rushed to help, as she hollered back, "The boat has an emergency first aid kit, but not enough medicine and bandages for all these wounds."

Sarah added, "We've got alcohol for antiseptic, and we can cut up clean sheets or pillow cases for bandages."

Mark spoke softly, "I'll get the alcohol and a bowl of clean water."

Charley added, "And I will follow him to make sure he doesn't try to take off again."

Jack nodded to that statement.

Kate rushed to the smaller boat and retrieved an armful of the casino men's weapons. Soon Kate helped the two casino fellows get cleaned and bandaged, and Sarah tended to Jack. She wanted to hold him, kiss him, and tell him she loved him, but the sad looks he gave her caused her to refrain from speaking. She continued until his bandage was secure, and then took the bloody bowl and rag away to the galley.

Jack saw her look over her shoulder at him, but he didn't move from the seat.

Charley pointed for Mark to sit where he could be seen by everyone, and then asked Jack, "How did you find him, and who are these other two fellows? They don't appear to be detectives."

"They are employees of a big wig at the Mirage. Their boss is Kate's uncle and their job was to make sure nothing happened to Kate. There were two others; one was killed, and the other wounded last night by NSA agents. Hopefully, they weren't the real ones, because they are dead. Four more of their suited buddies are lying around the bathroom at the marina. They will be joining their cohorts in hell."

He grimaced with pain, but continued, "I recognized, Mr. Wonderful there, as he came out of the john."

Sarah heard his words and knew what he was referring to. They cut like a knife into her heart.

"We were trying to take him into custody so he could lead us to you guys, but those four guys in suits appeared with weapons drawn. We returned fire including this guy, Mark. When the last enemy fell, I grabbed Mark's weapon, and now we are here."

Jack saw Sarah turn and walk to the front of the yacht, as he heard Charley, "That means the bad guys know we are in this yacht somewhere on the water. When those last four don't report in, reinforcements will be sent. Ten bucks to a dollar some of them will be in helicopters and/or speed-boats."

Kate finished the last wrap on the casino leader's arm, and walked away with her bowl and bloody towels.

Charley told the casino guys to keep an eye on Mark, and turned to Jack. "I need to make a call and see if I can speed up the extraction time. Looks like it will include extra choppers for our new guests."

Charley walked toward the side of the boat away from everyone. Jack saw Kate join him, as he began making his call on a burn phone.

Sarah was out of his sight, so he struggled to his feet and went toward the front of the boat. When he found her, he saw her sobbing as quietly as she could. When he came up behind her, he spoke softly, "I don't think I have ever seen a tear in your eye. You were always the hard case. Are those tears for him?"

"No, asshole," she answered bitterly, as she turned toward him. "Jack, I'm sorry. I made a lot of mistakes. If I could do it all over again, I wouldn't make them. It tore me apart, knowing I'd hurt you." As her voice trailed and broke, she began uncontrollably sobbing and shaking.

He hated to see her this way. He wrapped his good arm around her and pulled her body to his chest. He let her get it out of her system, as he stood solid, letting her cry it out.

When her tears began to subside, he finally spoke, "We all make mistakes, Sarah. My main concern, from the time this all started, was to find you and make sure you were ok. You are my partner, and it was driving me nuts not knowing."

She raised her head, wrapped her arms around his neck, and kissed his lips hard and long. Jack relished those lips pressed against his, and enjoyed the moment. He slowly pulled away, saying, "This isn't over yet. We are still in a bucket of rattlesnakes, and it's going to be hard to keep from getting bit."

She released his neck, but her arms went around his waist, "All that matters to me right now is you are here with me."

His free hand went behind her head as he kissed her forehead.

Kate and Charley came toward them. Charley spoke, "Satellite pinpointed a flat area not far from our present location. I have the coordinates and will enter them in the yacht's guidance system. There will be enough room on the choppers for everyone. Jack, you and the two casino men will be taken to a secure medical station to be treated. Kate, Sarah, Mark, and I will be picked up separately. The military needs Mark ASAP."

"Oh! Hell! No!" Sarah interrupted in an angry tone of voice. I'm not leaving, Jack again. Charley, it isn't happening."

"That's your decision, Sarah, but you might be safer with us. I still have to try to square things with your boss."

"I don't give a damn. I'm not leaving Jack's side, until I know he is ok."

"So be it," Charley answered, with Kate holding onto his waist and smiling at Sarah. "Kate and I are heading for the controls to get this yacht underway."

Sarah kept her arm around Jack's waist, as they watched Charley and Kate walk away. She started to say more to him, but Jack put his finger to her lips, "Later, it'll keep for now. I'm glad I found you."

She was satisfied with his statement, as they walked back to the others, with her arm still around his waist.

Mark took notice, as soon as they came into view, but didn't comment. His facial expression said it all. It indicated that he knew what a lucky man Jack was.

Jack informed, "We are headed to a rendezvous. CIA and/or NSA choppers will take us wounded to a medical facility off the grid. Sarah here will accompany."

"What about Kate?" the Casino leader inquired, knowing his job was to keep her from harm.

"She will accompany her companion. That is out of my control. She'll be surrounded by friendly armed agents and taken to a safe undisclosed location. Your boss will have to be satisfied with that."

Jack turned toward Mark, and added, "He'll be taken straight to the military. They need him for information on a secret location. That also is out of my control," as he glanced into Sarah eyes. She showed no emotion at his statement.

They heard the motors crank and the yacht began to slowly move, when Kate came running stating, "Speedboat approaching fast with two men in suits."

Sarah, Kate, Jack and the Casino guys armed themselves. Jack gave an order to Mark, "If you try to escape, or interfere, I will shoot you." As he finished his statement, he heard a voice coming from the boat with its engine gearing to idle, "We are NSA and request permission to come aboard," as the two held hands high to be seen."

Mack grabbed a bowline and tossed it to Kate. Jack spoke sternly, "You can come aboard, but I suggest you keep your hands far away from your weapons."

As they climbed aboard, Jack recognized the agent he met twice before. "You and I just keep running into each other, don't we?"

"Seems that way, Jack. We are only here to confirm our subject is still in Decker's custody," as he glanced toward Mark. "I wasn't sure, after we saw the results of your meeting with those guys at the marina. Sorry we didn't intercept them in time, again. I see you took a few hits," as he glanced at the bandages.

Charley was now joining, "How did you find us so quickly? There was no boat visible behind Jack's."

"Figured Jack rented a boat. Got the information of the letters on the craft from the rental man. I knew your original extraction coordinates, so I just headed in this direction hoping I'd get lucky. Speaking of lucky, Jack, this makes strike-three for you."

Sarah looked to Jack inquisitively; as she heard, Jack, "Let me worry about that. By the way, if you are going to continue trying to save me, I need to know your name."

The agent grinned, "Conners."

"Is that a first name or last name?"

"It doesn't matter, Jack. All you need to know is I am one of the good guys."

Charley nodded to the others and they lowered weapons, but kept them at handy reach.

They all sat and discussed the situation.

Sarah placed her arm around Jack's waist again. She wanted to be as close as possible. She couldn't help but whisper to him, "Strike three?"

He just grinned saying lowly, "I'll tell you about it later."

No sooner had he finished his statement, they heard choppers approaching. As they drew closer, Charley felt the hair on the back of his neck rise. He said, "I doubt very seriously if those are ours. Mine had to come from Nellis, and they could not have gotten here this soon. They are not transport helicopters and there is no gunship accompanying."

Everyone readied weapons again. They and the two NSA agents took up shooting positions wherever they could find something to get behind.

Mark hurriedly pleaded, "Give me a weapon."

Charley gave him a stern look, but handed him a pistol.

Men behind machine guns were seen in the doorways of the choppers. Front firing holes manned by the pilots could also be seen.

A voice on a loud speaker, "This is the NSA. Lower your weapons and take your craft to the shoreline. Prepare to be boarded."

The group looked at each other and almost simultaneously shook heads. It was evident no one was going to take orders from these guys no matter what.

"If you do not comply, we'll be compelled to open fire."

The casino leader suddenly stated, "I'm about tired of these assholes." He swung his rifle around and opened fire on the nearest helicopter killing one guy in the open door.

The hand had been dealt, so to speak, and now it was time to play your cards. The others opened fire at the helicopters.

Taking bullet hits, the choppers rose to regroup.

They didn't hear the Stealth fighter, but they saw it open fire, and blow both of the helicopters to bits. Just as quickly as it appeared, it disappeared.

Jack turned to Charley and grinned a little, as he stated, "You and I need to have a long talk. You've got some serious friends."

Charley grinned in return, "Sometimes it's good to have friends in high places. Let's get this yacht to the extraction point before something else happens." He turned and pointed his gun at, Mark, "I'll take that weapon now."

Mark hesitated for a moment, but saw the others train their weapons on him also, so he relinquished, handing it to Charley.

Jack's arm was killing him, now that the adrenalin high had gone away. He sat down to hold his shoulder.

Sarah rushed to his side to give him comfort.

The others waited until the NSA agents holstered weapons before putting their own down.

Soon the yacht slowly moved forward, and then gained speed.

Observing Jack's condition, Sarah put her hand to his forehead and told him, "You've got a fever. Infection might be setting in. Your bandages are blood-soaked and I need to change the dressing. I'll get some more sheets, but we need to get you to a hospital."

She started to rise, but he clasped her arm pulling her back down to her seat, "Just get enough to wrap over the top of this bandage. I'll make it till Charley's people pick us up to take us to the medical facility."

Concerned, she angrily answered, "You are so damn hard-headed."

"And you aren't?" he replied trying to force a grin.

She kissed his cheek and hurried away.

While the NSA agents and casino men kept lookout for any more trouble coming their way, Charley came over to Jack.

"How are you holding out, Jack?"

"Pretty painful and I'm starting to get a little woozy. Hope we aren't far from extraction time."

"Not long at all, Jack. As you can see, Kate already has us underway. The point of extraction is only two miles from here. Our helicopters will be waiting. Is there anything I can do for you?"

"Nah! Just try to make sure nothing else happens. I don't think I could be of much help," as he grimaced with pain.

"I'll do my best, old friend. Here comes Sarah with more bandage material."

Before he could leave, Jack requested, "Could you bring me a bottle of that whiskey that I see? He nodded toward the cabin."

As Sarah passed him Charley said, "Sure, Jack I'll get it."

"Get what?" inquired Sarah, as she began wrapping the new sheet strips over the soaked ones. She flinched each time she saw him grimace.

"Pain killer," he answered, just as Charley handed him the whiskey bottle and Sarah the top. Jack took two big swigs and held it in his lap. Sarah started to replace the top but he said, "Not yet." He took two more big gulps shaking his head at the burning sensation going down his throat. Then he nodded for her to put the cap on.

Jack said, "Sarah, you need to call Chandler and fill him in before we are airlifted out of here. I don't know what kind of restrictions we'll be under when CIA is in control. There are two burn phones in my jacket."

"I've got a couple in my cabin if we need them, but I'll grab one of yours for now." She rose and retrieved one of the phones from his jacket. She hesitated, as she observed the bullet hole in the jacket shoulder and the blood. She felt sick inside knowing she had caused all this to happen.

She returned but didn't initiate the call.

Jack had his eyes closed but felt her presence. When he didn't hear her voice, he slowly opened his eyes. "Did you find the phone?" That's when he saw the tears running down her face. She held the phone in her lap looking at him.

"Jack, I'm so sorry this happened to you. All of this is my fault. Every damn bit of it. I wish I could go back in time and change it," as she continued to cry.

"Sarah, we've already had this conversation. What's done is done. We've just got to move forward from this point, and try to get out of this mess we are in; call Chandler on his personal cell."

She dried her tears with a piece of sheet and dialed the phone. She tried to keep from crying when she heard him answer, "Chandler, who is this?"

"Captain, its Sarah."

"Where are you, Sarah? You are in a lot of trouble. Everybody and his brother are looking for you, Jack especially, but he hasn't checked in today." More softly he inquired, realizing her voice sounded tearful, "Are you ok?"

"I'm ok. Jack is with me, but he's been wounded. He was shot in the shoulder."

More seriously he demanded, "Where are you? I'll send Medivac, ambulance, or whatever you need."

"I can't tell you where we are, Captain, at least not yet."

"Damn it, Sarah! Is Jack able to talk?"

She didn't answer. She just handed the phone to Jack. "Yeah, Captain. I'm here."

"Jack, how bad is the wound?"

"Took a bullet through the shoulder, but you ought to see the other guy."

"Don't try to be funny. You ain't no damn comedian. Where are you?"

"All I can tell you is that Sarah, Kate, some others and I, are safe for the moment, but we are not in control. NSA, CIA or whatever agency is involved has taken jurisdiction. We are less than a mile from where we will be airlifted to some secret location and medical facility. After that, I'm not sure we'll be allowed to check in by phone. We also have the stranger from the station shooting in custody. Or should I say they have him in custody?"

"Jack, tell me where you are. I'll send some of our guys to help you."

"Trust me, Captain. You don't want to get any more of our people involved in this crap. I'm sure if you turn on the news, it won't be long before you know where we are, or where we were, if they get us out of here. Just listen for news reports on two downed choppers and four dead NSA agents prior to that."

"I'm reading you, Jack, I'm reading you."

He knew the captain would know now at least the vicinity of the location, and know Jack had something to do with what he would hear on the news reports. "I just wanted to bring you up to date. Don't know when we will be able to check back in with you. If you don't hear from us before too long, you know to start asking questions from upper echelon. Never know what these guys are liable to do."

"Got you, Jack. I'll find you. I'll raise so much hell they'll have to return you. We'll straighten all the rest of this shit out when you and Sarah are returned. Get that wound taken care of. You are a hell of a detective, Jack. I knew you'd find Sarah if anybody could. Now, don't let her out of your sight."

"She isn't going anywhere, Captain. Right now she's taking good care of me."

Sarah took the phone from his hand and spoke in her normal tone, "Not that good. He's stubborn as hell, as usual. I'll try to make sure he lives. I know I'm in a world of shit, Captain. I'll have to answer for my mistakes. Right now, my priority is to get Jack and me to safety and get his wound tended to. After that, I'll turn myself in."

"You do what you have to do, Sarah, but this time, try to do what's right. I want both of you sitting in front of me as soon as possible."

The yacht headed to the shoreline and the noise from helicopter blades was getting louder.

"Captain, It's time for us to end this call. Hopefully, you will hear from us soon." She tossed the phone overboard and looked toward Jack, only to see his eyes closed. She placed a hand on his arm and removed the bottle of whiskey from his lap. He opened his eyes slowly to look at her, but closed them again.

Two unmarked transport helicopters sat waiting on the shore. One heavily armed chopper circled the area above. Off in the distance, Sarah saw the glint of other helicopters, and by the size, she guessed they were news people.

Kate almost grounded the yacht and had to put the engines in reverse. Charley and the NSA agents, with the help of Mark, made sure the anchors held. Charley took the binoculars and checked the faces in both helicopters. He'd specifically requested two pilots he trusted, and wanted to make sure it was them.

Putting the binoculars down, he stated, "They are our people. Get the wounded in the boat first. Take as many on the first trip as possible. We need to make this a short stop."

The casino leader and one of the NSA agents helped the other casino man into the small boat.

Conners helped Sarah get Jack into the boat. As she sat holding him to her chest, Conners just shook his head. He then piloted the craft to the ones waiting on shore. When the wounded and Sarah were lifted away on one Medivac, he returned for the others.

His other agent, Mark, Kate and Charley climbed aboard. Conners got them to the shore and secured the boat line to a rock.

Armed men in tactical uniform surrounded and escorted them to the other Medivac.

Soon it also lifted, followed by the gunship chopper.

Conners and his buddy stayed behind and watched the helicopters disappearing in the distance. They saw news helicopters coming toward them.

Conners motioned toward the speedboat. As he fired up the engine, his partner untied the rope, and they headed down the cove. The other agent asked Conners, "What about the yacht?"

"I'll send someone over later. The keys were left in the ignition. I just need to find someone I trust to drive that expensive toy. I don't want it damaged too much, and on my expense account."

The agent grinned. He knew his leader had an open expense account. He'd seen him make larger purchases than a yacht, when needed for some cases. He was high up the food chain, so to speak.

Conners continued, "I promised I'd bring this boat back and I keep my promises, good or bad."

When they arrived at the marina, it looked like a county fair. There were police, state troopers, FBI, CIA, ambulances, fire trucks and countless numbers of news vehicles and cameras.

He docked the craft at the rental area. He saw his men had done their job. The four fake NSA victims were gone and so were his men. They used NSA jurisdiction to gather the bodies, evidence, and get the hell out of Dodge, so no one could ask them any questions. He saw they left the SUV for him, and got another ride.

Conners and his associate quietly went inside, returned the boat key, and told the owner thanks.

They were soon in the vehicle, eased out of the parking area, and headed to open road.

His agent began to speak his mind, "That Caruso fellow was in bad shape. He couldn't hold his head up there toward the end, and I heard the woman say he was running a high fever. Even when he was fully conscious, he wouldn't let her change his bandages."

Conners gave half a grin, as he explained, "Caruso knew what he was doing. He knew how bad he was wounded and bleeding. He knew if he let her remove the blood-soaked sheets, he'd start bleeding worse, and the blood already coagulating would be disturbed. It's not his first rodeo. He's been wounded before. He also knew from experience he'd start running a fever soon and the loss of blood would cause him to become less coherent. He was barely awake with that pretty lady holding him. It is very possible he'll pass out completely, before they get him to a medical facility, even with EMS on that Medivac. They will shoot him up with morphine to kill the pain."

The relatively young agent added, "That guy is pretty tough."

Conner nodded, "When he's well, he is definitely someone you wouldn't want to make angry. He's sent quite a few guys to an early grave, since he's been in law enforcement. They were all have to cases, of course. I've followed his career since the first day I saw him at the police academy. I was a young instructor. He had that look in his eye. The kind that made you think someone will be lucky to have him as a partner. He trained hard and wouldn't give up on anything we threw at him. There were times I could tell he wanted to tear my head off, but he kept his anger in check. He graduated with honors and the head of his class. He earned his way to detective and he's been an inspiration to everyone he's worked with. Well, except this Sidwell. I think he must have been thinking with the wrong head, if you know what I mean?"

"Who could blame him? She's a hot looking chick. I don't think there are many guys on the force who would pass up a chance to tap that."

"You have a point," Conners agreed.

"What will happen to Caruso and the others?"

"Decker is very high in CIA. I doubt if anything will happen to him, especially since he completed deliverance of the target suspect. His girlfriend, Kate was in a little trouble because of her actions, but Decker will most likely get that all smoothed over. The two casino guys will be treated, thanked for helping catch the objective, released, and told to keep their mouth shut, if they don't want to go to prison for ten or twenty years.

Jack has been working under the directive of his boss from the start. He most likely will be presented a medal before this is all over, and upped in rank and pay.

Sidwell, well the jury is still out on her. She was always a good detective, but she's broken so many rules and destroyed people's trust in her. Even CIA can only make some things go away, not everything. If she was a Nobody, they would probably shit-can her from the force, and/or put her in jail, but she's been in the public's eye for a good while. Interviews on TV, news articles, promotions on the force, and that kind of thing made her a celebrity of sorts. She was a shining example for women wanting to join law enforcement, but now she may have blown all that. I'm not sure how things will unfold for her."

The agent remained silent and only nodded as they continued on their journey.

(On Sarah's helicopter)

She was still holding Jack against her breasts. He managed to raise his head, look into her eyes, and then it was lights out for him. Even the medics had left his bandages in place, when Sarah explained she used whiskey to clean the wound during her initial bandaging. They gave him morphine, and placed an oxygen mask over his face. His vital signs were monitored on a screen near him.

The two casino men had their bandages replaced. The one with the leg wound was also given some morphine. The one with the arm wound was given a lesser type of painkiller. Both were traveling comfortably. The chopper hurried to an undisclosed medical facility.

When the Medivac landed on a heliport, medical personnel rushed toward them to extract the wounded. Two men with a gurney tended to Jack. Sarah trailed along behind them, as they entered the building and down the halls. At the doors of what was evidently an operating room with nurses and doctors waiting inside, she could not enter. She was told where there was a waiting room, and that someone would be talking to her soon.

Sarah found the room and sat down in a chair with her head between her hands. There wasn't another soul anywhere near. There was a TV, but it wasn't on. She saw a table with coffee pot and amenities. She rose, poured herself a hot cup, and returned to her seat.

For a good while, she sat there dumbfounded, sipping on her coffee.

Finally she stood and found the TV remote. She turned it to the news channel. As luck would have it, the first thing she saw was Danah Polero reporting the shooting at the Lake Mead Marina, and how NSA agents had taken the bodies away giving no explanations.

The screen showed footage of the yacht and the choppers she and the others had been on, off in the distance. Danah had been in one of the news choppers at that time, and it showed her mentioning her pilot had been threatened not to follow the other helicopters.

Then Sarah heard what she really didn't want to hear. Danah reported, "There is still no sign of, Sarah Sidwell. Information we received, is she and Officer Kate Brewster were on one of those helicopters you saw flying away. Of course, since her mysterious disappearance, there have been a lot of rumors being reported. We can only hope these fine officers of the law are not in any great danger. We look forward to their return."

"Shit," Sarah uttered aloud, and switched news channels. She heard somewhat the same thing on two other stations. It wasn't anything she didn't already know, so she turned the TV off again.

She took another long sip of her hot coffee, sat it down on the table, and leaned back, closing her eyes with her hands behind her head. It had been a hell of a long night and day. She felt the tiredness in her aching muscles, and before she knew it she was asleep.

She heard someone speaking her name and touching one of her arms that were now by her side on the seat. She raised her head to see a female in scrubs with a bag in her hand.

As she opened her eyes wider showing she was more awake, the woman began, "I'm, Doctor Calley the surgeon treating Mr. Caruso. He is sedated but doing fine. It was a nasty wound, as you well know.

We had to give him several pints of blood while I worked on his shoulder. The bullet didn't hit any bone but severed surrounding muscle tissue and tendons. He will not lose use of his arm, but it will be extremely painful if he tries to use it too soon. The arm will be in a sling for about five weeks. He may be out of that sooner according to how he heals. He will need to contact his normal primary care physician to have him connect with a surgeon. When Mr. Caruso is moved from here, he will not be able to return for treatment."

Knowing what she meant, Sarah only asked, "Can I see him?"

"Yes, he is out of intensive care. They are taking him to room 102. He will be hooked to monitors, IVs, oxygen and that sort of thing, but he should be resting comfortably. I'm afraid he won't know you are there till sometime in the morning. It will take a good while for the sedation to wear off. When he comes to, he might think he is better, but that will just be the effects of the morphine. He'll begin to feel the pain more as they begin the weaning process, and switch him over to some strong but normal pain medication." She handed Sarah the bag, saying, "These are his personal effects minus the clothes, of course. I hope I have attended to all your concerns."

"Yes, Doctor! I appreciate all your information and thank you for taking good care of him."

The surgeon shook her hand, turned, and headed out the door.

Sarah looked for room 102. She noticed an armed guard at each end of the hallway. When she found it, Jack was already in the room hooked to all the equipment. She rushed to his side looking down at him putting her hand on his arm.

She softly spoke, "I'm right here, Jack. You are doing fine. They say you'll be good as new in no time." She knew he probably couldn't hear her, but it made her feel better saying the words, just in case.

For awhile she stood watching him, as she touched his face and arm tenderly. Finally her legs began to tire, and she sat in the cushioned chair near the window. She sat the bag with his belongings on the floor beside her.

A nurse came through the door to take his vital signs and check his IV and monitors, "Is there anything I can get for you, Miss Sidwell?"

"Not right now, but thank you." At first it surprised Sarah that the nurse knew her name and knew she wasn't Jack's wife. Just as quickly, she remembered this was a government basically secret facility, and they had to know everyone coming and going.

Before leaving the nurse added, "There is a nurse's station on the left down the hall. Across from that you will see our amenities, coffee, and that kind of things. You may help yourself at your convenience, or if you prefer, any nurse assigned to this room can bring you any of the items. In a couple of hours a nurse will come around to take patient's meal selections. They know you are here and will be in to get yours. We are not overrun with patients at the present, and we find the food excellent. It's not what you might receive in some other facility."

"Thank you. I'll check out the coffee station for sure, and I'll be here in the room when the nurse comes with the selection sheet."

The nurse smiled, nodded and left the room.

She sat for a time thinking over all that had transpired.

Occasionally, she'd stand at his bedside, watch and touch him again.

Back in the chair she felt her eyes grow heavy, and she jerked back into consciousness. She wasn't ready to fall asleep. Coffee was what she needed. She went to find some.

When she returned with the brew, the food nurse entered the room from the other direction. She handed Sarah the selection list and a small pencil. "Miss Sidwell, I will pick up your food order on my return route. Is there anything I can bring you when I return?"

Holding her coffee up Sarah answered, "I have everything I need right now, and by the way it is good coffee," as she accepted the paper.

"I think you'll find the meals enjoyable. The food is pretty good here. I guess it's our tax dollars at work." The nurse soon departed.

Sarah glanced down at the list and muttered, "Damn, this will be like ordering at a restaurant." She sat down in the chair and placed her coffee on the stand. She went over the list and made her selection. She noticed her full name, date of birth, social security number, detective badge number, and a short description, typed at the top of the page. She realized everything about her was probably known, and figured she was being watched right now. She glanced upward with her eyes scanning the room. She saw the small dark glass bubble and knew the camera was behind it. She grinned a little and looked back at the list. Finally she laid it aside and went to stand beside Jack again.

She'd look at him and then to his monitors making sure there were no changes in what she'd already seen appearing on those screens.

When she returned to her seat, her holster touched the armrest, and she adjusted it out of the way.

She wondered if Jack's holster and weapon were in the bag. She realized she hadn't even noticed if the hospital bag was heavy or not. She reached down, removed things from inside, and took mental inventory.

Not only was his service weapon and holster in the bag, his spare Glock was also inside and several clips. His wallet and flip leather ID was there. She saw his small pocketknife; nail clippers and change lying loosely in the bottom of the bag, and a folded piece of paper. She picked up the paper, and unfolded it.

It was a sheet off of a pad from a hotel room. She saw it was a note for Jack, and her eyes went to the bottom to see who wrote the words. She didn't recognize the name, Lillian, and her eyes went back to the top of the page. There was a date written small in the top right hand corner.

She slowly started to read. As she continued, her eyes began tearing, and she felt pain and tightness in her chest. By the time she folded the note and dropped it into the bag, she had to pull tissues out of the box on the table. Tears streamed down her face.

She realized by the date, it was several days after she'd started screwing up and went off the grid. She felt it was all her fault. Jack would have never been with another woman if things had been different. Sarah couldn't stop the tears. They kept coming and coming. "God, what have I done?"

Through tear filled eyes, she looked toward Jack and wondered if there was any chance to save their relationship.

She rose and went to his bedside. Holding his hand in hers, "Jack, I'm sorry for everything I've done. Please don't stop loving me. Please give me another chance to make things right between us." She didn't know if he could hear her or not, but she wanted to try.

Two men in suits entering the room interrupted her words and thoughts. Her instincts told her they weren't doctors. As she used the tissue, she felt her tears subside.

One spoke calmly introducing, "I'm Lieutenant Thomas, CIA, and this is Lieutenant Perkins with NSA. First of all, I'd like to say we are glad your partner will make a full recovery. Secondly, I need to ask you a few questions. The timing may seem inappropriate, but I'm afraid it is a must. You may feel the need to not answer our questions and that certainly is your prerogative. However, it would probably be in your best interest to answer the questions as honestly as possible."

With a wad of tissues wiping her nose, she asked, "What are your questions?

He continued, "I don't think I have to tell you that the subject, Mark Wakefield, is special, for a lack of a better word. We know some things about him but we need to know much more. I assure you it is a matter of national security. During your time in his presence, did he disclose information of what he experienced at the facility where he was held?"

With tears dry now, she answered, "Yes! He related how he and other male and females were held in captivity since they were very young." She felt she might as well tell them everything. "He disclosed how they were given injections, possibly with alien DNA. They were given specific food groups and almost daily, learned information from screens. They were taught to use all types of weapons, and the use of martial arts for self-defense. They were also taught to use their mind to do several things. I'm sure you already know he was able to heat the weapon of the shooter at our station and make him drop it. We've already seen how he can use his mind to throw people around. I've personally seen bullet holes on his body heal themselves. I'm talking about wounds that should have taken months to fully heal."

She was interrupted by the NSA guy removing his phone from his jacket, saying, "Excuse me I have to place a call and he left the room."

Sarah continued, "Mark had an alien tracking device in his leg, but we removed it. Charley said he and Mark placed it in the back of an open rock truck bed as it passed under an overpass."

Now the CIA man interrupted, "That explains the reported UFO sighting at a road improvement location, which scared hell out of all the men working that night. Please continue."

"There's not much more to tell. I'm sure you already know about the attack at Charley's cabin and the men we left dead on the floor. I hope they weren't yours, or your friend's who just left the room."

"No! They were not ours. Let's just say they were receiving orders from a rogue group."

Sarah knew he was referring to the Majestic group, but to disclose her knowledge of that, she would have implicated the information came from Charley.

She continued, "After the attack, we stayed on the lam, and through Kate, we made our way to the yacht on Lake Mead. You know the rest of the story."

He began again, "Speaking of the cabin. The evidence collected by CSI indicated you and our subject engaged in sex."

A little angrily she admitted, "Yeah, I screwed him. I screwed up a lot of things lately."

"I wanted to tell you personally, before you are allowed to leave this facility, you will be given some specific examinations on your female organs. I wanted you to be aware of the situation, before you were subjected to the procedures. I assure you will not be harmed in any way."

Sternly, she spoke, "If you are wondering if I'm going to get pregnant and have a half-alien baby, I'm afraid you are barking up the wrong tree. Unfortunately, I can't have children even if I wanted to."

"We know your situation, but we still have to run the test."

"And if I refuse?" Sarah questioned.

"I'm afraid you will have no choice in that matter, Miss Sidwell. For now, just enjoy your time with your partner. It helps a patient recover sooner, when someone special is near them. I know from experience. We'll leave you two alone for now."

She could care less what they did to her, but she wondered what they were going to do with her partner, "What about, Jack? What are you going to do with him when he is better?"

He smiled, "I assure you we will do nothing detrimental to Mr. Caruso. When he is able to return to work, he will be allowed to with our encouragement. People like him are always in need in the world of law enforcement."

Before she could speak again, he informed, "I'm sure you are wondering about yourself. We are dealing with that situation, and working on getting the results of your recent actions straightened out with the proper authorities. You made it very difficult, of course, but I think things will be resolved in the end. I assure you, it is the desire of both NSA and our agency for you and your partner to be back on the job."

He stuck out his hand for her to shake, "You won't be seeing me again, Miss Sidwell. It has been a pleasure meeting you."

Without further speech, she shook his hand and watched him leave the room.

She wondered what kind of tests they'd be giving her. She also hoped she could believe the man about getting her back on the job. It would be one hell of a blessing if that took place.

She went to Jack's bed and held his hand again, but wasn't speaking.

The nurse came in to check on Jack and informed, "We can arrange for you to sleep in an adjacent room, or we can have a smaller bed brought into this room if you prefer. The couch over there makes into a makeshift bed, but it isn't very comfortable."

"I'm ok for now, but I will probably take a shower later in this room. Would it be possible for you to bring in some kind of hospital gown for me to wear after my shower?"

"I could, but I imagine you would prefer your own clothes. I'm informed two female agents are at your home collecting clothes and other items for your comfort. They'll be arriving before bedtime."

She wanted to say, "I wonder what else they are looking for in my house. These guys have no boundary." However, she knew the nurse had nothing to do with it, and just said, "Thank you. That will be nice."

As the nurse left, Sarah sat back down in her chair. She looked down at the hospital bag. She wanted to take the note and tear it into a million pieces, but she left it alone. In a whisper to herself, but directed toward Lillian, "You might have had a one night fling, but when I get the chance I'll make him forget all about you."

(Back on the other helicopter that left Lake Mead)

The transport chopper with Charley, Kate, Mark and armed soldiers was headed straight for a location to meet up with General Gilliam.

Kate kept her arm around Charley's waist, as she observed the stern blank faces on the armed men around her. She hadn't protested when they shackled Mark to one side of the helicopter with armed men all around him. She saw the futile look on Mark's face, as he sat quietly saying nothing. As a matter of fact, she saw no one was uttering a word. She knew they'd been given previous instructions and were following them to the letter.

Charley had his arm around her shoulder. Even he had only uttered a few words, when he told her, "Everything will be alright, Kate. I promise."

She could only hope he was able to make that come true.

Chapter Eighteen

With the two brothers now in their custody, the military sped up operations in the area pointed out by the two men. Just in case they weren't telling the truth about the entrance location, the military was strung out everywhere.

Tanks, APCs, jeeps with 50 caliber and 30 caliber machine guns, saturated the area like ants on an anthill. Helicopters were so thick in the air, collisions looked almost imminent.

Air Force and Navy jets flew low and continuously. Stealth fighter-bombers sat on tarmacs at nearby bases, armed to the teeth and waiting.

Big guns, with calibers like 175s and 105s were mobile and approached the target point.

There were more military personnel of all kinds in the area, than there were people in Reno Nevada. They were well armed, and ready for anything.

General Gilliam was at a command post in the rear, and barking orders to the different squad leaders, until he felt they were all in place. Then he gave the order for everyone to hold position.

His purpose was to let three Special Forces units try to make it through the entrances, and radio back to him. Those three units were on the move.

What the units found, and what kind of resistance they encountered, would determine Gilliam's next move. In the meantime the general deployed every available type of military force to back them up. They were in position and waiting for the next order.

The general got a personal three-way call. The head of NSA and the head of the CIA had some pertinent information concerning his attack on the facility. He was informed that the male escapee from the alien compound was in custody, and a scheduled extraction had been arranged. It was almost certain this subject could give the general insight as to the interior of the facility, and what his soldiers might encounter. It was suggested the general hold off his attack until the escapee could be brought directly to Gilliam for questioning.

Anxious to get the show on the road, he wasn't happy about putting all his troops in a holding position, including the Special Forces. Realizing it might save lives, he agreed, and immediately had his aide contact the Special Forces squads on the ground to continue a holding pattern and wait for his orders.

Hours seemed to pass; but finally and aide came to him reporting, "Sir, the subject is being delivered. They will land at our makeshift heliport in 15 minutes."

The general nodded and returned his salute, "Bout damn time."

When the Medivac and gunship landed, the general and other soldiers were waiting.

Kate and Charley watched the soldiers preparing Mark for debarking. He was in handcuffs and leg chains like a convicted prisoner.

Mark saw the hurt look in Kate's eyes, and he spoke, "It's ok. I'll be all right. I understand. I appreciate everything you did for me."

She and Charley could only nod, as they ushered him off the helicopter. They sat for a good amount of time quietly, when Kate finally asked, "Charley, what are we supposed to do?"

"Nothing, Kate, until they tell us what to do. Just be patient. I know that isn't one of your virtues, but try harder this time," as he wrapped an arm around her shoulders.

Two soldiers came to the door motioning for them to exit the helicopter. One said, "Agent Decker, we are to transport you and your companion to another location where some of your own will be waiting."

He nodded, as he and Kate climbed out of the helicopter.

The soldier led him to another regular army helicopter and soon they were in the air again.

Charley knew by the terrain and direction they were headed, it was toward Reno, Nevada.

To calm any concerns Kate might have, he grinned stating, "I should have taken more money out of my safe. It looks like we are heading for Reno."

She smiled a little, "I've got a brand new activated credit card."

This time he managed to laugh.

Kate asked, "Why Reno?"

"Not sure," he replied, "But I know we have a couple of offices there. Let's just enjoy the scenery from up here along the way."

Kate was obedient and remained silent the rest of the way, as her eyes took in the beauty on the ground.

They landed at a small army post on the outskirts of Reno. They were met by one CIA agent, and saw his vehicle.

The agent stuck out his hand as the army chopper rose in the air, "Decker, nice to see you again. I see you are in the company of a very pretty lady" as he shook her hand.

Charley spoke, "Preston, glad to see it was someone I knew. What do they have in store for us?"

Preston said, "Let's get to the vehicle. It's noisy and hot as hell out here." Soon they were enjoying the AC and headed out the gate of the army facility. Charley and Kate were in the back seat.

Now Preston continued, "In answer to your question, there aren't any plans for you two at the moment, while the big wigs spin their wheels and do their thing. You know what I mean. I've got you accommodations at a casino hotel, not under your names, of course." He reached over the seat handing Charley the little colored envelope with the room keys. "I wrote the number of your room backward on the edge of the envelope."

Charley accepted the room keys, but saw him reach back over the seat with a valet ticket. "Here is the valet slip for a red SUV under the name of Nicholson. By the way, your room is under the same name. You two are Mr. and Mrs. Nicholson, and you are booked at the hotel for a week. Clothes from your cabin and from Kate's home are already in the room; even bathing suits and amenities." Being facetious, he grinned, "Your mission, Mr. Decker, should you accept, is to lay low, gamble, swim, and have fun until you are contacted."

"Cute, Preston, are you checked in also?"

"I wish, Charley. I sure need a vacation. When I drop you off, I have a plane to catch. I've got a little something to do out of country."

"Too, bad," Charley smiled, "It would have been nice to have some drinks and catch up on what's been happening."

"Yeah, it would." Looking in the rear-view mirror at Kate, he grinned, "I'm sure you will have an enjoyable time without me."

They arrived and said goodbye to Charley's friend. They found the elevator and located the room. Several changes of clothes for both were in the closet. Two suitcases sat on luggage stands along one wall.

Kate inspected the suitcases while Charley looked into the small fridge, "Well, they could have put some booze and mix in here."

She grinned, "I'm sure there is plenty down stairs." She made her way to the bathroom and saw a lot of her toiletries, Charley's razor and his things. "It looks like they thought of everything," as she came back out of the bathroom.

"Not a bad view either," as he stood looking out the curtains.

When she passed the dresser, she saw a card in an envelope. She opened it and found a Master Card with the name Charles Nicholson, along with a driver's license with the same name. A note with the card simply said, "Have fun. You earned it." By the time she finished reading, "Charley was looking over her shoulder. She handed the credit card to him. He said grinning, "Time to shower, change clothes and go do some gambling."

"I'm hungry," she smiled.

"Ok! We'll go eat and then do some gambling." He wrapped his arms around her, and pulled her to his chest. Her arms went around his neck and they locked in embrace, as lips mashed against each other's.

"Thought you were hungry?" He grinned.

"Not that hungry. Let's take a shower and climb in bed for a little before we hit the casino."

"Sounds like a plan to me," and they started shucking clothes. The shower didn't take long and soon they were under the sheets and making love.

Chapter Nineteen

Mark was taken under guard to a room where General Gilliam and his aides were to question him.

"Take those damn shackles off the boy. Hell, he's here to help us," Gilliam ordered, and an MP hastily obeyed.

Looking toward Mark, he said in a softer voice, "Have a seat, son."

Mark also obeyed as he rubbed his wrists.

Gilliam continued, "From what I've learned, you could have easily gotten out of your confinement anytime you desired. That lets me know you are here because you really want to help your friends still being held in that underground facility. What can you tell us we could use to get to them?"

Mark thought for a minute or so, as the other men in the room remained silent. "You already know; or will know the delivery entrance, although, I'm not sure of its location. There are two other entrances, or exits, that I am aware of. One is a flat area high on the side of the mountain where they allowed us to sunbathe. By the rising and setting of the sun, I could tell it was on the west side."

As he spoke, one soldier in the room wrote everything on a tablet.

"The other was a smaller flat area where we target practiced at stationery targets and clay pigeons. I know the targets were taken back inside when we were through, and stored until the next time. That opening was on the northeast side of the mountain."

The general commented, "You are doing good, boy, real good. What about inside?"

"No way to tell east from west inside, of course. We had a lunchroom where we ate, training rooms, sleeping quarters, and some type of medical facility where we were treated for injuries. There was another smaller room with alien equipment that we were hooked to, one at a time, and frequently. While hooked to the machines, blood was drawn automatically. They would never explain anything, of course, but it didn't take a genius, as we grew older, to figure what they were looking for. I'm sure they were checking to see how their experiments on us were developing. We were never allowed in any other rooms; however, we know there had to be some for the aliens where the aliens stayed."

"You getting all this," the general questioned the soldier writing.

"Every word, Sir," he acknowledged.

"What do they look like, son? What are we up against?

Mark began again, "I know first hand they can use their minds to do certain things, like throw people and objects in a specific direction." Mark noticed extra pens on the table by the soldier's pad. As he looked toward one of the pens it rose, flew through the air, and stopped, touching the facial hair on a guard at the door. The guard turned drawing his weapon and pointing it at the pen hovering in the air.

"What are you going to do, shoot the pen? Put your gun away. If he wanted that pen embedded in your head, that's where it would be."

As the soldier complied, holstering his 45 caliber weapon, the pen dropped harmlessly onto the floor.

Mark looked toward and empty chair. It went flying across the room and up against a wall. The noise made two more soldiers enter the room with hands on their weapons.

As the general held up his hand in the stop position, he smiled toward, Mark, "Verbal explanations will be sufficient. Active demonstrations are not necessary. Please continue."

Mark had a little grin, and he continued, "I'm really about to reach the limit of my knowledge of your adversary. I'm sure you already know they can heat objects. In answer to a description of the aliens, most are shorter than me, but a few were as tall. They were thinner, gray-looking skin, head that looked like a cross between human and the alien UFO sightings you are accustomed to seeing."

"You have no idea the things I've seen, son. What else can you tell us about them? Did you see any of their weapons?

"They didn't need weapons to control us, however, when we were escorted out of the mountain into the flat areas; there was always an alien guard on each side of the opening. These guards had both a side arm and rifle looking weapon of alien design. We were never shown or trained on any of those weapons. Therefore, I have no knowledge of their weapons' capabilities."

As Mark hesitated, the general looked toward the writer and waited for him to look up and nod, signifying he had all the information down on paper.

Mark continued, "I became familiar with one of the female aliens. She would never tell me the name of their home planet, but she once admitted it was not in our galaxy. To travel that distance, they must surely possess much knowledge and most certainly great power. With the ability of space travel between galaxies, they had to harness an immense amount of energy. I fear your efforts to free my captive companions will be met with devastating force. Also, I have thought many times, if they weren't just dropped off on this planet, there has to be another opening of sorts, for whatever craft they came in, to come and go."

The general once again glanced toward the writer for a few seconds, until Mark spoke again.

"The aliens didn't eat our type of foods. We never saw them eat anything. That would indicate they have some type of food processor, or their type of food is delivered via an alien craft."

When he stopped talking, the general calmly asked, "You are a pretty bright fellow. Any thing else you can think of?"

"No. That is the extent of my knowledge."

The general nodded at the guards and they approached, as he stated, "I appreciate all your information. Hopefully, we can free your friends. I'm not going to have you shackled, but I want you to go peacefully with these men. Let me be perfectly clear. If you try to escape and any of my men are harmed, I will track you down and kill you myself."

Mark nodded and stood, but suddenly turned to him and asked, "Could I be allowed to fight alongside your men? Those people are my friends, and the only family I have known since I was six years old. I observed the contour and layout of the hilly area, when we were allowed outside in the sunlight. I might be of some help to find those entrances more quickly. Once inside, I might also be of some help."

The general looked deep into Mark's eyes, as he thought for a minute. He turned to the guards saying, "Get him to the Special Forces. Suit him tactical, weapons and all."

He turned to Mark stating, "I'm taking a chance here. You better keep your word. If you can aid my men and women in any way, do so."

Mark nodded, as the general motioned with his head for them to lead him out of the room.

When the door closed, Gilliam turned toward one of the other aides sitting quietly during the whole process. "Notify the S. F. guys. As soon as this fellow is delivered to them, they have a green light."

The aide snapped to attention and saluted, "Immediately, Sir, but I felt compelled to mention the NSA may take objection to your actions. They most definitely would want this man returned to their possession."

The general answered, "I know you are looking after my best interest. That's your job. But you need to know that I don't give a shit about what NSA wants. That boy has been a prisoner all his life and experimented on by aliens. When NSA gets their hands on him, he'll be back in the same predicament, and maybe worse. If he can help our soldiers in that mountainside achieve their goal, then he should be given a chance to do so. I'll deal with NSA. It was my decision and mine alone."

The aide's hand went to the salute position. The general returned the salute, and the aide hurried out of the room.

Gilliam looked at the aide closing his tablet and putting his pens away. "Get all that information to ground control. They need to know what they are up against."

The man also snapped to standing attention and saluted, "Yes, Sir!" and quickly exited.

"The rest of you do what you do best. The hour is at hand."

They stood, saluted and filed out the door, followed by the armed MP.

No one was left in the room now but Gilliam, standing quietly, and staring blankly. Slowly, he turned toward the flag in the corner and said softly, "God, help us." He came to attention and saluted Old Glory." Soon, he was also out the door.

Chapter Twenty

Later in the evening, Sarah slept lightly in the chair. Two of Jack's monitors began beeping. She jumped to her feet and rushed to his side, glancing at the monitors and to him.

A nurse came calmly through the door, "Figured those IVs would be running low about now." She shut off the beeps and began changing the bags.

Sarah felt her heartbeat slowly getting back to normal. She looked down to see Jack's eyes opening.

"Ah! You are coming back to the conscious world."

He didn't answer but glanced around inquisitively.

"You are in a government run medical facility. The surgeon who patched you up assured you are doing fine. Do you understand what I'm saying?"

He nodded a little. With a scratchy voice, he slowly answered, "Yes."

"She wanted to make sure I told you the morphine is taking care of your pain. You may feel better, but you need to keep your wounded shoulder stationary as possible. If you tear something, they'll have to start all over again."

This was not the time to mention she'd read the note. She hoped she'd never have to mention it. It wasn't the time to mention she'd have to be given some test because of her sex with Mark. He didn't need to be reminded of that screw-up.

"You had me pretty worried for awhile. How do you feel?"

With a rasp, he answered, "Tired, groggy."

"That's a good thing. It means the morphine is doing the trick. The Doc assured me you would be back in top form in no time. Well, maybe four weeks or so," as she placed his hand in hers.

He opened and closed his eyes as if he was trying to focus on her face.

"Can you see me?"

"Yeah," He answered, with his voice a little more prominent.

She smiled saying, "If you can see, how many tits do I have?"

"Four," he said forcing a grin, "Big ones."

"Yeah, you're getting better," as she raised his hand placing the back of his palm against her breast. "There are cameras in here or I'd let you play with them."

He turned his hand, so it cupped and squeezed one of her breasts softly.

She didn't move the hand. She just put hers over it saying, "When you get out of here, they are all yours to play with any time you want to."

It was his wounded shoulder and it felt weak, so he slowly released her breast. She lowered the arm to the bed, but kept his hand in hers.

"What about the others?"

"You were mostly out of it, when we got on the transport. The two casino guys are somewhere in this building being treated, but I haven't seen them.

Charley, Kate and Mark were in another transport, heading to some general's location. I haven't heard anything about them."

"What about you?"

"I'm ok. I slept some in the chair over there. I've been keeping an eye on you."

"How long are they going to keep me here?"

"That depends on how well you do, the next few days. Hopefully, you won't cause any complications by moving around too much too soon. I know how hardheaded you are."

"Have you talked anymore with Chandler?"

"I haven't tried using my burn phones in here. I'm almost certain it would set off alarms if I even had a signal, and armed men would come running to haul me off. I'm in no hurry to leave your side, Jack."

"Help me sit up. I hate lying flat on my back."

She adjusted his bed to the propped up position. "Is that better?"

He nodded and inquired, "Did you hear anything about what they are going to do with us?"

"Yeah, NSA and CIA guys were in here earlier. Apparently they still want us out there fighting crime. They are still working on straightening out my screw-ups, of course. These guys seem to have a lot of power. I hope we can both be back on the job together soon. That is, if you still want me as a partner."

"Of course, I still want you as a partner. I wouldn't want to work with anyone else."

Those words brought a beaming smile to her face and a glint of hope in her heart to patch things between them.

She continued, "They said they could set me up in another room or they could bring a rollaway-bed in here for me to sleep in. I figured I'd wait until you woke up and ask which one you wanted me to do."

"I want you in here with me."

Those were sweet words to her ears, as she said, "I was hoping you'd say that."

"You can sleep in this bed with me," he said with a sheepish grin.

"Yeah, right, that's all we need. Have a round of hot sex, tear loose that wound again, and you be in here for months. Just get well and I promise you I'll give you all the hot loving you can handle."

"I'll hold you to that."

She wanted to push any thoughts of this "Lillian" he may have, completely out of his mind, "I'm serious, Jack. I'll make love to you anytime, anywhere, as soon as you get well."

"I can picture me looking like a skinny dried up prune from having so much sex," he giggled.

"That's ok, too. I like dried prunes," she laughed.

A nurse coming through the door interrupted them, "Apparently you are feeling better, Mr. Caruso. I've been waiting for you to fully awake, so I could explain that I have to start reducing the amount of morphine you are receiving. Are you in any pain?"

He answered, "No, just tired and weak."

She reached for the controls on the machine, saying, "Good, then I'll just drop the amount down a tad bit. However, we don't want you in pain, so let us know immediately. Your call button is at your bedside."

He nodded, and she started to leave, but was stopped by Sarah saying, "Jack prefers that small bed be brought in and put next to his, if you don't mind."

"It's already on its way, Miss Sidwell. I've arranged for extra sheets, pillows and blankets to be delivered with it." She turned toward Jack, "Miss Sidwell's food will be arriving soon along with yours. However, yours will be a restricted diet for a few days. So, don't go stealing her food. As you probably have learned, these walls have eyes and ears, so I will know." She grinned as she left the room.

Sarah looked at him, "Guess we'd better watch what we say, too."

"Only if you give a shit about what they hear," he said very sternly.

They were interrupted by two men wheeling in the bed for Sarah. They gently moved Jack's bed closer to the door, and placed hers on the other side of his bed. They hesitated, and asked, "How close to the other bed do you want this one?"

Jack answered for her, "Butt it up against mine. I might want to jump her bones later tonight," with a grin on his face.

A little embarrassed, but not to be outdone, "Yeah, sure. He's so weak and shot up; he probably couldn't even play with himself."

They grinned, but refrained from comment, as they placed the bed next to his and left the room. The bed was completely made, and just as the nurse mentioned, there were extra sheets, blankets and another pillow. There were also several extra towels and washrags.

No sooner than the male attendants were out the door, a female came through the door with a suitcase in her hand. Another woman carried clothes on hangers.

Sarah surmised these were the two agents the nurse had mentioned earlier.

"We brought you every thing we figured you might need. I'm sure it will be enough to get you by until you are back home again."

"Thanks, I really appreciate it."

They hung the clothes in the closet and sat the suitcase on the floor, "If there is anything else you really need from your home, please tell one of your nurses. They will make sure we are contacted."

"I'm sure it will be plenty, thanks again."

They both smiled and left the room.

Jack said, "Looks like you are moving in."

"Sounds like a good idea to me," she answered, grinning back at him. She opened the suitcase to see what they'd crammed into it. Satisfied they had indeed brought every thing she would need, she removed pajamas. Holding them in the air, she said, "I'm going to take a much needed shower and get comfy. If you need me, just holler."

"I'll wait till I think you are completely naked, and then I'll holler for you."

"Unless you want whoever is watching to see me naked, I wouldn't advise that."

"Ok! Maybe I'll wait till we get out of here."

"You can have me naked any time you want then."

"Oh! This is coming from the woman who always wanted us to be hidden somewhere."

"This is coming from the woman who has changed a lot these last few days. This is coming from the woman who wants you in her bed anytime she can get you there." She looked up at the camera saying, "I'll bet that made your ears perk up. If you have a camera in the shower, you are fixing to get an eye full." She smiled at Jack, taking a towel, washcloth, and her PJs with her to the shower, and closed the door.

Jack had been forcing himself to stay awake to talk to her. He felt tired and sleepy. He heard the shower water running, as he closed his eyes and drifted to sleep.

Sometime later, Sarah, in her nighttime attire, was waking him, "Sleepy head, your food is here."

He opened his eyes and adjusted his body, as she swung the tray over in front of him. She removed the lids off everything, as he picked up a fork with the hand the IV was in. It was awkward for him to try to eat.

"Oh! That isn't going to work and I don't want you using the other arm, so guess what, Mr. Macho, I get to feed you."

He didn't object, but frowned, as she put a spoonful of food to his mouth.

Seeing her tray by her chair, he swallowed saying, "Your food is going to get cold. You can feed me after you eat."

"It will be fine, my dear. It will stay warm enough in the containers. Anyway, this is something new for me. I've never fed a man before. I'm glad you are the first," as another spoonful came his way.

He was hungry but felt full fairly quickly. Soon he only wanted the tea to sip on.

She sat down, uncovered her food, and began to eat.

"What did they bring you," he inquired.

"I don't think you want to know. I'd hate to torture you. This looks delicious. Besides, you couldn't have any. The nurse already said she'd know, because these walls have eyes and ears."

"Ok, Greedy. I'm ready to go back to sleep, anyway."

With those words, she laid her tray aside and hurried to the side of his bed, "Not until I get a goodnight kiss, you aren't."

He grinned, as her soft lips met his, and they kissed tenderly.

"Now you can get some sleep," as she looked over her shoulder on the way back to her food.

He closed his eyes and went into dreamland.

When he opened his eyes, he saw her asleep next to him holding his hand. He was still in the propped up position, and was looking down at her peacefully sleeping. Thoughts started trying to enter his mind, but he didn't want to think. He just wanted to lie there and watch her, knowing she was right there by him. He felt the urge to relieve himself and get to the bathroom. He looked at the monitors and IV bags. They were all on one movable table on legs. He removed his hand from hers and was trying to try to get out of bed.

She immediately rose up in bed. Realizing where she was, she asked, "What are you doing?"

"I need to go pee."

She jumped out of bed and rushed around to the other side of his bed. She scrutinized the monitor station and located the locks on the wheels. She helped him out of bed and to the bathroom. The IV and monitor cords attached to him were purposely long enough for the occasion, with the whole station moved closer, but the door had to stay open.

When she began to hear him urinate, she also heard him say, "I'm kind of weak. You want to come hold it for me?"

She was just as quick with her comeback, "Don't tempt me. Remember the cameras." She heard him stifle a laugh, and she couldn't help but smile, too.

When he finished, she helped him back into his bed, and locked the wheels of the IV table.

"Well, that went pretty well, don't you think?"

"Yeah, we always did make a good team."

She felt her face getting warm, as she beamed with pride at his words. He could always make her feel special. She had to change the subject, because her thoughts were beating her up again, over what she'd done to destroy their relationship.

"Can I get you anything? Are you thirsty or hungry?"

"Not right now. I am feeling a little pain in my shoulder."

The nurse came in twice while you slept and lowered the amount of morphine. I'll push the call button and have her come increase it a little."

"No, I want to get off that crap as soon as I can. If the pain gets too bad I'll let you know. Did you get any sleep?"

"I slept like a baby, knowing I was lying next to you and holding your hand."

There wasn't a clock in sight. He realized his watch wasn't on his arm and asked, "What time is it? Looks like they took my time piece."

Looking at hers she answered, "It is 8:30 a.m. Your watch and all your belongings are in that hospital bag over by my chair. Do you want me to get it for you? She hoped he wouldn't want the whole bag. He'd see the note and maybe read it again. She wished she had torn it up and discarded it in a trashcan.

"Nah! I don't need it as long as you've got yours."

Relieved from her thoughts, she said, "I imagine they'll come around for our breakfast order, or at least mine," as she grinned.

"Rub it in will you. Even what they had for me tasted pretty good. If I ever get shot again, see if you can get me in here."

"Yeah, sure, I'll just give them a call, and they'll come running to haul you off to this government facility that probably nobody out there knows about. Besides, I don't want you getting shot again."

"Hmmm, you have a point there." His words made her frown disappear.

More seriously, he told her, "We need to contact, Captain Chandler."

"I'll check with the nurse as to what the rules are in here for outside phone calls. One should be coming around soon. I'm not sure if I can make the call, or what we'll be allowed to convey to him. We sure can't tell him where this place is, or when we'll be allowed to leave."

"That's not important. What is important is we keep him in the loop and let him know we are still alive."

"I'll take care of it if I can. Now don't get your panties in a wad, Jack."

Realizing she was correct and he was getting too serious, he changed his tune. "These drugs are making me loopy. Did we have sex last night?"

"Twice," she answered smiling, "And it was so good. It put you right to sleep."

"Hmmm, I've got to make sure I stay awake, next time.

A voice on the room intercom interrupted their playful comments. "Miss Sidwell, could you come to the nurse station at your convenience?"

"Yes. I'll be there shortly." She pulled her housecoat out of her suitcase and slipped it over her PJs. "Don't you go anywhere, Jack. I'll be back in a little bit." She gave him a quick kiss and headed for the door.

He frowned, "I'm not going anywhere."

When she got to the nurse station, one was waiting for her. "Miss Sidwell it is time for those tests you were told about."

"I'm ready for your tests, but can we just change the Sidwell stuff to just Sarah?"

"Sure, we can do that. Please follow me."

Soon she was in an x-ray room, and then naked on a table, as female doctors examined her and the x-rays. A nurse drew vials of blood, put a band-aid on the needle location, and hurried off with the vials.

Afterward, she was allowed to dress and sit in a waiting room. It didn't seem too awfully long before the nurse reappeared, saying, "Got to get another small blood sample. A clumsy tech dropped one of the vials. I'm sorry for the inconvenience," and she started prepping Sarah's arm.

Sarah didn't complain. She just halfway smiled saying, "Happens sometimes, I guess." Then she was left alone in the room, to sit and ponder on things taking place. It was good to be around Jack again, and things seemed to be working out. She felt she had a good chance to make things right with him. It seemed forever, before one of the female doctors returned with a chart in her hand.

She looked Sarah in the eye and said, "You have what I'd like to say is an increased level of HCG."

Nervously, Sarah asked, "What is HCG?"

She answered, "Human Chorionic Gonadotropin; a hormone made by the placenta."

"What does all that mean?"

"First of all, I said I'd like to say it was increased HCG, which would indicate you are pregnant."

Sarah interrupted, "That's impossible. I can't get pregnant. What do you mean you would like to say it is increased HCG?"

"The test indicates you are in the early beginning of pregnancy, however it is not indicating HCG, but what we can only classify as UCG. We've had to name it Unknown CG. It appears you are in the beginning pregnancy of a child that will be born not totally human."

Devastated, but knowing it had to come from Mark, she still protested, "This can't be possible. I only had sex one time with the only person this could have happened with. That was almost a week ago. I can't be showing signs of pregnancy this soon. Your test must be inaccurate."

"Sarah, we ran the test three times and they were all the same. You are pregnant with his offspring. What you do from this point on will be totally up to you, and the government individuals who run this facility. I wish I could have given you better news. You will be taken back to your room shortly." The doctor left her alone and Sarah sat there in shock.

She kept telling herself this can't be happening. Now she was in a room with Jack, trying to patch their relationship, and pregnant with a part alien child in less than a week. The thoughts running through her head were mind-boggling.

The nurse came in to escort her back to the room, but Sarah broke down bawling. The nurse sat down on the bench beside her, put her arm around her shoulder, and let Sarah cry. When the tears finally began to subside, the nurse helped her to her feet, and said, "We'll take the long way back and give you time to compose."

Sarah wiped the tears almost continuously, as they walked. Even when she was at the door, she was still wiping final tears. She entered the room and thanked God that Jack was asleep.

She sat in the chair looking his way. She didn't want to go to his side and wake him. She didn't want him to see she had been crying and start asking questions.

She definitely wasn't going to have this baby. She'd get an abortion as soon as possible, but how could she possibly keep the information from Jack? Things were going so good with him in here, and now this new twist.

Darker thoughts entered her mind. What if these government assholes wanted to have this freak baby so they could study it? Shit, that wasn't going to happen, no matter what she had to do. She wasn't going to give birth to a part human part alien. She convinced herself to take her life, if they tried to make her go through the pregnancy and birth.

She heard Jack groan, wiped her tears, and rushed into the bathroom. She stood looking at the mirror, and the tears came again, as she muffled her sobs. It took her a good amount of time to straighten herself and come out of the room.

Jack saw her and said, "I didn't know you were back. I guess I fell asleep again." He noticed she looked as she'd been crying, "What happened? Are you ok?"

The lie flowed from her lips, "I tripped in the hall and hurt my ankle. It was painful and brought tears, but the pain is going away."

"I'll push the call button and get someone in here to take you to have it looked at."

She grabbed his arm, "No, really, it's feeling better already. I'll be all right. I'll ask the nurse for some Ibuprofen. That should take care of it. If it starts to swell, I'll have it examined." How quickly one lie leads to another, she became well aware of.

As she held his hand and looked into his eyes, she felt everything she'd hoped for these last few 24 hours starting to slip away. She pictured him hating her, and not wanting to have anything to do with her, when he found out the truth. She was torn between wanting to stay there with him and running away. She knew she couldn't get out of the facility. Her brain felt like it would explode. She knew she'd be losing it soon and the tears would flow.

"You know what, Jack? The pain is starting to return. I'll go down to the nurse station and see if they can arrange for someone to look at it."

"Now you are talking some sense. Get them to check you out before it starts swelling and gets worse."

She bent down and kissed his lips slow and longing. When their lips parted, she faked a limp toward the door, and forced a smile over her shoulder.

Outside the door, she placed her hand over her mouth, as her back fell against the wall.

A nurse came down the hall, led her to another room, and let her sit down in a chair.

Through tears Sarah said, "I can't go back in there. I can't face him anymore. You've got to contact whoever you need to terminate this pregnancy. I'm not going to have this freak. I'll kill myself first."

"Stay here till I return, Sarah."

When she returned, the surgeon and a man in a suit accompanied her.

The surgeon introduced the gentleman as a CIA agent.

Sarah looked him in the eye saying, "You are not going to make me have this baby. I won't be a guinea pig so you can study a half alien-baby."

"Calm down, Sarah. No matter what you may have heard, we are not monsters. We can understand how you feel. Yes, scientist would love to study a child born part alien, but we are not in the business of supplying samples for study. If you want to terminate the pregnancy, we will arrange it. The scientist can study your blood samples and DNA from the termination. They'll have to be happy with that."

The surgeon butted in, "You are past the point of the morning after pill working. Tests show your female organs are changing rapidly. If termination is your choice, then it must be done soon, and I mean real soon. Also, I have to be honest. Even after the termination, you'll have to remain in confinement, for the period of time it takes for all indications to show you are clear of any effects of the semen that caused you to get pregnant. It will entail many tests, over a long period of time."

"I don't care. Terminate it. Get it out of me and over with. Start it now if you can. I can't go back in that room and face, Jack. Not right now." The tears began to flow again.

The surgeon nodded to the nurse who had just walked in, and she placed an arm around Sarah's shoulder, "We'll set you up in another room and began the procedures tonight. We'll have all your things transferred from, Mr. Caruso's room, and brought to yours." She led her out and down the hall.

"He must not know. Please don't let him know."

"Sarah, we'll tell him we had to operate on the ankle, and move you to another room, so that you could be monitored. That should suffice for a couple of days, but then we'll have to come up with some other excuse for him not to see you."

As they entered a room empty of patients, she asked Sarah to wait there, while they arranged to bring her belongings. It would be her room during her stay at the facility.

When the nurse left, Sarah began crying again.

Chapter Twenty-One

While Sarah battled her situation, General Gilliam began his. Mark was delivered to the Special Forces, and they'd been given the green light. There was one contingent of SF on the ground near the delivery entrance. There were two more in helicopters. Mark was in one. As they circled around the mountainside, he pinpointed the opening where they target practiced. Close inspection by the chopper proved his location was correct. They saw pieces of clay pigeons scattered down the mountainside. The other helicopter remained hovering near that section. Mark led the chopper he was in to the other flat area where they were allowed to sunbathe, and pointed to the concealed opening.

With all three entrances now located, it was time to act. A short radio call back to Gilliam with this new information, and they heard, "SF One, two and three, Code Green."

The pilot didn't wait to hear anything else. He guided the helicopter to the flat area, and they saw the other pilot doing the same with his. When he landed, the men jumped out speedily and surrounded the rock colored door in a half circle. A demolition man placed a charge on the door.

Mark was armed and in tactical attire exactly like the others.

The demolition soldier took several steps to one side.

The team leader received word the other teams were ready. He spoke into his mouthpiece, "Three, two, one, go."

The soldier at the door ducked his head and set off the charge. The mountainside seemed to shake as it blew a hole in the opening.

Almost simultaneously, they heard the other blast, and the ground under them shook again.

The leader gave the advance signal and men rushed through the opening. Immediately they met resistance from the aliens. The weird part was they were using normal military pistols and rifles.

His men suffered casualties and the rest shifted to heavier artillery. They began using grenade launchers and throwing hand grenades, as they continued advancing. They put extra bullets in the creatures that didn't seem to want to die.

Inside the mountain, when they weren't firing, they heard their counterparts' weapons discharging in other areas. They were also meeting heavy resistance.

With more of his men wounded, the team leader radioed for back up. The team leader at the other entrance also needed more men, and radioed for help.

Mark was hit in his left leg, but continued the charge with his team. He fired at targets left and right. He used his mind to throw other aliens against the tunnel walls, who were getting the best of some of the other soldiers. It gave them time to regroup and kill those aliens.

The team that entered the target shooting entrance had worked their way through aliens into a large opening, and continued to battle the enemy amongst strange looking equipment. That team was losing more men fast; the aliens had stronger weapons. Laser type rays hit around and in the soldiers. The rays were either going through them, or taking chunks out of their bodies where they hit. That team leader radioed the information to the other team leaders, and learned they were experiencing the same.

The SF going in at the delivery entrance suffered heavy casualties. Only the first few guards had military weapons, the others used alien technology. The team leader and his men were thrown, flying through the air, from just an alien's thoughts. Yet, they returned fire from whatever position they landed, after bouncing off a cave wall, or skidding across the floor. They noticed the alien's eyes got bright red each time before they did the tossing trick. The team leader ordered his men, "Fire at the head. Concentrate firing at the aliens' head."

His men followed orders, and more aliens fell, mortally wounded.

The team leader with Mark heard the other team leader's order, and instructed his men to also fire at the head of the aliens. Mark and the others chose head targets.

Suddenly, Mark was hit in the left upper arm with laser fire. A chunk of skin flew out to the side causing him to drop his rifle, and grab his arm with his free hand. An alien closed in for the kill, but the team leader put three bullets in the gray's head.

As the gray dropped his weapon when falling, the team leader ordered, "Their weapons. Get their weapons and use them." He grabbed the weapon off the floor. He'd gotten glimpses of the aliens when they were firing. He soon found the trigger mechanism and fired the laser, killing another alien. An SF out of ammunition for his rifle picked up that alien's weapon. He soon adapted to the weapon and killed a few more of the enemy.

Other soldiers stowed their weapons and picked up alien rifles. Soon the tides ebbed, and the battle was on a more even basis.

It got even better when regular army men came running in behind the SF to join the fight. More grenade launchers were fired, and more grenades were thrown. One monster of a guy held a 50 caliber machine gun, and shell casings ejected, as he advanced forward. His bullets went straight through the aliens. He yelled over the noise, "Eat this you ugly bastards."

With the fight more in their favor, the soldiers pushed on. A medic quickly bandaged Mark and gave him morphine shots. Mark nodded and pushed him aside. He moved a soldier off the top of an alien, and used the alien's laser rifle. He limped hurriedly to catch up with the others.

When the advancement came to a sealed door, an explosive charge blew a big hole in it. The team leader and the soldiers went through the opening. A soldier beside the team leader had laser fire go straight through his chest, as he slowly collapsed to the floor. A soldier on the other side of the team leader returned the favor, and blasted a hole through the alien with one of their own weapons.

Mark saw this was their lunch room, but there were aliens everywhere with weapons. He couldn't help from saying aloud, "Where did all these bastards come from?" He blasted a hole in one.

The team leader had a chunk blown out of his leg, and fell to the floor. Mark and another soldier put holes through that alien, and nodded to each other. The soldier hollered for the medic, who came running.

The aliens retreated through a doorway. The door came down and closed.

As the medic wrapped bandages around the team leader's leg and gave him morphine, he still gave orders, "Get a charge on that door. We've got to get in there."

In no time, the door was destroyed. Mark and the soldiers busted through. Mark immediately hollered, "Hold your fire. Hold your fire."

The soldiers fanned out left and right in what Mark knew was the original sleeping quarters. It was a large room with a tall ceiling with beds jutting out from the walls.

Everybody's weapons were trained on four aliens, who had their weapons pointed toward the men and women Mark had left behind. The women were behind the men. Even with the visor down on his tactical helmet, he saw her. It was, Kathy. After he escaped they must have brought her back to the others. With his weapon lowered, Mark stepped in front of the others, and approached, "It's over. Drop your weapons. It is futile to continue. They will die. You will die. What purpose will you have achieved?"

He recognized a man about his age. They'd trained together, often. Mark raised his visor and stared into the man's eyes. He saw the friend had a folded piece of paper in his shirt pocket. Mark concentrated on the paper, and it lifted. The fellow looked down, saw the paper come out of his pocket, and watched, as Mark made the paper lower to the floor. Still looking at the man, he nodded his head slowly twice.

One of the aliens glanced toward Mark's friend and saw the paper settling on the floor. He realized Mark had given the man a signal, just as the fellow called out to the others, "Hit the floor."

As they followed his order, the alien swung his weapon around at Mark. He and Mark fired simultaneously at each other. The alien got a hole through his chest. Mark got a hole through his left side big enough to see through, as he collapsed.

The other three aliens turned and fired, but they were outnumbered by the soldiers using confiscated weapons, and the aliens met their maker.

The soldiers hollered for the medic and he came running to Mark's aide. As some soldiers made sure the aliens were dead, others stood looking down at the medic and Mark. They watched Mark take his last breath, as the medic looked up, shaking his head.

The men and women rose from the floor, as soldiers rushed to help them.

Nervously, the medic jumped back, saying, "What the hell?

They noticed tentacles, coming out of Mark's wound. It appeared they were trying to pull the wound together. He seemed to be growing new tissue in the wound.

Mark's eyes opened and his head turned toward his old friends. His left hand went out, palm up, and he weakly called out, "Kathy!"

The very pregnant woman stepped from behind the men, hearing her name from a familiar voice, "Mark?" She saw the hand out, and now saw his face. "Mark!" She started toward him.

Two soldiers only wanting to keep her from seeing the terrible wound stepped in front of her, with their hands in the stop signal. They were thrown through the air and across the floor in different directions, as Kathy passed between them.

She dropped to her knees at Mark's side and put his hand in hers.

His pain was evident in his face, as he looked up at her and forced a smile. "Kathy, I know what love is."

"Mark, I've always known, and I always loved you." She bent down and whispered something in his ear. She saw a smile on his face.

A sharp pain made Mark jerk and gasp. His eyes started to roll back in his head, but she brought him back, "Mark, hold on. Let the healing mechanics in your body take over."

Mark opened his eyes slowly, looked at her, and said weakly, "I love you." His head went backward and his eyes glowed bright red. The redness faded and his eyes closed for the last time.

Kathy fell on his chest, crying.

The soldiers brought the others forward. As they led them past Mark's lifeless body, they each looked one more time at their friend. He had escaped and brought help to rescue them. As the soldiers escorted them out to safety, they kept trying to look back for one more glimpse of Mark and Kathy.

The team leader limped up beside his men. Looking down, he ordered, "Take her out of here to safety. Get a stretcher in here. Get him out of here.

Get our other people out of here. This battle is over."

Noise from two sides of the room, made him and the other soldiers swing their weapons around. Some dropped to their knees in firing position. The noise was two doors that looked like rocks, opening. They were relieved to see it was the other two teams, who'd completed their part of the mission. They also had some of the hostages.

Some soldiers exited the delivery entrance. Kathy and the others waited just inside, out of harm's way. A group of soldiers were to the rear of them, and prepared to defend, if any more aliens showed.

They heard all the noise and explosions outside. When they cleared the opening, they saw four alien craft flying over the battlefield firing at the troops. Tanks and heavy artillery fired at the low flying craft.

Soldiers on the ground used every weapon they had, both large and small. They were strafed by alien craft. Many were killed or wounded, but the remaining fought fiercely.

Tanks were destroyed, as others took their place to continue the battle.

Big guns, like 175 calibers, and 105 calibers continuously fired, and shells connected with an alien craft. The big guns were also strafed by the aliens, and suffered similar consequences.

There was an explosion on an alien vessel. It went down at an angle as it crashed. Soldiers hurried to it, fired inside, and made sure the pilots were dead.

Stealth fighters and other jets engaged the alien craft left and right. A Stealth fighter was hit and slammed into the mountainside. His pissed off buddies, one male pilot and the other female, both fired at that alien ship and destroyed it, blowing it to pieces. They joined the others, as they engaged the remaining two alien ships. There were aircraft of every size and shape, but there were no news choppers anywhere in sight. As a matter of National Security, a civilian no fly zone reached for miles in every direction.

Other jets took hits. One exploded in mid air, and two crashed into the mountain. Another was hit and it went down among friendly troops. As it exploded, several soldiers were killed or wounded.

Another alien craft suffered damage, and went spiraling down in smoke, off in the distance. When it hit ground, it exploded.

As the general and others around him viewed the aerial battle, two unknown craft joined the fight. They fired at the Stealth fighters and the other jets.

"What the hell?" The men heard him exclaim, "They look like stealth fighters, but more sleek. They have laser weapons like the aliens."

Just as quickly, two other unknown types of planes appeared on the scene. They attacked the new enemy fighters, causing one to burst into flames, and slam into the mountainside. These new planes were not only using conventional weaponry, they were also firing with lasers. They also had another little trick up their sleeve. Periodically, they disappeared, and reappeared in another location.

Gilliam removed his binoculars and looked questioningly to the aide on his right, for he'd never seen the type of plane that was now helping to fight the enemy. He damn sure had never seen one disappear, and reappear.

The aide leaned closer with a half grin, and whispered, "Auroras."

"And the magic act?"

"General, do you remember the Philadelphia Experiment, by the Navy, in 1943?"

Gilliam looked at him, and sternly said, "When this is over, you and I are going to have a big conversation," as his eyes returned to the lens of his binoculars.

Suddenly, the main alien craft came out of the side of the mountain and headed upward.

The last alien fighter shot up toward it. A door in the larger craft opened.

Two Stealth fighters, the Auroras, and four different jets pursued the smaller craft, as it entered an opening in the mother ship. They continued firing at the larger one, until it shot off into space, out of their capabilities.

The Auroras hurriedly disappeared from the sky above, and would soon become just a memory.

When the other Jets came back into view, they made victory rolls. The remaining Stealth fighters did low flybys, as all the soldiers on the ground hollered cheers.

At his command position, General Gilliam also looked upward. Those near heard him, as he said, "This time we won. God help us, if there is a next time."

The cheering got even louder, when the hostages eased out of the entrance, with soldiers bringing up the rear.

As Gilliam looked toward the commotion, one of his aides reported, "We've got the hostages. We got all of them. They are unharmed."

Gilliam didn't bother to return his salute. He just jerked his hat off and waved it in the air yelling, "That's what I'm talking about. We saved the hostages and kicked ass. It doesn't get any better than this."

At his words and actions, the ones around him followed suit. They removed hats, waved and hollered even louder.

The general placed his hat back on his head and barked more orders. "Get the wounded to the hospitals. Cordon off the hospitals and don't let any news people in the area. Radio ahead and alert the hospitals to be ready for our men. Collect the bodies of our good men and women. Make sure every one of those gray bastards is dead. Get those alien bodies to NSA, so they can come up with some lame explanation that this battle never took place. Get some heavy equipment. Get the pieces of those alien craft loaded and out of here. Make sure you get the parts of those other two assholes' planes that came to help their alien buddies. I want to see them personally."

As the aides around him nodded, he continued, "I want reports on my desk on everything; and I do mean everything, before the sun sets."

They all nodded in agreement.

Chapter Twenty-Two

Jack's eyes were closed and there was rapid movement under the lids. He dreamed of his night with Lillian. He was reliving their time in the shower and making love. Just before he got his hospital gown and the sheets all sticky, he woke up. He glanced around the room. The door to the bathroom was open. Sarah was nowhere in sight. For the moment he was glad, for he might have called out Lillian's name while asleep.

A nurse came through the door, saying, "Ah! Good, you are awake. What's that shoulder pain on a scale of one to ten?"

He moved his arm and then lifted it. He felt a little but answered, "Probably a four right now."

"Good. I'll lower the morphine injection a little more. You are doing well. I lowered it some while you slept."

If she knew about the alien battle that was taking place, she wasn't mentioning it. There was no radio and no TV. There was no way for Jack to know it was even happening.

"Are you getting hungry?"

"Yeah, a little, I guess. Do you know if Sarah got someone to look at her ankle? I don't know if she came back in here while I was sleeping or not."

"She did. It was swelling, so they packed her ankle in ice and took her to x-ray. She hasn't returned yet. It takes awhile some times for the doctors to look over the x-rays. I'm sure they will know something soon." It wasn't hard for the nurse to continue Sarah's lie. Nurses are trained to do that sort of thing to avoid giving a patient bad news.

"Ok, thanks," he replied, as she smiled and walked out saying, "I'll send the food nurse in to get your order."

He nodded and she left the room.

She wasn't gone long before the other nurse appeared with the menu list. "I've got good news and better news. Which one do you want first?"

"The good news."

"Ah! You are saving the best news for last. Today you get to eat more normal food, and steak is on the menu."

"If that's the good news, what is the better news?"

As she handed him the paper and pen, she smiled, "This IV and the monitors are coming off of you now." She started unhooking the monitors from the patches stuck on his body, as he looked over the menu. She interrupted him just long enough for her to remove the IV and the port. She had him hold a finger on the folded gauze until she could tear off some tape and place it solidly over the gauze. "There, now wasn't that the better news?"

"Yep!"

She removed a clipboard with a chart at the foot of his bed. She took the list from him and placed it under the clip. "There, that will make it easier to write. Have you made your selection? You can have anything on the menu today, or everything, if you want, but I wouldn't advise it, of course."

He nodded, marked his selections, and returned the board to her.

She looked over his choices. When she put the board back where it hung, "I see you left room for dessert. It's not on the menu. We have chocolate cake, carrot cake, peach cobbler, strawberry and whipped cream, annnnnd (she drug out the word) you can have vanilla ice-cream with either."

"Is the peach cobbler hot or cold?"

"It is kept in the fridge, but I can heat it for you."

"No. I like it cold, and I'll take the vanilla ice-cream with it."

"I'll be back soon. The other patients ate while you slept. You are the last to be served. She waved over her shoulder as she exited.

Jack felt the urge, so he eased out of bed, trying not to move his shoulder too much, and made it to the bathroom. His bladder was full. Once he started, he felt like he was never going to stop.

When he came out, he went over to the chair and sat down. He pulled the bag around in front of him, and moved things around. His wallet, change, ID flip and watch were clearly visible. He removed the watch and placed it on his wrist, as he observed the time and date. Glancing back into the bag, he muttered; "Guess they didn't put my weapons in here. I'll have to remind myself to ask them about it, when they let me out of here." He had no way of knowing they came and removed his weapons while he was sleeping. They weren't taking any chances of him getting mad, when he found out he couldn't see Sarah, and go on a rampage. Sarah hadn't told him the weapons were there previously.

He picked up his wallet, opened and counted the visible money. Seeing it was all there, he checked the other compartments for a folded stack of bills he kept hidden. Yep, it was all there. He put it back in the bag and came out with the envelope with his stash of $100 bills. He guessed they were pretty honest, for it, too, was all accounted for. When he closed the envelope and placed it back in the bag, he saw the folded piece of paper. He immediately knew what it was. At first he didn't unfold the paper. He just held it in front of him. As he stared blankly, his mind raced back to her handing it to him when they said goodbye. He pictured himself up on the observation deck watching her plane rise into the sky. He remembered keeping his promise not to read it until she was in the air. Slowly he unfolded the paper and read her words again. He remembered the tears in his eyes when he read it that night, and now there were tears in his eyes again.

He couldn't let Sarah see him this way. He folded the paper smaller. He opened his wallet and crammed it into one of the compartments. Then he placed the wallet back into the bag. Maybe Sarah wouldn't see it now.

Suddenly, he wondered if she'd already seen it. Nah, he thought, she would have been pissed.

He decided he'd stretch his legs and walk down the hall. He didn't get very far, when two armed men in suits intercepted, "I'm sorry, Mr. Caruso. Patients are not allowed out of their rooms unless accompanied by a nurse and a guard. I'm sure you can understand, considering the type of facility you are a guest in."

He didn't answer; he just slightly nodded and returned to his room.

He went to the window and moved the curtain. It was impossible to see anything through the smoked glass. He started to unlock the window and raise it, but he figured that would set off alarms and the men in black would come running. He began to feel more like a prisoner than a patient. He wondered if he was really going to get out of here soon. He consoled himself with the thought that he would play their game until he got better.

Looking at Sarah's empty bed, he hoped they would return her soon. He went over to it and placed his hand on the pillow where she'd laid her head. He picked it up and placed it to his nose, so he could smell that perfume she wore. He was already missing her presence, as he laid the pillow back in place.

The food nurse came in with his selections and dessert, "Where would you like to eat?" as she glanced toward the bed and to the chair.

"I think I will take it over here," as he sat down in the chair.

She sat the tray on the over-bed table and rolled it over to him. She adjusted the height until he said, "That will be fine. Have you heard anything about Officer Sidwell?"

"I heard she'd been taken to X-ray, but I'm just the dietician nurse. They don't tell me everything. I will check on it for you, though."

"I'd appreciate it," he commented, as she walked away.

As he removed the covers over his food, he couldn't help but say aloud, "Damn, You don't get food that looks this good in some restaurants." He cut off a piece of his steak. After swallowing, he said aloud again, "Or taste as good, either."

He looked up toward the camera and said louder, "Hey! Guys and/or Gals, this is some good food. You know how to put on a spread here."

Of course, he didn't get a reply, so he went back to eating.

He was just wiping his mouth after finishing his last bite, when a nurse came in with a syringe. "Got to give you an antibiotic and pain killer mix. I figured I'd wait until you finished your meal."

She rolled the table away from him, and said, "I need you to stand. I have to give this shot in your upper hip area."

He complied, turned around with the open back of his gown exposing his rear.

She used an alcohol wipe to clean the area. When she gave him the shot, it didn't hurt much. Evidently she'd learned the art well.

"I'll get this tray out of your way and replace the cart by your bed. The shot might make you a little woozy. You might want to climb back in bed until it wears off."

He already felt it taking effect and decided to follow her suggestion.

When he climbed in bed, he drifted into sleep.

(Hours later)

When he awoke in the propped position, his eyes searched for Sarah. Her bed was gone. Looking around, he saw her suitcase was also missing. He climbed out of bed, still feeling a little woozy, but looked in the closet. Her clothes on hangers were also gone. When he turned toward his bed, he saw it was back in its original position. He was about to hit the call button, when a nurse came through the door. He didn't wait for her to speak, "Where is Sarah?"

The nurse faked an innocent look, as she softly answered, "When the doctors examined her x-rays, they found she'd severely cracked a bone. They decided to operate, and put a pin through her ankle for support. Otherwise, she might break it worse and be crippled for awhile."

"Why are all her things gone?"

"She's a patient now, Mr. Caruso. It is standard procedure for each patient to have his or her own room. She should be coming out of the anesthesia soon and taken to her room."

"What's her room number?

"That's another rule here. Patients can't be going to other patients' rooms. I know that is an inconvenience for you two, but that's the rules. However, knowing your closeness, I will try to arrange for you to see her, when she is settled in her room."

Her choice words were enough to appease him for the moment. "Please let me know as soon as I can see her."

"I will. I was just coming in to check on you. Are you feeling ok?"

"Yeah, I'm ok. Just feel a little spaced-out."

"That is understandable and normal. I'll check on you, later," and she left the room.

He sat on the edge of his bed and made a decision that he wasn't going to let them give him any more shots. Especially not one of the last ones they gave him. He stretched out on the bed and continued to think.

There was nothing to do. Sarah's burn phones went with her things, so he couldn't call Chandler. Not being able to contact him, like he'd promised, made him wonder if he still had a job. He made a mental note to inquire if he could call his boss, but he doubted if he was allowed.

He wondered about Charley, Kate and Mark. What was happening to them? Mark should have been delivered to the military by now. He felt a little sorry for Mark, but was glad Mark was going to be out of his and Sarah's life, at least for now. He'd been the cause of Sarah's walk on the wild side. He didn't feel any great loss with Mark's departure.

With Charley's connections, he figured he and Kate were safe somewhere. He was definitely going to sit down and have a long talk with that boy. Jack had taken Charley way too much for granted.

There was so much to think about and not a damn thing he could do about any of it.

A knock at his door caused him to look up. "Mr. Caruso, I'm here to take an x-ray of your shoulder," as he came through the door with his machine. He took a clipboard from under his arm. "What's those last four of your social?"

Jack rattled them off.

"Yep. That's you," as he came toward him with the x-ray plate. "If you can rise up, I need to slip this behind your back."

Without speaking, Jack sat up to let him do his job.

"I'm going to prop the plate against your back. You may feel the coldness in some spots," as he saw the bare skin in the back of Jack's hospital attire. "Please try not to move and I'll get this ordeal over with quickly."

He stepped back behind the insulated protection at his machine, "Take a deep breath and hold it."

Jack obeyed, and then heard him say, "Ok! Now you can breathe. That's all there is to it," as he removed the plate.

He hesitated when Jack suddenly asked, "Are you the one that took the x-rays of Sarah Sidwell's ankle? She's is my partner."

"No, I haven't done an x-ray on an ankle today. Was her x-ray taken today?"

"Yeah, that's what I've been told."

"That is strange. There are other techs that take the x-rays, but I am the only licensed technician to read them. However, some of the surgeons are qualified. Sometimes, they request x-rays to go directly to them. Maybe that was the case."

"Possibly. Thank you."

"You have a good day, Mr. Caruso," and he soon headed down the hall.

A suspicious feeling entered his detective mind. However, there was nothing he could do to investigate right now. Since the guys in black didn't come running when they heard him ask the question, it was reasonable to assume he might be feeling suspicious for nothing. He placed his good arm behind his head and closed his eyes. His last waking thoughts were to wonder what he'd find when he woke up the next time. Every time he came to, things were different.

Chapter Twenty-Three

Jack's nurse hadn't completely lied. Sarah had been taken away for surgery. Her pregnancy termination was not going to be anywhere near normal. By the time they got her sedated, a sonogram depicted the well formed shape of a fetus. The surgeons were somewhat shocked and began cutting her open.

Clipping the umbilical cord and removing the miniature fetus was easy enough, but when they did, Sarah went into cardiac arrest.

The operating surgeon gave the fetus to an assistant, "Get this to the proper authorities." He quickly turned back to Sarah, and motioned for the nurses to give her shock treatment. It took twice to get her heart beating again. The surgeon could see the old damage to her female organs, and the new organs that had grown around them, enabling Sarah to get pregnant.

He turned to the standby female surgeon, who was watching the screen. "All of this from one load of semen," and he shook his head. "Unbelievable." He noticed little sprouts starting to protrude from different parts of her female organs, and began removing them. As he handed them to the assistant, they were laid on a stainless tray.

The surgeon was beginning to sew her, when the assistant tapped him on the shoulder pointing to the tray. The sprouts were growing, even when exposed to air and removed from the body.

"Get those damn parts out of here. Put them in a quarantine chamber. Contact scientists who deal with this kind of thing; it is way over my head." He turned back to Sarah, "Right now, I've got to try to save this woman's life."

When he finished operating, he looked to the two female nurses standing, waiting, "Get her cleaned up and back to her room. I want a nurse by her bedside 24/7. I want monitors reading every part of her body. Do I make myself clear?"

He looked to the female backup surgeon, "Close the wound." As he removed his gloves he spoke sternly, "What you saw today, you didn't see. None of this ever happened." He looked at each one until they nodded in agreement, and then he left the room.

When the suturing was finished, the female surgeon turned things over to the nurses. They rubbed the area with antiseptic, and placed a bandage over the cut. They finished cleaning her, redressed her, took her back to the room, and hooked her to the monitors.

One nurse took her turn to observe Sarah and the other nurse left.

The one remaining made sure Sarah came out from under the anesthesia without any complications. Soon, Sarah was breathing normal and resting.

After checking her pulse, temperature and other vital signs, the nurse sat in a chair with her eyes glued to Sarah's monitor screens.

During her twelve-hour shift, she checked Sarah's vital signs often. Sarah began running a fever. She administered medicine in her IV and kept a cool pack wrapped in cloth on her forehead. Sarah had also been given morphine, and slept through the whole ordeal.

Hours later, when she woke up, a nurse was standing by her monitors. Softly she said, "You are in your room. You made it through the operation fine. Your pregnancy termination was successful. How do you feel?"

"No pain, just groggy."

"It will wear off soon. You still shouldn't be in any pain. You are being given pain medicine. Just as with your partner; we need to try to start weaning you off of it, as soon as you feel up to it."

"Yeah, I know. It was the same with Jack. How is he?"

"The monitors and IV are out of him, and he's up and walking around. He is also becoming more adamant about finding out where you went. He had to be stopped in the hall already. If you don't want him to see you, we need to tell him something to deter him from trying."

"No! I don't want to face him. Tell him I contacted staph, and no one is allowed near me."

"I doubt that alone would stop him from trying. Maybe if you talked to him and assure you are ok, it would ease his mind."

"How do I do that, there are no phones in these rooms."

The nurse smiled, "That doesn't mean there aren't any phones in this facility. I will arrange it. He is asleep at present. We will take care of it when he wakes."

The nurse stated, "I'll hang out with you to make sure you continue doing well."

Sarah was still drowsy. She closed her eyes again and fell asleep.

(In Jack's room)

Jack was having a bad dream. In his mind he relived an earlier shootout with a criminal. His body movements made him hurt his shoulder causing him to jerk awake in a feverish sweat.

A nurse entered his room with extra towels and a cool-pack in her hands. "Bad dream huh?"

"Yeah," He answered and held where he was injured.

"Do you need a shot of pain medicine?"

"No! I'll be ok in a little bit," as he accepted one of the towels and wiped the sweat on his arms.

The nurse placed the cool pack on his shoulder bandage, dabbed the other towel on his forehead, and the top of his head.

"How is Sarah?" He inquired, as he took the other towel and dried the areas himself.

"She's resting peacefully."

"When can I see her?"

"I'm afraid there has been a complication. She somehow contracted Staphyloccus, commonly called Staph infection. They have it in check, but no one is allowed near her."

Now he was angry, "This is a bunch of bull shit. One minute she's fine in a bed next to me, and now she's been operated on and contracted Staph."

He began getting out of bed, "I want to see her and I want to see her now."

The armed men in suits entered but stood near the door.

"Jack, Sarah is fine. I promise you. When she wakes, I have arranged to get phones to both of you, so you can talk. That is the best I can do for the moment. I'm sure you will be able to talk to each other in person in the near future."

He sat back down on the bed, exasperated.

Feeling a confrontation had been avoided, the two at the door disappeared.

The nurse also felt it was time for her to take her leave.

He was still sitting on the edge of the bed with his head in his hands, when he saw pants legs. He looked up to see Connors.

"Are you becoming a problem, Jack?"

"I can become a big problem."

Connors laughed a little, "I imagine you could."

"What are you doing here, Connors? Do I need saving again?"

"Hell no; you are in good hands here. You'll be checking out in a few days. I'm not here on business. I guess you could say this is a friendly visit."

"What kind of friendly visit?" Every time I'm around you there are bullets flying."

"Hey now. Don't blame all that on me."

"Why are you here, Conners?"

" It seems you impressed a lot of people in high places." He held a manila envelope in the air and handed it to him. "Inside you will find two applications. One is for the CIA and one is for the NSA. Recommendations have been included with both, along with my signature. Seems that people in high places think your talent is being wasted at your present job."

"I may not still have a job."

"Everything is fine with your job. Chandler has been contacted and told you are being taken care of. He was informed he would be contacted as soon as you are released."

"What about Sarah's job?"

"That was a difficult task, but it has been resolved. Her position is still secure. That is, if she still wants it."

"What the hell do you mean by that statement? We were just talking about it yesterday. Of course, she still wants her job, and for us to work together."

"I'm not going to get into that, Jack. It is something you two will have to work out."

Looking down at the envelope, Jack added, "I like what I do and I'm good at it. Sarah is, too. We make a good team."

"I'd have to agree on all of your statements. However, you now have two more options to consider. I just want you to think about it while you are recovering. Another thing to consider is the jump in pay grade."

"Hell, I don't have time to spend the money I make now."

"That's another thing to think about. In either of those two agencies, you will start off with four weeks vacation. In two years, it jumps to six weeks."

"Damn, you guys get that kind of time off?"

He answered, "Yes and it is all paid vacation. Your pay doubles and triples under certain conditions I can't disclose. Sometimes an unlimited expense account comes into play."

Looking toward the camera, he added, "No one is listening or watching. I sent them on break so I could speak freely."

Jack halfway grinned, "So far, everybody I've had to kill brought it on themselves. My shootings were all justified. Word is you guys have a license to kill."

"You've been watching too many movies, Jack. It's hard to get anything by the media or other eyes these days. However, I need to make this perfectly clear. If it came down to protecting this country and what it stands for, you would be expected to pull the trigger if it was deemed necessary. I can't stay any longer, Jack, I've got to be somewhere in an hour. I just wanted to get this envelope to you."

"I'll consider these offers, if you answer a question for me?"

"Ok! Ask?"

"Is Sarah really ok, and what about Kate, Charley and Mark?"

"You added a lot into that one question, but I'll answer it. Sarah is resting fine. I looked in on her. Kate and Charley are on paid vacation having fun. Kate's job is still waiting for her when she gets back."

"You didn't finish answering my question."

"Mark is dead. He was killed in a battle with aliens at the underground facility. He went down fighting hard alongside our troops. He is credited with personally saving several of our soldiers. Because of him, all the people held hostage were safely freed. Of course, they still won't be released back into civilization just yet. They'll have to find out exactly what effects the alien experiments achieved."

Connors watched Jack's blank face, but continued, "You may as well know the rest. Three alien craft were destroyed. One alien fighter made it back to the main craft and they shot off into space."

Jack's detective mind made him interrupt, "Why didn't the alien mother-ship join the battle?"

Connors grinned, "See why the big wheels want you? No babies were found anywhere at the facility. Our people are still tearing that place apart looking for anything. It is assumed the aliens took all the offspring with them, and didn't want to take any chance of not getting away."

"Logical," Jack agreed.

"Now, I've answered your questions and you know you have to keep your mouth shut about most of my answers. I've kept my part of the bargain. You keep yours and consider those applications."

He stuck out his hand. Jack shook it, but made no comment.

Connors nodded and left the room.

(Next morning)

The next day the nurse kept her word. She walked into the room with a cell phone. Jack was sitting in the chair looking at a picture of Sarah he kept hidden in his wallet. The nurse dialed a number and handed the phone to him. He heard it ringing and smiled when he heard Sarah's voice say, "Hi!Jack!"

"Sarah, are you ok? Are you making this call under any type of duress?"

"No, Jack. They are taking real good care of me." Here came another lie, "They had to operate on my ankle, and of course, I had to screw that up, too, and somehow got a case of Staph. They have it under control, thank goodness, before I woke up one day with missing extremities. I've heard of that happening."

"It's good to hear your voice, Sarah. I can't begin to describe how depressed I've been, since I woke up and you weren't beside me."

"I know how you feel, baby! That's been the hardest for me to adjust to. One day I'm enjoying lying beside you, and now I'm stuck in a room all by myself. They say it won't be long to get clear of the Staph infection. They are talking a week, maybe a little longer."

"If they hadn't let me talk to you, I was about to start causing one hell of a commotion."

She laughed a little, "Then you would have been in leg irons. I'd never have gotten to see you. I'm ok, and I hope to get out of here real soon." Now she felt the tears starting to appear in her eyes, "Not as soon as you, of course. They said I could be the one to tell you that you are going home tomorrow."

"Why can't I put on some kind of Haz-Mat suit, or something, so I can at least come to your room and see you?"

God she so wished he could, but she couldn't bear to face him. "Awe, that makes me feel good that you would have done all that for me. I'll be fine, but missing you, of course. Make sure you tell Chandler my condition and explain why I can't show up yet."

"If you are not back at the station within two weeks, Sarah, I'm going to bring in the National Guard and find you."

Able to smile a little, but still watery eyed, She agreed, "You probably would, too. Believe me, they wouldn't want that. They'll get me out of here as soon as they can." She hesitated a bit, to collect herself, "Jack, I'm getting the nod that it's time for me to end this call. Evidently the nurse went against the rules to get these cell phones where we could talk. You just get back out there and start busting criminals, but don't you even think of getting another partner."

"Nobody could take your place, Sarah. I'll be going it alone until you get back on duty."

It was now or never if she was ever going to get him back. "Jack, I love you."

His silence was almost heartbreaking until she heard, "I love you, too, Sarah."

She was getting close to the point of bawling, as she quickly ended the call with, "Wait for me, Jack," and pushed the end call button.

As the nurse took the phone, Sarah cried profusely, sobbing hysterically. The nurse held the phone in her lap and sat down beside Sarah. She put an arm around Sarah's shoulder and let her cry it out of her system.

Jack handed the phone to the nurse in his room and just sat there, stupefied.

Trying to cheer him a little, the nurse explained, "They'll be bringing your clothes this afternoon. As Sarah mentioned earlier, they will take you home tomorrow morning. It is extremely important that you use that shoulder and arm the least possible. We don't want you tearing anything and be back in a hospital somewhere."

A little bubblier, she said, "You get another delicious meal this evening, and a big breakfast before your departure tomorrow. Soon you'll be back out there fighting crime. That reminds me, I want to thank you and Sarah for all you do to keep the streets safe for us."

He hadn't been looking her way until he heard that statement. He looked up at her, and said, "Thanks."

The nurse seemed to be satisfied that she had accomplished her mission. She said she'd see him in a little while, as she left the room.

He had to admit to himself it was a good feeling that he was getting out of here tomorrow. That is, if they were telling the truth. He'd just have to wait and see. It irked the shit out of him that he wasn't going to see Sarah before he left. He consoled himself, thinking he'd better not make any waves, or he might never get out of this place.

There was nothing else to do, no books or magazines; so he opened the envelope and looked over the forms Connors left for him. He sat reading and thinking, until they brought the meal he'd ordered. Laying the papers aside, he uncovered the food. He had to admit he was going to miss the meals.

He was just finishing his meal and wiping his mouth, when an agent in a suit came through the door with pants, shirt and jacket in one hand, and a duffle bag in the other. He sat the bag down and hung the clothes in the closet.

Jack didn't recognize the jacket so he walked over to him, "That doesn't look like one of my coats."

The agent informed, "The pants aren't either. We figured you earned some new ones. There are a couple more outfits in your closet at your home. Just consider them earned compensation."

When the agent left, Jack removed the outfit holding the pants up to him. He slipped on the expensive-looking jacket, and it fit to a tee, with room for his weapon.

He opened the duffle bag. His weapons weren't in it, but it was full of new items. There were new underwear, socks, ties, white tee shirts, expensive shoes, a pair of colorful PJs, and unopened packages of amenities. His favorite cologne, toothpaste, mouthwash, and other little goodies were in view. Raising the package of PJs out of the bag, he looked at the camera and said, "Cute."

The thought entered his mind, "If they are trying to bribe me to take one of those jobs, they are doing a fine job."

He noticed a small envelope, pulled it out of the bag and opened it. Inside were a note and a new MasterCard. He inspected the card front and back. Seeing his name, he grinned a little and opened the note.

The note said, "Just a little bonus for all your hard work, and taking a bullet." Conners' name was at the bottom.

He couldn't help whispering aloud, "I wonder how big a bonus?"

Soon he retrieved his wallet from the hospital bag and placed the card in one of the slots. He brought the bag and the duffle close to each other, as he sat in a chair and began opening all the new packages. He felt a few pains, as he pulled the plastic coverings off the items, so he reached in the bag and pulled out his penknife to make it easier.

Before long, he had all the new toiletries in his bathroom. He moved everything from the hospital bag to the duffle. He folded the hospital bag and placed it in the garbage can.

He walked over to his bed and pushed the call button. Shortly, the nurse appeared.

"I'd like to take a shower, but I assume I can't get the wound and bandages wet."

"You assume correct. It would be best for you to take a sponge bath, making sure the bandages don't get damp. We wouldn't want any kind of infection setting in."

"I need a real bath to make me feel human again. Isn't there anything you can do so I can?"

"I can, but you may not like it. We have waterproof bandages that we can place over the wounds, but they stick to the skin real well. They are normally only used for emergencies. I assure you it will be very painful when they are removed. You will need assistance to remove the one I put on your back."

"I'll endure the pain. I'll find someone to help remove the one I can't reach."

"Very well, I'll be back in a few minutes with the bandages. I'll remove the normal ones and replace them with the waterproof. It was time for me to inspect your wound anyway." She left the room.

With the good news about the shower, he seemed more at ease.

She returned, changed the bandages, commented the wound looked good, and left the room.

He opened the package with the pajamas and laid them on the bed. He headed to the shower and adjusted the water. It felt great with the hot water cascading over his shoulders and head. He mostly had to soap with one hand, because it hurt to lift the other arm. It didn't matter. He was glad to feel really clean again when the shower was over. He had a little trouble drying with the hurt arm, but soon got it done. He came out, put on the pajama top and bottom, and lay back on the bed. Feeling clean and tired, he drifted to sleep.

When he awoke the next morning, he followed a morning ritual. When he came out of the bathroom, he had all the amenities in his hands and under his arm. He placed them in the duffle bag.

The food nurse walked in with a big breakfast on a tray. He was hungry and practically gulped down the food, chasing it with coffee. When he finished the meal, he immediately prepared for his departure. He laid all the clothes he was going to wear on the bed, and dressed. Getting the socks on was the hardest part. The shoes fit like a glove on a hand. There was a little pain trying to slip the pullover shirt on, but soon he tucked the tail into his pants. When he buckled the belt, he realized it wasn't a cheap one, either. Finally, he was completely dressed except for the jacket.

His nurse came through the door with a syringe in her hand, "Well, look at you, Handsome. One last little shot here, before they come to get you. It's got to be in your upper hip, so you'll have to drop those pants a little."

"Is this one going to knock me out like the other one?"

"Yes! It will probably leave you unconscious for a little while. They don't want you knowing how to get back to this facility."

He didn't object; in case it was true he was getting out of here. He turned and lowered his pants enough for her to give him the shot. As he buckled, she discarded the syringe in the container on the wall. She came toward him and lifted his jacket off the bed, "Let's see how the jacket looks on you."

When he slipped it on, he started to feel himself get woozy, and she helped him sit down on the bed. In a voice that seemed to be fading in the distance, he heard her say, "When you wake up, you'll be in the comfortable surroundings of your own home. Take care of that shoulder."

In a few seconds, if the world came to an end, he wouldn't have known.

When he woke up, he was sitting in his favorite recliner, still in the suit he'd put on earlier. However, there was a new addition to his attire. His arm was in a black sling. When he sat up, he glanced down at the open duffle bag. When he inspected the contents, both of his weapons and the clips were laying in the top. Everything he'd put in the bag was also there. He removed his wallet, seeing the new MasterCard and everything of his still in tact.

When he stood, he still felt a little unsteady. He went to the fridge, reached in, and as the door closed, he twisted the top off of a beer with his good hand. As he took a big swallow, he noticed his phone on the counter. Remembering throwing it in his trunk, he went to the window. His unmarked detective vehicle was parked in the driveway. He looked back at the counter for the keys. Not seeing them he reached into his pocket. Sure enough, there they were. He just shook his head.

He finished the beer and decided it was time for him to show up at the station. It felt good to be cruising down the street, and soon he was in the station parking lot.

When he walked through the door, uniformed officers and detectives came to welcome his return. They were all careful not to touch the arm in the sling.

Hearing all the commotion, the chief was standing in the doorway. Jack saw him and headed in that direction.

"Bout time you showed up. I'm informed Sarah will be awhile yet. Come on in, Jack."

As they sat down, he said, "I know you've had a rough time of it, but we're glad you are back. Of course, you'll have to see the company shrink, and the company doctor, to find out when you can be released for duty. Hasn't stopped your checks, of course, they are still on auto deposit. As far as the books go, you haven't been absent."

"Thanks, Captain."

"How is the shoulder?"

"Ok, if I don't move it; painful if I do. I never was much for pain pills, although they gave me a large bottle of them."

"You might need them for awhile. What can you tell me about Sarah?"

"She tripped in the facility where I was being treated. She hurt her ankle bad and they had to operate. Then she got some kind of Staph infection. They wouldn't let me near her, but I did get to talk to her via phones, the day before I left. I don't know whether to believe all that shit or not. I probably won't believe anything, until she shows up in this office, and I can see her, face to face. She sounded normal enough on the phone."

Chandler interrupted, "I'm told CIA is clearing up some things on Kate. Seems like, she was operating under their discretion. They say her stint with them is almost over, and they'll let her come back to work. Damn men in black think they can just do anything they want with people. She's a good officer. I'm looking forward to her return. What about that weirdo, Mark? I haven't heard any more about him. I can't get any info on him at all."

"Let's just say that we won't be seeing him again."

"Speaking of him and his claim about aliens; the papers and news on TV are reporting a big military exercise in the mountain area. Of course, the military swears it was just one big training exercise, which involved several branches of the service. Supposedly, it was practice to see how they worked together, if there was an external threat from another country. Sounds like the usual bullshit they hand us, when it has something to do with UFOs, or aliens. In Polero's news reports, she's blasting the government for not coming clean about what happened out there, and for restricting the news people from covering any of it. What do you think, Jack? Reckon there was any truth to that fellow Mark, and his claims?"

"How would I know, Captain, I've been laid up in a hospital?"

"Yeah, in a frigging hospital we couldn't find."

"The food was great!"

"Get the hell out of here, Jack. Let me know when the doctors clear you for duty."

Jack grinned and headed for the door. As his hand touched the knob, Chandler called out, "Jack, welcome back!"

He just nodded and closed the door.

Chapter Twenty-Four

At the government medical facility, Sarah was
going through a hell of an ordeal. Each time they
ran tests on her female organs; there were changes
from the alien interference in her body. To keep her
from screaming with pain, they had to keep her
sedated and supplying pain medicine.

Normal procedures, to try to kill the enzymes
and alien DNA that had infected her body, were not
working. Her body kept neutralizing the antibiotics.

Medical scientists working for the government
were brought to the facility to try to find a cure.

Days turned into weeks. At times, it seemed the
alien effect was determined to kill her, since the
fetus was taken. It tried to set up her organs for the
next semen donor. The more they worked to get rid
of the alien DNA, the more it rejected the attempts.
Several times, her bodily functions failed, and there
was no heartbeat. She had to be brought back to life
and put on life support.

The scientists struggled to find an antibiotic for
what they called the disease. Finally, during one of

their experiments, they found that Biocin mixed with DMSO "Dimethyl Sulfoxide" killed the alien DNA in the samples they removed. It was surmised the DMSO sped the Biocin to the target point too fast for the alien DNA to produce an antibody. There was a waiting period on those samples, while more samples were collected and submitted to the same procedure. The scientist became satisfied with the results.

Now it was time to try it on Sarah. She was still sedated with no idea what they were doing to her.

There was no known mixture to go by, so they made educated guesses, and flooded her female organ area with a DMSO/Biocin mixture. Her body reacted violently. Even in an unconscious state, she fought at her wrist and ankle restraints until she collapsed. Once again there was no heartbeat and she had to be bought back to life.

For the next three days, they kept running blood samples and giving her new blood platelets. By the end of the third night, the doctors and scientists began cheering. The alien DNA cells that had made it into her bloodstream were dead.

The nurses began the process of reducing the morphine, and by the end of the fourth day, she was very weak, but awake.

Her nurse was extremely happy to tell her the attempts were successful, and she was normal again. "We are going to keep you here for three more days just as a precaution, as we continue to check your blood. If the blood keeps turning out negative, you'll be able to go home."

She looked at her watch and squinted at the date. Realizing how many days that had passed, she pleaded, "Can I call Jack. Please, let me call him."

"I don't have any problem with you calling him, but give it a couple more days, until you are stronger and more yourself. I promise you can call him then. You can use one of those burn phones you came in with. However, you know the shut off time limit. We don't need them tracing the call. You will be home soon enough to talk to him all you want."

She nodded her head in agreement, as the nurse continued, "For now, you need rest and food. I'll bring you something to eat in a few hours. Of course, it won't be one of those scrumptious meals you had before, but I'll make it as nutritious as I can."

"Thanks," Sarah answered weakly with half a smile as the nurse disappeared. She closed her eyes and fell asleep. She dreamed of times before, when she and Jack were making love. Her intended dreams were interrupted by flashbacks of it being Mark, instead of Jack. She woke up aggravated and disgusted.

The same occurrence took place several times over the three days.

The nurse kept her word and told her she could call Jack, but Sarah decided to wait until she was in her own home, where they couldn't hear the conversation.

The three days finally passed. She was dressed and combing her hair, when the two female agents who had brought her things before, walked through the door. "We are here to help you get home, and situated, Sarah." They carried her things and escorted her to a door, where a helicopter was seen sitting on a heliport. They stopped at the door, turning to Sarah, as one stated sternly, "You saw how to get here when you arrived, not like, Jack, who was out of it. It is a matter of National Security that you do not speak of this place and everything that happened here. It doesn't exist. Do you understand what I am telling you, Sarah? It is imperative that you do."

"Yeah, I know the drill. I'm just glad to get the hell out of here and get back to a normal life."

They nodded and led her to the waiting unmarked chopper.

It took her to the top of a building in downtown Las Vegas. From there she was taken down the elevator, and out a side door to a waiting black SUV. The vehicle arrived at her home outside of Pahrump, and the two agents helped her get inside, and settled in. They instructed; she would be picked up once a week to be taken back to the facility; to make sure things were remaining copacetic. She would be notified as to where and when the pick-ups would take place. Later, they said goodbye and were soon down the road.

All the extra moving around had caused a lot of pain in the area where she'd been defiled. They sent her home with a bag of medicines, antibiotics, pain pills, and the rest she hadn't even looked at. She drew a glass of water, took two pain pills, and then went to lie down in her own bed.

Six hours later her eyes opened. She was in a curled position, and had somehow managed to pull the covers halfway over her body while sleeping. She eased out of bed and felt the pain. Her first agenda was to take another round of pain pills. With the glass of water still in her hand, she began an inspection of her rooms. By the time the water was finished, she was satisfied that everything was still intact.

Thoughts of calling Jack entered her mind. She sat in her recliner, turned on her cell and crossed her legs. She was beginning to dial his number, as her eyes saw her bare feet. She never finished dialing and ended the intended call. Stark realization set in. After all the lies she'd told, how was she going to explain no operation on her ankle? She was at a loss as to what she was going to say to him to explain everything. If she ever made it into his bed again, he'd see she lied. He'd want the truth. He could always read her face, if she wasn't telling the truth.

She was home, she was safe, and her life still seemed to be in a mess.

The words on the note to him from Lillian were blazed into her brain. Every time she wanted to be with, Jack, and make him forget the other woman, something happened to destroy her efforts. She slung the phone across the floor, as her eyes began to tear. She curled in the chair and cried herself to sleep.

Chapter Twenty-Five

Jack was back on the job. His arm was out of the sling. He was on light duty, so he wasn't allowed to work cases on the streets. He was going over paperwork at his desk, and stopped to look at Sarah's empty seat.

Not a word from Sarah, or anyone about Sarah, had been eating at him. He closed the case file and threw the pen in his hand haphazardly on the desk. He considered searching for the facility and finding Sarah. He knew he could get in a lot of trouble, but he was beginning to not care about that. His partner was still missing, and he didn't know if she was alive or dead. Sure, her words on the phone led him to believe she was ok, but they could have forced her to say whatever they wanted.

He reached in the top drawer, picked up his weapon and secured it in his holster. He stood and slipped his jacket off the back of his chair and put it on. He didn't know where he was going, but he needed to get out of the office. He needed to see something different, take a walk, or something.

When he was outside, he looked up at the sky. It was going to be a nice day. He looked left and right, but no direction to go entered his mind. Like most humans, who come to a stop sign and don't know which way to go, he started walking to his right, down the sidewalk. He didn't seem to be paying any attention to anything happening around him as he walked, though his head occasionally looked left or right.

A car's brakes squealed, as it slid to a stop at a red light. Auto reflex made him slide his hand to the butt of his weapon. Seeing it was just a woman who'd been on her phone, and almost ran a red light, he continued his stroll. Up ahead, he saw the café, where he and Sarah often ate lunch together while on duty. When he reached the door, he went inside and sat at the booth where they often dined.

"Officer Caruso, are you eating alone today?"

God, he wished she hadn't put her question in those words, "Yeah, I'll just have a cup of coffee for now."

The waitress nodded and walked away.

He looked across the booth at the emptiness, and pictured the smile on Sarah's pretty face discussing a case with him, or talking about how they were going to sneak off together. He had a sick helpless feeling inside, because he couldn't do anything to go find her.

"Are you dead set on being alone, or do you mind if I sit down?"

"What are you doing here, Conners? You are becoming a pain in my ass."

As he sat, he held up two fingers barely apart, "Yeah, but I'm only a little pain."

"Is someone coming to kidnap me? Did you come to save me again? Should I be drawing a weapon and looking over my shoulder?"

"Ok, Caruso, get it out of your system. I just wanted to know if you considered the applications."

"I read them."

"Did you have any thoughts on either agency?"

He answered a little angrily, "You know, I'm having trouble concentrating on anything. You assholes have my partner, and I'm not sure if she is alive or dead. The latter better not be the case."

"Your partner," he answered defensively, "Was released and taken home two days ago. It's not my fault that she hasn't contacted you."

"You are lying. She would have called me right away. What have you done to her?

"Nothing was done to her that she didn't want us to do."

"What are you talking about? You're not even making sense."

"I didn't know she hadn't contacted you. As a matter of fact, I assumed she had. I was worried she might have talked you out of considering the applications."

The waitress sat Jack's coffee on the table. Looking at Conners, she asked, "Are you having coffee, sir?

Jack stood and said, "He can have mine." Looking toward, Conners, he added, "Make sure you leave a good tip. I always do.

He headed toward the door, as Conners drug his coffee over to his side of the table, and asked the waitress, "Could I see a menu? I think I'll have some breakfast."

When she moved away, he looked toward the door where he saw Jack leave, and shook his head.

In less than a half hour, Jack got his car and drove to Sarah's house. He parked in the drive and walked toward her door. It opened and she stepped out, about to close it behind her.

When she saw him, she couldn't believe her eyes at first, but said, "Jack, I was just headed down to the station to see you."

"Really, Sarah? From what I hear, you've been home for two days. You've got to know I've been worried sick about you." His eyes looked her up and down and before she could answer, "I don't see a bandaged ankle. What the hell have you been pulling on me, Sarah?"

"Jack, it's extremely complicated," grabbing his arm she began dragging him inside, "I was coming to see you to tell you the truth."

"The truth; why the hell would you need to lie to me? You're the one person in this world I thought would never lie to me."

She closed the door, "Please sit down, Jack; and calm down; this is so hard for me. I promise I'll tell you every sickening detail."

For a second, he jerked his arm away, but her sad looking eyes beginning to tear, made him take a seat on one end of the couch.

Sitting down beside him with her hands in her lap, "Jack, I didn't know how to tell you. I couldn't bring myself to face you."

What could be so bad that you didn't want to face me, Sarah?"

"Jack, I was so happy being in that bed beside you in your room. I loved taking care of you."

"Then why the hell did you disappear?"

"They made me let them run some tests on me"

"What kind of tests?"

"Please, Jack, just listen, ok? This is hard enough for me as it is."

When he didn't frown at her again, she explained, "They ran tests on me because of having sex with Mark that one time. The test showed I was in the beginning of pregnancy."

Now he spoke, "You always told me you couldn't get pregnant and we never used protection. You have sex supposedly one time with this guy and you magically got pregnant. Is this another lie, Sarah?"

"No, Jack it is not a lie. Somehow, his semen affected my reproductive organs. In less than a week I was beginning pregnancy. I couldn't come back in your room and face you after they told me. They also told me the tests showed they needed to terminate the pregnancy in a hurry. When the operation was done, they found my female organs were changing, and alien DNA had entered my blood stream. For days; they tried to counteract the effects of the alien DNA on my female organs. Scientists from everywhere were brought in to try to find a cure. With each new experiment, the alien DNA would counteract. Finally they were able to destroy the alien antibodies. They said I died at least three or four times during all the procedures. They kept me a few more days running tests to make sure the alien effects were neutralized. Even now, I'll have to go back to the facility once a week for them to run tests, and make sure it doesn't come back on me."

She hesitated and placed her hands on his arm, "Can't you understand, Jack? It made me sick inside, thinking you would hate me, if I told you the truth. It's tearing my guts apart, telling you now. Please don't hate me, Jack. Please don't hate me." Her tears flowed down her cheeks.

"I could never hate you, Sarah. If all this is true, it just makes me hurt and angry that you didn't think I would understand, and that you thought lying to me was the answer. We've been through some tough shit together. You didn't even give me the benefit of the doubt that I would care enough to understand."

"I know I screwed up Jack; just like I screwed up everything else, lately. I'm trying to make it right. Please forgive me. Please say you'll forgive me."

"Sarah, I don't know what to feel. My brain is going round and round right now. I would have understood. I wouldn't have liked any of it, but I would have been by your side, through it all. Instead, I was left to worry and wonder, sick at my stomach, because I didn't know where you were, or if you were alive or dead."

"Jack, I'm sorry, I'm so sorry. I love you. Please don't let this tear us apart." She tried to put her arms around his neck, but his hands went to each of her arms, pulling them back down, as he stood.

"Give me some time, Sarah. Give me time to get my head straight, and figure out what I feel. If I promised you anything right now, I'd be telling a lie. My insides are churning, and my brain feels like a battlefield. Give me some time."

She stood, and quickly kissed his cheek, "Jack, I love you and I'll be praying you can forgive me. I'll be here for you, if you'll have me."

He didn't answer. He just turned and walked out the door.

As it closed behind him, she sobbed profoundly. Once again, she cried herself to sleep on the couch.

Jack got in his car and drove aimlessly. His head, his heart, and his insides felt like they were all going round and round at once.

He considered going to a bar and getting smashed, but in his condition, the slightest thing would set him off. He'd probably either end up beating hell out of some guy that mouthed off, or shoot him. He decided he'd go back to work. Sarah was safe. That had been his main worry. All the rest of the crap would just have to work itself out.

When he got to the station, he walked straight to his desk. If anyone had wanted to say something to him, they refrained, when they detected the mood he was in. At his desk, he opened the file he'd closed earlier, and forced himself to concentrate on the words. He was actually focused for a short time, but soon his thoughts drifted back to Sarah, and all the things that had happened. Before long, he was staring blankly.

A folded piece of paper being thrown on the desk in front of him caused him to look up and see Chandler.

"Caruso, you are a basket case. I don't want part of you here; I want all of your concentration on your work. That isn't going to happen right now; I can see that. The paper is an approved two-week vacation. You've got more vacation time built up than you could ever use. If you need more, give me a call, and I'll change the dates. Go somewhere. Do something different. Find somebody to have a long talk with. Get laid or something. The two weeks will give your shoulder time to better heal. Don't come back until your head is clear. I want my best detective back in top form."

Jack started to say something, but was stopped, "Don't say anything. No excuses, ifs, ands or buts. Just get out of here, Jack, and get well."

As the captain walked away, Jack picked up the papers. Today was Friday, and the vacation papers started next Monday. He stood, slipped on his jacket and crammed the papers in an inside pocket.

Normally he would have put up an argument and talked his way out of a vacation, but this time, he figured it might be a good thing to go somewhere and get away from it all.

He must have even looked in a better mood, for a few people spoke to him on his way out. Barry asked where he was off to. Jack just smiled and answered, "Vacation."

On his way home, he ran possible destinations through his mind. None of them sounded that interesting, but he figured he'd think of something when he got home.

In the house, he threw the empty suitcase on his bed. He opened drawers and laid things inside. He strategically tried to have outfits for any type of action he might decide on. He even pulled a garment bag out of the closet and put dress shirts, dress pants, belts and jackets in the bag. He made sure he had plenty of $100 bills, his extra weapon and clips just in case. If he was going on vacation, he was going to do it up right. He went to the kitchen and made a list of things to take. He might be gone two or three weeks; he had no clue. Soon, he'd put a check by everything on the list, and it was all packed. Satisfied with the job he'd done, he called a cab to take him to the airport.

In the cab and on the way, the cabbie inquired, "What airline, sir?"

He realized he hadn't even decided what airline, or where he was going. "I don't care. Pick one."

"Are you serious, fellow? You want me to just drop you off at any airline?"

"Yeah, either one."

"Ok! It's your dime." When he reached departure, he asked, "Southwest ok?"

"Yes."

The cabbie took his suitcase out of the trunk and handed him the garment bag. Jack laid it across the suitcase and took out his wallet.

"That will be twenty-one dollars and fifty cents."

Jack handed him a hundred, "Keep the change. I hope it helps make a better weekend for you."

"It will be a big help, fellow. Things have been awful slow so far this evening for a Friday. Have a good flight, wherever you are headed."

Jack forced a smile, and the cabbie pulled away.

He threw the garment bag over his good shoulder, and pulled the suitcase with the hurt arm.

Inside, he stopped to read over the list and times of departing flights.

North, south, east or west; which way was he going? Who was he going to go see, and what card was he going to use to buy the tickets? He had plenty of cash, but who knows he might need it all.

He remembered the MasterCard Connors had given him, and checked to see if it was still in his wallet. He figured he'd use it, and see if there was enough on the card to pay for these short-notice tickets. He imagined they'd be pretty expensive. Just before closing his wallet, he saw the corner of Lillian's note he'd folded away in one of the compartments. He removed the note, put his wallet in his back pocket, and read it once again. He folded the note and put it away in his jacket.

He trudged along to the ticket counter, "I need a one-way ticket to Jacksonville, Florida. Suitcase and garment bag, and I want to check both."

"Got you all checked in, Sir. Here is your ticket and your baggage stubs are stapled at the bottom. Your flight will be boarding in twenty-seven minutes." She informed his gate and location. He nodded and strolled away.

His departure was right on schedule; and soon he was in the air. Staring out the window, he wondered, "Jack, are you nuts? You haven't called her. You don't even know exactly where she lives, if she's married, has a boyfriend, or if she is even home. You have no clue if she even wants to see your face again. The note made you think she might want to see you again, but you've found out how some people can lie pretty good."

He decided he would land, and just play the cards he'd drawn. What the hell? He couldn't be any worse off than he was already. There had to be plenty to do in Florida.

The flight was non-eventful and the stewardesses were pretty, so it was a good flight.

When he got off the plane, he went to the nearest car rental desk, whipped out the same MasterCard, and secured a luxury car. If he was going to vacation, it was going to be in style. He pulled out his smart-phone and located the nearest police station. Using the GPS app, he was on his way.

At the station, he checked in at the desk, asking to see whoever was in charge. A phone call was placed and he was soon led to a Detective Farrell, who shook his hand, "What brings you to our beautiful city, Detective Caruso?"

Time for him to tell a little white lie; what the hell, everybody else does, he thought. "I'm following up on a subject, who could be involved in a case I'm working on. I'd appreciate you pulling wants and warrants on females with the name, Lillian White."

"Man, she ran a long way from Pahrump, Nevada. Hey! If you'd feel better pulling the information yourself, there is an empty desk and computer over there," as he pointed.

"Thanks, I'll be out of your hair in a few minutes."

"Take as long as you like. If you need anything else while in town, just let me know."

Jack was soon at the computer searching. There was quite a list, but he finally found the Lillian that had to be her. He clicked on the name, her picture and all her information was in front of him. He printed the information, bid his adieu, and was on the road again.

Now it was time to start thinking of what he was going to say when he knocked on her door. Everything he practiced saying, sounded stupid. When he located her house and pulled into the driveway, he still wasn't sure what his opening words would be.

The car in the driveway bore the license number on the printout. Now, he felt a small adrenalin rush. Her car was there, she might be there, and she might not be alone. How was he going to handle that kind of situation? What the hell? He'd come this far. At the worst, all she could do was tell him to get lost. So, he started walking toward her door. As he reached toward the doorbell button, the door opened. Evidently she was headed somewhere, for her purse and keys were in her hand.

"Jack, I can't believe you are here. What a wonderful surprise. Come on in. How did you find me?"

"I'm a detective, remember?"

"Are you here on business?"

"No! There's been a lot of confusing stuff going on in my life lately and driving me nuts. It's been hard for me to concentrate on anything. The only thing holding my thoughts was the best night of my life. The night I spent with you."

"Jack, that wonderful night is all I've been able to think about since we parted." As her words stopped, she reached her arms up around his neck and their lips met. He flinched a little at the pain she caused in his shoulder.

Realizing something was wrong, she pulled away looking concerned.

"A recent bullet hole in the shoulder."

"I'm sorry, Jack. I didn't know."

"The kiss was worth the pain."

She grinned, took his hand and led him to the couch. "You mentioned you have been really bothered about something. I'm a good listener."

"Yeah, those opening words weren't anything like I'd practiced on the way over here."

She laughed a little, but shifted to concern, "Tell me what's bothering you."

"Lillian, I'm not sure where to start, but I know I want to tell you everything. I want to be perfectly honest with you and explain it all. When I'm done, if you want to kick me out the door, I won't ever bother you again."

"That's highly unlikely; give it your best shot, Jack."

"First of all, I'm not even sure if you are in a relationship with anyone."

"That one is easy. No! I'm not in a relationship with anyone. You are still the only man I've slept with since my divorce. After being with you, I didn't feel I wanted anyone else."

He grinned a little at her statement, but turned serious, "Ok! Here goes. I guess I'd better start a few days before we met. I've got to get all of this off my chest, and I wanted you to hear everything."

When she placed his hand in hers, it gave him the courage to begin.

An hour later he finished, "That's it. That's everything, Lillian; from then till now. I just want you to know that no woman has made me feel the way you do."

She looked into his eyes, as if she was reading his soul, "Now it's my turn. First of all, ever since that night, I'd assumed you were in a relationship, and I'd never see you again. Secondly, nothing you have told me has made a dent in my feelings for you. When I got on that plane to leave, I knew I'd fallen in love with you, and sadly figured there was nothing I would ever be able to do to win your love. Now that you are here sitting in front of me, I'm telling you I love you and want to be with you."

Her words warmed his heart and whole body. Right then and there, he also knew, "I was stupid to ever let you walk out of my life. There was just too much going on, and I couldn't think straight. Now that I'm here, I know I fell in love with you that night, and I still feel that way."

Even though it hurt, he placed his arm behind her on the couch and pulled her to him. When she kissed him this time, there was no doubt in his mind about his feelings, or hers.

When their lips parted, he said, "I'm on vacation and I want to take you somewhere, anywhere. Can you get some time off?"

"Jack, its July. School is out. I'm off till the first of September."

"Then pack a bag. Hell, pack several bags. Where would you like to go? Do you want to go to some other country? I'm serious, I've got money, and I'll take you anywhere you choose."

"Jack, I don't care where we go, as long as I'm with you."

"Pick some place," he said excitedly.

"I've always wanted to stay at a fancy hotel on Panama City Beach."

"Done, do you have a computer?"

"Laptop," she laughed.

He quickly dug out his wallet and handed her the same MasterCard, "Here, make us reservations at whatever hotel you want."

"I can't believe this is all happening. It's like a dream come true. If I'm dreaming, I don't ever want to wake up."

"Me neither. Get that laptop."

She returned with it, sat down beside him, and began looking up the hotels. He looked over her shoulder, as they both discussed the amenities. Finally she picked out the one she liked most, but when she clicked on "reserve a room", the prices somewhat shocked her. "I guess it's their busy season, Jack. I didn't think about the cost. The rooms are expensive."

"Don't worry about the cost; just book us a room for a week."

"A week; you're talking about a small fortune, are you sure you want to do that? I'd be happy being with you right here. We don't have to go anywhere or spend any money."

"Worry wart. Am I going to have to take that card back and do it myself?"

"Ok, if you are sure," as she saw him smile and nod.

As she entered the information, she stopped, saying, "A double bed is cheaper."

"Oh! Hell no! I want a lot of room in bed, and see how much of it we can use."

Now she really grinned and continued. Soon she entered his card number and read the confirmation.

Returning the card, she said, "Ok, Handsome, the room is booked and our vacation is on. I'm going to throw some things in a suitcase. Don't you go, anywhere."

As she headed toward her bedroom, he hollered, "Pack clothes for every occasion. There's no telling what we'll be doing."

He heard dresser drawers opening and closing, as she answered, "Ok!"

Realizing the happiness he was feeling warmed him all over, "You need any help?"

"No! If I let you come help we'd end up in bed, and I want to get on the road before I wake up from this dream."

"Ok! It's your loss. Do you have anything to drink?"

"There's tea, beer, water, wine and soda in the fridge. Help yourself, but keep talking, so I'll know you're still out there."

He laughed and went to the fridge, "Ok! I'm talking. I got a beer. I'm opening the beer. I'm throwing the cap in the empty garbage can. I'm taking a big swallow," as he turned the bottle up to drink.

She came running in, "Ok! Smarty, you can stop talking now and kiss me again. I'm done packing."

As he pulled her to him, "That didn't take long. Are you sure you've got everything?"

"Yep." Their lips met and the kiss was wanton, until she pulled away half breathless, "When we make love. It's going to be in a bed on the beach in Panama City."

"Ok! It's going to be hard for me to wait that long. Let's get going."

In hardly any time, her suitcase, garment bag, and women's toiletry bag with hair dryer, and all the necessary equipment were in the rental vehicle next to his.

He felt like a boy on his first date, as they drove and talked about things they each liked, or would like to do. Though it was a long drive, and stops along the way, it just didn't seem long at all to him.

Finally, they were at the hotel, checked in, and inspecting the room and the view.

"Now, Detective Caruso, I will keep my promise." She kissed him tenderly, then backed away and removed her blouse and bra.

He took the cue and shed his clothes. Once again he viewed the lovely body he'd been dreaming about. Now, it was for real again, and his manhood stood proud for the occasion, as she approached, grinning.

Their roll in the hay was tender and slow, until it kicked into high gear near the end, and they collapsed beside each other.

She was the first to speak. "Jack, I've missed being with you so much. I can't count the times I woke up frustrated because it was a dream and you weren't beside me."

"And you think I haven't been going through the same?" Hell, I've almost made the sheets wet and sticky several times."

She laughed and kissed him again, "Let's shower, get on some beach clothes, and go walk by the water."

"Yes, dear," he grinned, as he got up to join her in the shower.

The moon was full and bright, as they walked along the water's edge, and dodged the incoming waves. It was a romantic walk, hand in hand, with stops to lock in embrace. They were gone a long time, and stopped at tiki bars for drinks. When they finally made it back to the room, they took a shower together to wash off the sand, and then round two in the sack.

Chapter Twenty-Six

Two days later, they sat by the pool, enjoying mixed drinks and looking at Lillian's laptop. They were oblivious to anyone else, as they laughed and talked. Pants legs came into view, and they looked up through sunglasses.

Jack spoke, "Don't you ever get out of that suit?"

"Yeah, when I'm not on duty."

"Lillian, this is Connors. I don't know if it is a first name, last name, or in-between. He is NSA."

He gently shook her hand, "Last name; and it's very nice to meet you."

"I had a sneaky feeling you'd be showing, if I kept using that card."

"I was in the vicinity and thought I drop by and see if you'd considered those applications."

Jack looked toward Lillian. She reached in the beach bag, and pulled out a set of papers, handing them to Jack.

He handed them to Conners. As he unfolded and looked over the papers, Jack stated, "She helped me pick CIA, but let me say this. If you expect me to hide anything, or lie to her, then tear up the papers and throw them in the nearest trashcan when you leave."

He didn't answer. He folded the papers and put them in one inside jacket pocket. He removed a white envelope from the opposite pocket. "It's about time you figured out where you belong." Looking toward Lillian, "And who you belong with." He tossed the bulging unsealed envelope on the table.

Jack just handed it to Lillian, to confirm he wasn't keeping anything from her.

She was a little surprised at his actions but opened it, and began pulling things out. First was a folded sheet of paper. As she read, "Jack, it's an acceptance form into the CIA at an office in Jacksonville," with excitement in her voice. "I know the street."

Jack looked up at Conners, who was wearing a half grin, "You kind of jumped the gun. What if I hadn't picked either one?"

"Let's just say I figured you finally had the right kind of guidance."

She pulled another item out and handed him an ID badge on a dog chain, "It's got your picture and information to clear you into the building."

Conners had been silent but said, "Keep digging," as he grinned at Lillian.

She pulled out three pictures and two keys on a ring. The pictures were of a beautiful brick home, two-car garage, landscaping, a glassed in pool and lanai.

They both looked up at him, kind of confused.

He grinned, removing more folded papers from his jacket. This time he handed them directly to her. "You two closed on that house yesterday. It's in an upscale section of the city." Reaching in his pants pocket, he came out with two sets of keys. These are keys to the two cars in that garage. Both of your names are on the license registration," as he laid them gently on the table.

Lillian said, "Jack, this is a deed to the house made out to Jack and Lillian Caruso. As you read on where the names go, it reads Mr. and Mrs. Caruso."

"It has a good ring to it doesn't it?"

She quickly hugged his arm, "Oh, yeah! Real good."

"What's the catch, Connors, who do I have to kill."

That statement made her a little nervous, but she held onto his arm.

"No catch. Higher ups wanted you; and wanted you to be happy. I just made it happen."

"Why me?"

"They've been watching your never-give-up attitude for a long time. Welcome to your new job, Jack."

It all seemed surreal, but he shot back softly, "I'm on vacation."

"Yeah, I know and you deserve it. You've been through a lot and that shoulder needs to heal. You've got three weeks from yesterday, but that Monday, be in that office on the fourth floor at 9:00 a.m., sharp. Your desk is by the window; and your team is anxious to make your acquaintance. Now, I have someplace I need to be."

"Whoa!' Jacked stopped him, "Explain my team."

"You'll be head honcho over four new recruits. I can tell you already, they are going to need some guidance."

"I don't know anything about what you guys do, except show up at times, and become a pain in the ass."

"Not much different than what you've been doing for years. You have cases to work on. It's just that the cases are, uh, a little more involved, for a lack of better words."

He shook Lillian's hand again, "It's extremely nice to have met you, lovely lady. Take care of my man, there."

"You don't have to worry about that. I'm going to take care of him forever," as she wrapped an arm around Jack's.

"Now that's the kind of woman I'd like to find some day. I'll contact Chandler and let him know you are changing jobs. I'll wait a few days, and let him get used to you being gone, before I break the news to him. He isn't going to be happy." As he walked away without turning around, he said, over his shoulder, "By the way, Jack. You haven't even made a dent in that MasterCard." Soon he was around the corner and out of sight.

"Jack, this is all way over my head, and completely hard to believe. Can all this be true and really happening?"

"Those guys can do anything. Hey! We've got three weeks and you don't have to be back to school. You want to go on a cruise? I've never been on a cruise, but always thought about it."

"I've never been on one, either, and a cruise with you sounds wonderful. However, before we go riding the waves to some exotic place, I want to go see our new house."

He laughed, "Ok! After we finish our week here, we'll check out the new house. Then we'll go on a cruise and make love while we're riding the waves."

Her face lit up and she kissed him again. When their lips parted, she grinned, "Wonder what kind of cars we now own in that garage?"

Now he busted out laughing and hugged her.

Chapter Twenty-Seven

When they arrived at the new house, they took a stroll around outside. The house was built on a small hill. It and other houses surrounded a lake in an upscale neighborhood.

Working their way back to the front door, he handed her the key. She unlocked and pushed the door open. She could see the new flooring in the empty living room. She turned, "If you didn't have that bad arm, I'd ask you to carry me across the threshold?"

Though she protested, his weak arm went around her waist and his strong arm lifted. He carried her inside, eased her to the floor gently, and closed the door behind him.

"Your arm? Is your arm ok?"

"It's ok! It was worth it," as he kissed her forehead.

"Oh! I love the colors," as she started her inspection, and headed toward the other rooms with him in tow.

The master bedroom seemed huge to her. The large bathroom had a walk-in shower, and in one corner was a large hot tub. The floors were all vinyl and shining. She flipped on the light switches one at a time. Some were for the ceiling, some for the lights over the mirror at the long vanity, and some were for subdued lighting in the shower and over the hot tub.

"I can't wait till we get in that hot tub together."

His face showed agreement, "It sure looks inviting."

She led the way back into the main room and to the kitchen, with a long bar, separating the kitchen from the living room.

Excitedly, she exclaimed, "Jack, look at all this counter space, new cabinets, and new appliances," as she opened the double door fridge. "I can't wait to fill this thing, and fix our first meal here together."

While her back was to him, he'd picked up the manila envelope on the bar and looked at the items inside. There were catalogs, with furniture, bedding, and a folded note. As he looked at a note, he spoke, "You might want to take care of this before you start fixing that meal."

She came to him and thumbed through them. "There are some beautiful items in these pages."

He handed her the note and she read, "Pick out the items you want. Write down the item numbers and call the number at the bottom of this note. Everything you have selected will be delivered as soon as possible. Welcome to your new home."

It was signed "Sheri."

She folded the note, and her eyes began to tear heavily. She tried to wipe them with her fingers.

He snatched out his handkerchief asking, "What's wrong?"

"Jack, I've never owned anything new like this. I'm scared it is all a dream, I'll wake up, and find it and you gone."

He pulled her to him smiling, "We can't both be dreaming. It's real; you own it, and you own me."

She put her arms around his neck and kissed him.

When they parted, "Dry those tears and let's go look at our pool.'

He found the proper button on the wall, and the long curtain retracted, exposing three large sliding-glass doors that led to a covered lanai and pool.

She unlocked the door and Jack easily moved the glass doors, until they disappeared into the wall, leaving everything open all the way to the pool.

"Jack, I've never seen anything like that. This is amazing," as they strolled through the lanai and to the edge of the pool. She hugged him, as they stood watching the water cascade off a waterfall on the other side of the pool. At one end, there was a bubbling spa, with rising steam.

Here came the tears again, as she turned and buried her face in his chest.

"If you are going to spend all day crying, I'm going to have to call them to take all this back."

Quickly pulling away and drying her eyes, "Oh, no, you're not," as she saw him grinning.

He pulled one of the car keys out of his pocket, "Let's go see what kind of new vehicles we own."

That statement made her eyes dry quicker; as they opened the door to the garage.

Inside, sat two brand new BMW's. She looked back at him in total disbelief. One was a black sedan and the other was a red hardtop convertible.

"Can I have the convertible?" she smiled up at him.

"Does that mean I don't ever get to drive it?"

She laughed, as she hurried around the other car and eased into the leather seat of the convertible. He stood, peeking in, as she pointed out all the bells and whistles. In the console, she found the registration and their names. She grinned. "Let's go for a ride in this beautiful thing."

"Hey, we haven't even looked at our other vehicle yet."

She giggled and got out, as he walked back around to the driver's side of the other vehicle. Just as they climbed in, his phone rang. It kind of unnerved him; because the only call he'd gotten was a message he found from Chandler. His message said he was sorry to lose Jack, and he'd take him back in a minute, if Jack wasn't happy with the new job. The ID showed unknown name. He answered, "Hello."

"Jack, it's Charley. Hang on a minute there is someone at the door." He soon returned to the phone, "Sorry about that, Jack. It was just UPS delivering something that I ordered.

"Charley, glad to hear from you." He turned to her, whispering away from the phone, "It's Charley I told you about."

She answered, "Yeah, Charley and Kate. Do you want me to go inside while you take the call?"

"No. I told you, Lillian, no secrets and no lies," as he hugged her.

Charley continued, "I was afraid you wouldn't want to talk to me, after what went down."

"Charley, don't talk crazy. We've been friends for a long time. Lillian is here beside me. I'm going to put you on speaker phone."

"Hey, Charley, I've heard a lot about you. I hope we get to meet someday."

"I heard from Connors that Jack had a new job, a new life, and a lovely, wonderful lady to share it with him."

"That's sweet, Charley."

Jack interrupted, "I didn't know how to contact you, Charley. Your phone number didn't work anymore. How is Kate?"

"I had to change my number because of all the calls. She's fine. She went back to work, but she said it just wasn't the same around there. I convinced her to quit and come live with me. I've got plenty of money and investments. I never had the time to spend much of it. She agreed; so we moved her stuff from the apartment to my cabin. She spent one night there and had nightmares, so we went out the next morning and rented a large apartment. To tell the truth, I really didn't feel right living out in the boonies anymore. I had a realtor friend put the cabin on the market yesterday, and she already has a solid contract. Seems she got several offers from people who had seen it on Polero's news clips after the shootout. Kate and I have already been looking at new homes."

He hesitated, then continued; "I guess there are some people you might not want to hear about right now."

Jack interrupted, "I know who you are referring to. It's ok! I've told Lillian all about Sarah," as he looked toward her.

"Sarah showed up at the station the day after you walked out on vacation. They gave her the job back and a new partner. She appeared to be trying to make it work out, but when she got the news that you quit, she handed in her resignation."

"Why?" Jack asked inquisitively.

"She'd been harboring an offer from the FBI for a long time. She never wanted to tell you about it. Once again, Kate and I were doing her bidding, when she made us promise not to say anything to you. Sorry about that."

"It's ok, Charley, I understand."

"She's going through training at the FBI office in Las Vegas. When her training is over, she'll be working out of an office in Dallas Texas."

"Training? She doesn't need any training."

"You and I know that, and I'm sure they do, too. I think it was to assure she was fully over her ordeal, and really fit to continue in law enforcement. I assume Lillian knows about Mark."

Jack said, "Yes, as I said, she knows about everything."

Charley continued, "Connors told me that you know Mark was killed at the underground caves. We were sad to hear that news. The military considers him a hero."

He hesitated for a moment, and then continued, "I hope I'm not opening a can of worms for you, when I say this over speaker. Sarah said she told you all about the tests she has to take once a week. The last one was negative. If it remains that way, when she heads for Dallas, she won't have to do the tests anymore."

"Yeah, Lillian knows all that, too. I told her everything, Charley; and I do mean everything. If our relationship was going to last, I wanted to be an open book for, Lillian. No secrets."

"I feel the same with Kate. Speaking of my lovely live in, she just walked through the door. Kate, its Jack, and Lillian, on speaker."

"Hey there, handsome, and you, too, lucky girl. You've got a good man there."

"I know! You are right, I'm very lucky," Lillian answered cheerfully.

"I heard you have a beautiful woman with a big heart. You better hold onto her, Jack."

"Trust me. I'm happy as can be. I don't intend to ever lose her. I hear you and Charley have been looking at new houses."

"Yes. We just put a bid on a lovely home on the outskirts of Vegas. The closing is tonight at 7:30. It will work out great, if it goes through. Charley has a job to do at a facility not far from the new house. I'll hand the phone back to Charley and let him tell you about it. It's great to hear your voice, Jack, and nice to meet you over the phone, Lillian."

"You, too," Lillian acknowledged.

"Yeah, Jack. They are finishing building a new long-range signal security facility. They want me there to get things rolling. Seems they want to get an ace up, in case our friends from the sky come back angry. I'm anxious to get started, but I was told this morning the facility wouldn't be ready for me for another month."

Kate was back on the phone, "We are going stir crazy in limbo with this job and house thing."

Lillian chimed in, "I've got a great idea. Jack and I were going tomorrow to sign up for a cruise ship out of Jacksonville Beach. It would be wonderful if you two could join us. It would be more fun with someone with us, and I could get a chance to meet you both."

"That sounds fantastic! Charley is shaking his head up and down like it is about to fall off. How are we going to connect?"

Lillian continued, "Grab a pen and paper. I'll give you the info on my old house and my phone number. When you get your flight set up, give us a call, and we'll pick you up at the airport. I'm looking forward to meeting you both and having a great time."

Jack jumped into the conversation, "When you get here, we can show you our new house. Of course, it doesn't have any furniture yet," as he laughed.

"Charley is already on the other phone calling the airport. Soon as we get the itinerary we'll give you a buzz. I know he'll be hollering for all my information. Ok, I've got the pen and paper."

Lillian rattled off her address and home phone number.

"Got it. So, we'll call you soon. I'm already getting excited."

"We are, too," Lillian quickly added, "Hurry back with that call."

Soon the call ended.

"Thanks for making my friends feel at ease." Jack said seriously.

"They are going to be our friends pretty soon," as she hugged him.

They checked out all the amenities of his new vehicle.

"Ok! Are you ready to take your convertible car for a tour of the area?"

Her grin was wide as could be, "Yes, and if you are a good boy, I might even let you drive on the return."

He laughed as they got out and climbed into the convertible.

Chapter Twenty-Eight

Five and a half months had passed, since the four enjoyed each other's company on the cruise. They were like four peas in a pod.

Both couples put in some flying hours back and forth from Jacksonville to Pahrump, visiting each other at the new homes.

Charley's cabin sold quickly. Jack and Lillian had solid contracts on their old homes.

On one of the trips, the four went to the Mirage, in Las Vegas. Lillian wanted to show Kate and Charley the exact spot where she and Jack met, since she'd already told them about it, and get in a little gambling.

When she pointed at the machine she was playing that night, and turned around, Jack was holding an open ring box, and the diamond glittered. "I figured this was the perfect spot to ask you to be my wife."

Tears of happiness flowed, as she removed the ring from the box and put it on her finger. Her arms went around his neck, saying, "I will and will forever." They locked in embrace, as Kate wrapped arms around both, in congratulation.

Kate suddenly realized Charley wasn't saying anything, and turned toward him. He was standing grinning, holding an open ring box of his own. "I was hoping you might consent, and we could make it a double wedding."

Nervously, she eased the ring out of the box and slipped it on her finger. Her eyes were teary, too, as she smiled, "God! Yes, Charley! I love you," Their lips met, as Jack and Lillian wrapped arms around both of them, in congratulation.

A boisterous, happy voice interrupted the hugging, "Now it's my time to wish both of you couples congratulations."

It was Kate's Uncle Bob, the casino boss. "Jack told me what he and his friend Charley here planned to do tonight. If you said yes, he wanted me to come to the wedding. Now that you both said yes, I have a surprise."

Maybe it was because Kate was his favorite niece, or maybe because he felt guilty having to disclose Kate's location to the NSA, he definitely had a big surprise.

"If you are agreeable, I'd love for you to have the wedding here at the casino in the dinner show room. The whole room would be exclusively for you and whomever you invite. I will pay to have all the food and drinks for the wedding. Anyone coming from out of town can have large discounts on any available rooms. Of course, the two married couples will have separate honeymoon suites, compliments of the house. So what do you think?

Kate and Lillian glanced at each other, and heads went up and down. They both rushed to Kate's uncle, and kissed him on the cheek from each side."

Jack and Charley stepped forward to shake his hand. Jack laughed, saying, "I guess that means we graciously accept your wonderful offer."

"It's a done deal then. Just let me know ahead of time, when the wedding is to take place, so I can make sure everything will be perfect for you."

The girls kissed his cheeks again, and he laughed, as he walked away.

(Nine weeks later)

The gala event took place flawlessly, with wedding decorations everywhere around the room, and on the tables. The women wore exquisitely beautiful wedding gowns and the men looked sharp in full tux.

The room was full of all their close friends. Chandler, Barry, Susan and a few others from Jack's old station happily attended.

CIA agents from Jack's new team occupied four of the seats.

A group of Charley's CIA and NSA friends attended.

Connors was there to share in the happy couple's event. He had a beautiful redhead on his arm. He pulled Jack aside, and whispered that the military found two Majestic men in the caves. Both had laser holes through their chest, by the aliens. One had a trigger mechanism in his hand that could have detonated a nuclear bomb. They found the bomb and those two men behind a fake wall.

Both Connors and Jack knew everyone was extremely lucky, at the outcome of the battle. It also made Jack more of a hero, in the eyes of his superiors.

Though Jack was very glad the bomb didn't explode, he didn't consider himself a hero.

Caruso was very happy that Tony was able to attend, with Nancy. He was healing great.

Kenny's smiling face was there with the gorgeous Diane.

Teachers from Lillian's school were there to share in her happy occasion.

At the wedding party table sat the three casino guys who were wounded helping Jack. They were surprised and elated to be invited.

Sarah didn't attend, although she was sent an invitation to her new home in Dallas. She did send a congratulations card, saying she was sorry she couldn't attend, and that she was on a case out of country. The envelope was stamped from somewhere in Bolivia.

Kate's uncle was the one to give Kate away, and Chandler had the honor of delivering Lillian to the bridal stand.

Barry was Jack's best man, and one of Charley's buddies was his.

Soon the four repeated their wedding vows and nervously exchanged rings.

When the preacher announced the two couples as man and wife, they locked in happy embraces and kissed.

When they turned and the preacher announced, "I now present you with Mr. and Mrs. Caruso and Mr. and Mrs. Decker," the place went nuts, with everyone standing and cheering.

The reception was held right there, after they were announced to the crowd. Waiters and waitresses brought in the salads and drinks. The two couples walked around to each table, and thanked each friend for coming to be part of the wedding.

When the main course came to come to an end, and waiters picked up the plates and replaced them with clean ones, they announced it was time to cut the cake.

On a table to itself was a five-tier cake with two sets of figurines on the top under a bridal arch. Around the cake on each tier were expertly crafted edible figures, such as a couple sitting on stools at casino machines, which, of course, represented the night Jack and Lillian met. There were figures of cops, detectives, and men in black on the lower tiers.

There was a figure of a teacher pointing at a black board, and on the tier below were figures of four students sitting at desks.

The one figurine that most friends didn't understand was one tall gray alien. Of course, there was plenty who did know what it was referring to, but no one was saying anything.

Soon they all four were around the table and slicing the cake. They refrained from pushing cake all over any of their faces.

After everyone stood and cheered again, the two newly married couples eased into two separate side rooms, and changed into more comfortable attire.

The rest of the night, they partied and danced, until the final person left the four alone in the room. Waiters were cleaning up the leftover mess. The four stood facing each other and made a toast of their own, with drinks, wishing each other continued happiness and vowing to be friends forever. They laughed and commented about the honeymoon they would take in two days, on their second cruise together.

Lillian turned toward her new husband, "I want to go sit on that same seat where we met and relive the moment. But first, I want to go to the room and change into the same outfit I had on that night."

"Just so happens that I packed the same clothes I was wearing," as he grinned.

Kate interrupted, "Ok, you two lovely people. That is a special spot for us, too, now. We'll go put on some gambling clothes and meet you there."

They were all four laughing, as they headed to the elevator.

When they stood waiting for the elevator door to open, the two couples turned to each other, and locked in tender embrace.

"A note from the author"

Be sure to check out "Under Watchful Eyes 2" when it is published. You'll find out more about what happened to Sarah, and I have some surprises in store for you.

"Other books by this author and comments"

1. CYRSTALS-Cyrstals was my first book, about a Florida State Trooper and his family abducted by aliens. The book spans over twenty-two years, as the family deals with each predicament. Other than the sex maybe being a little too descriptive, I think you'll enjoy the story. You can tell I had a lot of learning, to get under my belt.

2. Crystals 2 "A New Earth"-Carries old and new characters deep into space, making new friends and enemies, and helping new friends establish a home, on another planet.

3. Existence After 2020-A family in middle Tennessee, uses a run of good fortune, to build a fortress in the mountains of their state. For years, they have to defend what they have, after the U.S. is attacked with nuclear bombs.

4. COLT MAGUM-Here's a clue. The name of the book has nothing to do with the gun with the same name. The book is about an FBI anti-terrorist unit, trying to prevent terrorists from exploding bombs, in Atlanta, Georgia.

5. Blessed or Cursed-After a traumatic childhood, a soldier getting out of the military, inherits a farm. While making repairs, he has to deal with Russian spies, the law, and a serial killer. Or, is he the real serial killer?

6. A River's Fork-The main character finds himself at the beginning of a divorce, dealing with amnesia, and fighting off drug dealers; with the help of some unlikely friends.

7. Whitetail Deer Myths "Facts and Stories"-I had a lot of fun writing this book. By combining previously learned things about hunting, debunking most of those, adding facts as I now know them, and things that happened while hunting; I think you'll enjoy reading. I also hope that the book will help some established hunters, and those wanting to learn the sport.

   Most of all, I want to thank you for reading my book, or books; and I hope you enjoy them. All of my books are on Amazon under my name, except CRSTALS. It is under C.R. Loftin.

   Carlton Loftin

98037067R10258

Made in the USA
Lexington, KY
03 September 2018